THE LAST POST

THE KNOCKNASHEE SERIES

BOOK 7

JEAN GRAINGER

Copyright © 2025 by Jean Grainger

All rights reserved.

No part of this book may be reproduced in any form or by any electronic or mechanical means, including information storage and retrieval systems, without written permission from the author, except for the use of brief quotations in a book review.

NO AI TRAINING: Without in any way limiting the author's [and publisher's] exclusive rights under copyright, any use of this publication to train generative artificial intelligence (AI) technologies to generate text is expressly prohibited. The author reserves all rights to licence uses of this work for generative AI training and development of machine learning language models.

This book is dedicated to my dear friend, Sandy Perceval, whose advice on such an array of topics, always delivered with kindness and humour, has improved every book I've written immeasurably.

CHAPTER 1

Knocknashee, County Kerry, Ireland

5th June 1944

Dear Grace,
      Something about writing those two little words changes how I feel. It always has. Those words mean I can be me. No matter what else is going on in my life, no matter how confusing or upsetting anything is, when I write to you, I can be honest, I don't have to pretend. You understand me and I understand you. We are kindred spirits, Grace, you and I; we are meant to be. I know you realize this, but that letter Doodle found on the beach at St. Simons has changed my life. I can only believe that this is how it should be, because a life for me without you is unthinkable.

So often over these past six years, I was in despair, thinking that you and I would not ever be together—often through my own stupid fault, but sometimes through fate—but here we are. Tomorrow I will wait for you at the top of the aisle of the Knocknashee church, where you will come to marry me. I can't believe it. I have to keep pinching myself. Grace Fitzgerald is going to marry me! It's amazing and wonderful, and I don't think I have ever been this happy.

I won't be able to sleep—I'm too excited. Nathan is laughing at me, saying I'm like a kid going on his first date, checking and double-checking everything. My family has never seen me like this. I just want everything to be perfect for you.

I promise you I'll be the best husband I can. And I'll spend my entire life trying to make you happy. Because you are my whole world.

I can't wait to see you tomorrow, my darling girl.

I love you, Grace.

So much.

Richard xoxoxo

PS Don't be too late. I know brides are allowed to be late, but I'll be such a nervous wreck thinking that something has gone wrong—we do have some history in that regard! Please don't prolong my agony any longer than it needs to be.

Grace folded the letter with a smile and put it in the biscuit tin by her bedside, which bulged with years of her correspondence with Richard Lewis.

She pulled her notepad towards her and filled the fountain pen with her signature lilac ink. Charlie was downstairs, having brought her letter. He'd kindly told her he'd deliver a reply if she wanted to write one.

Dear Richard,

I know what you mean. I'm the same. Is this really happening? Are we getting married tomorrow? I know we are, but it feels a bit like a fairy story. Are we finally getting our happy ever after?

Getting your letter – hand-delivered by Charlie (I have friends in high places, you know) – gave me the same thrill I always get when I see an envelope with your lovely handwriting.

I love you too, and I'm so grateful to Agnes for being so mean that day I wrote that first long diatribe of complaint. If she'd not been so awful to me, I might never have written it, and then you and I would never have met. We must be the most unlikely pair on this earth, but here we are.

I won't sleep either, and I have to go downstairs shortly for another fitting because Lizzie and Peggy are not one hundred percent happy with the fall of my hem. I'd love to tell them that you don't give a hoot about hems.

All I really need for my wedding day is to see your face at the top of that aisle in the morning.

And this time tomorrow, I'll be Mrs Lewis, and I'll say things like, 'Oh, I'll just tell my husband, Richard...' My husband. Richard Lewis is going to be my husband. Eeeeeekkkk!!! I can't wait.

Don't worry, I won't be late. I'd go to the church now if I could, just to be sure. But I know what you mean – we've had a lot of near misses, so let's leave nothing to chance.

Try to sleep a bit. I need you full of energy for tomorrow!

Your very-soon-to-be wife,

Grace xxxxxxxxxxxxx

She chuckled as she closed the envelope. That last sentence was a bit racy, she knew. Agnes would be horrified. But Grace did want Richard full of energy. These last months had been wonderful but also a bit of torture for them both, and she was so looking forward to being Richard's wife in every way.

She went downstairs to give Charlie the letter.

He took it with a wink and a grin. 'Special delivery,' he said as he left the house and climbed on his bike.

Her home had been a hive of female activity these past days, everyone busy with the preparations for the most exciting thing to happen in Knocknashee for years – maybe ever.

The Infant of Prague statues were out on the back step of every house in Knocknashee to ensure a fine day for the wedding. It was a tradition so far back that nobody could remember how it started. Everyone was going to such trouble for her.

'Right. In here, Grace,' Lizzie Warrington instructed, leading Grace into the sitting room where Tilly O'Hare, Dymphna McKenna, Peggy Donnelly, Sarah Lewis and Grace's nieces were waiting. 'I will not sleep until that hem is perfect.'

Grace laughed and stood on a milk crate in the centre of the room as Lizzie and Peggy, both with their mouths full of pins, went to work.

There was a loud knock on the front door.

'That better not be him,' Tilly warned as she went to answer it. 'There have been enough mishaps and cross-purposes with you pair to last a lifetime. So the groom gets to see the bride the night before the wedding over my dead body.'

Voices from the hall told Grace it wasn't Richard. Instead it was young Mikey O'Shea dropping off a huge bouquet of flowers, which which Tilly returned. It was so large, she could hardly be seen behind it.

'This is from Mikey,' Tilly said, setting the bouquet down on the table. 'He grew them all himself and said you might like them for your bridal flowers. And for the bridesmaids and flower girls too.'

'Ah, isn't that lovely?' Lizzie sighed, admiring the roses, lilies, hydrangeas and agapanthus in a huge array of colours. 'Is he a pupil of yours, Grace?'

'He is.' Grace was so touched by the boy's gesture. 'Mikey's a pet, there's nothing he can't do with plants. He's only twelve, but he's able to grow anything. He supplies the hotel in Dingle and does the church flowers and everything. He says he's going to get a job in a big house when he's old enough and learn to be a proper gardener.'

'He never forgot you for saving him from the *caill*...' – Peggy Donnelly blushed as she stopped herself from using the nickname everyone called Grace's late sister, Agnes: the *cailleach*, the witch – '...your sister, Agnes, that time, and he only a little *garsun*.'

'You were a hero that day for sure, Grace,' Tilly stacked some gifts that had arrived on the table.

Grace didn't confirm or deny it, but the slightly crooked smile and all-knowing look in her friend's unusual grey eyes said it all. Sticking up for Mikey O'Shea had been the first time Grace challenged her sister, who had been slapping the little boy for nothing.

Molly and Cáit, Grace's nieces, were admiring the beautiful flowers. 'Will we put them in water, Aintín Grace?' eight-year-old Cáit asked.

She and Molly were two of Grace's five flower girls and desperate to be involved in the preparations. They were on strict and dire warnings from their mother that the peach organza dresses – supplied by

Richard's mother, Caroline Lewis, and by far the fanciest things anyone in Knocknashee had ever seen, currently hanging on the curtain pole in the sitting room – were not to be touched on pain of death. The remaining three dresses were for Richard's nieces, Naomi, Stella and the youngest, Megan, who they worried might balk at the sight of the crowds and refuse to walk up the aisle.

'Do please, darlings.' Grace blew them a kiss each from the crate. 'I haven't a vase big enough, but maybe put them in a bucket outside the back door for now and we can make them into bouquets later on.'

'I'll help you,' Sarah said, and followed the two little girls outside into the yard in search of a suitable bucket for the flowers.

'Are you nervous, Grace?' Dymphna asked. 'I was a bag of nerves before I married Charlie. I don't know why, but I was. Yes, your daddy, love,' she murmured to baby Seámus, who was wriggling to get down from his mother's lap. At almost two, he was beginning to walk and growing into a fine, strong boy.

'I'm nervous something will go wrong. You know us,' Grace answered truthfully. 'But I'm excited and over the moon. I can't believe it's finally happening.'

'Nothing is going to go wrong, pet,' Dymphna soothed. 'Charlie and Maurice are managing everything between them, and sure Richard will be safe in Dingle staying at the hotel with all the rest of the Americans.'

'Yes. He said it was lovely. Did you know that the hotel owner is the woman Agnes thought would be her mother-in-law? Remember she had hopes of marrying in there? Gosh, that feels like a thousand years ago now... But anyway, nice or not, how the Dingle Harbour Hotel will live up to the very high standards of the Lewises, I've no idea.'

Grace had to admit she was a bit worried about that. The American side of the wedding party was huge. That everyone had come astonished her. Wartime meant civilian travel was severely curtailed, but the rules didn't seem to apply to people like Arthur Lewis. He'd arranged passage for everyone, including the entire Lewis family from Savannah – Arthur and Caroline, Richard's parents; Richard's brother, Nathan, and his family; his sister, Sarah; as well as Esme, the family housekeeper.

Mrs McHale, the bishop's housekeeper from New York, was here as well. Not to mention – inexplicably – Richard's ex-girlfriend, Miranda Logan-Smythe, who had divorced her husband, Algernon, and decided she wanted to see Richard tie the knot. Then, at the last minute, the Maheadys had decided to come too.

The entire entourage crossed the ocean, arriving in Cobh, County Cork, earlier that morning. Grace and Richard had been on the quayside at Cobh to greet them, after staying with Lizzie and Hugh Warrington the night before, and a fleet of cars had been arranged to convey the American contingent all the way to Dingle, where they were booked in at the hotel. They'd all make an appearance in Knocknashee tomorrow for the wedding, and the whole place was being sent sideways with the excitement and drama of it all.

It was hard to believe people had gone to so much trouble for her and Richard, but everyone was so happy for them, it was infectious. Even grumpy Pádraig O Sé managed to tell her earlier today that she was glowing. She'd waited for the barbed afterthought – Pádraig always had something – but no, he seemed genuine. He'd even gone so far as to say that with so much bad news about the war all the time, it was lovely to have something cheerful like a wedding going on.

He'd further astonished everyone by dropping over a pair of shoes, built up as Grace's had to be because of her polio, but dyed cream to wear on her wedding day. He refused to wait so she could thank him. Tilly had opened the door, and he'd just scurried off.

Lizzie squeezed her hand. 'They'll be fine, Grace. I'm sure they'll love it. The Dingle Harbour Hotel is a lovely, charming old place, and they probably don't have things like that over there. Anyway, they're here to celebrate your wedding, not to do a hotel inspection,' she said, lowering her voice as the back door opened and Sarah came back into the kitchen.

'The girls are doing a great job of looking after the flowers,' Sarah announced with a grin. 'There was nothing for me to do, so I made myself scarce.'

The women laughed, and then Lizzie smiled at Grace. 'Now, I was thinking about "something old, something new, something borrowed, something blue".'

'Oh, I forgot that,' Grace said.

Lizzie held up a neat box with a ribbon on it. 'Well, you can say no if you don't want it, pet, I won't be insulted, but I brought my veil, the one I wore when I married Hugh, and if you'd like to wear it, it could be your something borrowed?'

Grace heard the slight hesitation in the older woman's voice as she opened the box and extracted the veil from its protective covering of tissue paper. She held up the delicate cream lace into the light, and Grace gasped. 'Oh, Lizzie, it's so beautiful. And just the right colour too.'

Lizzie blushed. 'Thank you,' she beamed at Grace. 'But I'd understand if you didn't think a veil was appropriate for this wedding. Not to wear it as a veil, but I thought you might be able to use the lace in your hat or something, but I wasn't sure…'

'Why wouldn't it be?' Sarah looked bewildered.

'I dunno, some silly old notion of a widow not looking like a first-time bride or something?' Tilly explained.

Sarah snorted her clear disgust for such nonsense. 'Well, I say wear what you want, Grace.'

'Same here,' Tilly nodded as she fixed her own hair in the mirror..

'Nothing to worry about,' Peggy Donnelly's mouth was full of pins but she could still talk. 'I have a lovely pillbox headpiece I can fix up for you. I'll make a birdcage for the front with some of that beautiful lace. A few stitches, a bit of ruching, and I'll have you looking like that Rita Hayworth film star, love.'

'Oh, Lizzie, if you're sure,' Grace said. 'I'd love to wear it. Thank you.'

Lizzie beamed and brushed away a quiet tear as Grace bent down to hug her.

'Well, since we're on the subject…I brought you this. I wondered when the right time might be, but it seems that would be now.' Sarah pulled out a long black velvet box from her handbag and handed it to Grace.

Inside was a small diamond bracelet.

'Sarah, it's… Oh my goodness… It's too much…' Grace felt herself tear up.

'Not at all, and it's your something new.' Sarah helped her put it on, and Grace marvelled at the sparkles on her slender wrist. She blinked back a tear and hugged her soon-to-be sister-in-law. Sarah was not soft and gushy, but she was incredibly kind, always had been. She was so worried about her own husband, Jacob Nunez, who had stayed behind in Switzerland to help fight the war, but was here now doing her best to make Grace's wedding feel special.

'Right, we have borrowed and new, we just need old and blue…' Lizzie tapped her lip with her index finger, a gesture Grace remembered from her childhood.

'I know!' Tilly winked and ran to the back door. She returned with two beautiful blue agapanthus blossoms from the bouquet Cáit and Molly had placed outside in the bucket as Grace had instructed. 'All thanks to Mikey O'Shea. Eloise will be able to pin these like a brooch in the morning, so we have something blue.'

'So something old is all we need,' Sarah said.

Grace looked down at her left hand. She had been thinking she would take off Declan's wedding ring in the morning; it didn't feel right to wear it when marrying Richard. Not that he would mind; he understood how much Declan's memory meant to her.

She slipped the ring off her finger. 'Could we stitch this into my dress?' she asked Peggy.

'Of course we can, Grace,' Peggy replied. 'That's a lovely idea.' She took it from Grace and deftly snipped the stitching on the cuff of the dress before inserting the slim gold band into it and then sewing it up again.

'Now, then, that's perfect.' Dymphna beamed. 'You're all set.'

There was a sudden commotion outside, and Tilly went to investigate.

'Nothing to worry about,' she reassured the women when she returned. 'They're just bringing up the new bed.'

Grace's brother, Maurice, had built the couple a new bed, a beautiful thing, as a wedding present. It had a carved oak frame, oiled till it shone. The mattress had to be ordered specially from Dublin. Tilly's friend Eloise had been sent to lie on it in the shop to make sure it was comfortable. Maurice had built it in the workshop behind Charlie's house, and they were installing it now, ready for the honeymooners' return.

Grace felt a frisson of pure anticipation as the women fussed around her. She was ready for this, and the time was almost here. Only a few more hours left to wait.

CHAPTER 2

Fitting complete, and the outfit finally ready to the satisfaction of both Lizzie and Peggy, Grace was told to get herself off to bed. The bride needed a good night's sleep.

Tilly was in Grace's bedroom, helping Maurice to heave the heavy mattress onto the new bed.

'Oh, Maurice,' Grace breathed, 'it's so beautiful.' She'd only seen parts of it up to now. 'Thank you so much.'

'You're more than welcome, Grace,' her brother replied. He laughed. 'I think the mattress is comfortable, but you can blame Eloise if it's not. Now, ladies, I better let you to it. See you in the morning, Grace. Sleep well.' He gave her a quick hug and was gone.

Sometimes when Maurice smiled or looked out of the side of his eye in a particular way, she felt she could be looking at their father. Here now, surrounded by family and friends, it was hard for her to imagine that her brother had been a stranger to her until last summer, when he and his family turned up on her doorstep.

'It's a beautiful piece of work.' Tilly ran her hand over the curved footboard.

'It's truly gorgeous,' Grace agreed, sitting on the bed.

Tilly O'Hare and Grace had been best friends since they'd first gone to school and sat beside each other in baby infants. They had no secrets from each other.

'So, Grace, this is it? No cold feet?' Tilly grinned, knowing the answer.

She made a face. 'I've got polio. I always have cold feet.'

Tilly rolled her eyes. 'Very amusing, Miss Fitz. But seriously, how are you feeling?'

Grace felt a wave of affection for her lionhearted friend. God might have taken a lot from her – her parents, Declan, her health compromised by polio – but he gave her Tilly, and nobody on earth had a more loyal champion. She knew that if she did have a change of heart – not that she would, of course – Tilly would be in her corner.

Tilly caused regular scandal in Knocknashee because she only wore trousers, never skirts, she never put a touch of lipstick or rouge on her beautiful face, and her hairstyle was now a crew cut, like the men in service, which showed off her perfect angular bone structure. She could farm her land as well as any man, and she had, over the years, gained the respect of the farmers and fishermen around here who thought of Tilly now as one of them. It had come as a surprise to Grace to learn that Tilly was interested romantically in women. Nobody ever said it, but Grace now knew that was what Agnes had been driving at that terrible day she had shamed them as they got off the bus from Dingle all those years ago.

'I can't wait, Til,' she answered. 'Honest to God, I just can't wait to be his wife.'

'I'm glad to hear it. Because you nearly gave us all ulcers between the jigs and the reels with the pair of you. If you brought your story to Hollywood to make a film of it, they'd say 'twas too far-fetched. So I'm delighted you've no doubts about marrying the poor man and have done with it.'

She laughed. 'Did anyone ever tell you you're a right old romantic, Matilda O'Hare? Is Eloise here yet?'

Tilly shook her head. 'She's at the mercy of Bobby the Bus, and there's a huge funeral in Ceann Trá this evening. The last one of the Heffernan sisters finally died. She must have been a hundred.'

'Do you remember when we went to the removal of the middle sister –Florence, was it? – and Marion the other sister, told us if we were going to be standing around doing nothing, we could make ourselves useful by tidying out the cutlery drawer, and she had the Murphy sisters ironing sheets?'

'I do!' Tilly hooted. 'Remember when she asked if any of us wanted to sleep in the room with the corpse?'

Grace giggled. 'They were totally daft.'

'Marion died last year, and I think the last one was Ursula. She's the one that just died. Anyway, Bobby the Bus will be stopping there to pay his respects, no doubt – everyone knows the Heffernan sisters made sloe gin. Eloise had hoped to get down in time to get a lift from Cork with you, but she was involved with a play in the Gate Theatre and had to wait till closing night, so Bobby the Bus it is.'

Grace and Tilly rarely talked about Tilly's long-standing romance with Eloise Meier, a Swiss woman now living in Dublin, but Grace knew that it was a relief to Tilly to be able to mention Eloise without fear of anyone making dangerous assumptions or judgements.

'Oh dear, and you know Dinty Collins, one of the Collins brothers, he died yesterday as well, so Bobby will definitely be stopping at that wake too. The brothers made the best poitín on the peninsula.'

'Excuse your cheek, *I* make the best poitín on the peninsula.' Tilly exclaimed archly. 'Though how Dinty Collins survived this long is the mystery. The bust-ups he had with his brothers every night of the week – and they all jarred off their heads on second-rate poitín, clattering seven shades of muck out of each other – were legendary. Then after all that, 'twas a kick from the donkey and that did away with him. Life is very strange sometimes.'

Grace knew Tilly had no time whatsoever for the five bachelor Collins brothers after they sent the matchmaker Miah Danny Gurteen up to Tilly to arrange a match for her with the middle brother, who was sixty if he was a day. She'd been highly indignant that they had the audacity to even ask and gave Miah Danny the road with a flea in his ear.

'Don't be worrying about the Americans, by the way – they're having a great time. Arthur Lewis and Mrs McHale ended up in a pub in Dingle earlier, did you know that? And my mother was in there for whatever reason, best not ask, and she noticed that Caroline Lewis was limping a bit and found out she had a corn. And sure enough didn't Ma have a potion for it and insisted on taking her back to the hotel and treating it, paring it down and dressing it and what have you. So apparently all is well with the mother of the groom's foot, and all is well with the world.'

'I hope so. I just want it all to go well.'

'Of course it will. Besides, this is about you and Richard, not anyone else. But I know what you mean.' Tilly sat on the new bed and pulled her legs underneath her. 'Honestly, Grace there's nothing to worry about.' She counted off on her fingers. 'Sarah is lovely, a pure dote, and she is so obsessed with finding the mother of that kid in the orphanage in New York and trying not to fret about her husband that she couldn't care less if you fed her boiled eggs up a tree. Arthur Lewis is weak for you – you can see it when he looks at you. He's as mad about you as his son is, so he's not going to say or do anything bad. Nathan seems delighted to be here. Did you hear him oohing and aahing over all the castles and ruins and the lot? And his girls are sweet and dying to play with all the little ones. They'll be slobbering all over Bríd Butler's caramel apples tomorrow and delighted with everything. Mrs McHale thinks the sun shines out of your bum, and anyway she's Irish, so she's grand. The Maheadys are so relieved they didn't lose Lily to either Charlie or Fiachra O'Flynn and are so excited to spend time with Charlie and Dymphna and the kids that you and your nuptials are only a bit of the story for them. Which leaves Caroline Lewis, Miranda Whatshername and Rebecca, Nathan's wife.'

Grace winced. 'Those three are exactly who I'm worried about.'

'Leave them to me. I'll charm them. Caroline thinks my mother is magic, and Charlie has a way with her too. You said that yourself, that when you were over there, she was all about him. Even this evening she was lit up talking to him. So he'll manage her as well. As for Rebecca, she might be fine. She looks a bit stuck-up, but Nathan is nice and her girls are lovely, so maybe we're judging prematurely.'

'And what about Miranda Logan, who looks like a film star and calls Richard "the one that got away"?' She could only admit her fears to Tilly.

'What did Richard say when he heard she was coming?'

'She wrote and asked if he'd mind. He asked me how I felt, so of course I had to say she could come. But I suppose I just imagine everyone looking at her and then looking at me. I can't compete with her, Til. She's like a different species to me.'

'But if Richard wanted her, then he'd have had her. You told me he said she admitted to him that letting him go was a mistake, and now she's single again, she might be going to have another crack at him. I don't think she would, but she might.' Tilly was nothing if not truthful; it was why Grace trusted her so implicitly. 'But the truth of the matter is, even if she got down to her lacy smalls and did the quickstep in front of him' – Grace giggled at the thought – 'he wouldn't pick her over you. You know he wouldn't. So you're perfectly safe.'

'I know.' She still had butterflies in her stomach. 'Richard wouldn't think that, but I just hate the idea of his family feeling he could have done better.'

'They won't. And look, it's not about her anyway. Or anyone else for that matter. It's about you and Richard, and you both finally getting to tie the knot. And believe me, every person that knows either of you knows how longwinded you were about getting here, so all any of us will feel is happy, blessed relief.'

Grace laughed. 'Thanks, Til. I believe you.'

'I should hope so,' her friend replied with a grin. 'Now I'd better get myself off out of here and let you get your beauty sleep. You've an important day ahead of you tomorrow, Grace Fitzgerald.'

With Tilly gone, Grace sat for a while, listening to the happy chatter of the women downstairs still busy with wedding preparations. Then she dressed for bed and slipped beneath the covers, stretching out to ease some of the ache in her bad leg after all that standing for the fitting earlier.

The bed seemed huge and strange in comparison to what she was used to. It was a proper bed for a married couple. And tomorrow, that's exactly what she and Richard would be – a married couple.

She smiled, soaking up that deep contented thought for a moment. *This is it, Grace Fitzgerald. This is really it. Tomorrow you get to marry the man of your dreams.*

CHAPTER 3

The wedding was at eleven o'clock the following morning. Father Iggy and Father Lehane would concelebrate it, and the whole church was spectacular thanks to the supply of flowers from Mikey and others, combined with the work of the postmistress, Nancy O'Flaherty, and her band of women who decorated the altar. Miss Fitz's wedding was a special one.

Grace had had a sleepless night, excitement coursing through her veins for most of it. Relief that the day was finally here flooded over her as the pink dawn painted the summer sky.

She rose at five thirty in the morning, and after making a cup of tea, went out into the back yard, past the bath house Declan had built for her, where she could bathe her bad leg and do her exercises. She set the cup on the small table Maurice had made for her and watched as the morning began to brighten in a clear sky.

'Thanks for the fine day, Mammy and Daddy,' she whispered. 'I wish you could be here yourselves. You'd love Richard. He's wonderful.'

The little yard soon filled with bees and butterflies, buzzing and fluttering industriously among the raised vegetable beds near the bath house. Cáit and Molly were growing rhubarb, spring onions, cabbage and carrots in one bed, and Maurice's wife, Patricia, had set potatoes, strawberries and tomatoes in another.

It was a beautiful day; the azure Atlantic calm, and tiny white clouds scudded across the cerulean sky. The still air scented with the honey-sweet smell of wild furze mixed with seaweed – the aroma of home. Grace sipped her tea, enjoying the peaceful moment before the biggest day of her life. Soon the army of people would arrive and she and Richard would become the centre of everyone's attention.

She could hardly believe she was going to have Richard all to herself for a whole week while they were on their honeymoon. He'd probably have to go back to London then – he wasn't sure yet – but she was going to have a whole seven days with him with no interruptions. It felt like sheer bliss.

Since they got engaged, Richard had been back to America to tell his parents and Sarah in person that he was back from the dead. Grace's heart had gone out to him having to tell Sarah that her husband, Jacob, had chosen to stay in Switzerland rather than come home. Sarah took it surprisingly well, all things considered. She'd thought Jacob was dead, so the realisation that he wasn't was a huge relief. She didn't blame Richard for taking that flight back without her husband; she knew it was exactly the kind of thing Jacob Nunez would do.

Richard's newspaper editor, Kirky, had taken advantage of him being in the United States and sent him to report on a train crash in Pennsylvania, where 79 people died and 116 were injured. It was horrific, and Richard had done several pieces on it, two of which had been syndicated all over the country.

He had managed to get to Knocknashee for Christmas, which was magical, but once the New Year came, he had to return to London, and from there to Italy, to report on the Allied advance in the wake of the unconditional surrender of the Italians.

Grace taught with Eleanor as normal, and Maurice had taken up a position teaching in the boys' secondary school in Tralee. It seemed silly to try to make any plans while everything was so up in the air. The war was not over, but the feeling was that it would be soon – it was just a matter of time. With Richard being busier than ever and sent all over the place by Kirky, even if she'd gone to live with him in London, he wouldn't be there most of the time. So they had decided it was best that Grace stay in Knocknashee and he'd come back when he could. It wasn't ideal, and being married wouldn't change the situation much, but it was the best they could do for now.

'You'd say it if you wanted the place to yourself, though, wouldn't you?' Maurice had offered last week again. He was terribly concerned that he and Patricia and the girls would outstay their welcome or expect too much, but Grace had told him that she liked the company. Maurice and his family would move out eventually, she knew they would, but she didn't want them to feel under pressure to do so.

Her brother had been busy all morning setting up the tent on the village green – a huge thing worthy of a circus, borrowed from some parish up the country where Father Iggy knew the parish priest or something. Inside the tent were trestle tables, heaving with food despite the rationing. The Lewises had begged Grace for a list of things they could bring with them. 'Add to it,' Arthur Lewis had demanded several times when she sent him her modest requests. But at no point was an American wedding mooted, for which Grace was grateful.

Eloise arrived about seven o'clock. Grace went inside to greet her and succumb to her expert hairdressing and make-up skills. Grace almost never wore make-up, and her copper curls were a law unto themselves – the best she could usually do was tie them back with a ribbon. However, Eloise had much more detailed and complicated plans to put manners on her mop, which involved pinning it up on her head but allowing tendrils to fall seductively – as Eloise put it – to frame her face.

On top of the curls, Eloise placed the pert pillbox headpiece Peggy Donnelly had magicked up, from which one section of Lizzie's veil draped down Grace's back in an elegant ruche while the other section formed a stylish birdcage veil that could be pulled down to cover her face in the church.

The Swiss woman, who herself exuded elegance out of every pore, was in charge of Grace's wedding make-up too. 'Subtle but striking' was her goal, and according to herself and Tilly, in the practice run, she had achieved it. She'd coloured Grace's eyelids in a glistening gold colour, which caught the amber flecks in her green eyes. A light dusting of powder, brown mascara, and then the use of an instrument that looked like a medieval torture implement but that made Grace's eyelashes curl upwards. Eloise even plucked her eyebrows into a delicate arc, which really hurt, but Grace was given no sympathy.

'Beauty is pain, my darling Grace,' Eloise had cackled wickedly as she plucked without mercy.

From then on, the morning went by in a flurry, but even Grace herself had to admit that the end result was amazing. She was speechless as she stood looking at herself in the mirror, Tilly, Eloise and Lizzie behind her.

The dress was different to the one she wore to marry Declan. It was not really a wedding dress at all; it was a cream pencil skirt that stopped below her knee, and a matching boat-neck jacket with pearl buttons that cinched in at her waist. At first, being self-conscious about her twisted leg, she had said she wanted something floor-length, but she realised she didn't want to re-create the look of her first wedding, so she decided instead she would just have to accept that people would see her bad leg and get on with it. The outfit, chosen with Eloise's and Tilly's help from a boutique off Dawson Street in Dublin, was beautiful in a grown-up, refined way. Grace felt very sophisticated in it. And Caroline Lewis had very kindly supplied silk stockings from the United States, which were wonderful and made her feel less self-conscious about her leg.

The nerves of last night had finally dissipated. Tilly was right – this was a day for her and Richard, not for showing off or trying to make Knocknashee into something it wasn't.

'Well then, we'd better go,' Eloise said. 'See you in the church, my dear.'

As she and Tilly left, Lizzie said, 'Hugh can bring the car around if you want, Grace.'

'No, Lizzie. I think I'd prefer to walk. But thank you, though. For everything.'

Lizzie Warrington's eyes were bright with tears. 'I'm so happy for you, Grace, and I know your parents would be so proud of you today.'

She smiled. 'I know they would, and they'd be very grateful to you, Lizzie, for stepping into their shoes. You've been like a mother to me most of my life, and I thank God every day for you and Hugh. I've been so lucky to have you both.'

'It's we who are the lucky ones. You're like a daughter to us. I wish you all the love and luck and happiness in the world.'

Hugh arrived then, and when he saw her, he too was overwhelmed. 'Oh, Grace...' He seemed lost for words. His lovely Yorkshire accent had soothed her since she was a girl, and it was doing the same now.

She grinned. 'What? Won't I do?'

'You look beautiful, really and truly. You are so lovely. Richard is a lucky man.'

'He'll be a frantic man if we don't get a move on.' She laughed. 'You scrub up well yourself, by the way.'

Hugh was dressed in a pale-grey suit, and his iron-grey hair had been cut for the occasion. When she was a small girl, Dr Warrington had reminded her of a bear, a huge man with a beard and straggly hair, but now she realised he was just above normal height, and like everyone, time was taking its toll on him too.

'Lizzie wouldn't let me put butter on my toast this morning for fear I'd get grease on me.' He chuckled. 'Do I recognise that veil?'

'You do indeed.' She grinned. 'It's my "something borrowed" for luck.'

'Well, if you and Richard are as happy as Lizzie and I have been, then you'll be very fortunate indeed.' Hugh met his wife's eyes, and Grace saw that same love there. They had it, and she and Richard had it too, she just knew they did.

'Well, you look very handsome,' she said, taking his arm. 'Now will we get this done?'

'We will. And thank you for asking me, Grace – it means a lot to me.' His voice was gruff with emotion.

'Oh, I'll have you do it at *all* my weddings.' She laughed again as they walked down the hall.

They followed Lizzie to the front door, but as they reached it, Grace stopped and turned to Hugh. 'You're the perfect person to do this, Hugh. And I wanted to say this. When my parents died, I was in a fog of grief. And then to get polio and have to be in hospital for so long… You were so kind to us all. You made all the children feel like we were important to you personally. Not many doctors do that.' She looked up at him, her gaze sincere and direct. 'Not seeing you and Lizzie every day was one of the hardest things to bear when I came home here to Knocknashee. And then Agnes telling me not to be writing to you and bothering you…'

His kind eyes looked sad. 'But you were special to us,' he replied earnestly. 'And you still are. Even then you knew it on some level.' His broad vowels had never shortened despite over forty years in Ireland.

She smiled at him. 'I'm so glad we reconnected. I don't think I would have survived these last years without you and Lizzie.'

Hugh put his hand on her shoulder. 'You would have, Grace. You're the bravest, strongest person I know. But we're glad to have been part of it. And being here today, seeing you marry Richard, well, it's very special. I'm not a religious man, as you know, but I do think there's more to it all than this. So if he's anywhere, Declan is right here too, and your parents, and perhaps even your sister – all cheering you on, Grace. If anyone deserves to be happy, it's you. So go now, love, and grab your happy ever after.'

Grace didn't trust herself to speak, so she just nodded. Besides, Eloise would kill her if she smudged her make-up.

Hugh opened the front door for her, and they walked out together, heading for the church that sat on a small hill overlooking the bay and the village of Knocknashee.

CHAPTER 4

To Grace's delight, when she emerged from her house, she saw that under Eleanor Worth's management, the children in her school were lined up on each side of the street to form a guard of honour for her. They were all playing the tin whistle, and the beautiful wedding tune 'Tabhair dom do Lámh' rang out in the still, warm air.

Tears threatened again but Grace beamed instead, waving to the children as she walked arm in arm with Hugh through the ranks of their sweet, scrubbed faces. All the neighbours, and everyone from miles around, invited or not, would be in the church today to see Miss Fitz get married to her big, handsome American. The walk only took a few minutes, but she drank it all in.

Outside the church, the breeze blew her hair, but the lacquer applied liberally by Eloise kept Grace's curls and veil in place.

Waiting in the porch for them were her bridesmaid, Sarah, and her maid of honour, Tilly. They were both dressed in salmon-coloured shot silk because Tilly had agreed to wear a dress on this one occasion, although Grace had told her she didn't have to. Beside them, Maurice's girls, Cáit and Molly, and Nathan's daughters, Naomi, Stella and little Megan, were all dressed in their peach organza.

'Grace, you are radiant,' Tilly said and Grace laughed.

'I feel it. And you don't look too bad yourself.'

Tilly grinned and twirled the hem of her dress, which, like those for the flower girls, had been brought from America by Richard's mother, as such fabric was simply unavailable in Ireland.

Nathan, who was Richard's best man, came out to enquire if they should start. He was like Richard but slightly less handsome. 'Grace, you sure do look so beautiful,' he said. 'My brother is like a cat on a hot tin roof in there, so we better put the poor guy out of his misery.'

She returned his grin. 'I'm ready.'

'Great,' Nathan said. 'I'll give the reverend the thumbs-up.'

Mrs Devereaux, the old church organist, had retired, and the hunt for a replacement was ongoing. But Father Iggy had insisted on Grace walking up the aisle to the bridal march played on an organ. So he had asked his friend Reverend Hilliard, the Church of Ireland vicar from the next parish over, to do the honours.

It was very kind of Reverend Hilliard to agree, and apparently he'd said he was delighted to do it for Miss Fitz. His little granddaughter, Kitty Hilliard, had asked to go to Knocknashee school because the nearest Protestant school was in Tralee and she would have to board and didn't want to leave home.

Grace's sister, Agnes, who was headmistress in Knocknashee before her, had given no such accommodation to Kitty's older brothers, as she refused point-blank to have people outside of the Catholic faith attend the school. But it hadn't been a problem for Grace, who was happy to have Kitty at the school and had welcomed her with open arms.

Now Kitty Hilliard was having a wonderful time in Knocknashee, although she did find some of the aspects of Catholicism strange. Grace had had to intervene a few weeks ago when she stumbled across six girls performing an unofficial baptism on their little Church of Ireland friend in the girls' cloakroom. She'd gone to see Yvette and Geoff Hilliard, the girl's parents, to explain what had happened, and they couldn't have been nicer about it. And the would-be ministers of the sacrament of baptism were given a stern talking to, but Grace had softened when she realised they meant no harm. Quite the opposite actually. They were fearful for Kitty's immortal soul. It later emerged that Kitty wasn't their first bootleg baptism. They'd performed similar ministrations previously on the three Worth girls.

'Come on, girl. Let's get you sorted.' Tilly's voice brought her back to the moment.

As Tilly and Sarah helped her to adjust her birdcage veil, Hugh squeezed her arm and gave her an affectionate kiss on the cheek.

'Are we ready, girls?' Grace asked the little ones.

All nodded enthusiastically. Cáit was going to hold hands with Naomi, and Molly with Stella and Megan. They had a little posy of flowers each to carry, and they were taking their roles very seriously. There had been a lot of practice with Lizzie on the path outside Grace's house earlier this morning: step together, step together, as they tried to walk in unison.

Grace shut her eyes and offered up a silent prayer to her parents and to her guardian angels to watch over her and Richard. Then she exhaled slowly. She would remember this wonderful day for the rest of her life.

The church organ started up with a flamboyant wheeze, and with the sun shining through the stained-glass windows that lined the nave, a joyful burst of organ music filled the cavernous church as Grace and her little entourage entered. It was filled to capacity, and Grace glanced from side to side as she made her way up the aisle, leaning on Hugh for support.

To her right she saw Eloise with Odile on her lap, Mary O'Hare beside her – firm friends, but as unlikely a pair as you could meet. Mrs McHale and the Maheadys were on the groom's side, just to balance things up, and Grace smiled as Joey Maheady gave her a huge wink. He and Sylvia stood proudly with their daughters, Lily and Ivy, and she was glad to see that Lily had chosen to sit with them rather than with Charlie and his family.

The O'Donoghues were there, Biddy looking conspicuous in a cerise dress that gathered at the waist. Peggy Donnelly was at pains to tell Grace she'd done her best to talk her out of it, but Biddy had her eye on it and wouldn't listen to reason. Grace thought Biddy looked nice; it was a very cheerful colour even if the cut wasn't ideal.

Peggy herself sat with Bríd Butler; they were both single so went to a lot of things as a pair. Peggy was of considerable girth, even with the rationing, but she said she was happy to be a bit plump because it made selling clothes easier. According to Peggy, no woman wanted to buy a dress from someone slimmer than them because they felt judged.

Sergeant Keane was there with his wife, Maureen. He gave Grace a nod and a smile, which she returned. Dr Ryan was there too, with his wife, a woman who looked always on the brink of losing her temper. Her brow furrowed naturally, but she was actually very kind and made sure everyone who needed to saw the doctor, whether they could afford to pay or not.

Eleanor Worth and her three girls beamed at her from their seat, while on the other side, almost the entire O'Shea clan had turned out for Miss Fitz. John, the father, had drowned with Grace's first husband, Declan, and Seán O'Connor, the local publican and undertaker, on that terrible night in 1941. Catherine O'Shea, the mother, had sent a lovely present of a linen tablecloth and a note of apology to say she wouldn't make the wedding because she had to go to Cork to have her varicose veins looked at.

Grace's heart gave a little flutter as they neared the top of the church. Her brother, Maurice, his wife, Patricia, and Lizzie Warrington sat in the front pew on the bride's side, with Charlie and Dymphna McKenna and their children behind them. Paudie and Kate were smiling broadly, while little Seámus waved happily and gave her a cheeky grin that showed off his one front tooth.

Peggy and Nancy sat together, and they both gave her an encouraging nod as she passed.

Arthur, Caroline and Rebecca Lewis sat together in the second pew on the groom's side. Behind them sat Miranda Logan, Richard's former girlfriend, and Esme Carter, the Lewises' housekeeper and Richard's surrogate mother for most of his childhood.

It had been touch-and-go that Esme would even make it over.

She'd never left Georgia, let alone the United States, she didn't have a passport, and it wasn't clear that they could get her paperwork sorted in time.

'Black people are entitled to apply for a passport,' Richard explained to Grace. 'But the reality is that they are often stymied by systemic discrimination, especially in the South. There's even a school of thought that questions the very citizenship rights of Black people, even though the Fourteenth Amendment was passed. The Nationality Act of 1940 should have helped, but legislation won't change people's habits or ideas overnight. So Esme and other coloured folk still have to deal with prejudice. And when that's built into an administrative practice or system, the rights of people like Esme are too often the casualties.'

But Richard had been determined that Esme Carter would make it to Knocknashee for his wedding, and with the combined clout of Arthur Lewis and Kirky, whom Richard had asked for help, they made it happen. Esme was now the proud owner of an American passport declaring her to be a citizen of the United States of America. She'd shown it proudly to Richard, with tears in her eyes, the moment she arrived.

Of course, no one in Knocknashee had ever seen a Black person before, so Grace had been worried about how the local townspeople would react to her. It wasn't that people would be rude to Esme. Well, not intentionally anyway, she hoped, with the possible exception of the local cobbler, Pádraig O Sé. But then he was rude to everyone.

When Grace expressed her concerns to Richard, he just smiled.

'Esme is a coloured woman living in the state of Georgia. There is nothing anyone can do or say that would shock her. Don't worry, Grace – we'll look out for her. And if I know Esme, she'll have them eating out of her hand within an hour of arriving.'

Grace needn't have worried. People stared – there was no getting away from that. But there was an innate dignity and kindness in Esme Carter that everyone in the village seemed to pick up on. They may have been taken aback at first, but when she smiled at them, they had no option but to smile back.

Little Seámus McKenna took to her immediately and insisted on clambering onto her knee, much to Dymphna's embarrassment.

'Oh, don't you fret yourself, Mrs McKenna,' Esme had said. 'Why, this little man is just peachy, and we all are getting on like grits and gravy.' Seámus gave a loud chuckle at this, which made everyone, including Dymphna, laugh.

Esme also answered Paudie McKenna's curious questions about why her skin was brown with grace and patience.

'Well, young man,' Esme said, 'this is how the good Lord made me, and I can no more change that than you can your lovely blue eyes. Nor would I want to,' she added.

Paudie nodded solemnly to her. 'Thank you, Mrs Carter,' he said, depositing that information into his already huge store of knowledge.

This morning in church, Esme was wearing a beautiful amethyst-coloured silk dress and coat, with matching hat – paid for by Caroline Lewis. Grace had been touched by the gesture, but Richard was sceptical of his mother's motives. He thought she just wanted people to see how well the Lewises' help was treated to quell any nasty comments about prejudice or segregation. Whatever Caroline's reasons, Grace thought, Esme looked wonderful.

Grace's breath caught in her throat as she looked towards the top of the aisle, where her future husband was waiting for her. He was so tall, broad and handsome – more like a film star than an ordinary person – and yet, there he was, waiting to marry her. Richard's blond hair had been expertly cut by a famous barber in Cork yesterday, and he was clean-shaven. He wore a dark-grey morning suit, tailored like it was made for him. Nathan had brought the suit with him from America because Richard, who had no love of fancy clothes, didn't own one. Seeing him there, Grace felt a surge of pride that this gorgeous man was soon to be hers. Was it any wonder that every woman for forty miles away had come to see this wedding?

Hugh shook Richard's hand as they reached the top of the aisle, and Grace turned to Richard. He towered over her, but she lifted her chin until their eyes met, his indigo blue, hers green with amber.

'You came,' he whispered with a grin.

She smiled. 'I did.'

'You look so beautiful. I…I'm lost for words.'

Father Iggy leant over and whispered, 'Just as long as you remember the "I do" bit, you'll be grand,' and the three of them laughed.

Sarah led the little girls into the front pew on the right of the church, Tilly bringing up the rear and sitting on the outside of the seat so she was free to sign the register with Grace. As they settled themselves, Grace could feel the eyes of the entire congregation on her. But she only had eyes for one person: Richard Lewis.

After six years of writing, crossed wires, she marrying Declan, he being engaged to Pippa Wills and so many near misses, they had finally made it here.

She and Richard Lewis were getting married.

This was really happening.

CHAPTER 5

'Friends,' Father Iggy began, 'you are all very welcome to Knocknashee to celebrate the wedding of two very special young people. I know we have family and friends from all over the world joining us, and we are so glad you could make the journey in these perilous times. As we pray the sacred Mass today, we pray for the happiness of Grace and Richard, but we also pray for peace in our world.

'We'd especially like to welcome Richard's family and friends to our town, and we hope that you'll feel at home here. I know Grace and Richard have explained that we usually speak Irish, but everyone is going to make a concerted effort to converse in English, so please bear with us – the language can be a bit rusty with us, but we'll do our best.'

He looked around, making eye contact with many of the congregation, and it struck Grace that being a priest was a lot like being on stage. She recalled meeting the famous Peter Cullen of Cullen's Celtic Cabaret years ago with Tilly in Dingle; he'd been charming but a consummate showman, able to hold an entire audience in the palm of his hand. It was a unique gift.

Amazingly, last week Charlie had delivered an envelope

containing a wedding card and two tickets in the royal box to see the cabaret at the Domhain Theatre in Dublin as guests of the Cullens, because Eloise had met Peter and May Cullen at a theatre event in Dublin and had mentioned Grace was getting married. Grace was surprised they remembered her, but they did and sent the tickets as a gift. She and Richard were staying in the Shelbourne hotel in Dublin for their honeymoon, so they would go to the show when they were there.

Grace and Richard listened and gave the responses in Latin as the priests concelebrated the Mass, their backs to the congregation. Throughout the church, many of the villagers said the rosary while the Tridentine Mass was intoned, as was the tradition. People didn't speak Latin of course, so it was permissible to say one's own prayers as it went on. Grace didn't dare turn around to catch the eye of the Lewis family to see what they made of it all.

Richard kept stealing glances at Grace as the priests said the Latin prayers, and each time he did, she met his gaze. They were positioned a foot apart, on separate chairs and kneelers at the top of the altar. She longed with all her being to move closer to him, to hold his hand, to be right beside him. Instead she had to force herself to concentrate on the Mass.

Once holy communion was over, Father Iggy and Father Lehane turned to the congregation and came down to where she and Richard knelt.

'This is my favourite bit of the job,' Father Iggy joked, reverting to English, and there was a ripple of laughter.

'As you all know,' the priest continued, 'Grace and Richard's story was not a straightforward one. So I would like to offer a special prayer of thanks to St Jude, that patron saint of hopeless cases, who played a significant role in their relationship. It just goes to show that the power of prayer can move mountains, or in this case, cross vast oceans.'

Once again, Grace could sense the congregation smiling behind her.

The priest leant forward and whispered to her and Richard, 'There's no backing out once this bit is done. Are you both sure?'

'We are,' they murmured in unison, and with such certainty, it made them both laugh.

Father Iggy grinned mischievously. 'Well, don't say I didn't warn you so.' He cleared his throat, adjusted his thick-lensed glasses – he was blind as a bat without them – and the congregation behind them went silent as he addressed the couple.

'Dear children of God...'

He'd mentioned to Grace earlier that he would use his own words for the rite of marriage rather than the more archaic standard ones – if that was all right with her. Of course she'd agreed.

'You have come to pledge your love before God and before the Church here present today in the person of the priest, your families and your friends. In becoming husband and wife, you give yourselves to each other for life. You promise to be true and faithful, to support and cherish each other until death, so that your years together will be the living out in love of the pledge you now make.'

Richard caught Grace's eye once again, and she felt such love there, she had not one single reservation. This was right.

'May your love for each other reflect the enduring love of Christ for his Church. As you face the future together, keep in mind that the sacrament of marriage unites you with Christ, and brings you, through the years, the grace and blessing of God our Father.'

Grace felt her eyes well with tears as Father Iggy spoke. He was one of her oldest friends and had been with her through some of the hardest times of her life, never preaching or superior, just always there, comforting, helping and doing his best. She felt so grateful to have him in her life– and now in Richard's as well.

'As you are about to exchange your marriage vows, the Church wishes to be assured that you appreciate the meaning of what you do, and so I ask you – have you come here of your own free will and choice and without compulsion to marry each other?'

Without touching or looking at each other, they answered in unison, 'We have.'

'And to the congregation here gathered, do you know of any lawful impediment why this couple should not be joined in holy matrimony? Speak now, or forever hold your peace.' Father Iggy paused for a moment; you could hear a pin drop. Then the priest smiled. 'All good so,' he said with an impish grin. 'That can be a hairy moment sometimes.' The crowd laughed again.

'So now then…' He turned to them both. 'Will you, Richard and Grace, love and honour each other in marriage all the days of your life?'

Grace and Richard spoke together. 'We will.'

'Are you willing to accept with love the children God may send you, and bring them up in accordance with the law of Christ and his Church?'

Grace didn't dare hope such a thing would happen. Hugh Warrington had always said every other part of her was in perfect working order, so there was no reason she wouldn't live a full life, but she worried. She and Declan had not managed to conceive. Admittedly, they had barely any time as husband and wife…but still.

'We are,' they chorused, as Grace offered up a silent prayer to God to give them a baby. At least bringing their children up Catholic wouldn't be a problem. Father Iggy had supervised Richard's instruction for his conversion from Episcopalian to the Catholic faith. Richard had said the priest was very lenient on points of doctrine, so he had passed with flying colours.

Father Iggy extended his hands. 'Then I invite you to declare before God and his Church your consent to become husband and wife. Hold each other's hands. Richard Harold Lewis, do you take Grace Margaret McKenna as your wife, for better, for worse, for richer, for poorer, in sickness and in health, all the days of your life?'

Richard squeezed Grace's hands gently, his blue eyes locked with hers, oblivious to everyone else in the church. 'I do.'

Father Iggy then turned to Grace.

'Grace Margaret McKenna, do you take Richard Harold Lewis as your husband, for better, for worse, for richer, for poorer, in sickness and in health, all the days of your life?'

This was it. The moment she had never dreamed would happen. Time stood still, and all at once, she felt the presence of her parents, Agnes and Declan at her back, urging her on. 'I do.'

'What God joins together let no man put asunder. May the Lord confirm the consent you have given and enrich you with his blessing.'

Father Iggy then turned with a smile to Nathan. 'Have we rings?'

Richard had insisted on wearing a wedding ring as well as Grace. It was traditional for just the woman to wear one, but Richard said he wanted the whole world to know he was a married man with a wonderful wife. Grace had been touched but had said she trusted him, so it wasn't necessary.

'I know it's not necessary, but I want to. Do you mind if I do?' he'd asked. She'd agreed, and they'd bought two gold bands in a jeweller's shop in Cork.

Nathan fumbled for a moment, then blushed slightly, before locating the velvet ring box in his inside suit pocket.

'That's another hairy moment survived,' Father Iggy quipped again, to another ripple of laughter.

Nathan handed the box to Father Lehane, who held it out so that Father Iggy could perform the blessing.

'Almighty God, bless these rings, symbols of faithfulness and unbroken love. May Richard and Grace always be true to each other. May they be one in heart and mind. May they be united in love forever through Christ our Lord.'

'Amen,' the congregation responded.

Father Iggy handed Grace's ring to Richard and gave him the nod to place it on her finger.

'Grace, wear this ring as a sign of our faithful love. In the name of the Father, and of the Son and of the Holy Ghost.'

Grace then took the other ring and placed it on Richard's finger. 'Richard, wear this ring as a sign of our faithful love. In the name of the Father, and of the Son and of the Holy Ghost.'

'All right, this is the best bit.' Father Iggy opened his hands again, beaming joyfully at the gathered crowd. 'I think we should all say it together. Doing so is not exactly part of the rite of marriage, but in this case particularly, I think it's deserved, because God knows we've all waited long enough for this moment. Are we ready?' He waved his arms as if conducting an orchestra. 'One, two, three…'

The entire congregation spoke as one. 'I now pronounce you husband and wife.'

A burst of spontaneous applause erupted through the church, and Father Iggy beamed as he invited the couple to sign the register, which Father Lehane had placed on the altar. Tilly signed beneath Grace's signature and Nathan beneath Richard's. Then the organ started to play Mendelssohn's 'Wedding March' as Grace and Richard, hand in hand and beaming at the gathered crowd, walked down the aisle, finally a married couple.

CHAPTER 6

As the wedding party milled around in the churchyard, the bride and groom greeted and congratulated, nobody noticed a woman in a dark-green coat and hat in the gathered crowd. She lurked at the back, trying not to look conspicuous. Typically a stranger in Knocknashee would draw attention. However, given today's circumstances and the presence of a number of unfamiliar faces, she was hoping people would presume she was an acquaintance of the American groom.

The woman knew the person she had come to see was the tall, willowy, dark-haired woman in the beautiful silk bridesmaid's dress, and she suddenly felt a wave of panic. *This isn't the right time.* She shouldn't disturb the woman today. Maybe she'd slip away and try to see her another day. Or maybe not at all. Because if she approached this woman, if she told her who she was, then closing that can of worms would be impossible, and she had no way of knowing what would happen. It might work out, and how she dreamed – no, *longed* – for that to be the case, but there were a million ifs and buts and maybes, plenty of things that could go wrong, and she would have exploded a bomb in her own life for nothing.

And it would be a devastating bomb. She was under no illusion about that.

A tall blond woman, wearing what looked like a very expensive and expertly cut midnight-blue silk trouser suit, and who spoke in a European accent, was herding everyone onto the steps of the church for a photograph. The bride, with her alabaster skin and copper curls, was radiant in a cream two-piece, and the groom was a very handsome man. The bride, she noticed, walked with a limp; one of her bridal shoes had a built-up sole to compensate for the shortness of her leg. She barely reached her husband's armpit, but when she smiled up at him, it was as if she were glowing from within.

The woman was fascinated by the groom's family. With their fine clothes, expertly done hair and white teeth, one knew straight away they were American. She'd never been to America. Never imagined for a second she would ever go there. But maybe that would change now?

She watched from the side as more photos were taken. She paid particular attention to the photo being organised with five adorable flower girls. She only had sons herself, and she wondered what it would be like to dress a daughter. To put ribbons in her hair and have her wear a pretty dress so she could twirl and be admired.

The bride was with an older couple. The man was tall, almost as tall as the groom, kind and attractive in an older-man kind of way. The woman beside him – she presumed she was his wife – was plain, dumpy really, with a large nose. They seemed mismatched. But as he helped her down the steps after they'd had their picture taken, he did it with such tenderness and kindness, it made her take notice. Nobody had ever taken her hand like that or helped her down steps with such obvious tenderness or care.

Then it was the Americans' turn. The well-dressed couple were clearly the groom's parents. The groom's resemblance to his father was unmistakable; although the older man's hair was grey, he had the same blue eyes as his son. His wife beside him wore her hair – suspiciously dark for a woman her age – in an elegant bun at the nape of her neck. Her dress and coat of silver silk were not like anything the woman had ever seen before, and unlike the groom's father, his mother seemed tense.

A younger man, clearly the groom's brother, along with his wife and children, joined the couple in posing for the photograph.

The woman watching gave a soft gasp as the couple called another woman forward. She was an older Black woman, elegant in purple silk, who looked both overjoyed and reticent at the same time. But the couple insisted, coaxing, cajoling, until she joined them, and they all smiled joyfully for the camera. The groom put his arm around her shoulder and kissed her cheek, saying something that made all of them laugh.

I wonder who the Black woman is. Whoever she was, the jealousy in the groom's mother's eyes was unmistakable.

The woman's heart began to pound as the American party returned for one more family photograph, all together – father, mother, brother and his family, the Black woman and finally the groom's sister – the tall bridesmaid she had come to see.

The group began to move down the chapel steps. She knew where they were headed – along the main street to the village green, where tents had been set up for the wedding feast. She had peeked in earlier before going to the church. It was the most extravagant thing she had seen in years – if ever. All those piles of food – her boys' eyes would be out on stalks at the sight.

As she pondered what to do next, she heard a band begin to play. For some strange reason, hearing the happy music made her shiver.

This is not the time.

She would leave it. It was stupid anyway. She knew that. Why couldn't she just leave well enough alone? But she also knew, even as she was saying the words to herself, that leaving it wasn't an option. Not any more. Not now that she knew.

Would she have been better off if her husband, Frank, had never met Tom O'Donoghue that morning? Or if they'd met and discussed something else? But that wasn't what happened. Frank had met Tom at the wholesaler's in Killarney, both men getting stock for their respective grocery shops, and the conversation had come around to the excitement in Knocknashee. Frank had remarked that Tom seemed to be stocking up, and he'd explained how it was because of this enormous wedding in the village – a local girl to an American. Then Tom had told him about Sarah Lewis, the groom's sister, and how she was a fine-looking woman apparently.

She'd wrinkled her nose in disgust. Trust Tom to remark on that, as if it was relevant or he had even a chance of a look-in with her. Tom explained how the good-looking woman had come over to Knocknashee a bit earlier than the rest of the family because she was doing a bit of research.

She'd been in the kitchen mashing the spuds as Frank, sitting at the kitchen table with his cup of tea, had droned on in that terrible monotone voice of his. Not that he had a clue how awful it was. Sure his favourite sound was his own voice.

'Yes, this American woman is over here because she and some other aul wan, who is Irish, I think, but has lived for years in the States, are doing a bit of digging. The postman in Knocknashee had his children taken off him by Canon Rafferty when his wife died – he hit the bottle and they were not safe with him – but they were reunited recently, I believe. Now this American woman is trying to reunite another child placed for adoption by the canon in America with the woman who had him. Of course, I'm assuming it's a boy. Tom didn't say.'

Frank had sounded disapproving, but then he was disapproving about most things. 'I mean to say, that's only poking noses where they're not needed, typical female behaviour, if you ask me. If a child was lucky enough to have been adopted in America and saved from a life of shame and ridicule – because let's call a spade a shovel, that child will have been born to a girl who was up to no good...'

She stopped mashing the potatoes as her husband threw her a sly, malicious look that made her sick to her stomach. 'Nice girls don't find themselves in that kind of predicament,' he continued. 'You may be sure of that. The offspring should be delighted and grateful for what he's got and leave well enough alone.'

She'd swallowed, trying to keep her voice light but interested.

Frank had keen hearing for any tone he considered insolent or dismissive. 'And did the canon have many children adopted, do you think?' She would flatter Frank by asking his opinion. Of course he wouldn't know, he knew nothing, but he liked to think he was an authority on everything.

'Oh sure, loads, probably,' he said imperiously. 'The man's a walking saint, and all that business a few years back about him working for the Germans is a load of rubbish. I know him well, and he was a devoted servant of Christ. He was set up.' Frank's mouth curled up in a contemptuous sneer. 'Most likely by some slut of a girl who let men do what they wanted to her and then blamed the poor canon for her downfall.'

The *poor* canon. No. That man was a lot of things, but poor wasn't one of them.

'And this American woman is trying to find these children, is she?' She was being deliberately vague and unsure. Frank hated it if she knew something he didn't.

'Foolish woman, yes. Apparently she and this other interfering old biddy are trying to find a woman who had a child here that the canon had adopted. The adopted parents died or something, and the child is now in an orphanage.' Frank had sighed as he changed his cardigan from the shop to the one he wore at home. As they were both the same dull beige colour, she often wondered why he bothered.

'Did you say the child was a boy or girl?' she asked again, as casually as she could manage.

'Ah sure, didn't I say I didn't know?' Frank snapped. 'I tuned out of listening to Tom O'Donoghue and his nonsense. The man can be a right bore – the gospel according to Tom O'Donoghue every time I've the misfortune to run into him.'

Takes one to know one, she thought.

CHAPTER 7

'Reminds me of your wedding day,' Richard said to Sarah. He knew she was trying to put a brave face on everything but that she was sick with worry about her husband, Jacob.

'Don't let the people of the Savannah Yacht Club hear you say their spread was equal to a tent in Ireland.' Sarah smiled, but it didn't reach her eyes. It never did these days. 'Are you enjoying yourself?' she asked.

He nodded. 'It's wonderful, and everyone has gone to so much trouble. I know it's because they all love Grace so much, but it's nice. How about you? You doing OK?'

Sarah sighed and nodded. 'It's the not knowing that gets to me the most. Sometimes I tell myself he's dead. That way it's at least certain. At least I know. But I can't let my mind go there. It's too hard. So I hang on to hope – false hope, most likely – and that doesn't feel any better... Sorry, I shouldn't be moaning to you, especially on your big day. Ignore me.'

He sat beside her and put his arm around her and gave her a squeeze. 'It's not false hope, Sarah. We thought he was dead last time – and look how he turned up for us. But I know what you mean about the not knowing. It's a killer, I have to admit. Truth is, I miss him too. Not a day goes by when I don't think maybe I should have dragged him onto that damn plane. Or let him go and me stay or something.'

She laughed. 'Don't be crazy, Richard. First, Jacob Nunez does exactly as he pleases, we both know that, so he wouldn't have allowed it. Second, he wanted to stay.' Her eyes were bright with unshed tears. 'Fighting that damned war is all he ever wanted to do, and he was never going to give up an opportunity like that.'

He gave her another small hug. 'Look, I'm not going to go over old ground. We've talked about this to death, I know, but if Jacob stays in Switzerland, he'll be fine. Truly, he will. Germany is not going to invade Switzerland or anywhere else at this stage – they're on the run and they know it. So if he stays there, he'll survive.'

Sarah reached into her purse, searching for a handkerchief. 'That's a big if, though, isn't it? And if Jacob is working with Alfie O'Hare now, as you think he is, then he won't stay in safe old Switzerland, will he?' Sarah was nothing if not a realist. 'He's a Jew, and he wants to do his bit. We both know he won't have gone that far to sit in safety in Switzerland. And even if the Germans are losing, like you seem to think, it doesn't mean they'll just allow an American Jew to roam about freely.'

He sighed. 'True, Sarah, and I'm not saying there's nothing to worry about. But if Jacob does do any kind of work, it will be underground and subterfuge – the kind of thing Alfie is involved with. And Alfie O'Hare is still alive, despite all the odds, so he's with good people.'

Sarah gave a pale smile as, a few feet away from them, Paudie McKenna beamed in delighted surprise as he bit into a ripe, juicy peach, shipped all the way from Georgia. Surely his first time tasting one.

Richard nodded. He got it. She didn't want to discuss it further.

Everyone milled around, filling their plates with the astonishing array of food, most of which had either never been seen before or hadn't been seen since before the war.

'Daddy sure pulled out all the stops, didn't he?' Sarah said.

'Yes, he did. People here haven't had treats like this for years.'

'And credit where it's due, Mother got involved too. She went to the City Market downtown herself to supervise the purchase and shipping of fruits and vegetables and chocolates and all sorts. You can imagine it. The traders never had such a bumper day of sales – she practically cleaned them out. Then she and Daddy paid a small fortune to ship it all over here. But it's her way of saying she approves of you and Grace. Because, as we know, she's emotionally constipated.' She giggled at their running joke.

He smiled. 'She gave Grace a sapphire necklace that belonged to her grandmother as a wedding gift.'

Sarah grimaced. 'Look, I know I'm Caroline Lewis's worst critic,' she said, 'but that girl of yours sure melted that iceberg. She succeeded where almost everyone else failed.'

Richard was about to agree when he heard his name being called. The band was gathered, and a large circle of people had formed around the makeshift dance floor.

He pecked his sister's cheek and stood. 'Got to go, Sarah. I have to dance with my wife.'

Grace was waiting for him at the side of the dance floor, laid by Charlie and Maurice last night, and he thought she had never looked more beautiful. He almost had to pinch himself – was this really happening? The girl who six years ago had put a letter in a bottle, which found its way to him – after so many wrong turns and crossed wires, here they were, about to dance together as man and wife for the first time.

They'd practised. Grace had told him how Peter Cullen, a famous Irish showman, had danced with her in Dingle and told her to never limit herself. Polio didn't stop Grace; she was such an indomitable spirit. But he knew she was nervous about this dance.

The showband played regularly in the hotels around Killarney for the tourists and had been prepped to play the song that had been bittersweet for them over the years.

Janie O'Shea, who had a voice like an angel, was going to perform, and the band leader was happy to step aside. 'If we can't have Vera

Lynn here, we have the next best thing.' He chuckled, giving Janie an encouraging wink.

The brass section of the band began the familiar melody of 'We'll Meet Again', and Janie caught Richard's eye and opened her mouth to once again sing the song that meant so much to the couple. He had managed to get a gramophone and a copy of the record for Janie to listen to, the young woman now had the forces' sweetheart's sultry alto almost to a T.

As Janie sang her heart out for them, Richard waltzed slowly with Grace. He could smell her shampoo, as he put his face to her hair. How he longed to be alone with her. After a few minutes, Charlie cut in on their dance, so Richard marched straight up to Esme and asked her up. Rebecca looked shocked at this, and his mother arched a perfectly plucked eyebrow at him, but Miranda Logan raised her glass in a toast as he passed her. Esme looked as proud as any mother as she beamed on his arm as they approached the dance floor. Together they waltzed in perfect time. Esme had been the one to teach him to dance when he was a little boy, so dancing with her was as natural as breathing. This would cause some gossip back in Savannah, Richard had no doubt.

As Janie and the band really got into the swing of it, everyone joined in. There wasn't a family untouched by this war, and as people took to the dance floor, they were all thinking of their people gone, some to the British forces despite Irish neutrality, many more to work in England in the factories and on the farms.

Richard looked down at his wife. He had to keep saying the words 'my wife' to himself every time he looked at Grace. 'Is this real?' he whispered.

'If it's not, I don't want to ever wake up,' she whispered back.

'How soon before we can go, do you think?' he murmured in her ear. The last ten months had been bliss and hell simultaneously. He'd been away from her a lot, first to go home and later staying in London for Kirky. He had used every chance he had to get back to Knocknashee, but even with a press pass, civilian travel was fraught, and Kirky hated him being away from London as the war heated up.

He'd come back to do his instruction to become a Catholic, and Father Iggy had been flexible about his classes, fitting them in when it suited Richard. Once or twice Grace had come to Dublin to meet him; if he only had a few days to spend, then Knocknashee was too far away. She'd stayed with Marion, Tilly's sister, and her family in Malahide, and Richard had stayed in a hotel. But being so close to her, even when chaperoned, meant he was going mad with desire.

Grace was a devout Catholic, which meant no sex before marriage, and Richard had thought today would never come. He was enjoying the wedding, but more than anything, he wanted to take Grace to bed, to be alone with her in the hotel room in the Metropole in Cork, before they took the train to Dublin for their honeymoon. At this stage, it was all he could think about.

Of course she knew exactly what he meant. Once or twice over the last months, the ferocity of their desire for each other – it was a two-way street, he knew – had almost made them break the rules. But they hadn't. Grace had been married before and so wasn't a virgin, and neither was he, but making love to his wife was all he could think about.

Grace giggled. 'We have to cut the cake, and I've to throw my bouquet and all sorts yet. Besides, Hugh and Lizzie are taking us to Cork, and I'll have to change for going away, so we'll need to wait for another while anyway.'

Richard groaned and dipped his head to kiss her there, in front of everyone. It wasn't the done thing, public displays of affection like that, but he didn't care. He'd waited for what felt like forever for this moment.

CHAPTER 8

Sarah stood in a line of women waiting. The wedding guests were using the restrooms at the school, and there was a long wait for the ladies' facilities. Yet another example of the inequity of the world, she thought. The men didn't bother waiting, availing themselves of a bush or an alleyway to take care of business.

There was nobody waiting for the men's restroom, and Sarah wondered if she'd cause a scandal by suggesting the women use both.

She swung around as she heard someone call her name. 'Yes?'

Facing her was a slight woman in a bottle-green coat and brown hat. She had been pretty once, but the wild salt winds of the west of Ireland had carved lines in her face, and her hazel eyes held a deep sadness.

'How can I help you?' Sarah smiled, and the woman seemed to relax a little. But Sarah sensed she was coiled tight as a spring.

'I was wondering if I could have a word…?'

Sarah nodded and moved out of the restroom line, putting enough distance between herself and the queue to prevent being overheard. She had little doubt that the other women waiting would be very interested to hear what was going on, and some sixth sense told Sarah this woman wouldn't want to state the reason for seeking her out in front of the whole of Knocknashee.

'It's a bit...well...' The woman wrung her hands and had the look of a hunted fox, as if any moment she expected someone to lay a hand on her shoulder and lead her away to an uncertain fate. 'I'm sorry to disturb you today,' the woman continued, 'especially at your brother's wedding. But I didn't know if I would get another chance...'

'In relation to what?' Sarah asked.

'The child in the orphanage in New York,' the woman said quietly.

Sarah exhaled. *Thank God.* It wasn't to do with Jacob. 'Of course. Come with me,' she said. She ushered the nervous woman across the street to Grace's house. She was sure her new sister-in-law wouldn't mind her using the privacy of her home for whatever this woman wanted to tell her. And besides, Sarah could use Grace's bathroom.

The door was unlocked as always, and Sarah directed the woman towards the sitting room. 'This is the bride's home,' she explained, 'but she won't mind us using it. I'm right in presuming what you want to talk to me about is not general information?'

The woman nodded and Sarah smiled. 'I'll be back in a moment,' she said. 'I have to use the restroom.' She caught the look of bewilderment on the woman's face. 'Or what is it they call it in London, the *loo?*'

The woman still looked puzzled, and she wondered if her strange companion would still be there when she got back.

When she returned to Grace's sitting room, she found the other woman standing in front of the empty fireplace, her old but polished handbag over her forearm.

'Won't you have a seat?' Sarah had found that, like Richard, she had a knack for getting people to open up, to relax. She didn't know exactly how she or Richard did it, but something about their demeanour put people at their ease. Usually.

'Thank you.' The woman sat, perched uncomfortably on the edge of the sofa, as the sounds of merriment from the wedding wafted across the street.

Sarah tried to break the ice. 'This is the wildest wedding that

Knocknashee has ever seen, I'm afraid. We Americans are not known for our subtlety.'

'It all looked so magical,' the woman said. 'And the bride and groom are clearly very happy.' Sarah noted as she spoke that she had a different accent than Grace and the other villagers in Knocknashee.

'They are happy, which we're all thrilled about,' she replied. 'Although to tell you this wedding was a long time coming would be to understate it. Now what can I do for you?'

The woman wore a plain wedding band, no other jewellery or adornment, and Sarah could see her dark hair under the hat was inexpertly cut.

'Well, I don't know, to be honest. I...' The woman swallowed and seemed all of a sudden tongue-tied.

'OK, let's start with an easy one. What's your name?'

'Hannah Monaghan...Mrs Nunez,' the woman managed.

'Well, since neither of us are a hundred years old, why don't we begin with me being Sarah and you being Hannah?' Sarah laughed, hoping it would help the conversation to flow more easily.

'Er, yes, all right...Sarah. My husband is Frank, Frank Monaghan – Monaghan is my married name. I was Kelly before. Hannah Kelly.'

'From around these parts?' Sarah asked.

Hannah shook her head. 'No...I... Frank is from here. Well, near here, closer to Dingle. I'm from North Kerry, near Ballybunion.'

'So you came a long way?' Sarah was trying to loosen her up but something was making this woman reticent, and it was as if she was teetering on the edge of bolting out the door any second.

'Well, yes...'

'And you wanted to speak to me about the girl in New York?' She found it was best to build on information given with a reluctant source rather than go off on her own tangent.

The woman's eyes brightened. 'So it is a girl? In the orphanage in America?' she whispered.

Sarah nodded, her interest now piqued.

'Well, then, yes. I want to speak to you about the girl... I think so. I...I'm sorry, I must seem...' She leant forward suddenly and let out a loud, nervous whisper. 'My husband doesn't know I'm here, you see, and...'

'He wouldn't approve?' Sarah guessed.

The woman inhaled through her nose, her skin pale and her eyes terrified.

'Hannah, if you're in danger or –'

'No...' Hannah gave a half smile. 'No, nothing like that... I...' She exhaled a ragged breath.

Sarah smiled again in a way she hoped was reassuring. 'How about you take a nice deep breath, a few of them actually, and tell me the whole story? I promise you, I won't repeat any of it if you don't want me to.'

The woman's gaze locked with hers, and an unspoken conversation passed between them. Something told Sarah that what this woman was about to talk about was not something she'd ever discussed with anyone, and her journalistic instincts tingled.

Hannah gulped and started to speak. 'I was sold into marriage after having a child out of wedlock. A deal, nothing more, nothing less. My father wanted to be rid of me because I was a disgrace to the family, and so he made an arrangment with Frank Monaghan.'

The words were rehearsed, and yet delivered with such bitter hurt, it was hard for Sarah to hear them. 'To the baby's father?' she asked gently.

'No. A different man. I was disgraced and my family were disgraced. I was sent to a place in Cork, a convent, and I had the baby there. A little girl. The child was taken from me. I wasn't given a say. Then, after a few weeks, I came home. My father couldn't bear to look at me, and my mother...well, she was not a woman to speak up. But I had nowhere else to go.'

'That sounds awful,' Sarah said, moving to sit beside Hannah on the couch.

'Yes, well, Frank Monaghan was approached by an intermediary, known to both Frank and my father. My husband was...he *is* much older than me. He had spent his life living over the shop with his elderly parents, so he wasn't in a position to marry before that, but now his parents were dead and he had the shop. So he wanted a wife and family. He needed someone younger, as someone his own age would be too old to bear his children. Which is why, through the negotiator, he offered my father a deal.'

'What kind of a deal?'

'Two hundred pounds for my hand – one hundred to be paid on the date of marriage, and the other hundred when I gave him a son.'

Hannah's words hung in the air.

'How old is he?' Sarah hated to think. *This poor girl.*

'Seventy-five this year. And I'm twenty-nine. We married when I was seventeen, and we have four sons.'

Sarah tried to hide her shock. The woman facing her looked a lot older than twenty-nine, but this life she described did not sound like a bed of roses. So she was married when she was seventeen to a man of... Sarah quickly calculated in her head. *Sixty-three? Surely not?*

'I heard...well, actually, Frank spoke to someone who was talking about you trying to find the mother of a child who was in an orphanage in America. He said the adoption was arranged by Canon Rafferty.'

Something about the way she said the man's name struck Sarah. The woman's voice was full of loathing. That said, if the canon had stolen a child of hers, she would probably loathe him too.

'I am,' she confirmed. 'Charlie McKenna, who is the postman here and a friend of Grace's, had his daughter taken by this Canon Rafferty guy when she was a baby. Charlie was reunited with her last year. In fact, Lily is at the wedding today with her family. But I knew there were others too, and I've taken an interest. One girl in particular is bothering me because the people who adopted her were killed in an accident, so she's now in an orphanage. She's thirteen and very lonely. I thought I would try to find her birth mother in case there was any way she could have her back, even at this late stage.'

The woman stared at Sarah with a mixture of fear and hope. 'Does she...this girl...have a birthmark on the inside of her right ankle? Almost a star shape?'

Sarah's mouth went dry. The child had been taken to America, and given to a couple to adopt, for a fee of course, the Canon had a nice business going in babies, but her adoptive parents had been killed and now she was in an orphanage in New York. As she read the notes on the child something had struck her as fortuitous. In a box on the form marked 'distinguishing features', there had been an entry stating the girl had a birthmark on her ankle. She didn't know if it was star-shaped or not, but this was as close as she'd come to finding the child's mother. 'I think she has a birthmark, but as to the shape, I don't know...'

'Well, my daughter would be thirteen years old now, and when she was born, she had a birthmark on her ankle. I remember seeing it. They let me feed her, after she was born, and I saw it then. She had a big head of dark hair and blue eyes...but I think all babies have blue eyes.'

Sarah thought of Carrie Dwyer in the Graham children's home in New York. She had dark hair, sleek and straight as an arrow, cut in a kind of bowl shape. She was a sweet girl, quietly spoken, with a slight lisp. She exuded forlorn and lost, and each time Sarah visited, she hated to see the light of hope in the child's eyes dashed when Sarah had to admit she'd gotten no further.

The only information Sarah was sure of was that the canon placed the child with her adoptive family, presumably at a cost. He was the only person who could give her any other information about Carrie's origins, but he had vanished without trace, and nobody could or would say where he was. Grace had asked Father Iggy, but he didn't have a clue, and Grace said she believed him. Sarah had every intention of approaching the bishop and asking him, as well as the local cop here, who arrested the canon on suspicion of being a German spy. There had been no mention of a trial or anything since then; it was as if he was simply spirited away.

But if this woman was Carrie Dwyer's legitimate mother, and she knew about the birthmark, then would that be proof enough for the orphanage? To do what? This poor woman was unlikely to be in a position to be reunited with her daughter or give the child a home. Reading between the lines, her husband wasn't a compassionate man.

But perhaps Sarah was jumping to conclusions, because she couldn't accept a man who thought marrying a seventeen-year-old when he was in his sixties was all right.

'And if Carrie – that's her name, Carrie Dwyer – is your child, I don't know how I would prove it without the corroboration of Canon Rafferty. So what do you want to do?'

Tears filled the woman's eyes. 'I don't know. I just know I can't bear the idea of her alone in an orphanage. But Frank would never allow me to make contact, let alone offer her a home with us and the boys. He has no idea about Carrie, but he has strong opinions about things like that. And my sons…well, they're young and take up all my time. But I…'

Hannah stood suddenly and made to leave the room. 'I'm sorry. This was stupid of me. I should have thought it out better. I'm sorry, Mrs Nunez – Sarah. I shouldn't have come here…'

Sarah also stood and caught her hand before she reached the door. 'Please, Hannah, don't go, please. Nobody is going to force you to do anything, and this conversation won't go beyond these four walls, I swear to you. But please, let me help you.'

'There's nothing anyone can do,' Hannah replied, every word a knell of hopelessness.

'I don't agree.' Sarah led her back to the couch. 'When we're in a dark place, sometimes we need another person to see the way out. We get blinded by all the problems, one piling on top of the other. But there's always a way, Hannah – always.'

'My husband would kill me if he knew I was here. He's very… strict.'

Sarah scowled. This guy was obviously not just a predator but a total jerk into the bargain. However, she held her tongue.

'If this girl is my daughter,' Hannah continued, 'then I have nothing to offer her. I always comforted myself with the knowledge that she was better off, with a family who loved her, but now…knowing she's alone, and I…' Emotion overtook her and she couldn't go on.

'All right, here's what we'll do,' Sarah said. 'I'll check on the birthmark, find out if it is a star shape. Though to be fair, she's thirteen years old now and would have grown, so the shape of the mark could have changed. Do you remember what date she was born?'

'The sixth of February 1931,' Hannah said with certainty. 'That's my birthday too.'

'You gave birth on your own birthday?' Sarah asked incredulously.

Hannah nodded. 'She was so perfect, so beautiful…'

'I'm so sorry this happened to you, Hannah. I can't imagine the loss you must have felt.'

The woman nodded. 'I knew I couldn't keep her – none of the girls in that place could, it was just how it was – but it was so hard to let her go…'

Her voice was raspy, and Sarah offered her a napkin from the sideboard to dry her eyes, as she didn't have a handkerchief. Gratefully, Hannah took it, dabbing away her tears.

'They took her when she was only two days old. Usually the babies were left with their mothers for a few days at least, but *he* arrived – Rafferty – and arranged to take my daughter. He came to see me, and he warned me not to look for her. He said she was better without me, now that she was starting a new life away from me.'

'Did he come to take babies from that place regularly?' Sarah was beginning to wonder if this wasn't a much bigger story than she'd first thought.

Hannah's mouth twisted in a way Sarah found hard to interpret. Was she going to cry? Laugh? Was it horror or amusement?

'No, I don't think so. None of the others knew who he was, and some of the women were there for years. He took a special interest in this case. He was the one who negotiated my marriage – he brokered the deal.' She spoke quietly. 'I think he was cut in on it, financially.'

Sarah struggled to understand this. Girls got in trouble – it happened all over the world, and they were ostracised and parents were ashamed. But the fathers of these children seemed to almost get away scot-free – as if these women and girls did this all on their own, another universal truth.

This woman had her baby in Cork, a city eighty miles away from here, and she wasn't a parishioner of the canon's, so Sarah failed to see how he was so involved. 'Was he a friend of your family? Or of your husband's? Given that he was the one arranging all of this?' she asked.

'Not a friend, but they knew him. At least my parents did. And Frank knew him as well. The canon filled in for our parish priest for a few weeks when he was in hospital.'

'Was this a business for him? The sale of babies?'

'Possibly. I don't know. But I do know why he was so involved with my case.' Hannah had stopped crying now, her voice steely and cold.

'Why is that?'

Long seconds passed, and Sarah could see the inner turmoil in the woman sitting beside her.

'Because he was my child's father.'

CHAPTER 9

Richard and Grace walked arm in arm along the beach at Knocknashee. It was early evening, and the wedding celebrations were in full swing. They had slipped out together, leaving their families and friends deep in song and story. It had been a wonderful day, and yet both of them, unspoken, had felt the need for some fresh air and a little breathing space. The beach seemed like the ideal spot. It was mostly deserted this summer's evening, with many of the locals attending the party in their wedding tent on the village green.

They stood together, Richard's arms circling Grace's waist, listening to the sound of the gentle lapping of the ocean and the occasional screech of seagulls. There was no need to talk. Instead they each basked for a few precious minutes in the simple peace and comfort of the other's company.

They were both relieved the day had gone so well, but there had been some surprises as the day progressed. Richard in particular had been flabbergasted to see his father take to the stage and accompany his mother on the piano while she sang the George Gershwin love song 'Someone to Watch Over Me' in a sweet soprano voice.

'I still can't get over it,' Richard said. 'I knew my father could play piano, but I've never heard my mother sing before.'

Grace smiled. 'There you go. And she has a beautiful voice. And they obviously practised, because your father was such a support to her.' She leant back against her husband, resting her head on his chest. 'I think it was beautiful that they dedicated the song to us. I mean, after all they've been through, to still be standing side by side. Marriage isn't easy, but your parents are obviously people who stick it out, despite all the ups and downs. I think that's great.'

He nodded and kissed the top of her head. 'You're right, of course. It's just strange that I found out only today that my mother is musical. That said, she did force us all to learn piano when we were kids.' He chuckled. 'I was the only one the teacher got exasperated with and finally admitted defeat.'

She laughed. 'But neither Sarah nor Nathan can play now and you can. Just goes to show.'

'I always wanted just to play,' he said. 'I hated the rote learning of it and being chastised for not getting it right. Or what the teacher thought was right.' He leant down and murmured in her ear. 'Promise me, Mrs Lewis, we'll teach our children to play, but not by rapping their knuckles.'

Grace felt that familiar pang of anxiety when the subject of children came up. 'Richard, what if we can't…? If *I* can't…?'

'Then that's fine too.' He pulled her around to face him. 'I love you so much anyway, Grace Lewis, that it won't matter a fig to me.'

'Are you sure?' she whispered. 'I mean, if we can't, then we know I'm the problem. You already…well, with Pippa and everything…'

As soon as she spoke, Grace wished she could take the words back. Why had she brought up the fact that Richard's former girlfriend had miscarried and that was the reason she stood here now as his wife? On this day of all days? Was it because it scared her to think that if the baby had survived, he would be Pippa's husband, not hers?

Richard became serious. 'Grace, listen to me. Everything about us is a miracle. I was supposed to be dead at least twice, you married Declan, I almost married Miranda and then almost married Pippa.

We've had so many chances, we're like the cat with nine lives. And all I feel is gratitude. Nothing more. I'm just so grateful to fate or God or whatever force is managing this whole world, that in the midst of all this carnage and chaos, the universe found time to put us together at long last. So if all I ever get from this life is being your husband, then I'm the luckiest man on the planet.' He leant over and kissed her, his lips soft against hers.

'I feel the same,' she whispered against his mouth.

Their kissing moved from gentle to urgent, until an embarrassed cough from nearby startled them out of their embrace.

'Eh, I'm sorry, Miss Fitz – oh, I mean, Mrs Lewis. Mr Lewis.' Fiachra O'Flynn, the young postman, was standing a little distance away, looking mortified at having disturbed them at such an intimate moment.

'Goodness, Fiachra, you startled us,' Grace said, unable to keep some of the irritation at the interruption out of her tone.

The young man blushed crimson red and stammered another apology.

'It's fine, Fiachra,' Richard said, taking pity on the youth. 'Is there something you want?'

The young postman nodded miserably. 'Well, yes, there is.' He plucked a piece of paper from his jacket pocket and handed it to Richard. 'Miss O'Flaherty went back to check the post office a few moments ago and found this. It's for you, Mr Lewis,' he added somewhat redundantly.

Grace could see that the buff-coloured piece of paper was a telegram, and her heart began to pound. Was it bad news about Jacob? Or Alfie?

Richard's face told her that he was thinking the same as he opened the telegram and scanned it. She was relieved when his expression turned from alarm to annoyance.

'It's from Kirky,' he said. 'The man has some nerve.' He handed the telegram to Grace so she could read it.

Congratulations, Lewis. Get to London, then France. Stop. ALONE. Stop.

Allied Expeditionary Force landed Normandy. Stop. Go immediately. Stop. Expect copy soonest. Stop. Kirky.

'Now?' Grace asked incredulously. 'He doesn't mean now this minute surely.'

Richard grimaced. 'You can bet your bottom dollar he does, Grace.'

'He sent a second telegram asking if the first was delivered,' Fiachra added nervously. 'Do you want me to ask Miss O'Flaherty to tell him yes?'

Richard nodded grimly. 'Yes, do that,' he replied. 'Otherwise Kirky will keep sending telegrams until he's sure,' he added for Grace's benefit. 'Oh, and Fiachra…'

'Yes?'

'Not a word to anyone. Not just yet anyhow. Miss O'Flaherty too.'

Fiachra nodded. 'You can rely on me, Mr Lewis,' he said. 'I'll be off now and tell Miss O'Flaherty to telegram back like you said.'

As Grace watched the youth make his way over the dunes towards the village, her new husband deep in thought, she recalled a conversation she'd had with Sarah some days earlier.

'Things are going to heat up in Europe soon, Grace. I have it from a good source in London that certain lines from the French poem 'Chanson d'automne' by Paul Verlaine will be broadcast on the BBC. Apparently that's the signal to the Resistance that the invasion of the continent is imminent.' Sarah's eyes had shone with hope. 'If that's true, then Richard and I could go to report on it, and hopefully make contact with Jacob or Alfie or someone. I know it sounds naive, Grace. It's a huge continent in total disarray. But sitting here, waiting, doing nothing, is driving me crazy.'

Grace doubted Kirky would send Sarah to Europe – she was being naive if she thought he would – but her sister-in-law was right about one thing. If the Allies were landing in France, then Kirky would have no hesitation to send Richard there in a heartbeat. He just had. And Richard had to go. She had to accept that.

The thought of losing him again so soon filled her with a mixture of terror and heartbreak, but she reminded herself that all over the world, women were going through the exact same circumstances.

Why should she be different? Even if Richard refused to go on account of her, it wouldn't be the right thing. He had a job to do, it was vital he did it, and she was resolved not to stand in his way, no matter how hard it would be to let him go.

They made their way up the village main street towards the wedding tent in silence. Kirky's untimely telegram had thrown everything into disarray. They had planned to travel to Cork with the Warringtons tonight and take the train to Dublin in the morning. They would spend a week in the Shelbourne hotel, go to the theatre and travel out to Bray to go on the rides at the fairground there. Mostly they planned just to be together. Alone. To eat and drink and gaze into each other's eyes. Was that all to be cancelled now? It seemed so. Richard was right – when Kirky said immediately, he meant immediately.

Grace took Richard's hand in hers as they reached the edge of the village green. The band was playing Irish dance music, and they could hear the happy chatter and cheers from inside the tent as their family and friends continued to celebrate.

'When will you go?' she asked.

She could see the battle raging within him: his longing to stay, be a husband to her for at least the length of their honeymoon, but also wanting to go. He was a journalist, and the final push of the Allies back into occupied Europe was too big an event for him to miss. She knew it.

'It's all right, Richard,' she said softly. 'You have to. I understand.'

He squeezed her hand tightly and whispered, 'I wish I didn't.'

But they both knew that what he said was only half true. This was the life he had chosen, and by extension, it was her choice too.

'Sarah will want to go with you,' she said quietly.

Richard shook his head. 'She can't. Kirky won't allow it. There's no way he would get her a press pass for this. And I'd only admit it to you, but I'm relieved.'

'She thinks she can find Jacob.'

He sighed. 'I know, but she can't. It's just not possible.'

There was nothing left to say, so they stood together in silence once again, the decision already made.

Then Richard murmured, 'I'll ask Hugh and Lizzie if they can take us both tomorrow. I can catch a train from there to Dublin. You could come as far as Cork, and then maybe stay for a couple of days?'

She gave him a small, pale smile. 'I'll see,' she said.

'Okay. And I have a favour to ask.'

'Anything. You know that.'

'Take care of Sarah for me, will you? She's going to be frustrated when she learns she can't go. I know she's putting a brave face on the fear she has for Jacob, but she's broken inside.'

'Of course I will.'

There was a brief pause, then he pulled her close to him and whispered, 'I have another favour, Grace.'

'What is it?'

He nestled close to her and planted a soft kiss on her ear. 'Let's not tell the family straight away.'

'But...' She looked up at him, puzzled, then as the realisation dawned on her, she grinned. 'Oh. Oh, yes.' They were within yards of her front door.

Richard glanced around him. Seeing no one about, he picked Grace up in his arms and carried her up the path. She giggled, her copper curls bouncing freely about her face as he elbowed open the front door of her house and practically galloped up the stairs into her bedroom.

'Gosh,' he said as he put her down on the new bed. 'This is amazing.'

'A present from Maurice and Patricia.'

'Well, thank you, Maurice and Patricia,' he said, his voice husky and raw with desire.

Grace held her breath. The moment she had dreamed of had come. But for a brief second, it was as if they both held back. They'd shown so much forbearance – although the temptation was overwhelming sometimes – that now they were alone and legally man and wife, neither could believe this was happening.

Richard made the first move, undressing her, his fingers brushing softly against her skin. She reciprocated, and then all at once, they were standing there together, naked.

Grace was shy and self-conscious, and a little anxious. Richard had seen her wasted leg often. After Agnes's death she had stopped wearing the floor-length skirts her sister insisted on, adopting the newer knee-length styles that were in fashion, but Richard had never seen her fully exposed like this before.

Sensing her nervousness, he drew back the covers on the bed, and they climbed beneath them together. He was so much taller and broader than her that she felt tiny. It was so different to Declan, who had been a much shorter and slighter man. But as they lay together, his arm around her waist, his warm breath on her hair, she allowed her trepidation to fade away. This was Richard, her closest confidante and dear friend. The development of their relationship from pen friendship to genuine friendship, and finally to romantic love and passion, had crept up on her. Circumstances had not allowed her to even consider him in this regard for so long. Their lives had been so diametrically opposed. He was wealthy, she wasn't. He was American, she Irish. He was able-bodied, and she had polio. He was Episcopalian, she Catholic. They lived thousands of miles apart, geographically, socially and in every other way. And yet some miracle had happened and here she was. In the arms of Richard Lewis, her husband.

They made love urgently at first, releasing the pent-up frustration of their engagement, but later more slowly, taking time to experience each other.

Afterwards they lay together in contented silence, enjoying the comfort and warmth of each other's presence. Mr and Mrs Richard Lewis savoured this precious time together, for a few short hours away from the demands of family and the distant but ever-present noise and horror of war.

CHAPTER 10

Their family and friends were naturally upset at the news that Richard had to leave for London the following afternoon. As Grace had suspected, once they were missed from the party, Charlie had quickly extracted the news of the telegram from poor Fiachra, and it had not escaped the couple's notice that everyone had stayed away from the house for a few hours. 'To give you some privacy,' as Tilly put it the following morning with a big cheeky grin on her face.

The news had spread a pall over the wedding celebrations; there was no getting away from that. Richard's family were particularly upset. Arthur Lewis had wanted to use his influence with Kirky to get him to rescind his instructions, but both Sarah and Richard cried 'No' in unison to that suggestion.

'Don't do that, Father,' Nathan had insisted. 'This is the final push to defeat the Germans, and Richard has an important job to do. He needs to be there. You know that. We all do. And if Grace can be brave enough to let him go, then we need to be brave too.'

It was the longest speech Grace had ever heard Nathan give, but she was grateful to him for it. She knew that Richard was too. It meant a lot to him that his elder brother supported him in this way. She could see he found it hard to look at poor Sarah, though. She had been distraught and disgusted in equal measure when she realised Kirky would not allow her to travel to Europe with Richard.

'It's so unfair,' she declared bitterly. 'I don't see why I have to stay here and twiddle my thumbs doing nothing like this, while you and Jacob –' She stopped herself, 'I just want you both to be safe,' she added, tears welling in her eyes. 'I just want you both to come home safe to me. To Grace. To us all.'

Richard hugged her tightly. 'We will, Sarah. We will come home to you.'

But his words felt hollow to Grace. Perhaps even to Sarah also. They both knew that he had no idea where Jacob was, and he could make no guarantees that his brother-in-law and best friend would come back.

Esme had wept at the news. Richard knelt down beside her to comfort her as she begged him to take care of himself and to come back to them all. Through all of this, Caroline Lewis stood to one side, silent and somewhat distant. But as Grace watched the woman, she thought she caught a glimpse of the anguish Richard's mother was feeling but doing a spectacular job of hiding. From her children, at least. She seemed far more concerned about her husband's distress at losing his son, resting her hand on his shoulder, urging him to accept this crushing news. It was strange, Grace thought. For all the acrimony in their relationship, Richard's mother was devoted to her husband. And not just for his money and his status. Grace could see she loved the man and was glad they had managed to weather their marital storm.

Her own heart was heavy with distress as the time for Richard to leave loomed near. He would return to Cork with Lizzie and Hugh and take the later train to Dublin from there. He was booked on an overnight ferry from Dublin to Liverpool and would reach London by train the following day.

It was another fine summer morning, and she and Richard had

elected to eat their breakfast together in the small courtyard outside the house, near to the flower and vegetable beds. Cáit and Molly, aware that Uncle Richard had to go away to a dangerous place, took it upon themselves to solemnly set the little table Maurice had placed outside with a white napkin and flowers from their garden. The little girls had been thrilled when Richard thanked them for making it all look so pretty for him and Aintín Grace.

Charlie had called over with a copy of the *Irish Times*, and Grace gasped at the bold headline: *Allies Advance Ten Miles into France*.

'Read it to me,' she said to Richard. She didn't add that she wanted to hear his voice, to imprint it on her memory, her heart, for these few precious moments of them being together here in Knocknashee before the world and its wars would tear them apart.

'"The world is living through tremendous days,"' Richard began. '"Almost immediately after the capture of Rome by the Allies – in itself an event of historic importance – Anglo-American forces have invaded the northern coast of France."'

'"The attack was scheduled to begin on Monday morning, but weather conditions were so unfavourable that it was delayed for twenty-four hours. The first news of the invasion was broadcast by the German radio early yesterday morning, when a substantial force of British and American airborne troops landed behind the Germans' Atlantic Wall near the mouth of the Seine."'

Grace listened as Richard read out the initial success of what Churchill described as a 'gigantic operation'.

Apparently the Allied losses were 'very much less than expected'. Naval losses, on the whole, were small, and the German opposition to the invasion was not so formidable as the experts had anticipated.

'The Germans must have been caught unawares, do you think?' Grace asked.

Richard shrugged. 'Maybe. There were rumblings but nothing concrete. It was top secret for a reason, and it looks like it worked. "All the Allied reports agree that there has been a remarkable lack of activity on the part of the Luftwaffe,"' he continued, '"although it is well known that the Germans have a substantial number of fighting aircraft in readiness. Yesterday, it is stated, 31,000 Allied airmen, apart altogether from the parachute troops, were in action over France, and it would seem that the Anglo-American air forces have achieved at least temporary mastery in the air."'

Grace could hear the pride in his voice at this last statement. From the start Richard had been writing articles to inform but also to help persuade the US to enter the war, and later, to stay in it. But she knew that the winning of this terrible war against the Germans meant far more to him now that he'd endured all he had. And endured by people he loved and admired. Men like Jacob and Alfie and little Odile's mother, Bernadette Dreyfus, all of whom were risking their lives to thwart Hitler's evil Nazi regime.

However, according to the article, 'Mr Churchill declared that the Allies were entering upon "a most serious time" and that the real struggle for control of northern France was only beginning.'

Richard smiled over at Grace as he read Churchill's words. "'We enter upon it with our great Allies all in good heart, and all in good friendship.'" But Churchill did not believe that the war was yet over, especially as the German propaganda minister, Dr Goebbels, had already declared that with the Allied advance, Germany's very survival was at stake.

Grace winced at this, as the dark reality of what lay ahead for him sank in. The Germans were not going to just lie down. They would fight tooth and nail, and her husband was going to be in the middle of it. One stray bullet, one shell, one bomb would be all it took to end this dream before it even began.

'Grace...' he began. But any words of reassurance would be hollow, they both knew.

'Keep reading,' she said, her voice unrecognisable to her own ears.

Richard inhaled and carried on. "'Furthermore, it is not yet known whether the invasion of Normandy represents the Allies' final effort to bring the war to an end or is only one of a series of projected assaults upon the continent. The world is watching these prodigious events with bated breath. It is far too soon yet even to guess at their outcome. One thing, however, is certain. Many thousands of young lives already have been lost, and no man can tell how many others are committed to their doom."

"'This hour is one of the most solemn and tragic hours in human history. Mankind's destiny has been flung upon a cruel hazard.'"

He got to the end of the article, and they sat in silence. Nearby, a bee buzzed in the flowerbeds, and a soft summer-morning breeze ruffled her hair. It was as if the universe didn't have a care in the world. But even as she and Richard sat there together, tens of thousands of young men were fighting to free millions of others from the clutches of a murderous, evil regime, hell-bent, it seemed, on destroying everything it touched, including, she thought with a shiver, her beloved Richard.

She stood up suddenly, alarming Richard.

'Grace, sweetheart? Is everything OK?'

She nodded, then went to him and murmured, 'Whatever happens, I will always have this moment.'

Then she leant in for a kiss full of love.

* * *

THE MORNING SEEMED to slip by far too quickly for Grace's liking.

Her one moment of amusement amongst all the chaos was seeing Mrs McHale so upset at Richard's leaving that she blessed herself multiple times and then blessed him.

'As if she was the pope himself,' Tilly spluttered.

Father Iggy, of course, had given Richard a proper blessing, and Father Lehane had gripped his hands tightly and told him to come back safe.

With all the comings and goings of family and friends to say goodbye to Richard or to commiserate with Grace, by ten o'clock that morning, she had a thumping headache.

As Richard busied himself with telegramming Kirky and the London office in preparation for his journey, as well as spending a last few minutes with his family, Grace went up to her – *their* – bedroom to rest. She was not best pleased when there was a soft knock on the door.

'I'm fine, Tilly,' she called. 'You don't have to be worried about me. It's just a headache.'

'It's not Tilly,' a voice replied, and Grace sat up on the bed in shock. She got up, opened the bedroom door and peered out. Sure enough, Caroline Lewis stood there, looking somewhat nervous, Grace thought.

'Is Richard with you?' her mother-in-law enquired.

She shook her head. 'He went down to the post office to send a telegram,' she said. Although she was sure the woman already knew that.

'May I come in and wait for him?'

Grace hesitated. The last thing she wanted was Caroline Lewis in her bedroom when Richard returned, but something about the woman's demeanour stopped her from refusing. She seemed tortured or vulnerable this morning. It wasn't something Grace could see, but she could feel it.

'Of course, Mrs Lewis,' she said, and stood back to let the woman enter.

Caroline Lewis looked entirely out of place perched on a small chair beside the bed in Grace's room. The older woman seemed in no mood for small talk, so Grace just smiled at her and said nothing.

The awkward silence was broken by the sound of Richard bounding up the stairs, calling for Grace. She jumped up and opened the bedroom door just as he reached it.

'Richard, your mother's here,' she said, pointing at Caroline, who had also risen as Richard entered the room.

'Richard, I...'

'Good morning, Mother,' Richard said, with somewhat forced cheerfulness. 'You look well rested considering how late the party went on last night. I hear you were tempted to try Tilly's moonshine.'

Caroline smiled. 'I did, and it was actually quite palatable, considering.'

Grace glanced at Richard. Was that a joke? It was so hard to know with Caroline.

Richard crossed the room to his mother and kissed her cheek lightly. 'Well, you don't seem to have suffered any ill effects anyway. So, what can I do for you?'

Caroline looked from Richard to Grace and then back again. Grace wondered if she should offer to leave, but they were in her bedroom, so she didn't see why she should.

Caroline cleared her throat and stared at her son anxiously. 'I know you have to go to France, my dear,' she said, 'and we will all worry until you are home safely once more. I am also acutely aware of the onerous task ahead of you, and that you will have quite enough to do without any distractions, but...' She hesitated.

'What is it, Mother?'

'It's Jacob. Sarah's Jacob.'

For once, Richard looked taken aback. 'I know who Jacob is, Mother, but what about him?'

Caroline was almost babbling now. 'You see, Sarah won't ask you herself, Richard. In fact, she doesn't know I'm here and will be furious with me if she finds out.'

'Ask me what?' Richard's face was unreadable.

'To find him,' Caroline replied. 'To find Jacob Nunez. For Sarah.'

Richard and Grace stared at the older woman in astonishment. She hated Jacob, so why...?

It was as if Caroline could read their thoughts. 'Sarah is distraught with worry, as you know, and until she knows, one way or another, what became of him, I fear she will simply fade away. I cannot bear it, Richard. I have to do something. My daughter is pining away in front of my eyes, and only Jacob Nunez can save her. If he's...well, if he's gone, then she will have to accept it and try to move on with her life. But this...half-life of not knowing that she's living is too much for any person to endure. So I just thought that maybe you could look for him when you're –'

Richard's voice was solemn as he spoke. 'I'm going to Normandy, Mother, and the last time I saw Jacob was in Switzerland. If he's in

France at all, he'll most likely be at the whole other side of the country, so I'm not sure exactly how much I can do, to be honest.'

Grace's heart went out to Caroline Lewis, who looked crestfallen at Richard's response.

'Of course, my dear,' she said. 'I understand if you can't, and the opportunity may not present itself, but I just thought… Oh, perhaps it was foolish of me, and please, Richard, please don't think I'm playing fast and loose with your safety. If anything were to happen to you, I don't know how your father and I… Or Grace…'

Richard's expression softened. 'I know that, Mother. Not at all.' He turned to Grace. 'It's been on my mind since Kirky sent me the word to go to France. I have to do what I can to find Jacob. Or, at least as Mother says, to find out if he's dead or alive.'

Grace fought the rising panic within her. What about her? The least he could do for her was not put himself into obvious danger. Going to France behind the Allied troops and reporting on the military operation was dangerous enough, but trying to find a Jewish man who was standing up to the Nazi regime in a part of the country still under German control…well, that was nothing short of a death wish. No, she couldn't let him do that. She couldn't bear to lose him again.

She closed her eyes and took in a deep breath to quieten herself. The truth was that Richard wouldn't be the man he was, the man she loved, if he didn't want to find Jacob. And Jacob Nunez would do the same for her if the tables were turned. No, Grace knew that no matter the danger, she couldn't stop Richard going to find his sister's husband, nor should she. But she didn't trust herself to speak, so she simply nodded.

Richard placed his hands on her shoulders as Grace blinked back tears. 'I'll be very careful,' he said. 'I won't take any unnecessary risks, and I will come back to you. I promise.'

She wanted to tell him not to make promises he couldn't keep, but she said nothing.

Then Richard did something she'd never seen before. He walked over to his mother and embraced her in an affectionate hug. 'I'll try to find Jacob, Mother, and thank you for asking me.'

Caroline looked as startled as Grace at first, but then she returned his hug with all her might, before pulling back and gesturing at Grace to join them.

Grace did so, and Richard locked them both in an emotional embrace.

'I'll be OK,' he murmured. 'I promise.'

And Grace hoped with all her heart that he was right.

CHAPTER 11

NORMANDY, FRANCE

15TH JUNE 1944

Richard sat in a beautiful church on the outskirts of Bayeux. It was one of the first places to be liberated after the Allied landings, and General Charles de Gaulle had given a speech there the day before. Richard had been sent to cover it for the *Capital* and had met his old friend Warren King, an Australian freelancer he'd known in London.

Word had been sent to the Allied bombers that the Germans had fled and there was no need to bomb the town, so it was intact, which made a nice change compared to the carnage everywhere else. The medieval streets were too small for the heavy artillery and tanks, so a hastily constructed ring road around the town had been created, and one could almost believe that the war was a thing of the past as one walked down the streets. The rapturous welcome the general got was such an outpouring of love, of loss, of grief, as if the whole town had been allowed to exhale after holding its breath for four long years. It seemed to give legitimacy to de Gaulle's leadership of France, not just in the eyes of the French but as far as the British and Americans were concerned as well.

The town had become a control hub for the Allies, so the place teemed with men in uniform.

'This is their version of a hotel, is it, mate?' the ever-cheery Warren remarked as, after the speech, Richard took him back to the church where he'd been sleeping.

'Not much in the way of the hospitality business, as you can see, and we're not anyone's priority,' Richard explained with a sigh. He was exhausted, really bone-tired, so he could sleep anywhere, and had done since he arrived in France six days ago. Six days? Was that how long he'd been here? It was hard to imagine it was only that long; it felt like years. 'The hospital is full, and any other public buildings, schools, convents, the seminary, they've all been taken over by either the army or the doctors.'

'So do we just doss down here?' Warren asked, pointing to a pew.

'Be my guest.' Richard smiled wryly.

'I'm glad I thought to bring a kit bag and not a suitcase. At least I can use it as a pillow. And the weather's not too bad.'

'It's improved. It's been awful since we landed – raining constantly, humid too. Made a quagmire of the whole place. But it seems to be drying up a bit now.'

Warren sat on the upturned bucket Richard offered, beside a tea chest he had dragged in as a makeshift table, and opened his sack, pulling out bread, a tin of spam and, amazingly, two bottles of beer. His friend laughed. 'In the absence of a prettier companion, care to join me for dinner?'

'No thanks, but keep your ration – you'll need it. I got some soup and bread earlier from a grateful French lady. I'm OK.'

'Let tomorrow take care of itself, mate. Come on, have a beer. You look like you could use it.'

Richard wiped his eyes with the back of his hand; they'd felt gritty and sore since the beach. He was convinced his eyeballs were scratched from flying sand, blasted at him as explosions went off all around him. It still amazed him that he was here and in one piece.

He looked at Warren, suntanned, fit and handsome, his fair hair combed and Brylcreemed perfectly. 'Did you come over with de Gaulle?' Richard asked.

'Yeah, hitched a lift with *la grande asperge*. Not that he knew it. The ship was full of Johnny-come-latelys like yours truly.'

Richard smiled at Warren's honesty. At least the Australian wasn't pretending he was there for the push into France like some of the reports Richard had heard about – eye-witness accounts of the beaches, written by men safely back in London.

De Gaulle was called *la grand asperge*, the big asparagus, on account of being six-foot-five, but Richard knew he towered over other men in more ways than height. He symbolised the rebirth of a proud nation.

After de Gaulle's speech, Richard had met with Guillaume Mercader, a Free French leader who was in the process of producing a newspaper that would be printed and distributed all over the country to keep the various Resistance cells informed and buoyed to keep fighting. Richard had agreed to help. Before Warren arrived, he had been about to pull out his new Smith Corona portable typewriter – incredibly, a gift from his mother – from its mustard-coloured hard carrying case to write his article on de Gaulle.

'So, tell me,' Warren said as he flipped the lids off the two bottles with his cigarette lighter, 'what was it really like?'

'You're interviewing me now?' Richard raised an eyebrow as they clinked bottles before taking a long swig.

'Well, I won't write about what you tell me if you don't want me to. And if I do have your permission, I'll be sure to point out I wasn't here and I'm getting this from someone who was.' He looked questioningly at Richard. 'Is that fair enough?'

Richard sighed. 'Of course, and there's no need to credit me. I don't care.'

'Mate, you look absolutely jiggered, and judging by the state of the place, I'm amazed you're in one piece at all.' His friend gazed at him, his face full of concern. 'By the way, weren't you getting hitched?'

'Yeah, we got married on the sixth of June, and I was sent over here the next day.' Richard took the hunk of bread Warren offered with a roughly cut chunk of spam inside it and bit into it gratefully. He'd lied earlier; he was starving.

'Bet your missus loved that idea.' Warren winked.

'Not exactly, but Grace knew I had to go.' He ran his hand over his hair, which was greasy with dust, sand and sweat. He'd tried washing himself in a fountain earlier, but he wasn't sure it was much of a success. He had no soap.

'She sounds like an understanding girl. Not like Darlene, a girl I was knocking about with. Her old lady found us in a compromising situation and assumed we'd get hitched, buy a house in Cronulla across the road from her, and that I'd spend the rest of my natural life writing about the Patrick Grant Rose Exhibition and who is on to take the Winter Trophy at the Cronulla Bowling Club this year.' Warren chewed his sandwich. 'Don't get me wrong, Darlene's a nice girl, but I'm not really the marrying kind. Not yet anyway. But her old man's a big Irish navvy – he'd make mincemeat of me if I stuck around, so I took off. I'm not a pro like you, mate. You have a way with words I'll never have. I'm a hack. You're the real deal. Anyway, sports writing is more my thing. I've no delusions about my skills. How I got this gig, I don't know. Maybe my ability to get myself into situations – balls of steel, my old man says. I can get the interviews, but writing about it after, that's more your thing. I'm not ashamed to admit it. I read everything you write, try to emulate you. My editor is putting the pressure on now. He reckons he's paying me to be here, and he wants decent copy, so that's why I came over, hoped by being here I'd do better.' He jumped as a rat ran across the floor inches from his foot. They, like everyone and everything else were running for their lives. He shuddered. 'I'll never get used to those buggers. Anyway, I'm a sports journo, racing, footy, cricket… But I convinced my boss I could do this, and I'm rubbish at it. Waaay out of my depth. He says I'm fired if I don't come up with something good, and soon. I should have thought it through better, I know. But it was go overseas or face up the aisle with Darlene and her mum. Reckoned I needed to scarper.'

'You didn't join the army like your brother?' Richard asked.

'Nah, mate. I would have, but I was writing for the local rag, and they offered me the job over here. Dunno why. Reckon the other blokes were old, with families and that, and I was chomping at the bit to go someplace that didn't have Darlene and her mum in it, so I got sent to London.'

'And your brother is in the Australian air force?'

'Yep, a wing commander, and a fair dinkum ace he is too.' Warren beamed with pride. 'He was in a dog fight, got hit with eleven twenty-millimetre shells into the fuselage, but not one detonated. He couldn't believe it. He had to coax the old crate back to Blighty, but when he got back and they took the shells out of the fuselage, they found there was no charge in them – only a note inside the casing of one, written in Czech. Some bloke on the base's mum was from Czechoslovakia, so he translated it. It said "This is all we can do for you now." Reckon the Czech fellas, forced labour, making shells, deliberately sabotaged them by not putting any explosive in. Brave buggers, eh?'

'That's an amazing story. You'll have to write about that.'

'Better not in case the Jerries are reading the *Sydney Morning Herald* and the poor Czech blokes cop it. Besides, I wouldn't have the turn of phrase you have. Take it, add it to one of your reports.'

Richard laughed. Warren was instantly likeable and so open and honest, but on the subject of Richard's writing, Richard knew his colleague was right. Something about the way he wrote captured imaginations. It was a God-given gift, no credit to him. But he was grateful for it.

'And you definitely won't use it yourself?' He didn't want to steal the guy's story, especially if he was struggling to come up with copy.

'Nah, I wouldn't do it justice, and anyway, my editor wants stuff on the landing and the push through France. He was very clear, so I'll have to cobble something together on it. Though how, I've no real idea. Anyway, don't worry about me. Tell me about your wife. How'd she take you going walkabout five minutes after getting a ring on her finger?'

'Grace is amazing. I just want to get back to her.'

'Can't you go now? You've done the hard bit. Surely they'll let you go back now?'

He shook his head. 'It's not that simple. Remember my buddy Jacob Nunez?'

'The photographer? Sure. Where is he? Not with you? You two were like peas in a pod, never one without the other.' Warren took another swig of beer, wincing as it hit his throat. 'The poms love warm beer, but I can't be doing with it… Disgusting.'

Richard chuckled. 'Couldn't agree more. If you gave someone in Savannah warm beer, they'd have you committed. I used to dream of a cold American beer, straw-coloured, fizzy, ice-cold, when I was in England. That warm, dark-brown stuff they call beer looks like molasses and tastes worse…' He groaned at the memory.

His friend grinned. 'Oh, I hear ya, mate, it's muck. Sometimes I wonder if I'll ever again have a cold schooner down the Cecil Hotel in Cronulla, watching the sun go down over the surf, all the girls out in their bathing suits and nothing to do but sink a few cold ones and admire God's beauty. Anyway, your mate, what's his story?'

Richard quickly outlined how Jacob had stayed in Switzerland and how he was going to try to find him.

'He's Jewish, right?' The words carried their own weight; there was no need to elaborate.

'He is. But I'm helping a guy here to set up a Resistance newspaper, and we have another friend, Alfie, an Irish guy who's been working against the Nazis since the fall of Paris. If I can find him, maybe through the Resistance guy's paper, there's a chance he'll know where Jacob is. He married my sister – Jacob, that is, not Alfie. I need to either find Jacob and bring him home, or' – Richard found even speaking the alternative difficult– 'at least find out if he died so my sister can grieve and move on.'

'That's your plan, is it? To stay here and try to find him? Or go to Switzerland?' Warren was leaning forward, hanging on every word.

'I suppose so. Honestly, I thought it was all over so many times, but if I can stay alive, I'll do all I can to find him.'

'Tell me what it's been like since you got here,' Warren asked, back in business mode. 'Oh, by the way, my flying ace brother Ed is somewhere here too. He took off from Dover a few days ago, I reckon. I'll try to track him down. He was doing supply drops all over, so maybe we can persuade him to let you hitch a ride if they're going over that way. He said he'd take me if I wanted, but my editor wants stuff from here. If you need to get over to the east, every inch here is going to be hard-won, so flying might save you some time.'

'Are you serious?' This was the first bit of good news Richard had heard in ages. He'd had no idea how he was going to get to Switzerland, or even eastern France, and that was where he'd last seen Alfie. The Allies were winning, but it was slow and harder fighting than anyone had ever thought possible. Getting ahead of the advancing Allies wasn't an option, not as a civilian, but if he could fly across the country, he'd at least be in the right place. It was dangerous, he knew, but he had promised his mother and couldn't face Sarah if he didn't try. Besides, Jacob was his best friend.

'Yeah, I reckon he would. He kind of owes me one. I got him out of a tight spot with our old man last year, and I'm happy to use up my favour if it helps to find Jacob. I always liked him. Top bloke. I need half-decent copy for my editor on this whole thing, though. He wants the real thing, not a soft-soap version. He's syndicating all over Australia, I reckon. Not that my wages reflect that. But anyway, I'll mooch around, see what I can dig out, and once that's done, I'll try to track Ed down. How does that sound?'

Richard thought for a minute. 'I can do better than that,' he said, going to his duffle bag and extracting a sheaf of typed pages. He unfolded them and passed them to Warren. 'If you can get me to Lyon, or Strasbourg, or anywhere in Switzerland, this is yours. No need to credit me. It's yours, you wrote it,' he explained as his friend skimmed the pages.

'I can't do that,' Warren objected. 'This is really good, mate. Like really, *really* good.' He laughed self-deprecatingly. 'Nobody would believe it was me, for starters.'

'Well, rewrite it in your own words if you want to, but if you'll get me on a flight across France, then it's all yours.'

'Are you sure? Don't you want to file this yourself?' Warren gazed at the typed sheets and then up at Richard.

'No, my editor rejected it, said it was too gory and upsetting. But if your guy wants the unvarnished truth, then that's it.'

'And I can have it? I'd get Ed to take you either way – I offered before you gave me this.'

'I know you did, but I'm sure. I have to try to find Jacob. I've sent plenty of copy from here, and my boss knows I'm going to try to find him, so it's all aboveboard. I just couldn't figure out how to get across France, so you're really helping me. Do we have a deal?'

'I reckon we do, Richard Lewis.' Warren grinned and slapped the sheaf of pages with the back of his hand. 'This is bonza, mate. Absolutely flamin' bonza.'

CHAPTER 12

Knocknashee, County Kerry

21st June 1944

'Owww!' Sarah Nunez had nicked her finger peeling potatoes at the kitchen sink as she helped Grace and Patricia prepare dinner. 'Stupid thing.' She flung the potato into the sink with force and glared at it sourly.

Grace exchanged a glance with Patricia, but they said nothing. Sarah had been frustrated and in terrible form for most of the past week.

As well as everything else she had on her mind, Sarah was convinced finding Canon Rafferty was the key to ensuring a happy future for Carrie Dwyer, but she was getting nowhere with her enquiries as to his current whereabouts.

The girl's mother – if the woman who turned up at the wedding was indeed her birth mother – was anxious to be reunited with her, but there were so many obstacles to overcome, and Canon Rafferty himself was the main one. Sarah had gone to the public records office in Cork but had found no trace of the child's birth in them. She went to the convent where Hannah said she had the baby, but the nuns wouldn't even open the gate, let alone the door, to a nosy American. She'd tried to get an appointment with the bishop but was told by his secretary that it wouldn't be possible – no reason given, just a flat no. Sergeant Keane had said – and Grace believed him – that he had no knowledge of the canon's case or whereabouts after the day he was arrested. And so Sarah's enquiries were being stonewalled in every direction.

Grace had huge sympathy for her sister-in-law. She knew Sarah was out of her mind with worry about Jacob, but there was nothing she could do to find him. She was still furious that she wasn't allowed to go to France with Richard. She'd even sent Kirky a curt telegram demanding she be given a press pass and got a one-word reply. *NO.* Since then she had been distracting herself by pouring all of her energy into finding a family for this young girl in New York.

Of course Grace herself was in the same metaphorical boat. As far as she knew, Richard was now somewhere in France. And the news on the invasion of Europe was terrifying. Far from D-Day resulting in the sweeping and fast capitulation of the Germans, it was proving to be a gruesome bloody mess. All she could do was pray with all her might that God wouldn't give her yet more heartache. Surely he wouldn't? It would be too cruel.

Sarah threw another baleful glance at the innocent potato. 'Maybe I should have gone home when my parents and everyone else did,' she moaned.

Grace and Patricia shared another look. They agreed that she probably should go home at this stage. Neither of them would say it to her, though.

'It's a beautiful day. Will we go for a walk?' Grace asked. Sarah was now prowling up and down the small kitchen, finger in her mouth, getting in Patricia's way.

Sarah sighed. 'Sure. Look, I'm sorry, Patricia. I know I'm being –'

'It's grand, Sarah. You've a lot on your mind.'

'Come on, let's go for a stroll.' Grace gently steered her American sister-in-law out of the house and onto the main street of Knocknashee. They waved at Fiachra, who was doing the afternoon-post delivery, although he looked more like he was on his way to the gallows.

'Lily Maheady left yesterday,' Grace explained to Sarah, 'and the lad's bereft.'

'They danced together at the wedding,' Sarah said. 'It all seemed to be going well then.'

'I get the impression from Charlie that Lily was trying to let the poor lad down gently. Apparently she told him before she left that she couldn't be his girlfriend any more as she had to focus on her studies. Being granted a scholarship to Vassar to study medicine is no small thing, and she couldn't be doing with any distractions. I don't think Fiachra took it well.'

'He certainly doesn't look happy, that's for sure,' Sarah agreed.

'He even asked Joey Maheady if he thought it would be a good idea for him to save up enough to go over to America and try to persuade Lily to change her mind. Joey was less than enthusiastic, as you can imagine.'

'Well, if he makes it all the way to the States on his own, then maybe she should give him another chance.'

'And what are the realistic chances of that happening, do you think?'

Sarah sighed. 'Look, if it's meant to be, it will be. You know that better than the rest of us, Grace. Oh, sorry, I'm going too fast for you.'

Sarah, like Richard, was tall, and her long legs out-strode Grace. She slowed her pace to give Grace a chance to catch up.

Sarah had agreed with Hannah Monaghan that she could tell Grace Hannah's story. Hannah wasn't happy about it, but Sarah was adamant that she and Mrs McHale would need Grace's assistance if they were to help her find the canon and reclaim Carrie, and so the woman had, reluctantly, given her permission for Grace to be brought into the small circle of those in the know.

'I can't get Hannah out of my mind,' Sarah said as they walked. 'I've written to the Graham School in New York, asking them to clarify about her birthmark and to confirm the date on her birth certificate. Though that, of course, might be wrong. But my instincts are screaming at me that we've found Carrie's mother, and Mrs McHale agrees with me.'

Grace smiled. 'Speaking of Mrs McHale…' She was grateful to see a grin on Sarah's face.

'I know, right? Who would have thought Mrs McHale would come to Knocknashee and get herself a beau.'

Having come so far, Mrs McHale was making a long holiday of it and was staying with the postmistress, Nancy O'Flaherty, who she realised was a distant cousin through marriage. Nancy, it seemed, enjoyed the other woman's company and assured her over and over it was no imposition for her to stay as long as she liked.

Not alone that, but to everyone's astonishment, Dinny McCafferty, a man who hadn't a word to throw to a dog in the normal run of events, had asked Mrs McHale up for a dance at the wedding. Then two days later, he invited her to have a cup of tea with his mother, who was as old as Methuselah and still alive, and for whom no woman was ever good enough for her only child, Dinny.

The pair had been seen at a dance in the church hall in Ceann Trá, and even at the pictures in Dingle. Yes, to everyone's utter astonishment, it would seem that Dinny and Mrs McHale were an item.

But now that the older woman was otherwise occupied with her gentleman friend, it left Sarah much more at a loose end. 'By the way, Grace, where are we going?' she asked.

'Up to see Father Iggy,' Grace replied. She had avoided involving her friend in Sarah's quest up to now, fearing it was asking too much of him, but as he often said himself, 'a dumb priest never got a parish', so there was no harm in asking. It was unlikely he could help, but you just never knew.

'I think we should tell Father Iggy what we know. He might have some ideas.'

'But he won't go against one of his fellow priests, will he? Charlie and I discussed it, and he was of the opinion that they close ranks.'

'Normally yes, I'd agree with Charlie. But Father Iggy is different, and this is very important. It's worth asking anyway.'

'I don't know if that's a good idea. I promised her I would keep her secret, and I will. Although I told her I would tell you. But I really don't know if she'd want me to tell a priest.'

'Father Iggy won't say anything to anyone if you ask him not to,' Grace said with certainty. 'And since no one has seen hair nor hide of the canon for ages, Father Iggy is our only hope. But if you don't want to, then I understand, but I'm not sure how else we can proceed.'

Sarah shrugged. 'OK, Grace, let's tell him. But maybe keep Hannah's name out of it for now. Until he has to know.' She threw Grace a smile. 'By the way, I'm glad you're saying "we". Mrs McHale said we'd need you – she said people know you and trust you, and they don't know either of us from Adam. But I didn't want to bother you, what with the wedding and then Richard gone and everything.'

Grace returned her smile. 'Well, I don't have much else to occupy my mind, and worrying myself half to death over your brother is serving nobody, so if I can help, then I will,' she said simply.

When Sarah had told her the story, her heart had gone out to Hannah. Some women had so much to endure, it was unfair. Most of the women Grace knew were strong – they had to be where they lived – and they wouldn't put up with any nonsense from their husbands or anyone else. But there were others, the minority, who had a sort of sheepish look. She'd seen it with some of the mothers at the school over the years. She recalled one woman from when she was in her first year of teaching, who asked that she never report any childish misdemeanour to her husband because she feared what he would do to the child. Grace had been shocked, but Agnes, who wasn't known for any degree of softness, said the father was a violent brute and it would be best to have no dealings with him.

For women like that, surely there had to be a way out, a way to be safe? But the Church was clear. Till death did you part – no exceptions.

Tilly's mother, Mary O'Hare, had another story about a woman out towards Cuan Pier years ago, whose husband was a terrible tyrant altogether. The poor woman worked her fingers to the bone, and he regularly took whatever she earned to buy drink, then came home and battered her and the children. So one morning early – according to Mary, anyway – she got a shovel, and when he was drunk, she gave him an almighty clatter to the head. Killed him stone-dead. With her eldest son, she dragged his body onto their cart and shoved him off the cliff, his body landing on the jagged rocks far below. Then she went out to the market and sold her eggs and a few bantam chicks she'd raised, and every woman there swore blind to the local sergeant that she'd been there since dawn. Someone even said they saw the husband staggering home on the road the night before. The sergeant, if he guessed the truth, never took it further, and the death was deemed misadventure. It was what Grace's father would have called 'an Irish solution to an Irish problem'.

'I told Hannah to divorce him, but she just laughed,' Sarah said, indignation written across her face at the rejection of what she saw as a perfectly reasonable suggestion.

'Sarah, we don't get divorced in Ireland. It's not legal here. So no wonder she laughed at you.'

She waved over at Pádraig O Sé, who was standing outside his cobbler shop scowling and looking for someone to criticise.

'What's the weather like up there, lofty?' he called at Sarah. Of course he was only trying to get a rise out of her. Insulting people was a hobby for Pádraig; it was what he lived for. But Grace knew her sister-in-law wouldn't be able to understand his thick accent anyway so decided to ignore him on this occasion. She also knew that he was being irritating at the moment because his sister, Gretta, who he nicknamed 'the squeaky hinge', had come to stay for what was turning out to be a dangerously protracted visit. She had been a cook for some wealthy family up the country someplace, but apparently she was let go. She said something about the family moving to England, but nobody believed that, especially now. More likely they got fed up of her constant whining and complaining.

Bed and board were part of the employment contract, it would seem, so Gretta was now out of her lodgings as well as her job. The house in Knocknashee had belonged to their parents, so technically she owned half of it. To Pádraig's disgust, she showed no sign of leaving, and it was driving the grumpy cobbler mad.

Gretta O Sé visited Knocknashee every summer, and nobody got along with her while she was there. She criticised everything and everyone, and the villagers wondered why on earth she came back at all if everything was so dreadful. But return she did. Every year. Religiously. And now Pádraig and the rest of the village were facing the unpleasant prospect of her being back for good.

Sarah was still fixated on Hannah Monaghan's situation. 'I know divorce is not common here, Grace, but this is an extreme case. Her husband is horrible, and she never consented to the marriage in the first place. She definitely has grounds for divorce. I'm sure she'd get custody of her children, and he'd have to pay alimony –'

Grace sighed. Sarah had a lot to learn about Ireland. She'd do as much damage as a bull in a china shop if she went blundering into Hannah Monaghan's life, full of outrage and indignation on the other woman's behalf.

'Sarah,' she said, 'you're not listening to me. Divorce isn't legal here. And even if it was legal in the state, they are Catholics, and there is no divorce in the Catholic Church.'

Sarah looked perplexed, as much by the sharpness in Grace's voice as what she'd said. 'I hear you, Grace. But Tilly's sister, Marion – I spoke to her at the wedding – her husband is divorced, right?'

'Yes, in England. His first wife, Angela, was English, and they married over there,' she explained. 'She wasn't Catholic, so they married in a registry office. That meant Colm was able to get a divorce when she, unfortunately, developed dementia at a very young age. She died in 1939.'

'And so did Colm marry Tilly's sister in the Church?'

Grace shook her head. 'No. They got married in a registry office as well. Colm and Angela had children together, and because the marriage was consummated, the Catholic Church acknowledged the union, and therefore in their eyes, Colm wasn't free to marry Marion, even though his marriage to Angela hadn't been a Church wedding.

Canon Rafferty was particularly vocal on that subject. He used to make all kinds of snide comments to poor Mary about Marion.'

'Well, that's just ridiculous,' Sarah exclaimed, and Grace had to smile. Sarah was like Richard in many ways, but she lacked his diplomacy. A small stab of pain hit her at the thought of Richard – she'd not heard anything from him in the two weeks since he had left for London en route to France.

Some of the schoolchildren were playing in the village green, their shrill, happy voices carried on the summer air. Girls picked daisies to make daisy-chain necklaces and bracelets, while the boys reinstated the rope swing that had been taken down for the wedding.

Grace sighed wistfully as they passed the Wooden Spoon bakery, which was now closed permanently because sugar was in such short supply. The owner, Mrs Doyle, had moved to Killarney to take a position as housekeeper in the Grand Hotel. But the bakery did provide her with a welcome change of subject from the absurdities, as Sarah saw them, of the Catholic faith.

'I remember when I was small,' she said, 'the aroma of Mrs Doyle's baking would waft all over the street. The smell was absolutely divine. My mother would buy me a sticky bun in there every Saturday as a little treat.'

'I can imagine how good it smelled,' Sarah said. 'We had Gottlieb's in Savannah. It was owned by a Jewish family, and they made the most amazing rugelach. Esme would let us have one each, and we'd eat it on the street as we walked home from town. If our mother knew we were eating in public, she would have had a fit, but we knew not to say anything.'

'What is rugelach?'

'It's a rolled pastry – sort of like a croissant – and filled with chocolate or apple or apricot. It's sooo good.'

Grace laughed. 'I don't know what a croissant is either.'

Sarah grinned. 'It's a French pastry, buttery and flaky, amazing. I miss treats like that.'

As they passed Peggy Donnelly's drapery, her large beige plaid-covered bottom was pressed to the glass while she arranged the display of clothing in the shop window. Even with coupons there was almost nothing to buy, but Peggy valiantly tried to keep her shopfront enticing, despite the increasingly deeper deprivations.

Creedon's pub was closed – it wouldn't open until the afternoon – but the empty barrels of beer were on the footpath for collection, and a sour smell of beer and pipe smoke hung around the whole area. The fact that there were two pubs – O'Connors and Creedon's – in a village as small as Knocknashee never struck anyone as strange, and both establishments did quite good business.

The parochial house itself was at the end of the town, a two-storied building with a garden. Grace would never approach it again without thinking of the day she and Richard broke in to expose the canon and all his wrongdoing. On this occasion Sarah and Grace walked straight to the front door and used the brass knocker.

Father Lehane opened the door in his shirt and trousers, his clerical collar untied. 'Oh, Miss Fitz, I mean…Mrs Lewis…' The priest was still very shy but had grown up a lot since coming here as a very green young curate a few years ago. Life under the canon had been so intimidating for the poor lad just out of the seminary, and it wasn't until Father Iggy came back to be parish priest that Father Lehane had begun to blossom. He'd even joined the local football team and was apparently a huge asset.

'Hello, Father Lehane,' Grace said, smiling to put him at ease. 'We're sorry for disturbing you. It's Father Iggy we were after actually.'

'We're just having a late breakfast,' the priest replied. 'There was a funeral Mass this morning out in Gortnaglogh, and Father Iggy did the ten o'clock here, so we're tearing busy this morning.'

'Ah, we don't want to disturb your breakfast. Sure we'll call back later…'

Grace was turning to go when Father Iggy appeared, wiping his chin with a napkin.

'Ara, stop with that old nonsense, ladies. Come in here to me and have a cup of tea. Since Mrs Coughlan left, we're having to fend for ourselves and making a bad enough job of it. Isn't that right, Donnchadh?' He chuckled at Father Lehane. 'But much as we miss Mrs

Coughlan and her baking and having clean shirts and all the rest of it, we must not stand in the path of true love, so we'll have to go on burning our toast till we get the hang of it. No harm to us too. A pair of grown men and we're not able to boil an egg between us. High time we learnt to be more useful.'

Grace and Sarah followed the two priests through the house and into the kitchen. Once there, Father Lehane sat down at the table to eat what might have been a fried egg, but it was burnt and had a slick of fat on it that made it seem most unappetising.

Father Iggy'd had the whole village in stitches for the last two weeks with his retelling of the culinary exploits of himself and Father Lehane since their housekeeper, Mrs Coughlan – a tiny, mousy woman who wouldn't say boo to a goose – announced that she was getting married to an octogenarian who had come back from England with a load of money and was looking for a wife. Miah Danny Gurteen, the local matchmaker, had arranged it all.

Mrs Coughlan had apparently made her interest in a husband known to the matchmaker, and when this man, who'd made a fortune in coal in the north of England, said he was after a lady who could keep a nice house, was nice to look at and wasn't going to make too many demands, all Miah Danny had to do was make the introductions and it was all signed, sealed and delivered.

According to Father Iggy, Mrs Coughlan requested an audience with himself and the curate, and while she'd hardly spoken more than ten words at a time to either of them in the years she worked at the parochial house, she'd announced that with all due respect, she had no notion of ending her days scrubbing floors and making apple tarts and nothing to show for it. So she took her leave of the priests and was now happily ensconced in a fine big house in County Limerick with a housekeeper of her own and the man of her dreams. Mrs Coughlan was of indeterminate age, something between fifty and seventy, but she would most likely see this old man off and then sit on a nice inheritance to keep her in comfort for evermore. Father Iggy didn't blame her one bit. There was no provision in the Church for retired housekeepers; they were expected to fend for themselves. And often they gave up everything for the priests in their care.

'Can you not get someone else?' Grace asked, glancing about the kitchen, which was in a right mess. Under Mrs Coughlan, it had been spotless, fragranced by a combination of Sunlight soap and scones. But Father Iggy was right – the two priests were making a terrible job of fending for themselves.

'Sure whatever poor misfortunate woman would take us on – if we could find one – would be in the same boat as Mrs Coughlan when she got too old for the job, and we're in no position to help. So no, we'll just have to figure it out. We tried cleaning the floor yesterday. There's something sticky on it, but we don't know what. If anything, our efforts appear to have only made it worse.'

He wasn't lying. Grace could feel the soles of her shoes stick to the floor as they stood in the kitchen. In the sink was a saucepan with the bottom burnt black with something or other. The men had put it steeping, but she could tell no amount of scrubbing was going to bring it back from the brink.

She looked around in dismay. Crumbs on every surface, the table sticky and grimy and the windows badly in need of a clean. The two priests also looked like some care wouldn't go astray. Father Iggy's trousers were too long, and his shirt was grubby.

'Ah, Father Iggy, this is madness. You are too busy, and surely there's someone who can help?'

The two priests shared a glance.

'What is it?' she asked. For her part, Sarah was taking in the whole fascinating scene as though it was something out of a Hollywood comedy.

Father Iggy looked sheepish. 'Well, we put the word out that there was a position, and we had an applicant, but...'

'Who?' Grace raised an eyebrow.

Father Lehane gulped and Father Iggy sighed.

'A certain cobbler's sister... Who I'm sure is a wonderful person, but part of the job of being a priest's housekeeper is dealing with people that come looking for us in times of need, and, well…that's a very particular skill and maybe it might not suit…eh…'

Grace felt for her friend who was trying to be diplomatic, but he was right. Having Gretta O Sé would be actually worse than the bad old days when Kit Gallagher ran the parochial house for Canon Rafferty and getting a papal audience would be easier than having five minutes with the canon.

'And you can't employ anyone else ahead of her?' Grace asked.

'Not really. Not without causing offence, and I wouldn't like to do that.'

Sarah laughed. 'Well, Father, if you don't mind me saying, you two aren't exactly doing a great job, so you might have to be a bit more ruthless.'

Father Iggy gave a loud chuckle. 'Ruthlessness isn't a trait we try to cultivate in the clergy, I'm afraid, Mrs Nunez. But sure, we'll figure something out. God is good, and I've passed this particular issue on to the higher level of management…'

'The bishop?' Sarah asked.

Father Iggy hooted. 'Hah. Sure the bishop doesn't care if we give ourselves dengue fever here. No.' He pointed a finger towards the ceiling. 'I mean the man above.'

'God? You're hoping God will send you a housekeeper?' Sarah sounded bemused.

'He's never let me down yet.' Father Iggy winked.

Father Lehane stood, draining his cup of tea. 'I better get moving, Iggy. I said I'd call on Murty Kelleher. He got a new anvil for the forge, and he wants me to bless it.'

Grace didn't even bother trying to explain to Sarah why the local blacksmith would need a big piece of metal blessed by the priest.

Father Iggy beamed at his colleague. 'Good man. And you'll call on Noirín Daly, will you? Her poor little one has a very weak chest and she's worried, so I said you'd call. I've to meet Jarlath O'Keeffe myself. He's closing the post office out in Ballyferriter to come in to me today, so I better be around.'

'I will, of course,' Father Lehane replied. 'Mary O'Hare gave Noirín an ointment to rub on the baby's chest, and she says it gave her a bit of ease. Which is as well, as Dr Ryan is trying to avoid putting her in hospital again.' He fixed his collar and pulled on a cardigan that had frayed cuffs and a strange stain on the front.

Grace smiled to herself. These were good men, she thought, trying their best to make the hard life out here on the western seaboard, battered by the wild Atlantic, easier for the people they served. They needed someone to take care of them, though. Dymphna McKenna was the obvious choice, but she was busy with Seámus. She had been the canon's housekeeper after Kit Gallagher, and then she had looked after the O'Hare farm for a time. But now Eloise was around so much and did all of that for Tilly and Mary instead. Also Grace was sure Dymphna wasn't that well herself at the moment – she looked very pale and tired of late – so Grace wouldn't even approach her. But there had to be someone other than the squeaky hinge.

'Now, ladies, is this a social call?' Father Iggy enquired as Father Lehane bade them goodbye and left. 'And if it is, let me say I'm delighted, if a bit mortified at the state of the place. Or can I do something for you?'

'Well, there is something, actually…' Grace said.

'Of course.' Father Iggy said with a smile. 'Then how can I help?'

Grace glanced over at Sarah, who nodded. 'We need to ask you about Canon Rafferty.'

CHAPTER 13

Father Iggy exhaled and looked so indescribably sad that Grace felt for him. He was a dedicated priest, a good man who tried his very best all the time to help his parishioners, but he was also loyal to the Church, and the behaviour of his predecessor was something she knew caused him deep pain.

'As I said before Grace, I don't know where he is, if that's what you're asking,' he said, and Grace was sure he was telling the truth.

'Well, it is what we're asking,' Sarah interjected, 'because we need to find him.'

'Why?' Father Iggy asked, his eyes, magnified through his thick lenses, fixed on Sarah.

'Because there is a child in an orphanage in New York City who needs our help. Her adopted parents are dead, and she has nobody to care for her. Her adoption was arranged illegally and for profit by Canon Rafferty. Pretty much like Lily Maheady's and several more. The thing is, I may have located her birth mother here in Ireland. But I will need to prove the child is the daughter of this woman, and with no paperwork to go on, Canon Rafferty is the only one who can corroborate the story.'

The clock ticked on the dresser as dust motes danced in the warm summer air. A fly buzzed, crashing repeatedly into the window.

'I'm sorry if this is putting you in an awkward position, Father,' Sarah continued, 'but this girl – Carrie is her name – has nobody…'

'And the woman you believe is her mother wants to regain the custody of the child?'

Grace hoped Sarah would be honest with him. If she wasn't, Grace would have to intervene.

She needn't have worried. Sarah was as straight as a die.

'No, the woman's situation is not easy. She was essentially sold into marriage to a man much, much older than she is. They have four children, and she didn't seem to think he would support her in trying to reunite with her child. In fact, it's not even clear that he knows of this child's existence.'

Father Iggy looked sad, his eyes full of empathy. Grace knew, though he would never say, that he saw the full gamut of life – the parts people wanted the world to see but also the parts they didn't.

'Then I'm afraid there won't be much you can do,' he said.

Sarah shook her head determinedly. She was not going to be defeated. 'No,' she said. 'I can't accept that. This child needs her, and she wants to be reunited. She has grounds for…well, if not divorce, then at least to separate. Look, she can't be forced into a life she didn't choose. But even if she won't leave him, she shouldn't be prevented from being reunited with her child.'

Father Iggy listened to Sarah's passionate declaration. Then he took off his glasses and polished them with a grubby napkin that was on the table, making them if anything, even filthier. 'Sarah, I know how it must seem to you – indeed, how it actually is – but there is a cultural context here that you don't understand any more than if I was to go to your country and express outrage at some aspect of how you live –'

Sarah tried to cut across him. 'With respect, Father, that's not it at all –'

Father Iggy carried on gently. 'You'd say to me, I understand what you believe, and you're right. But what would you think, for example, if I told Esme that she should go to the same restaurants or church or public building as a white person, that she has every right to, and she should just march on up there and demand to be treated equally. What would you say to me?'

Sarah stopped – the dawning realisation on her face showed she understood.

Grace marvelled at the priest's skill. He didn't condescend or try to belittle her position, but he did a much better job than Grace ever could of explaining how what she was proposing was not an option.

Sarah sighed and conceded defeat. 'I'd say that while you may be right, and while it might be the moral thing to do, that's not how it works, and Esme would be the one to suffer – not you, the person telling her to do it.'

'Exactly,' Father Iggy replied. 'And it's the same here. Should that poor girl have had her child taken from her? No. Should she have been coerced into marrying someone she didn't want to marry? Of course she shouldn't. But divorce, separation – whatever you want to call it – isn't an option. If she just left him – and people do if situations are intolerable, rarely, but it happens – she would be ostracised. So would her children. And under the law, her husband would retain custody of them, not her. She'd lose her home, her children, her dignity and any financial stability she has. I'm not defending it, Sarah. I hope you know I'm not. But we have to deal in this life with what *is*, not what we wish it to be.'

A look of anguish crossed Sarah's face. 'So what's to become of Carrie? Am I just supposed to go back and say "no dice, kid, sorry"? Because I can't do that, Father. I just can't.'

'No, I'm not suggesting that at all. But is another adoption an alternative for the child? Over there in America?'

Sarah shook her head. 'She's thirteen. Nobody wants to adopt a child that age. And she knows she has a mother in Ireland – her parents told her she was adopted. So she just wants to ask her if she can come home. It's heartbreaking.' Sarah's voice cracked, and Grace knew it was not just sympathy for this child but also the fear and worry over Jacob.

'Does the child's father know of her fate? Maybe he could…?'

Sarah caught Grace's eye. If she spoke the words, then they could never be unsaid.

'The father knows exactly where she is but has never done anything to help her,' Grace said quietly. 'Father Iggy, this woman was pregnant at fifteen and had Carrie when she was just sixteen years old.' She paused for a moment and looked at Sarah, who nodded. 'Canon Rafferty is the father.'

The priest paled, and Grace felt such guilt at upsetting him in this way.

'And you are sure of this?' The normally unruffled priest was visibly shocked and his voice shook.

'The mother has told us he is the father. As I said, she was only fifteen herself, a sheltered girl who'd never had a boyfriend. He had come to her parish to cover for another priest who was sick, and while there, he – well, she became pregnant.'

Nobody in the room was under the illusion this was a consensual relationship.

'I…' Father Iggy opened his mouth but closed it again. There was nothing to say.

Grace recalled how inappropriate the relationship between the canon and her late sister had been. He had her spend her money – well, Grace's money, actually – on entertaining him, but she had no evidence the relationship had become physical. Although it wasn't beyond the bounds of possibility, especially now they knew about Hannah Monaghan.

'What would tracking him down achieve? If it could be done?' Father Iggy had composed himself.

Grace let Sarah explain her thinking.

'Well, since divorce isn't an option, as you say, and this woman wouldn't be willing to give up her other children, I'm wondering if we might be able to make use of Rafferty's friendship with her husband. Perhaps he could be prevailed upon to convince this man to accept the child, to allow her into the family. It might not be ideal – to be honest, the husband sounds awful – but Carrie would be with her mother and her brothers and at least she'd belong somewhere. Of course we'd have to find the canon first, and he might not even be in the country.'

'And assuming you did locate him, and you could convince him to do as you want him to, surely if he did that, he'd be admitting…well, his actions.' Father Iggy's eyes were troubled.

'Not necessarily. He wouldn't do it out of goodness, we know that. But we could use revealing the truth as leverage. Tell him if he confirms the woman as Carrie's mother and then convinces her husband to welcome the girl and to be kind to her, then the identity of the girl's father remains a secret. But if he doesn't, then we tell him we'll blow his cover. I'll threaten to write about it in the papers.'

Grace spoke then. 'It's got some merit as an idea, but to be honest with you, Sarah, there isn't a newspaper in Ireland that would print such a story. So I'd advise against that particular threat because the canon would know that as well. But if he is under some kind of Church protection after the incident with the Germans, perhaps if the hierarchy knew of this, they might consider that a cut-off point for their support.'

Sarah couldn't help but show her exasperation. 'They'd back him even though he's a Nazi spy, but fathering a child would be the reason they'd drop him?'

'It's not a question of backing him. It's more a matter of reputational damage – not to him personally but to the Church,' Father Iggy said. But Grace heard the despondency there. He was horrified by what Rafferty had done up to this, and now, such exploitation of a vulnerable, young girl – it was too much.

'Does the mother definitely want the girl? If she could take her, would she?'

Sarah nodded. 'I think so. If her husband would agree, I believe she really would. But she wasn't hopeful that he would agree.'

'Do you have any ideas of what we can do next, Father Iggy?' Grace asked her old friend. She hated to put him in this position, but Sarah was right – the fate of this girl hung in the balance. In a world where there had been so much loss, so much grief, if they could help just one person, then that was something, wasn't it?

'I don't,' Father Iggy admitted, 'and that's the truth. But I suspect he is being sheltered somewhere. I don't have that on any authority – just an inkling I got when I went asking.' He turned to Sarah. 'I would like to discuss this further with the bishop – with this new information. Do I have your permission to do that?'

'What if he tries to bury the story to protect Rafferty?' Sarah spoke in her usual forthright way.

'He won't, I don't think. But I'm obliged to report this to him, and I'll suggest to him that he would meet with you. How is that? All I know is the canon was arrested in Knocknashee when Grace and Richard exposed what he was doing in helping the Germans and seemingly taking money for it. I didn't ask and I wasn't told, but I was in Cork then. When the bishop asked me to come back, he didn't refer to the situation with Canon Rafferty, and there was never anything in the newspaper about a trial, but…'

'The emergency powers act means the government have a lot more leeway now than they do in peacetime,' Grace mused. 'He could well have been tried, convicted even, and nobody would know. I wonder if he's in prison?'

'I don't think he is,' Sarah ran her hand through her hair. 'I did some research, spoke to some people in Dublin – I leaned on Irish contacts we had had from London – and nobody had heard of him.'

'Well, let me speak to Bishop Buckley, and we'll take it from there,' Father Iggy rubbed at a stain on his cuff. 'Now, Sarah, how are you keeping yourself? The worry about your husband is a heavy burden to carry. And I know you are worried about Richard too, Grace.'

'It's not the same thing, though,' Grace was quick to point out. 'Richard is with the expeditionary forces. He'll be behind the Allied lines and so has some protection. Last we heard Jacob was in Switzerland, possibly occupied eastern France, and being Jewish, that marks him out…'

'Indeed, indeed.' Father Iggy took off his glasses again to clean the lenses – with the sleeve of his jumper this time – and his face looked so different. Grace realised that without the spectacles, he looked more vulnerable or something. 'Thankfully, it looks at last like the end is in sight and that terrible regime in Germany is coming to an end. But there's more work to do, I know. We're living through extraordinary times, and while the evil in the world is on display for all to see, so too is the good. All those young men, coming to the rescue of Europe, putting themselves in harm's way to do the right thing. That's heartening, and I feel sure God is on their side.' He sighed wearily. 'I pray for them all, and I especially pray for Richard and Jacob, that they come home to you and you live the rest of your lives together in peace.'

'Thank you, Father Iggy,' Grace said as they took their leave. They'd taken up enough of his time. 'And we appreciate you talking to the bishop. If he wants to speak with us at any time, then of course that would be fine. Sarah is meeting the mother again later this week. Now that she's had some time to process the information, we should learn more about her intentions.'

'Yes,' Sarah confirmed. 'I left it that she would just think about it, but I am convinced that if her husband could be prevailed upon to take Carrie in, then she would be glad to have her daughter back.'

'And the other children that were sent over to America, have you located them?' Father Iggy asked.

'Well, Lily Maheady you know about,' Sarah replied. 'And there is another girl – a young woman now, actually, Edeline Congreve is her name – but she is well and happy and has no interest in finding her birth mother. It was her father who Mrs McHale was in contact with initially. Mrs McHale wanted the truth to come out to exonerate a priest named Father Noel Dempsey who was sort of implicated in the selling of babies – not blamed exactly, but he was seen as being somehow complicit with Rafferty's scheme. He wasn't at all, so Mrs McHale set about proving he was innocent. Then there's Carrie, and she's the one I can't get out of my mind. We know there are others, and if I do get to speak to this Canon Rafferty guy, I want to know who they are. But for now, if I could help Carrie, that would be worth it.'

Father Iggy shut his eyes briefly and placed a hand on Sarah's shoulder. 'I wish the blessings of the Lord on you, Sarah, in your work. Your heart is pure and your intentions are good, and I'll help you if I can.'

'Thanks, Father, I'd appreciate it.'

CHAPTER 14

Grace felt every muscle and sinew of her body relax as Charlie handed her the bulky envelope over the school wall. It was morning break, and the children were outside playing in the summer sunshine. Eleanor was inside making herself and Grace a cup of tea, though the dust at the bottom of the tea caddy would barely colour the water. Next week's ration was only a day away, but the day before the ration was due was always lean. Last night for supper they'd had potatoes and carrots. No meat and not even an egg. Tilly's hens were on a go-slow because the old cockerel, Rudolph, named after Rudolph Valentino, had died and Tilly'd had to replace him with a younger lad that the hens were none too keen on. Between Rudolph Valentino, the cockerel, and Clark Gable, the one-eyed ram, Tilly's male creatures caused no end of amusement. She also had a billy goat called Fred Astaire because he seemed more interested in dancing away from the nanny goats than doing the business.

Holding her letter, Grace realised how she'd been tense for weeks, her thoughts constantly going to Richard and how he was. Sarah had found out a piece he'd written about the Normandy invasion was printed in the *Capital*, and she thought another piece about Bayeux, the home of the famous tapestry, was by him as well, so at least he was alive then, but that was over ten days ago, and every second he was over there felt like a year.

The Irish papers too talked of nothing but the invasion, how the fighting was fierce but losses were less than anticipated. Though what did that mean? Precious little consolation that would be if your husband or son was among the fallen. As usual, the reporting was high on rhetoric and low on detail. Grace knew there was little point to fretting constantly. Dr Ryan had suggested she take a drop of poitín at night if she couldn't sleep, but she didn't think alcohol was the answer to the problem.

What she held in her hand now – this was what she needed. The worst thing would be a letter from the Lewises. Richard hadn't yet had a chance to register Grace as his next-of-kin, so a letter from his parents could mean that something had happened to him and they'd been informed.

But this was not that. This was a letter from Richard himself. She scanned his loopy writing. Before he left Knocknashee, he said he wanted her to keep writing to him, even if she didn't think the letters would reach him, and he would do the same. They spoke often of the time he was in France, when she was sure he was dead, and how they wrote to each other regardless. He in a cold cell in a French prison, with no pen or paper, would compose long letters to her in his head; she in Knocknashee, with her signature lilac ink and notepaper from Easons in Cork. None of the letters were ever posted, but just the act of writing them had connected them both during those terrible months.

She'd written to him every day since he left, posting the long missives faithfully each week to a box he had at the United Press office in London. She was convinced that was where they were gathering, unopened, but it didn't stop her. Richard had said if a passing newspaperman saw them, and he knew where Richard was, he'd try to get them to him.

She longed to read her letter, but she'd have to wait until after school.

She cast an eye over the children who were playing in groups. They'd had an English lesson this morning. They were reading *Treasure Island* by Robert Louis Stevenson, and she had told them how Captain Flint, the owner of the famous treasure map from the story, died in an inn in Savannah, where Richard was from, and how Richard told her that the inn was one of the most haunted places in Savannah. They found that bit of the story much more interesting than Stevenson's dense prose in a language they were preconditioned to resent. It was with sighs of relief the clock had ticked to eleven.

English was never going to be something the children enjoyed, no matter what the topic. Grace believed there was such a thing as generational memory, and though these children had never lived under British occupation, their parents and grandparents had, and suffered the brutality of it. As a result, the language instilled nothing but bitterness and hatred. But that thinking would get them nowhere if they ever wanted to go abroad for work. There was very little work here in Ireland, and they would be at a terrible disadvantage if they couldn't speak English.

She heard a yelp over by the wall and turned towards the red-faced culprit, looking guilty as sin.

'Billy Hennessy, tell me I'm seeing things and you were not about to stick that compass into Donal's arm?' she cried, as Billy hastily tried to change course. Eleanor had been teaching the older children geometry this morning, and Billy must have slipped a compass into his pocket.

Janie, the class monitor, had her hand out, and the young torturer sheepishly handed the jabber over. She smiled. 'I'm actually thrilled you did that, Billy. Because the weeds are gone pure wild behind in the school vegetable patch, so you'll have a great time pulling them after school.'

Her cousin, Mikey O'Shea, sniggered, and Janie rounded on him. 'And sure you can help, Mikey, since you find his antics so hilarious.' Then she turned on her heel, the compass firmly in her grasp.

'But we're going swimming...' Mikey began to complain, not enjoying being humiliated by his older cousin in front of his friends.

'So I'm not pulling weeds,' he muttered mutinously. His freckles and sticking-out ears always endeared him to Grace, but he, like all boys, had to save face.

Grace watched as Janie pretended not to hear him. Being selectively deaf was a necessary trait in a teacher. She herself had learnt that you didn't need to go to war on every single issue – just the important ones.

Eleanor appeared beside her, two mugs of watery tea in her hands.

Mrs Worth, as she was called in school, was English. Her husband had grown up in Ireland in a wealthy Protestant family, but Eleanor had never been to Ireland until the school where she was principal and their house were destroyed in the Liverpool Blitz.

Her husband, Douglas, was in the RAF, stationed in Italy now, and while she only heard from him sporadically, she said she was sure he was all right. Whether or not she really believed that, Grace was never sure. Eleanor was of the 'let's not borrow trouble' school of thought. Time enough to be distressed if something bad happened. Their three girls had settled into life in Knocknashee as if they'd been born and reared here and not in the heart of Liverpool.

'You got a letter!' Eleanor was so pleased, it touched Grace.

'I did.'

'Oh, that's wonderful. I heard from Douglas this morning too. He's fine and really thinks the end is nigh, thank the Lord.'

'Let's hope so, and then we can get our tea back – I mean, our husbands.' She laughed, gazing sadly at the almost opaque liquid in her cup.

'I know. Have you tried the chicory-root coffee? It tastes absolutely nothing like coffee and it's revolting. I bought a bottle of it but can't bring myself to drink it.' Eleanor pulled a face.

'No I haven't. I don't like coffee anyway,' she said. 'But I did try the powdered eggs. Biddy O'Donoghue gave me some off the ration. I don't know why she stocks it – everyone at least has a few hens, so they have eggs – but I used them to make a kind of pie with leftover potatoes and onions. Patricia got the recipe from the *Woman's Own*.'

'What was that like?' Eleanor asked, her face displaying her scepticism. Every 'recipe' suggested in the newspaper or magazines using wartime ingredients was almost always disgusting.

Grace winced. 'I made some gravy with the chicken carcass, which helped, but...'

'Dreadful?' Eleanor sympathised.

She nodded. 'Fairly awful, yes.'

'All right, let's do it,' her friend said, leaning on the wall. Grace knew exactly what she was talking about. It was their favourite game. They described their perfect meal in such glorious detail that it left them both ravenous, but it was worth it for a momentary taste memory.

'All right. Today I'm going to make a lovely roast leg of lamb, gravy made with the juices, with roast potatoes done in goose fat, buttered carrots with a pinch of sugar to bring out the flavour and cauliflower in a cheese sauce. Then for dessert I'm going to make Queen of Puddings, with cake crumbs to thicken the sweet custard, then a thick layer of strawberry jam and a fluffy meringue on top, baked until golden.'

Eleanor's eyes were closed. 'Mmmmm...I can taste it.'

'Your turn.'

'Oh, for us today it's going to be steak and kidney pie, with thick meaty gravy, full of onions and button mushrooms and big chunks of meat, all covered in flaky buttery pastry and served with a bowl of mushy peas. And for pudding, we're having baked rice cooked in milk and cream, full of fat juicy sultanas and dusted with cinnamon. It's going to be piping hot from the oven, served with a big dollop of ice cream. And when I've eaten all of that, I'm going to have a cup of tea so strong you could trot a mouse on it and a lovely Scottish shortbread biscuit to dunk in it. Actually, two. I'm having two shortbreads.' She sighed wistfully. 'Douglas loves shortbread. His mum used to send him a box when he was at boarding school. I always think of him when I see the tin. I use it for my sewing now, but when he comes home, I'm going to buy him a whole tin of shortbread just for himself.'

Grace smiled at the thought. She wondered if they would ever eat like that again. It felt selfish, considering all the people of Europe were enduring, but she would love to have a huge, delicious meal. One where you felt you had to just lie down afterwards to digest the food. It felt like a dim memory. She glanced at her friend, who was wiping a tear. It wasn't like Eleanor to get emotional, but Grace knew this was taking its toll on her, like everyone. They tried to put the bright side out, to hope for the best and make do with what they had, but sometimes it all felt like too much.

'I know you miss him, Eleanor,' she said quietly.

Her friend nodded, stuffing her handkerchief back up the sleeve of her cardigan. 'Not long now. He'll be home and driving me up the walls, and I'll be saying "Did I really miss him?"' She laughed and drained her cup and took Grace's empty one from the wall. 'Right, I'm going to do a gardening class. The carrots and peas are ready, and we can dig some spuds and summer cabbage too. So how about you take a few minutes to read your letter in peace while I make green-fingered gardeners of this lot?'

'Ah, it's all right, Eleanor, I can wait,' she objected, but her colleague insisted.

'Not at all. You must be dying to get to it. And anyway, the strawberries are ripening, so they need to be watched like hawks.' She laughed. The children showed much more enthusiasm for harvesting the small sweet strawberries and raspberries than the potatoes and carrots.

Grace took the opportunity gratefully and slipped inside the classroom, shutting the door behind her. The large map on the wall – its purchase her first act of defiance against her sister, aided and abetted by Father Iggy – had taken on a new meaning for her recently. Every day her eyes went to parts of Normandy in France – Caen, Cherbourg, Sainte-Mère-Église – places she had never heard of but that now played a pivotal role in her life because it was there that Richard and thousands of young men just like him from all over the world were fighting to rid the world of the spectre of German national socialism.

She sat at her desk and opened the letter. There were several pages, some typed, some handwritten. The postmark was London, she noticed. Perhaps he was back? Her heart quickened at the thought. If he was back in London, then perhaps she would see him soon.

CHAPTER 15

The opening line of Richard's letter dashed that hope.
Saint-Laurent-Sur-Mer, Normandy
Dearest darling Grace, my beautiful wife,
I pray this letter reaches you. I gave it to a priest I met out here, who was accompanying a group of badly wounded men home, and I asked him to mail it to you. His name is Father Mike Bell, and he's a Catholic priest from South Boston. I smiled when he told me his family is Irish, recalling your story about the cop you met in New York who told you his whole family was Irish yet could not name a single relative for three generations who had ever set foot there. Father Bell and I became good friends, because the padres and the journalists tend to get lumped together as non-combatants in the chaos of this godforsaken place.

This place. How to even describe it? Words fail me. The horror, the blood, the noise, the fear, the hatred, the chaos, the lack of a plan, the heroism, the boys crying for their mamas...

I wrote a piece for Kirky, but he rejected it, said it was too gruesome, that the mothers in America are not ready to hear the reality of what's happening to their boys. So I wrote a softer piece. Maybe I'm doing the wrong thing by sending you the original, but I have to tell someone. Someone who isn't here should know. I don't know why. Maybe I'm shell-shocked, or have gone crazy. It's hard to know over here. If you find this too hard to read, just stop. Maybe I shouldn't send it. I don't know. I don't know much any more.

It's terrible, Grace. Like hell. Honestly, that's the only way I can describe it. Hell on earth. I learned so much about religion and God and all of that so we could marry in the Church, but I have to be truthful with you and wonder what on earth God is thinking, allowing this.

It's hard to remember those Germans are just young men like me, with hopes and dreams and sweethearts and wives and children, because I'm only seeing this from one point of view. But the sheer damn waste of young lives snuffed out in blood and noise, lives left unlived, children unborn, things these guys would have achieved if they'd not been blown to bits on a godforsaken beach in northern France left unfulfilled.

There is something about dying on foreign soil too. I interviewed so many young men the night before they crossed the channel. I stayed up all night. Nobody could sleep anyway. Young men from Iowa and Oklahoma and Maine and Nevada, who up to that point had barely heard of France, let alone thought of going there. So many guys who had never been abroad before—hell, neither their parents nor grandparents either. For them to leave their farms and factories to come over here to die—I can't explain the enormity of it.

I know all the stuff, the need to defeat Hitler and all of that. I've seen more than most people what that regime is capable of. But to see a kid named Dan Calletto from Omaha, who worked in his old man's body shop with his brothers, who had a girlfriend named Alice, who was saving up to buy a plot of land to build a house on so he and Alice could marry, to see him die on Omaha Beach has changed me forever. He had no business here.

His mother will never see her son again. Alice will have to find someone else to marry. And for them, the defeat of Hitler is cold comfort. Germany, France might as well be the moon for the Calletto family. All they know is their boy Dan is dead. And this is repeated and repeated and repeated.

There will be reports of the valiant fighting, and Grace, I've seen some heroism, breathtaking bravery, but I've also seen those who didn't even get off the landing craft, those guys who were mown down by machine gun fire as the trap was opened, or the ones who drowned, caught up in the ropes and straps of their packs, the guys that turned the English Channel red with their blood, gone in the blink of an eye. They are heroes too.

I'm sorry if this letter is depressing. The situation here is so depressing. The soldiers have a word—fubar. It stands for "fouled up beyond all recognition." Some soldiers change "fouled" to another, more expressive word—you can guess, I'm sure—but it really does describe what we're going through. It's hard to imagine anything approximating normal life ever again.

I can't say much. This letter might not hit the censor, but even so. Just so you know, I'm relatively safe compared to the guys on the front lines. But the Germans are fighting back harder than anyone anticipated. The locals are starved, terrified and exhausted as they watch their towns and farmland reduced to rubble.

I think of your beautiful face so often. I picture you walking up the aisle to meet me there the day we married in Knocknashee. And if I die tomorrow, or if I live to be a hundred, that will have been the best day of my life.

I love you, Grace, and as I talk to these men just like me, I see we are all part of a club: the guys who have someone to love who loves them back. And to them, leaving their girls is as inconceivable as me leaving you. And yet they are doing just that, every single day, by the thousands.

Life is so precious, so fragile; we don't ever realize that. We think we'll all live forever and die old people in our beds. But this war has changed the world irrevocably. I can't see how we can ever go back to being as we were.

We had no time to plan for our lives after this madness, but now this feels critically important. I've said that as long as I'm with you, then I'll be happy, and that is true. But I would like to support us, and whatever family we have, and I'm not sure how I'd do that in Knocknashee. I think about all the various places we could go: London, Savannah, Cork, Dublin, Paris. I have a reporter friend here who is Australian, and he is always telling me how great that is, so I don't know. We can see. If leaving Knocknashee is not an option for you, then of course, that's all right. I'll figure something out.

To get a break from it all, whenever I have some time, I write a bit of my novel. I didn't expect to write a love story, but that's what it is. I can only imagine the ribbing Jacob would give me, but I just sit down to write whatever comes, and this is the story that's coming.

It's our story, really. With some bits changed. But I'm finding myself writing about us, and I don't know if it's good or awful. Maybe I'll let you read it someday. I can't imagine letting anyone else see it. I had dreams, I suppose, one time, of becoming a novelist, but I landed on journalism and it's been good to me. I'm writing our story just for us. Maybe our children or grandchildren will read it someday and wonder at how their old grandma and grandpa could once have been a pair of star-crossed lovers.

It's 4 a.m. now, and all I can hear is the booming of incendiaries, cracks of gunfire, and crunching of tank tracks in the mud. It's been really wet for June, turning everywhere into a quagmire—as if it couldn't be any worse.

I'm at a makeshift camp in the roofless church of this little village that might have been pretty once but is now destroyed. The whole back wall behind the altar has had a giant hole blown in it, and I can see the stars as I lie on my pack, gazing up. Those are the same stars that shine on you in Knocknashee. That thought makes you feel closer.

I can't wait to see you again and for this whole mess to end. I want to go home, Grace, and I don't care where that is, because my home is with you.

Lovingly,
Your husband,
Richard

Grace folded the letter and placed it carefully in the envelope to read again later. Tilly had given her and Richard a really beautiful wedding present of a large brass box, burnished and polished to a shine, with tiny, delicate hinges; it was at least twice the size of the biscuit tin Grace had been using for so long to store their letters.

She had kept every single one of Richard's letters over the years, and when Richard had gone missing the previous year and was presumed dead, Sarah had brought all his letters from Grace to Knocknashee. The combined stash of correspondence was far too big for the biscuit tin, so Tilly's brass box was now the new home of their love story.

The three carbon-copy typed sheets of Richard's rejected article sat on the desk. Part of her was glad he felt he could tell her anything. She wanted to be his safe harbour – as he was hers. There was nothing she could imagine she wouldn't tell him. But her worry about him was almost all-consuming as it was. She knew from Richard that the press, and the Irish press in particular, was scant on detail and definitely tried to adopt a cheerier tone about the progress of the war than was strictly accurate, and even that news caused her more sleepless nights than she cared to admit. Would she be able to rest knowing Richard was in the throes of whatever he'd written that Kirky rejected? Richard was not one for exaggeration or hyperbole – he was factual and balanced and tried to write with reason and compassion. But she also knew that once she read what he'd written, she could never not know what he was going through.

She listened to the voices of the children in the school playground outside – so innocent and full of enthusiasm, full of confidence that the adults around them had the world under control. But how wrong they were. All over Europe, all over America, Australia, Canada, India, Pakistan, New Zealand, even Germany and Italy and Japan – the list of countries went on and on – people waited to hear news of those they loved. For millions, their hearts would be shattered by loss, their precious husband, child, sibling lost to war on foreign fields, in the air or at the bottom of the sea. Given the horror of it all, how could anyone declare a victory? Loss was everywhere, the human cost and the very fabric of human existence destroyed. Grace knew only too well the torture of knowing a life, and all the potential that life held within it, was just gone. That was a universal feeling, not one unique to any country.

But Hitler had to be stopped. That was the crux of it. Could someone not just kill him and his henchmen who had unleashed this hell on the world? If they were so anxious for killing and dying, should they not be the first to volunteer? No, it was never that way. To Grace, the futility, the sheer unfairness of it all, suddenly seemed impossible to bear.

Old men sat around and dreamed up quarrels, instructed their subordinates to do the most appalling things to satisfy their own basest desires, but it was never those men who had to face the bullet and the bomb. It was young men like Richard and Jacob and Alfie O'Hare – lads who themselves had no reason to hate a lad from another country but yet must kill him or be killed – who bore the burden of these old men's wars. All on the whim of someone who sat comfortably in an office or a well-protected bunker, miles and miles from danger.

Time and again, it was ordinary people who suffered.

She was so weary of it all.

CHAPTER 16

Grace had taken her usual walk up to the Knocknashee cemetery after Mass that Sunday to visit the graves. The cemetery was situated on the hill the town was called after, Cnoc na sidhe, or its anglicised version, Knocknashee – the hill of the fairies. Grace knew each of the families in the town who had buried loved ones here for generations. It was like the place they came from, a thing that rarely changed.

She spent some time by her parents' grave, saying hello to them and Agnes, before making her way to Declan's grave. Of course, Declan wasn't buried there. He had been lost at sea and his body never found. But Charlie McKenna had added his son's name to Maggie's headstone, that of Declan's mother. No matter how much Grace loved Richard or how happy she was with him, there was a part of her that would always be connected to Declan, and she was grateful to have somewhere to go to remember him.

She stood for a while in the warm summer sun, chatting away, when Charlie passed the graveyard wall. It was unusual to see him out on his bike on a Sunday when there was no postal delivery. He usually spent the day with the family.

Seeing her, he waved. He leant his bike up against the wall and joined her, stopping first to fill a glass bottle at the freshwater spring just outside the cemetery gate. Leaning on the headstone, he turned his face to the sun and took a long drink of cool, clear water from the bottle.

He offered her a drink too, but she declined, so he pushed the rubber bung back in the glass neck and set the bottle down.

'It's a grand, fine day today,' he said, less cheerfully than Grace would have expected from him.

'It is surely. How have you all been keeping? I haven't seen much of you all since the wedding.'

'Ah, you know yourself. We're just getting ourselves back to normal after all the excitement. How are you doing? Not too worried about Richard, I hope?'

'Out of my mind worried,' she replied. 'But sure that's only to be expected. At least you got to see Lily again.'

He nodded. 'It was good to see her. And the Maheadys. They're good people.'

'Yes, they are. And Lily's doing really well at college, I hear.'

Charlie's eyes shone with pride. 'She is. She got her brains from her mother.' He ran his hand over the headstone beside him. 'God bless you, Maggie,' he said softly.

'I'm sure she got a fair few brains from her daddy as well,' Grace said with a smile.

He grinned. 'Maybe. Fortunately she got her looks from her mammy, though.'

They both laughed.

'And poor Fiachra O'Flynn is like a lost soul.'

'Ah, that fella would want to cop on,' Charlie replied. He sounded dismissive, and she was surprised. It wasn't like him. 'Going around the parish like a sick calf. Did you know he asked Joey Maheady if he could go over there to visit her, the big eejit? Even though Lily told him plain as day that she had no interest in him.'

'Well, I don't think she was that blunt, to be fair, but maybe just that it would be hard for them to have a future. But he's mad about her, so I suppose he just wanted to see if she would give him another chance,' she suggested gently.

'Mad is the right word. She's going to be a doctor, and she has expectations of life that that *oinseach* couldn't fulfil in a million years.' Charlie's mouth was set in a hard line.

'Fiachra's a decent, hard-working lad, Charlie. And he's honest and caring. Those are not qualities to be sneezed at – even for a doctor with a degree from Vassar, or anywhere else for that matter.'

To his credit, Charlie looked a little shamefaced. 'I know that, Gracie,' he admitted at last, 'but let's be practical here. Lily's miles out of his league, and he needs to forget about her and move on, set his sights on a more realistic option.'

Grace could sense those were Charlie's final words on the subject and there would be no point in pushing it further. In any event she had to admit Charlie probably wasn't wrong about the likelihood of Fiachra's success with Lily Maheady. One thing Grace had noticed over the few weeks the girl had been in Ireland was how driven she was. Lily had a strong determination to succeed and push the boundaries of what might be traditionally on offer for her. She had no intention of limiting her choices or expectations for her future. Lily was ambitious – something you didn't see in too many women in rural Ireland; mostly because, like Hannah Monaghan, and indeed Grace herself when her sister was alive, it was knocked out of them before they even got a chance to figure out what they wanted or to follow their dreams.

Grace sighed and changed the subject. 'How's Dymphna these days? I didn't see her at Mass. Is she keeping well?'

'She's in bed at the moment. She wasn't feeling too good and...'

The forlorn look on Charlie's face was so unlike him that it alarmed Grace. 'Charlie, what's wrong?' she asked.

'Ara, nothing, Grace. Don't mind me. I'm like a cut cat these days.'

'Ah, come on now. You can always talk to me, Charlie. Like I can always talk to you. If there's something on your mind, I'm happy to hear it. Two heads are better than one and all the rest of it.'

Her leg was aching after the long walk up, and she longed to sit down and take the weight off it. 'Will we sit on the wall here?'

He shrugged again but followed her as she picked her way across the graveyard past the assortment of headstones, many dating back to medieval times, their markings long eroded by the salt air and whipping winds of the peninsula, which made walking in a direct line impossible.

'Look, don't mind me, I'm grand. So what had young Mr Lewis to say for himself?' Charlie asked. 'How is he doing over there?'

'Awful, Charlie. The scenes he describes over there are just dreadful.' She shivered. 'We're not being told the full reality, that's for sure.'

'I'd imagine we're not. The government haven't told us the truth since the start, De Valera and the rest of them treating us like we're children as usual. Please God it won't go on much longer and they can all come home. My heart is going out to you both, and you only married barely five minutes…'

'I'm no different than the wives of all the millions of men from all over the world,' she replied.

Despite Charlie's questions, he seemed more distant and distracted than usual. Grace stole a sideways glance at him. He looked older than she had thought he was now. Deep lines ran either side of his mouth, and his hazel eyes, exactly the same shape as Declan's, were surrounded by sun-burnished wrinkled skin, his silver stubble contrasting sharply. The harsh weather was one of the reasons people aged out here faster than they did in cities, she thought. But it was more than just ageing with Charlie. There was something else troubling him, and she knew that it probably related to what was going on at home.

'What's the matter, Charlie?' she asked gently. 'You seem very low in yourself.'

'I shouldn't be burdening you with my problems,' he said, kicking at a pebble with the toe of his boot.

'Why not? God knows I've worn the ears off you often enough with mine.' She smiled and gave him a little nudge. Their lives were as intertwined as the honeysuckle around the dog roses that lined the boundaries of the graveyard. 'Come on, Charlie. I thought Lily going back would mean everything was back to normal at home?'

She didn't like to pry, but she knew that all was not well in the McKenna household. Kate McKenna had told Grace's nieces, Molly and Cáit, that Charlie and Dymphna had a big fight. Kate and Paudie had been scared, and baby Seámus started screaming in the middle of it. Molly and Cáit had, of course, immediately confided everything in their Aintín Grace.

Charlie McKenna was one of the most important people in her life, and he'd helped her in innumerable ways over the years. So Grace couldn't pretend not to notice how miserable he was.

'Ah, it's nothing, Grace. 'Twill blow over, I suppose.'

But she persisted. 'You can tell me to mind my own business if you like, Charlie, but if it would help to talk about it, then I'm here to listen. I don't know if I have any answers but...' To be honest, she felt a bit self-conscious about offering to help. Sure what would a girl of her age with no real experience of marriage really be able to offer a man of Charlie's years?

He took out his pipe and started cleaning the bowl. She'd noticed he always did that when mulling something over. Charlie wasn't impulsive; he thought things through thoroughly. He filled the pipe with tobacco from the well-worn leather pouch he kept in his pocket and lit it. The sweet aroma of the tobacco encircled them, and Grace was transported to a memory of herself as a small child, sitting on her daddy's knee one evening as he told her a story he had made up based on Irish mythology, about the magical people of the sidhe and the Tuatha Dé Dannan and the Fir Bolg.

Charlie sucked on his pipe, exhaling a plume of blue smoke. 'I know Lily didn't mean to cause friction by coming to stay last year, but she did. Herself and Dymphna got along well in the end. And more power to her, she even won Kate over, which was some feat in itself. But I knew, just from a "space in the house" point of view alone, it would be a relief when she went home. I foolishly thought this time when she came it would be only for the wedding and things would be fine, we'd all have a nice time together, but if anything, Dymphna is even more bad-tempered.'

Grace could see he wasn't comfortable speaking like this about his wife, but he had to get it out.

'I might not be a saint, Gracie, but I'm not a terrible husband. But to listen to Dymphna giving out and the way she is with me, you'd swear I was boozing every night of the week or being rude or lazy or something. Nothing I do is right. And she's very sharp with the kids too. It's not like her, Grace, not at all. I thought at first it might all have just been too much, maybe she was just tired after all the visitors for the wedding. So I suggested she go and have a lie-down – I'd feed the lads and look after Seámus. And what did she do? She ate the head off me, telling me that she didn't need my sympathy or my pity. And then she went on and on about Lily again. She was trying to make out that because Lily is mine and Maggie's, she's more precious to me than our own gang. She's jealous of the girl or something, I don't know – and me thinking that was all over and done with. I'm bewildered, Grace. Ara, I got angry then too, and I shouted at her that I didn't know what the hell she wanted and I wasn't a bloody mind reader. The poor children were scared, and I felt terrible after. And now I'm sleeping on the settle and we're not talking at all.'

'Oh, Charlie, I'm sorry...' Her heart went out to her old friend.

'Could you talk to her, Grace? I know you are good friends. Maybe she'd talk to you? I wouldn't ask, only I'm desperate...'

Grace thought she might not know much about marriage – her relationship with Declan hadn't lasted long enough for them to have any problems – but she knew that only the most foolhardy of people would go blundering into someone else's marriage. Her instincts told her that whatever was going on between them was for Charlie and Dymphna to work out. Nobody else could do it for them.

But Charlie was right about one thing: Dymphna wasn't herself at all. Grace had noticed she had been a bit tetchy while helping out with the wedding preparations, which was totally out of character. She hadn't been like that with Grace herself so much, but only because

Grace got the impression that Dymphna had been making a concerted effort with her. But there had been other things also.

Dymphna was highly capable and organised, but she had been forgetful lately and seemingly overwhelmed by even the smallest things. She blamed the hot weather for it – said the heat was getting to her. Also Dymphna normally didn't mind when the children were rumbunctious. 'Sure aren't they only children?' she would say. But recently Grace had noticed Dymphna snapping at them, often for no reason at all.

Something Patricia had said at the time stirred in Grace's mind. She and Tilly had talked about the change and how it affected some women very badly.

'I knew one woman in the Philippines who turned from being an absolute angel of a woman – the sweetest, kindest person I knew – to an absolute raging demon almost overnight,' Patricia had declared. 'That said, Dymphna McKenna's still only in her early forties, which is a bit young for the change.'

'Ma says it can happen much younger,' Tilly had said. 'All depends on the woman.'

Grace was no expert, but she had to wonder if Dymphna's problems might be due to the changes in her body rather than anything Charlie and the children had done. But she didn't know enough about the process to discuss it with Charlie McKenna. No, the best piece of advice she could give him was to send him to someone who might actually be able to help.

'My advice, for what it's worth to you, is to give Dymphna a bit of time and space, Charlie. I know it's hard, but if she's not feeling herself, that might be why she's reacting so strongly to everything.'

'Do you think I should send her to Dr Ryan?'

She shrugged. 'I suppose it wouldn't hurt,' she replied. 'But you know, it might be worth suggesting to Dymphna that she talk to Mary O'Hare. She's very good at helping women.'

'Mary O'Hare?' Charlie's eyes widened. 'Do you think it's something…? I mean…eh…well, you know…women's business?' He gazed down at his boots.

Grace understood exactly how he felt. This topic was proving embarrassing for her too. Such matters were not discussed out loud in public, and certainly not with a man old enough to be her father. Even pregnancy, which was obvious to everyone, was rarely commented on beyond a remark that so-and-so was expecting. How babies came or what happened as women aged – all as natural as the nature surrounding them – none of that was considered socially appropriate conversation.

'Sure I don't know, Charlie,' she replied. 'But I tell you what? Why don't I mention it to Mary O'Hare and see what she says.'

Charlie still looked a little shell-shocked. 'Thanks, Grace. I'd appreciate that. It might explain some of it anyway.'

'But in the meantime, maybe you could talk to Dymphna yourself? I'm sure she hates fighting with you and is just as upset as you are about the whole thing. Look, why don't you send the children over to us for their tea this evening. Cáit and Molly will be delighted to have them. Seámus won't know what hit him with all the minding he'll get. I made a big pot of stew earlier, so there's plenty for everyone. That will give you and Dymphna a bit of time on your own. Have a chat. See if you can sort it out between you anyway?'

He looked less than enthusiastic at the prospect.

'So what do you think, Charlie?' she asked gently. 'Will you send the children over to us this evening and have that chat with Dymphna?'

He sighed, then nodded and squeezed her shoulder. 'Yes, thanks, Grace, I will. But if there's any loud bangs or smell of smoke from our place, get Sergeant Keane, will you, though?' He gave a rueful laugh.

She smiled. 'I'm sure you can figure it out without the guards. That's settled then. Well, I'd better get off home and start preparing for our guests. Nothing but the best for the McKennas.'

Charlie was unusually silent as they made their way out of the cemetery. She waited by the graveyard wall as he collected his bike. As he joined her, he put his hand on her arm. 'You're a good person, Grace. Eddie and Kathy would be so proud of you.'

'Thanks, Charlie.'

Her eyes filled suddenly with tears and Charlie looked at her in alarm. 'Ah, Gracie, what is it? What's wrong?'

'It's not you, Charlie.'

'What is it then? Is there something about Richard you're not telling me? Something that's worrying you?'

He put his arm around her shoulder and drew her to him. The familiar smell of Charlie, fresh air and Sunlight laundry soap, gave her comfort as it always had. 'No, Richard's not hurt, and as far as I know, he's safe. It's just' – she threw him a half smile – 'women's stuff…'

'Richard has another woman?' Charlie frowned.

Grace had to laugh in spite of herself. 'No, of course not, you silly goose. I meant me. Women's stuff. Babies and that sort of thing.'

'Gracie, are you…?' Charlie's eyes widened, and the hope in them tore at her heart.

She shook her head sadly. 'No. I'm not.'

The tears welled up again, and she blurted out everything that was oppressing her. 'That's the problem, you see. I'm *not* expecting. And I never conceived with Declan either, Charlie. So there must be something wrong with me. Because of the polio. Hugh Warrington says the polio won't stop me being able to, but what if he's wrong? What if it never happens? What if I can't…'

He stared at her solemnly for a moment, then took her gently by the shoulders. 'It's not as easy as you might think, Gracie. Maggie and I were married for nearly a year before Declan was on the way and 'twasn't for want of trying, let me tell you…' He winked and gave a chuckle, and Grace felt some of the embarrassment dissolve a little, if not the anxiety.

'Look, I'm not going to say don't worry,' he continued, 'because that's the most stupid bit of advice anyone can give another person. If you could stop worrying, you would, of course. But the first thing you need is your husband home to you.'

'But what if he doesn't come back, or he does and I can't get pregnant?' She voiced her fears.

'Well, Gracie, none of us can tell the future, but Richard has got himself out of some fairly tight corners before this. He's no fool, and if any man is determined to come back to his wife in one piece from that place, 'tis him. And as to the baby thing... Well, love, you'll have to just be patient.' He gave another wicked chuckle and a cheeky wink. 'And sure, think of the craic you'll have trying!'

Grace couldn't help laughing. She certainly had not expected to be having this conversation on a Sunday morning.

She glanced over the wall at the grave where her parents and sister lay. Something told her that her parents would be like Charlie – she imagined them as earthy, loving people, who if they knew her as an adult wouldn't be horrified at such talk. Her sister, Agnes, on the other hand was probably spinning in the grave at the idea of Grace talking about sex with the postman outside a graveyard. The thought of it made her giggle again.

'What?' Charlie asked, and she told him, which made him laugh too.

'Indeed, then, Gracie, she's up there having a right conniption altogether, I'd say.' He guffawed. 'Or maybe she's finally after finding some angel or saint of someone to show her what she was missing...'

'If she was missing it,' she said, and then instantly regretted it.

'What do you mean?' he asked, raising a querying eyebrow.

She hesitated. She couldn't tell him the full details about Hannah Monaghan or the fact that Canon Rafferty was Carrie Dwyer's father because they had promised Hannah that they would keep her secret, but she could tell him her suspicions about his relationship with Agnes and that they were backed up by other stories that had come to light since about the canon fathering a child.

'You don't look shocked,' Grace said when she was finished.

'Ara, nothing about him would shock me, but I don't think she was the only one,' he said quietly.

'No, I think you might be right.'

Charlie sighed. 'I don't know what the truth is, Gracie, but I do know that I called to your house one evening – not long after you went away to hospital – and there was no answer. I had a parcel for your sister, but it was too heavy to carry with the usual round, so I brought it over specially. It was pouring rain, and I didn't want to leave it outside for fear she'd slaughter me altogether if it got destroyed. The front door was locked, so I went to put it inside the back door. And they were there in the kitchen. And, well...they were in a position you wouldn't expect to see a young woman and priest in, put it that way.'

Grace was simultaneously shocked and not at all surprised. 'Did they see you?' she asked, her voice sounding strange.

'I made sure they didn't. He and I had enough run-ins, and he wasn't at all happy I got the job with Nancy, so I didn't want to give him any cause to get me sacked.'

'I had hoped that... Well, I hoped that it wasn't that but...' She sighed. 'I know she was a difficult person, but he destroyed her. She was only a girl when he got his claws in her, too young for him, leaving aside altogether the fact that he was a priest who had taken a vow of celibacy.'

He nodded. 'I always thought it was a cruel demand for priests to be celibate. What harm would it do for them to marry and have families? It might make them better priests too, if they had some personal knowledge of what it was like raising a family, paying the bills, keeping shoes on their feet and dealing with in-laws and all the rest of it.'

'Wouldn't Father Iggy be a lovely husband and father?' she mused, trying to blot the image of Agnes and Canon Rafferty together out of her mind.

'Indeed, he would. But the Church would never allow it. They wouldn't want to pay for them. And if a priest had a family, they'd end up the responsibility of the Church. Not to mention it might distract them from the job.'

Grace didn't comment, but she knew Charlie, even though he went to Mass like everyone else, had not much time for the Catholic Church. She didn't blame him. The canon had almost destroyed him, and Declan had been treated so cruelly in that awful place he was sent to that was run by the brothers. Charlie liked the two priests who looked after the parish now, but as an organisation, he was less than enthusiastic.

'So what are you going to do about this little girl in America that Sarah was telling me all about the other day?' Charlie asked.

Grace was grateful for the change of subject. She didn't want to dwell on Agnes and the canon any more than she had to. She sighed. 'I don't know, Charlie, I honestly don't. But Sarah is determined to help her, and she can't do it here without someone Irish on her side. You know how people get on the subject of babies born out of wedlock. And as for mentioning the canon, well, again, you know yourself. But if we want to do something for the little girl in New York, it seems getting him involved – much as the idea of ever crossing paths with him again gives me the shudders – is going to be the only way.'

'Well, if I can help at all, I will,' he said. 'That poor little mite is on my mind since Sarah mentioned it. I got Declan back – although it was horrible for him all those years, and that haunts me to this day. But we got him home and he was happy with you and with me. And even if things can be a bit tricky with Lily and all the rest, I'm still so happy to have her back in my life. That little girl should be with her own flesh and blood, if it can be done at all.'

'We'll do our best, Charlie,' she said with a smile. 'Anyway, you've enough to worry about.'

'God, Gracie,' he said, the comical look of horror at the thought of what ailed his wife returning for a moment. 'When does it get easy, do you think?'

'I don't know, Charlie. I really don't. But sure we'll just keep pulling and dragging, as Mary O'Hare says.'

'I suppose we will, love. I suppose we will.'

CHAPTER 17

*G*race's first thought was that at least the children had all gone to the strand, it being the last day of school. The buff-coloured telegram envelope in Charlie's hand had stilled her heart, and she felt the blood drain from her face.

Seeing her distress, Charlie shook his head. 'It's for Eleanor,' he said quickly in Irish, though Eleanor was in the other room, tidying it for the holidays and putting everything away. The air in Grace's classroom was scented with the smells of school – ink and paint, milk and sandwiches – and the late-June sunlight beamed through the windows, buttery and golden.

'Oh no, Charlie.' Grace's hand went to her mouth; it could only mean one thing.

He nodded. 'I was there when it came in. I told Nancy I'd bring it over.'

'We'll give it to her together,' Grace said, taking the envelope from him. He followed her into the classroom next door, where Eleanor was standing on a chair, taking down some artwork the children had done during the year.

'Grace... Oh, hello, Charlie. Grace, I was wondering if we could salvage some of this paper, use the other side maybe. I know it's only –'

Eleanor hopped down, lithe as a goat, and in that moment saw the envelope in Grace's hand and the look on her friend's face.

'Eleanor, I am so sorry,' Grace said gently, moving towards the woman.

Eleanor shook her head, backing away. 'No. No, I don't want it, Grace. Don't give it to me… Please, I don't want it…' She flopped down on one of the desks, her breath coming in horrible gasps.

Time seemed to stand still as Grace stood in front of her friend, her hand on the other woman's shoulder. She knew this sensation: the horrible, gut-churning disbelief, the certain knowledge that, even though no other thought was clear, this one was. Life, as you knew it, was over.

'Read it for me…please.' Eleanor's voice was raspy.

Grace looked at Charlie, who gave her a slight nod of encouragement. With trembling fingers, she took the card from the envelope.

'"Immediate – Mrs Douglas Worth, Clochbán House, Knocknashee, Dingle, County Kerry, EIRE."'

'"Immediate – From Air Ministry Kingsway 43229 21/6/44."'

'"Deeply regret to inform you that your husband, Squadron Leader Douglas James Worth, lost his life in air operations at Amendola Air Base, Foggia, Italy, on 18 June 1944. The Ministry expresses its profound sympathy. Letter to follow with all known details."'

Eleanor did nothing for a moment. Then, her hand steady as a rock, she took the telegram from Grace and scanned the words that had changed her life forever. She made no sound, no movement, just stared, as Grace and Charlie stood by, helpless.

'Can you get my girls, please, Charlie?' Eleanor asked eventually.

'Of course,' he said, leaving the room.

'Eleanor, I'm so sorry…' Grace repeated. She knew the words were completely inadequate, but words were all anyone had.

Eleanor nodded and swallowed, breathing in and out, slowly and deliberately, as if forcing herself to remain calm.

'Two nights ago I dreamed he died, Grace.' She gestured with the telegram in her hand. 'I dreamed this. I'd never done anything like that before, but it was so vivid. He died quickly, in his sleep. But he…' Her voice faltered. 'In my dream, he came to me. The blanket had slipped off the bed, and he picked it up and covered me. He kissed my forehead and smoothed my hair. And then I woke up.'

'He came to say goodbye,' Grace whispered.

Eleanor's eyes filled with tears, fat, full tears that spilled over and down her cheeks. 'He did. He came to say goodbye.'

Grace made her a cup of tea, adding a heaped spoon of precious sugar, and handed it to her. The older woman took it gratefully and sipped.

'How will I tell the girls?' she asked, the loneliness, grief and loss showing naked on her face. Her voice was a monotone. 'We didn't have a perfect marriage. I told you before that we almost divorced. But when Douglas thought we'd been caught in an air raid, he was distraught. I suppose he realised how fragile, how fleeting, life can be. And do you know, Grace, once we decided to really make our marriage work, those were the best years. He was away for some of it, but not all. I got more of my husband in these past years than many servicemen's wives, and the girls had their daddy. He said once that we were like an old battleship, welded and patched but all the stronger for it. And though I teased him for not being very romantic, comparing us to a battered old ship, he was right.' She gave a watery smile. 'That which doesn't kill you really does make you stronger, and Douglas and I were strong as a rock.'

'I know,' Grace said quietly.

Eleanor ran her hands through her shoulder-length chestnut hair, now streaked with grey. She was a tall woman, with a strong bone structure, the sort of presence that imbued confidence – a person in control, a perfect school principal, which is what she was before coming to Knocknashee.

'We are so close to the end too. Rome has fallen to the Allies, and I really thought this war was all but over, that we'd be one of the lucky ones. I imagined us at parades to commemorate those comrades of his that didn't make it, that I'd be the one offering my sympathy to their widows and orphans, not that I'd be the one receiving the pitying looks, the widow's pension.' The words were slow, almost dreamlike, as if Eleanor were taking a stroll through her future, observing it with surprise.

Grace wished she had words, something to soothe, but she knew she didn't. She'd been on the receiving end of so many people's platitudes when Declan died. She would spare her friend that from her at least. Plenty of others wouldn't. They would trot out the well-worn lines soon enough.

The silence hung heavily on them, until the church bells began to ring out the Angelus at noon. Now, all over Knocknashee, people would say the familiar words of the daily prayer to the Virgin Mary, each with their own intentions, many of them connected to this infernal war.

'Father Iggy once told me that people who say things like "only the good die young" or "he's watching over you now" are not being flippant. They don't know what to say or how to be, and so what they are really doing is choosing their comfort over the reality you are living. So I won't say anything like that to you, Eleanor. I'll just say, I am here, I'll help you to endure this in any way I can, and I am so, so sorry that your lovely husband died.'

'What are those words that Charlie said at the Mass for Declan?' Eleanor asked. 'I didn't have much Irish back then, but I asked him to translate them for me, and he wrote them down. Do you know them?'

Grace nodded. 'May God grant him peace. *Ar dheis Dé go raibh a anam dílis.* May his soul rest at God's right hand. *Ní bheidh a leithéid arís ann.* We'll never see the likes of him again.'

Eleanor smiled. 'I've come to love this place, you know. Douglas remarked on it when he was last at home, how well the girls and I have settled here. He said he was so glad to see it. He'd loved growing up here, hated being sent to boarding school in England, and he was so pleased to see his girls running about like wild goats in Knocknashee, speaking this beautiful language, being free and full of life and joy as children should be.'

'He asked me if we'd stay,' Eleanor continued, 'after the war. We both agreed it was the best idea we ever had. He said he'd find work doing something. He'd have his army pension, and I have my job here. We could fix up the house properly and just live here, raise our children, be safe, be happy. But I don't know if that's what I should do now, or if I should go back and live in the country he died for, help to put it back together some kind of way after all of this hell. I had a letter from the chairman of the board of my old school saying they had bought a big house that they were going to use as a school and asking me to come back. But now… What do you think, Grace?'

Grace's heart was full. Eleanor was right. The three Worth girls were as much a part of Knocknashee as any child born on the peninsula. The idea of uprooting them and taking them back to live in Liverpool would be heartbreaking.

'I'll admit my answer is going to be based on some selfishness, because I don't want to lose you, Eleanor. But the way I see it, this is your home, this is your community. You and the girls are loved here, and if this place can do something well, it's that it looks after its own. When my parents died, and Agnes and Declan, people came together around me, held me up, in the big things and the little things. It made it bearable – just about. And I believe that support is what you and the girls need right now.'

Eleanor nodded, her eyes watery. Her voice cracked as she spoke. 'Yes, you're right, Grace. The girls need that stability now.'

Grace took her friend's hand. 'Eleanor, you don't need to think about any of this right now. All you have to do today is look after yourself and the girls. Olivia is fourteen, and she'll be a great help to you – she's such a sensible girl – but she will need you now. Joanne and little Libby too.'

She wasn't sure if Eleanor was really listening to her. When her friend spoke, she sounded dreamlike, as if drifting in and out of reality.

'If the girls were in England, this would be something they'd have seen a lot of – fathers killed in the war. But not over here. I remember when I arrived over, first thinking that I was somehow shirking, that it was wrong that my children and I got to live here in this peaceful place with enough food while my countrymen and women suffered. But not any more...' Eleanor put her hand to her mouth as a loud sob escaped, and Grace drew her into a hug.

'Charlie will be back with the girls soon,' she said as Eleanor grew quiet again. 'Do you want to tell them alone, or will I stay with you?'

Her friend pulled a handkerchief from her pocket, wiped her eyes and blew her nose. 'Thank you, Grace,' she said. 'I'll tell them on my own. I appreciate you more than you'll ever know, but this is something I have to do myself. They'll never forget this day until they take their last breath, so I need to do it the best way I can. Though how that would be, I've no idea.'

She released a ragged breath, and Grace knew the woman had not yet absorbed the devastating news herself. Something about a sudden death – it took a bit of time to sink into your cells. When Declan died, it was like Grace knew it had happened in her head, she knew logically, but it had been as if her core self couldn't – wouldn't – accept it yet. It had taken a long time to finally come to terms with it. Poor Eleanor was in the early stages now. There would be many others, but they could only be navigated one slow, painful step at a time. Grace's own default position, she now knew, was to withdraw, not speak, feel as if she were underwater. But Eleanor's was to spring into practical action. Everyone was different.

'Can I give you a bit of advice?' Grace asked tentatively, but she knew Eleanor was a person who was above all things rational and calm, even now, in these tragic circumstances.

'Please do.'

'When my parents drowned...I was ten years old. A year younger than your Libby is now.' For a moment, she was transported back to those days, when her precious, idyllic life changed forever. Nothing bad had ever happened to her before that.

'I can't remember exactly who told me what had happened – there were so many people milling around at the time – but I do remember that nobody said the word "dead". They said "drowned" and "passed away" and "gone to God" and "with the angels" and things like that. And I remember thinking that my parents were still alive but maybe somewhere else. It wasn't until afterwards, I can't remember how long after, I asked – I think it was Charlie – "Is my mammy dead?" He looked so stricken, so shocked that after all that time I would ask him that. But he took my hand and told me straight. "They are, Gracie, your mammy and daddy are dead."

'So my advice to you is do the context afterwards – whatever you want to say about where Douglas is now, or how it happened, or any of that – and open with the fact that he's dead. It's so hard to say the word, I know. But if someone had said that word to me back then, it would have spared me all the confusion and wondering. It's awful and hard and feels cruel, but the thing is, there is no way to soften this. So it's best not to try, I think.'

Eleanor squeezed her hand tightly. 'Thank you, Grace. That's good advice, I think.' She gave a pale smile. 'I would probably have gone down the "Daddy is gone to heaven route", to be honest. But I'll do as you suggest –'

Their conversation was interrupted by the high-pitched voices of her three daughters. They were teasing each other about being too scared to jump off the pier into the water – the rite of passage in Knocknashee school to be with the big boys and girls. Olivia, the eldest, had done it, but the middle girl, Joanne, had balked. Grace remembered Tilly writing to her about the first time she'd done it. Grace had been in hospital and could barely walk, let alone jump off the pier.

Charlie opened the door, and the girls ran in.

'What is it, Mammy? Mr McKenna said you wanted us, but Joanne said she was going to do the jump today, so we have to get back. Eileen O'Flynn did it, and she's six months younger than Joanne – she's not even thirteen yet...' Libby, the youngest girl, was also the most animated and vocal of the three.

'What happened?' Olivia, the eldest, had sensed something was wrong.

'Come on, we have to get back to the pier...' Libby insisted.

Joanne looked from her mother to Grace. 'Is it Daddy?' she asked.

Grace withdrew then, leaving Eleanor alone with her three daughters. She and Charlie waited outside. Through the glass in the door, they could see the girls standing in front of their mother, then all three clinging to her, then they heard the cries of grief. Eleanor was right – her girls would never forget this day for the rest of their lives.

As she stood there, watching the Worth family's loss and pain, Grace felt a rush of vile, venomous hatred for Adolf Hitler. The personification of the devil. Not happy until the whole world was plunged into despair and misery.

The war would end eventually. But for the rest of their time on this earth, the Worth girls would miss their father. They would marry and some other man would walk them down the aisle. They would have children who would never know their grandad Douglas as anything other than a faded photograph in a frame. And it was all the fault of that revolting little excuse for a man in Germany, may he rot in hell.

In time the girls' memories of their father would fade to just a few snapshots, like Grace's memories of her daddy. Frozen in time. It struck her that she never thought of Eddie Fitzgerald as anything but Daddy. Would she still be calling him Daddy if he'd lived? Would she have changed to Da as most children did as they got older?

Either way, she had been deprived of a father, and so now too were Olivia, Joanne and Libby, and as they wailed in their mother's arms, Grace knew that, like her, they would never fully get over this loss.

CHAPTER 18

BERN, SWITZERLAND

Richard stood outside the house at Herrengasse 23, Bern, and tried to process the fact that he was back here once more. The last time he'd been deposited at this door was by the Swiss police, who'd picked him up after he was sprung from a Nazi prison, narrowly escaped a German patrol and crossed the border from France. He'd been disorientated, with not a penny in his pocket, having been assisted by a mysterious man known to him only as Gabriel.

Allen Dulles was a US government official – his exact title had never been explained, but Richard surmised he was secret service at least in some capacity – and he'd been welcoming but a bit aloof. He'd handed Richard into the care of one of his staff, Steven Kempler, who had turned out to be much more than first met the eye.

Richard hoped he could find Steven again. He was a cheery, happy-go-lucky kind of guy on the surface, but Richard had come to realise that, just as Dulles and Steven had explained, nothing in Switzerland was as it seemed and one could never drop one's guard.

Richard had no idea if Steven had been in on Jacob's plan to stay in Switzerland when Richard had been picked up and flown out. Maybe Jacob had made that decision at the last minute. Or maybe that had always been the way it was going to happen. Alfie O'Hare or even Dulles himself might have made that plan – Richard had no idea. It had all happened so fast.

The door opened, and a young Swiss woman smiled at him questioningly.

'My name is Richard Lewis. I wonder if I could speak to Steven Kempler or Allen Dulles, please?'

'Come in.' She stood back, and he entered the dark-panelled, marble-floored entranceway. Four large dark wooden doors either side were shut, and marble stairs led upstairs from the back of the hallway.

'Follow me, please,' the woman said, and tripped up the stairs, Richard following behind. On the second floor, she stopped before three chairs placed against a wall beside another row of dark wooden doors. 'Sit, please,' she said, disappearing behind the nearest door and closing it behind her.

Time seemed to slow down, and Richard waited. Five minutes turned to ten and then fifteen. He wondered if the woman had forgotten about him. Nobody had passed up or down the stairs since he'd been here, and the doors were so thick, no sound emerged.

The jubilation on the west coast of France at being liberated was nothing more than news headlines over here, he realised. The Nazis were still very much a force to be reckoned with behind their lines, and this war was by no means a done deal. Warren's brother Ed, who had taken him here, had told him about how he'd picked up two escapees, resisters who had fallen into the clutches of Klaus Barbie. Known as the Butcher of Lyon, Barbie was nothing short of a sadist, and the condition of these two men was so pitiful, Ed had been doubtful they'd even survive the flight out. However, they had and were now recovering in England. Ed had been so horrified by what he saw, what they told him, he was hell-bent on doing as much damage to the Germans as he could, and he told Richard that if he ever got close to seriously hurting Barbie, he'd do it with relish.

Richard hoped that Alfie and Jacob never crossed paths with Barbie. He sounded like a monster, and it was particularly worrying that he had set his sights on resisters, communists and anyone else who sabotaged the work of the Third Reich.

Richard checked his watch. He'd been sitting here nearly half an hour. His plans for how to get back, to get out of Switzerland, were non-existent, and he feared that Dulles would be none too pleased at having to come to his rescue again, but he had no choice. He *would* find out about Jacob, and if he was alive but refused to come back – or try to get back, as was probably a more accurate assessment of their situation – then at least he could tell Sarah that Jacob was still alive. He had promised Grace he would try to find Alfie as well. His poor mother and Tilly were so worried, probably with good reason. Luckily they knew nothing about Klaus Barbie, but something told Richard that the infamous Nazi likely knew all about Alfie O'Hare.

He hoped it would be simple – find them, convince Jacob to go back, work out a way to get back, then everyone would live happily ever after. But knowing what he knew, he had to face the fact that, while it was his preferred outcome, it was also the most unlikely. If Jacob had got his way – and Richard was in no doubt that he would have – he was working with Alfie sabotaging the Germans, and that was an activity that had a directly negative impact on one's life expectancy. Either way, he had to be realistic. Jacob might well be dead. But whatever the situation, Richard had to know.

At least this time he was travelling with his American passport and a press pass, as well as plenty of money. He'd telegrammed his father to wire him some, so he was in a better position than the last time he'd been here.

'Mr Lewis, we meet again.' Allen Dulles, silver-haired, his pipe clenched in his teeth, appeared on the stairs from the third floor. He was dressed impeccably in a cream double-breasted suit. Single-breasted suits had become popular due to shortage of fabric, but

Dulles didn't strike Richard as a man who would have been affected by rationing. Rather, he exuded the air of someone who got whatever he wanted.

The man's tone was ironic. He was not exactly thrilled to see Richard – as Richard had expected.

'Thank you for seeing me.' Richard stood to shake his hand.

'Nothing to thank me for yet,' Dulles replied. 'I am assuming you are here because you need something, so whether thanks are warranted remains to be seen.' He gestured that Richard should pass him and go up the stairs ahead.

They didn't speak again until they were back in Dulles's office. It hadn't changed since the last time: long Georgian-style windows overlooking the river far below, a large walnut desk with matching chair, two chesterfield sofas and glass coffee tables on either side of an enormous marble fireplace dominating the large room. It looked more like his father's office in Savannah than a place in Switzerland, but Richard assumed Dulles had decorated it with items from the States.

'Please take a seat,' Dulles offered, and Richard sat on the nearest sofa. Dulles took a seat opposite him, crossing his legs as he sat back. He steepled his fingers and fixed his gaze on Richard. 'At the risk of seeming rude, what the hell are you doing back here? We went to considerable trouble to get you home safely, and yet here you are in front of me again.'

It felt like Richard was in the headmaster's office after sneaking out after hours, having been warned once before. 'I apologise. I wanted to return the cash you lent me.' He took an envelope from his pocket and handed it over. Dulles didn't open it; he merely accepted it and placed it in a drawer.

'And also, as you know, my colleague and brother-in-law, Jacob Nunez, didn't come ba –'

'*Chose* not to.'

'Well, indeed, he chose not to come back, and I'm here to find him.' *I lost my friend.* It sounded silly and juvenile even to his own ears.

'How did you get here?'

'I hitched a ride with an Australian air force supply delivery plane. He landed in a field near Saanen –'

'He was lucky the Swiss didn't shoot him down,' Dulles muttered. The Swiss, ostensibly maintaining their neutrality, had shot down both German and Allied planes, but Richard knew Dulles was well aware of the proclivities of his hosts. They helped the Allies to a certain extent but also allowed the Germans to store their ill-gotten gains in Swiss banks as well as allowed the Germans to transfer weapons and resources on their railroads, and they minted their coins. Richard wondered how the Swiss experience of this war would be written. Whatever way it was presented, it was unlikely to reflect the reality, which was that Switzerland looked after itself, in whatever form that needed to be.

'He's done it a few times. He's also picked up people, so he's adept at getting down and up again fast.'

Dulles didn't look impressed. 'So now what?' He raised an eyebrow at Richard.

'Well, I wanted to speak to Steven to see if he knew anything about Jacob or Alfie O'Hare.' Richard hoped he was coming across as a calm professional, not some dumb schoolboy trying to be a hero and failing.

'Mrs Gerhardt Gruber hasn't been seen for weeks. Did you know that?' Dulles asked, apropos of nothing.

'I didn't.'

'Our sources initially feared she'd been taken to Russia for "debriefing". That is not a fate as benign as it would seem. Comrade Stalin is very suspicious and believes everyone has it in for him. Which doesn't mean they don't, of course, but...' Dulles gave a small smile.

'Did Gruber find out she was working for our side?' Richard was worried for his old friend Bernadette.

'Tell me about the conversation you two had,' the other man said. It was an order, not a question.

Richard considered being reticent, but he was going to need this man's help and they were on the same side, so he decided to be frank. He inhaled. 'I knew her in Paris in 1939, before that city fell. She was Bernadette Dreyfus then, married to a Jewish communist named Paul Dreyfus. She and her sister, Constance, who was and hopefully still is Alfie O'Hare's girlfriend, took Jacob and I under their wing. We had a lot of meals at their house and became friends. When we left Paris as the Nazis were at the gates of the city, Alfie arrived at the train station. The plan was that he would get out with Jacob, my sister, Sarah, and me. But he didn't. Instead, he gave us Bernadette's tiny baby, Odile, to take care of.'

Dulles gave no sign of a reaction, but he was listening intently.

'We had no idea what to do with a baby, but they were sure she couldn't be kept safe. They thought the Nazis were aware of Paul, Bernadette and Constance – they certainly knew of Alfie. They were all outspoken communists, so they presumed they would be first on the Germans' list to be hunted down, and whatever hopes of survival they had alone, they had none with an infant. So we took her.'

Dulles nodded. 'Where is that baby now?'

He swallowed. 'In Ireland, where my wife lives. Odile is being cared for by Alfie's sister and his mother.'

Dulles stood and poured himself a whiskey. He handed one to Richard also, without asking if he wanted it. 'Go on.'

'So when I went to the party at Montreux with Steven and saw that Bernadette was now Mrs Gruber, I was shocked. I thought she'd turned to the Nazis. Gruber was a known collaborator, and they were living a very lavish lifestyle. Or it certainly looked that way anyway. So I challenged her.'

The other man examined his fingernails as he sipped his whiskey. Richard placed his on the coffee table, untouched.

'How did that go?'

Richard gathered his thoughts. 'She told me it wasn't how it looked, but that I'd have to meet her somewhere safer to talk. The next day we went for a walk, and she arranged for us to meet in a kind of chalet in the mountains. It was there I met Jacob again. I'd been told he was dead.'

Dulles nodded. 'That was the safest thing. O'Hare could only get one of you out, and he assumed correctly that a tall, strong, wealthy Episcopalian from Savannah would be easier to negotiate for than a sick, undernourished Jew. So he got Jacob out and left you to Gabriel.'

'Yes.' Richard said, realising that Dulles already knew this whole story. 'It was Jacob who explained that Bernadette was working with Alfie, but also for the Russians, using her husband's contacts in the top brass of the Reich to gather intelligence that would help the war on the Eastern Front.'

Dulles nodded again. 'Stalingrad might not have gone our way were it not for strategic people, even within Hitler's inner sanctum, feeding information to our side to ensure the German downfall there. They knew as soon as they gave him the ultimate power that it was a mistake, and the only way to oust him was to help his enemies.'

'And Bernadette was how that information got back to Moscow.'

'Indeed. But she was playing a very dangerous game.'

'I know.' Richard would never forget that conversation when he'd begged her to come back with him, to return to Odile. 'She said that. She was at risk if her husband found out who she really was, if the Nazis who wined and dined at their house knew or if the Russians suspected her of being a double agent, which they seemingly accuse everyone of. Everywhere she looked she was in danger. It was why I wanted her to come with me.'

'Not to mention what happens once our side pushes through. As far as they're concerned, Mrs Gruber is a Nazi-loving socialite, living high on the proceeds of the wealth of European Jewry.'

'But we would speak up for her. I mean –'

Dulles held up his hand. 'Let me explain something to you, son.'

Richard hated the condescension in the man's tone but had no choice but be deferential. Dulles stood between him and Jacob.

'Once the Allies liberate Europe, it's not going to be a nice orderly handover of power. As you've no doubt seen in France, it's chaos, and in that chaos people can' – he tapped his lips with his steepled fingers – 'shall we say, avail of the opportunity such a situation presents to settle scores, to deal with things in their own way. The Grubers may have powerful friends – for now. But they have even more powerful enemies. So you would be foolish to think the arrival of the good cops is going to be the answer to your friend's prayers. In fact, the Allied liberation of Europe could mean that the nightmare for her might well just be beginning.'

'But they're in a neutral country. The Allies have no jurisdiction here.'

'True, but as you saw the last time you visited this picture-postcard place, the war is being fought here just as fiercely as it is in Normandy. It's just being fought at dinner parties and in ballrooms. But be under no illusion, Mr Lewis, things are going to get very ugly here, just as in Germany, France, all over, and the Grubers, like all Nazis with the wherewithal, see how this is going. They will be in an advanced stage of planning their exit strategy. Whether they ever get to execute that plan, however, remains to be seen.'

'So Bernadette is doomed either way? Is that what you're saying?'

Dulles shrugged. 'Possibly.'

'And Gabriel, can't he help her?'

'Ah, Gabriel, the man of many names, many faces, many nationalities, many loyalties and none. He's as mercurial as a sprite and just as capricious.'

'You don't trust him?'

Dulles laughed then, the hearty sound breaking the tension. 'I don't trust anyone, Mr Lewis. It's why I'm still alive.' He drained his glass and placed it on the table. 'Now, why are you here?'

'To find Jacob Nunez and Alfie O'Hare if possible.'

'Both last seen here in Switzerland?' He sounded as if he was asking about the weather.

Richard stifled his frustration and swallowed back what he longed to say. *Of course they were in Switzerland. Of course, and you know that. Steven Kempler, who worked for you, Dulles, oversaw the whole thing. Stop pretending like you're in the dark here, because we both know you're not.*

'Yes. I last saw them in a field in the mountains outside Montreux. Alfie, Bernadette, Gabriel and Jacob.'

'I see,' Dulles said with a sigh, as if Richard were an irritating five-year-old who kept asking questions.

There was a gentle knock on the door, and he left to answer it. Murmured conversation, indistinguishable, with an unseen person, was all Richard could ascertain.

Dulles was gone just a few minutes and then returned. 'Steven is travelling at the moment. I don't know anything about your friends. Mrs Gruber is in her home in Montreux, we believe, but has not been seen out and about for weeks. Nor have the Grubers entertained as they usually do, I do know that. As for Mr Nunez and the Irishman, I don't have a clue. People in their line of work do not tend to keep the authorities apprised of their movements. Perhaps you should go to Montreux. Mrs Gruber might see you. Maybe she can give you what you are looking for.'

Dulles opened the door, the audience clearly over. 'Things are going on here that are far and away more important than your problems, Mr Lewis. Critical things for the outcome of this war. So I'm sorry I can't be of more help. But I wish you luck, and as Steven no doubt warned you, be careful. Just because this place isn't littered with tank traps and machine gun posts doesn't mean it's any less of a battlefield. I saved you once. I won't be happy if called on to do it again, so be careful.'

'Thank you,' Richard said, and walked past him. At least Bernadette was in Montreux. He would go down there and speak to her; it was a start.

Out on the street, two men of military bearing walked by, deep in conversation in German. They might well have been German-speaking Swiss, but some instinct told Richard they were not. They walked with the arrogance and swagger he'd seen in officers of the Third Reich. They approached Herrengasse 23 and pushed open the door, walking in. Richard had read between the lines that Dulles was in contact with everyone here – people from every faction of this war that was shaking humanity to its foundations – and now he knew it to be true. The man was right about one thing – this was not simple. The way people saw it back at home, the good guys and the bad guys, was naive and wrong. It was nuanced and complex, and nowhere more so than here in Switzerland. He would have to tread very carefully, because while finding Jacob was critical, getting back home to Grace in one piece was more important than anything.

CHAPTER 19

The chateaux on the shores of Lake Geneva was resplendent in the summer sunshine. Bougainvillea and wisteria tumbled from the balustrades, and the aroma and the riot of colour reminded Richard of Savannah. He felt a sudden pang of loneliness. How he wished he could take Grace to Savannah in peacetime, just to relax, go out to the cottage on St Simons, have Esme spoil them, walk on the beach, swim in the sea, eat shrimp and hamburgers and drink cold beer, and at night, lie with her in his arms, her luxuriant hair spread across his chest.

He'd sent her a letter and a telegram. She'd be worried if she didn't hear from him. He'd sent another telegram to his parents, just telling them he was all right.

The train ride south to Montreux had been uneventful but breathtaking in its beauty, the fresh green meadows of the Swiss countryside giving way to the glorious foothills of the Alps before the glistening aqua of Lake Geneva came into view. All around the lakeshore, well-dressed people sat at sidewalk cafés, smoking and drinking tiny cups of coffee. And just as before, he had to keep reminding himself there was a war on and that the idyllic sense was just that – an illusion.

He needed to gather his thoughts and make a plan, so he took a seat at one of the cafés in Montreux and ordered a *café au lait* and a *pain au chocolat*. The middle-aged waiter with a pencil moustache and a starched white apron down to his feet took his order. As he did, Richard pointed to the glorious façade of the Caux Palace Hotel, an incredibly beautiful structure nestled between the mountains and the lake. 'Is it still open for guests?' he asked in passable French. Last time he'd stayed at the Grubers' residence, but now he didn't have that option.

The man grimaced.

'No?' Richard asked mildly.

'If rumours are to be believed, a Hungarian Jew is going to fill it with refugees – bought them off Eichmann.' The man curled his lip in distaste, clearly unhappy at such a prospect.

'He who saves one life, saves the world entire,' Richard quoted, deliberately ignoring the man's tone. Jacob had told him this phrase; it was from the Talmud. 'I wish him luck.'

The waiter didn't comment further and stalked off to fill the order. Richard thought he was most likely going to spit in his coffee.

A younger woman, dark-haired, short and curvy, delivered his order in a china cup, with an exquisite flaky pastry on the side, the top golden and buttery, the filling oozing with liquid chocolate. Richard shut his eyes to savour the sensation.

'Mademoiselle, would you know of any place offering guest accommodation?' he asked as she cleared the table beside his.

She nodded, tucking her cloth into the belt of her dress and balancing a tray of dirty cups and plates on her hip. 'My mother has guest rooms. We live just up the hill there, that peach-coloured house. We have a vacant room for tonight because a couple just checked out.' Her smile revealed a crooked front tooth, and she reminded him of Tilly O'Hare. He would not go back to Knocknashee empty-handed if he could help it. He would bring them news of Jacob and Alfie.

'Thank you, I'll go up there right now.' He put some coins on the glass-topped table as a tip and drained his coffee that tasted like nectar. The pastry had been devoured in two delicious bites, melting in his mouth, gone far too soon. One day, he promised himself, he would bring Grace here, and they would sit at this spot, overlooking the lake, and have coffee and pastries, and the memories of all he'd seen and endured would fade, to be replaced by just the sheer unadulterated joy of being with his wife.

'What's your name?' he asked as he stood.

'Angelina Andros. My mother is Heidi. She'll be there if you go now. Later she will go shopping.'

'Thanks, Angelina. Nice to meet you,' he said, smiling at her as he walked away.

Heidi Andros was a plump, pleasant-faced woman in her fifties who showed him to a pretty room with a floral theme. The bed, curtains and lampshades were all white with tiny printed pink-sprigged flowers, and the floor was wide pitch-pine boards, polished to a shine. The room smelled of soap and flowers, and he knew he would sleep well here. It felt like weeks since he had slept in a bed. But first he had to go to the Grubers'.

He decided to reestablish the identity Dulles had assigned him last time he was here – Harry Anderson.

He walked along the waterfront, past the cafés and exclusive shops where women seemed to mill around, simultaneously looking both glamorous and bored.

The Gruber house was on a residential street, taking up an entire block, and he noticed the gates were locked. A sentry sat in a small box beside the gate.

He approached the box with confidence. 'Hello,' he said, 'I wonder if I might speak with Mrs Gruber?'

The man was overweight, in his sixties, and looked like he'd rather be anywhere but there. He wiped some crumbs from his mouth and then from the front of his jacket, a quasi-military kind of thing. 'Do you have an appointment?'

'No. She's not expecting me. We are acquaintances from years ago, and I just happened to be in Montreux and thought I'd drop by.' Richard kept his face open and his demeanour relaxed, but he knew his statement was as ridiculous as it sounded. Nobody just dropped by the Gruber house; it wasn't that kind of place. Invitations were issued and that was that. And an American was not likely to just be strolling around Switzerland, looking up old acquaintances for no reason. However, he didn't change his expression – he had to take the chance it would work.

'She isn't seeing anyone today.' The man wasn't rude exactly, but he certainly didn't exude any charm. He'd clearly decided Richard was a nobody, so Richard had to think quickly.

'I think if you let her know it's me, then she'll see me. It's quite important.'

The man thought for a moment. 'You got identification?'

He did, but as Richard Lewis, so he said, 'Please just tell Ghislaine that Harry Anderson is here. She will admit me.' He spoke in a voice that sounded both bored and imperious at the same time – the way he'd observed aristocratic people speak to staff sometimes. He also refused to drop his gaze, and the man seemed to be dithering.

The sentry picked up a receiver in his hut, cranked a handle and spoke in rapid French that Richard failed to catch. He stood on the sidewalk waiting. Mont JeanClare, the mansion the Grubers called home, was an old convent – an imposing building framed between the Alps and the lake and surrounded by a twelve-foot-high wall.

The sentry hung up the receiver and studiously refused to meet Richard's eye, gazing straight ahead until it rang. When it did, he answered and spoke quickly, then turned to Richard. 'You can go up.' He opened the gate, and Richard walked through, nodding his thanks.

The avenue was covered in white gravel chips that glinted in the bright sunlight, and Richard took off his jacket, the heat making his layers of clothing too uncomfortable. He longed to dive into the lake. Perhaps later.

Perfectly manicured shrubs and flowerbeds dotted the bowling-green-smooth lawn that surrounded the large red-bricked house. To his right, someone was pushing a wheelbarrow out of a Victorian-style greenhouse, and to his left, someone was pruning a fruit tree.

He walked up to the front door and pulled the scarlet silk rope he assumed rang the bell. He prayed Gruber himself was not there, and he wondered why Bernadette, or Ghislaine as he must refer to her here, had not been seen in society for weeks.

A short dapper butler with thinning dark hair and an aquiline nose opened the door. 'Monsieur?' he asked.

'Oh, hello,' Richard answered in French, ignoring the man's faint wince at his accent. 'I was hoping to see Madame Gruber?'

'Yes, your name please? And some identification?' the man replied, his words clipped.

Richard looked deliberately perplexed. 'Identification? This is a social call. Madame Gruber and I are old friends. My name is Harry Anderson.'

'And you do not have identification confirming this?' the man asked, but Richard felt he knew he was on shakier ground. He summoned his best Arthur Lewis energy – his father would dismiss this little guy as if he were a fly – and said, 'Of course I don't. What a bizarre suggestion when visiting friends. Now please tell Madame Gruber I'm here. I don't have much time.'

It flew in the face of all that he was to be so arrogant and haughty, but it seemed to have worked, because without another word, the butler ushered him into the hallway and left.

Richard stepped into the entranceway, delightfully cool after the heat of the day outside. The black-and-white-chequered tile foyer had an elegant double-width cantilever staircase with gold spindles off to the right, and dotted all around were alabaster nymphs, life-size and mounted on marble plinths. He remembered Steven telling him the last time they were here that there had been holy statues on the plinths when the Grubers bought the house but Gerhardt Gruber sent to Athens for the marble ones and dumped all the saints. On the back wall was a huge portrait of Bernadette, in an ivory gown, seated on what looked like a throne, and Gruber in a nondescript military officer's uniform standing beside her and looking stern. To the left and right were a series of large white-painted doors.

He heard footsteps on the tiles coming from what must have been a corridor off to the right at the back, and the butler reappeared.

'Madame Gruber will see you. She's out beside the pool. Follow me.' There was no friendliness or courtesy in his tone, which teetered instead on the edge of insolence.

Normally Richard would have thanked him, but this time he didn't. He simply followed the man down the corridor he had come from – a wide-open glass-roofed space – to a stone terrace full of urns with green succulents and grasses growing in profusion. The swimming pool was kidney-shaped and tiled in light blue and white. The effect was dazzling.

At the far end, there were two lounge beds, each with a large umbrella to shield the occupants from the sun. The butler stood back and gestured Richard should walk down.

Bernadette rose as he approached, and he was shocked by her appearance. She was even thinner and more gaunt than she'd been when he last saw her, and she seemed to have aged.

'Harry, how wonderful to see you again,' she said loudly in French.

'Ghislaine…' He kissed her on both cheeks as was the custom and sat in the wicker seat she offered, while she sat on the lounger, trying and failing to hide her discomfort and exhaustion.

'Lemonade?' she offered, pointing to a table where a crystal jug stood full of pale-yellow liquid with mint leaves and ice floating in it.

'Thanks, I'll help myself,' he said, realising that even the effort of getting up was too much for her.

She just nodded and shut her eyes.

He poured a glass and drank it down thirstily, then filled another. 'Can I get you a glass?' he asked, but she just shook her head.

He returned to his seat and looked at her. She couldn't be much older than he was – early thirties, at the most – but she looked seventy. Her pallor was yellow-tinged and her skin looked thin as paper.

'Bernadette…' he whispered, though they were completely alone. 'What's wrong?'

She opened her eyes, and there he saw all that was left of the fun-loving, curvy young woman he'd known in Paris. The adoring mother to her baby, Odile, the way she hung on every word her husband, Paul, uttered. How could it only have been four years ago that they were mopping up the delicious gravy of her *boeuf bourguignon* with crusty baguettes and drinking cheap red wine in their tiny Parisienne apartment? It felt like decades ago.

The huge diamond engagement ring she wore had slipped around her finger because her hands were now so thin, and her twig-like wrists were still adorned with gold bangles. She was wearing a long robe of delicate pink silk, everything so expensive, so decadent. But now that he saw her, Richard knew why she'd not been seen.

Bernadette was dying.

'How's Odile?' she asked, her voice barely a whisper.

Richard reached into his wallet and pulled out the photograph Eloise had given him of Grace and Odile on the beach in Knocknashee. The little girl was on Grace's lap, and they were reading a picture book. Her dark wavy hair was growing long now. She hated to tie it back, and Tilly didn't make her, so it hung around her heart-shaped face. He passed it to Bernadette, who stared at it without saying a word. After a prolonged silence, she spoke. 'That's Tilly?'

'No, that's Grace, my wife.' He heard the pride in his voice.

She ran her finger over the photograph. 'Odile looks so strong, so happy. She looks just like Paul, doesn't she?'

Richard nodded and smiled. 'She does, and she's such a sweet little girl. She's funny and brave as a lion, and she can speak Irish, English and French. She's loved by everyone.' Richard wanted to ease this woman's pain but was at a loss as to how to do it.

'French?' She sounded surprised.

'Yes, Tilly, Alfie's sister, is very friendly with a woman from here actually – Eloise is her name –' He stopped himself. 'They are together, in fact. And Eloise speaks French to Odile. Tilly and everyone else speak in Irish to her, and Grace and I speak English. So she's trilingual. It's hard to believe, but she'll be starting school in September. Grace is the teacher, so she's going to love it. She can almost read already.'

'And Tilly, she's happy to care for Odile?' Bernadette asked. 'She wasn't given much choice.'

'She loves her like a mother, so does Eloise. And Mary, Alfie's mother, is a wonderful grandma. It's hard to explain Knocknashee. It's a small community where everyone knows everyone else and the children are almost raised communally. Odile is a total native.'

She nodded again, handing him back the photograph.

'No, keep it. I brought it for you,' he said.

She hesitated. 'I shouldn't. In case it is found and I...'

Richard could see the conflict in her face. She wanted it badly – the only thing she had of her darling child – but in her position, it was dangerous. Even a simple photo could get her in deep trouble.

'I'll hide it,' she said, deciding. She placed the photo between the pages of a book that was on a small table beside her.

Bernadette sighed, exhaling a slow, ragged breath. Even breathing seemed to cause her pain. 'Cancer. I haven't got long.'

'Oh, Berna –'

'Call me Ghislaine, it's safer.' She smiled weakly.

'Ghislaine, are they sure? Is there anything that can be done?' He hated to have what he suspected confirmed.

She shook her head. 'Gerhardt has wheeled me before the best doctors in the country, but no, it's spread. They think it's everywhere by now. It's probably for the best. We both know I wasn't going to come out of this well, no matter what.'

'Are you still working?' he asked, not daring to elaborate.

'Not now, I can't. My friends in Moscow sent someone to check I was really sick. They didn't believe me. That's why the people at the gate were so suspicious. I said not to let anyone in. Gerhardt has no idea about that side of me, or indeed who I really am, but he is terrified now, knowing he backed the wrong horse.' She swallowed and winced. 'And he's very sad about me of course.'

'Does he love you?'

She nodded sadly. 'Very much.'

'And you him?' He was in dangerous waters, but he wanted to know.

'I will take him to the gallows myself, if I can. I'll watch as the rope squeezes around his neck and feel nothing but satisfaction.' The adamant way she spoke, despite the weakness in her voice, shocked him.

She chuckled. 'You seem surprised, my friend.'

'Well, I don't know. It's all so surreal. You living here, as his devoted wife, him devastated about your illness. I didn't know…'

'He's a Nazi. His friends are Nazis. Everything in this house, these rings, these clothes, that lemonade, bought with the blood and tears of innocent people. He's despicable and I hate him. At least the Nazis have the guts to wear a uniform, to show the world the scum that they are. He hides behind them but rushes in when they have done the dirty work to gorge on the spoils.'

'You're some actress in that case,' he said with a wry smile.

She shrugged. 'I did what I could, what I had to do. Everyone who remembers me will have an opinion. To some I'm a Nazi wife, to others a Russian spy, to more I married a Jew. To some others, I'm a heroine of the maquisards. To my parents and Constance, I'm just sweet Bernadette who made the best *clafoutis* in the seventh arrondissement. I'll never be remembered as Odile's mother, though, or Paul's wife. Those are the titles that matter to me.' Her tired eyes shone with unshed tears.

'I remember your *clafoutis*. I was telling my wife about it, how it melted in your mouth. She wanted to find a recipe.'

'It's easy. You just make a custard of eggs, sugar, flour, vanilla and cinnamon, chop up your apples, cook them with a little butter and sugar and place them on the batter to bake in the oven. I've been making it since I was six years old.' She gazed wistfully into the middle distance as if already leaving this world.

'Are you in pain?'

'Sometimes, but they give me pills. I don't want to take them, though. They make me groggy and I'm afraid of what I'll say. It probably doesn't matter now, but still. I'm glad you came, because I need you to get a message to Alfie. I can no longer do it, and all communications in and out of this house are monitored.'

'And Jacob? Is he with Alfie?' Richard almost held his breath as he waited for the answer.

'Yes, I think he was, but that was some weeks ago. We don't host any more. Gerhardt insists I rest, and I'm too weak to go out, so I have no way of meeting people. The Russians know I can't do anything for them any more, but I think they have a plan for me regardless. They don't like loose threads…'

'But surely I could try to get you out? Maybe Dulles would help…?'

She smiled and reached over to pat his hand. 'All we are arguing about here is geography, Richard. Wherever I am now, the outcome will be the same. Please don't worry. I'm astonished I survived this long. I hoped I might see Odile again some day, but she's happy and safe, thanks to you, so I can die without a worry.'

'What do you want me to do?' he asked, feeling helpless.

'Alfie and others are involved with getting people over the mountains, just as they did with you, but they need more money. You can get weapons, clothing, food here – whatever you need – if you have a way to pay for it. So I want you to make like you are helping me to bed. One of the staff will surely arrive, but I'll shoo them away. I'll give you what I have to give to Alfie. You should find him if you head to Chamonix, provided he's still alive. He runs the escape line from there, right around Mont Blanc and over the border. It's all I can do now.'

Richard recalled the story Warren told him about the empty shell cartridges, people risking what was left of their lives with such abandon to throw all they had at the war effort. Bernadette was going to fight to the last breath in her body.

'All right, let's get you inside,' he said, standing and helping her up.

'Gerhardt is not here, but the butler reports everything to him, so we are old friends from Paris. You're American – nobody would believe you're anything else with that accent,' she teased gently, 'and you're a jewellery maker. I told him the last time you were here that I knew you because you made some pieces for me when I lived in Paris. As if I could afford bespoke jewellery then. We could barely afford bread.' She grimaced at the memory, and he felt a guilty pang at how often he and Jacob had eaten in their flat. 'Just so we have our story straight.'

'Sure.' He gave her his arm to lean on, and they shuffled slowly off the terrace into the house.

CHAPTER 20

As Bernadette predicted, they were immediately approached by a matronly woman, stocky, with a stern expression and iron-grey hair twisted into a severe plait that wrapped around her head. Richard thought it the most ridiculous hairstyle he'd ever seen.

'Madame Gruber, please let me help you.' The woman glanced at Richard with ill-concealed suspicion.

'It's fine, Frau Huller, thank you. My friend Harry has come to pay a visit. He and his wife were friends of mine in Paris many years ago. He's going to accompany me to my room, and then he'll be on his way.'

Bernadette smiled and the woman softened; she seemed to hold the mistress of the house in genuine regard.

'Monsieur Gruber telephoned this morning to see how you were. You were sleeping, so he said not to disturb you but that he hoped to be home tomorrow.'

'Oh, that's wonderful.' Bernadette beamed. 'Thank you, Frau Huller. Please ask Emille to prepare *confit du canard* for him. He loves to come home to a nice meal. Ask him to make a *millefeuille* for dessert and take a bottle of the '27 from the cellar.'

'Very good, madame. And can we get you anything? Some soup, perhaps?'

'No, thank you, Frau Huller. I don't feel hungry.'

Richard could see the effort of conversation was taking it out of Bernadette; she was fading in front of his eyes.

'But madame, you have eaten nothing since yesterday, and even then just a tiny bit. Please, maybe a cup of broth, or a hot chocolate?' The older woman's face was filled with concern, and in that moment, she reminded him of Mary O'Hare, brusque and almost rude on the surface but within a deep kindness and empathy.

'Perhaps later. I'll ring once I've had a rest.' Bernadette smiled again. 'You are so very kind to me, Frau Huller. And please tell Emille that it is not his wonderful food I am rejecting. I just don't feel like eating anything, but if I was to eat, it would be his *mousse au chocolat*.'

'I'll have him prepare some right away. He worries about you too...'

'I know, and I hate to worry you all. I'm sure I'll be back to my old self in no time, eating like a horse.'

Bernadette squeezed Richard's arm to indicate she wanted to go, so he led her inside. They shuffled slowly down another wood-panelled corridor, the walls adorned with hunting scenes and majestic mountainscapes, until Bernadette indicated towards a set of ornate double doors. He opened them and walked into possibly the most exquisite room he'd ever seen. The floor-to-ceiling windows were bow-shaped and gave an uninterrupted view of the lake with the snow-capped mountains behind. It looked like a painting.

The bed was a four-poster, with ivory silk hangings, and the floor was covered in deep-pile snow-white carpet. A glass and gilt dressing table with an oval-hinged mirror was against one wall, and a matching closet and drawers were against the other.

Bernadette went immediately to the bed and lay down, shutting her eyes.

'Can you move the bedside cabinet and lift the carpet – there's a little trap door there. But first lock the door.'

Richard did as she asked, and sure enough, when he peeled back the carpet, he could see two small brass hinges and a knot in the wood that he was able to put his finger into to lift the trap door that was about a foot square. The space below was wide and at least a foot deep and filled with rolls of bank notes in a variety of currencies. There was also a black velvet box, a bit smaller than a shoebox, with various pieces of expensive looking jewellery, and finally, three pistols wrapped in a chamois. There was also an envelope, which he extracted and opened. Inside were at least ten identity cards with names and photographs, as well as ration cards and military service cards.

'Bring this all to Alfie, and also there...' Bernadette pointed to the dressing table. 'Take all the jewellery. I wish I could give you more, but you'll need to travel light. There's a rucksack in the bottom of that closet.'

He opened the closet full of gowns and velvet and furs and dug down to extract a canvas bag with leather straps. 'Should I put it all in here?' He was barely processing what was happening.

She nodded.

'Will your husband not notice?' he asked as he emptied rings and bracelets from the mother-of-pearl jewellery box on the dresser into the bag.

'Leave him to me,' she said. 'Now, take it all, but leave one pistol there.'

'Bernadette, I...' He wasn't going to refuse her, but the idea of getting back over the border into occupied France, finding Alfie and Jacob in a town he'd never been to, with a bag full of money, weapons and jewels, felt ridiculous.

'I know it's a lot to ask, but Alfie needs this. That' – she waved her hand in the direction of the bag, now full and on the bed – 'will save lives. Now more than ever, the Germans are open to bribes. They know it's all over, so they are trying to save their own skins. Use whatever you need to get through.'

'All right, but how will I –'

'Pass me that bag.' She pointed to a brown leather handbag hanging on the chair in front of the oval mirror. He crossed the room, took it and handed it to her. She opened an inner pocket and extracted a key.

'There's a car, a BMW 328, parked behind Claude's, the pâtissier on Avenue des Alpes. Take it. You will be fine until you get to the border. Then either ditch the car and try to cross on foot or take your chances driving through. If you try to cross late at night with some money in your passport – US dollars are best – you stand quite a good chance. If there are only one or two border guards, have the pistol loaded. You can shoot them if you must. After that, well, you'll have to rely on your wits.'

She swallowed, and he offered her a sip of water from the glass on the bedside cabinet. She allowed him to hold it – her hand was trembling.

Her voice barely more than a whisper, she went on. 'Chamonix is an important frontier post for the Germans. The ridges of the Mont Blanc massif have become a front line. You will find Resistance fighters, hopefully Alfie, at the Abri Simond hut on the Col du Midi. You can remember this?' she asked, and Richard nodded. He would.

'That region, the Vallée Blanche, is patrolled by experienced skiers and climbers, something the Boche are not too good at. So if you get there and run into someone, don't shoot – they are more likely to be friendly than not. The Germans prefer to stay low in the town. Or they used to, but I don't know how it is now.

'There's a hotel in Chamonix, Hotel de la Paix – it is being used as a children's home. If you go in and ask for Paulette and say the old violin is ready for collection, they will know I sent you. After that, if he is there, Alfie will be notified.'

He didn't reply; he was trying to absorb all she said.

'Richard, can you do this?' she asked, fixing him with a heartfelt gaze. 'I know it's a lot. You just came to check on Jacob and now you're drawn into this, but I am despairing. I have nobody else to ask, and time is slipping away. Gerhardt is back tomorrow, and I don't know how much longer I have – not long, I think. So it is like you were sent to me, an angel… But if you can't, or don't want to risk –'

'I'll do it. Of course I'll do it,' he said, thinking of Grace, and knowing by agreeing to this, he'd just considerably lowered his chances of getting back to her.

Bernadette lay back on the pillows and shut her eyes as a tear seeped out, running down her dry, pale cheek.

'Will your staff think it odd I am leaving with a bag?' he asked.

'Drop it out of that window. There's a large shrub below it, and the bag will fall behind it. Once you leave, go out the main gate, and further down the wall is a small garden gate. Later on, when it's dark, come back there. It's overgrown, but it opens. If you come back in that way, you can come and collect the bag. Nobody will notice.'

She seemed to have all the answers, and he sensed this was not the first time she'd done this.

He did as she instructed, opening the latch on the window and dropping the bag out. Shutting it again, he turned. She looked like a little child on the bed, she was so tiny, her weight barely indenting the mattress.

'All right, I guess this is it.' It struck him then – would he see her again? Probably not.

'Goodbye, Richard, and thank you – for everything. For Odile, for this, for it all.' Her voice was barely audible.

'Goodbye, Bernadette, I…' He choked up. This wasn't right. She was a young woman, she was a mother, and though he had not spent much time in her company, she felt like a dear friend. 'I wish I could help…'

She shook her head. 'It was never going to end with me dying as an old lady in a rocking chair, Richard, we both know that. I wish you well. I hope you get back safely to Grace. When Odile is old enough, please tell her that her *maman* never stopped thinking about her. Every day she was my first thought in the morning and my last before I shut my eyes. Thank Tilly and Mary for looking after her, and if you see Constance, tell her I love her, that Maman and Papa would be so proud of her.'

On her right hand, in contrast to the huge diamond ring and the cushion-cut emerald beside it on her left, she wore two simple gold bands, one with a tiny diamond. Her fingers were so thin, they slipped off easily. She pressed them into Richard's palm.

'Take these. Paul gave the diamond to me. Gerhardt thinks it was my mother's. Please give the wedding ring to my sister and the diamond engagement ring to Odile. Tell her that her papa proposed to me on the banks of the Seine – on Bastille Day, 1937. He was so nervous, and this was the best ring he could afford. He worked overtime for two months to pay for it. I never hesitated for a moment. They are the only things in this whole room that mean anything to me.'

'I'll see they get them,' he said, slipping them onto his baby finger.

He leant down and put his arms around her. She was so fragile, he was afraid he would break her. She held him and kissed his cheek, and he felt her tears on his neck.

'I did my best, Richard. Not enough, but I did my best. Maybe I should not have trusted Moscow, I don't know. But Hitler needs to be stopped, for the sake of the whole world.'

'He will be. And you played a huge part. People will live because of the sacrifices you've made, families will survive. I know you did all you could. You were so brave, so fearless… I'll make sure Odile knows her mother was a heroine.'

'Not fearless, I was always terrified, but I had good people around me, even if they were confined to the shadows. *C'est dans le besoin que l'on connaît ses vrais amis.* Paul always said that. "It is when we have trouble, we know who our friends are." You are a true friend, Richard. I wish you a long and happy life. *Au revoir*, Richard…' She exhaled and lay back, her eyes closed. She was worn out.

'Goodbye, Bernadette Dreyfus,' he whispered as he kissed her head. He remembered the old Irish blessing Grace had translated for him. 'May your soul rest at God's right hand.'

He crept out of the room and made his way back to the foyer, where the butler seemed to appear as if he moved on casters. 'Monsieur?'

'Madame Gruber is sleeping now. I'll go.'

The man eyed him as if he wouldn't trust Richard as far as he could throw him. However, he opened the front door, glancing at Richard once more as he exited, merely nodding his goodbye.

CHAPTER 21

KNOCKNASHEE, COUNTY KERRY

JULY 1944

Grace walked up to the door of the O'Hare's farmhouse but stopped before making herself known. Coming from inside she could hear Tilly's sultry alto singing the Bing Crosby song 'I'll Be Seeing You'.

She peeped around the door to see Tilly dancing with Odile in her arms, the little girl's head on her shoulder, her dark curls tumbling down her back. Odile was a bit big to be carried now, but Tilly had mentioned the child had been a little fractious for the last few days. She didn't have a temperature, but she wasn't her usual cheerful self.

The letter Grace had received that morning from Richard – this time with Swiss stamps on it – was written cryptically but the meaning was clear.

'It's all right, my love, don't be worrying. Everything is going to be all right,' Tilly crooned as Odile snuggled into her neck.

Eloise was at the stove preparing some food, and Mary O'Hare was nowhere to be seen. She was probably in bed. Tilly said her mother was tired a lot these days. Grace hoped at least some of the news would be good for the O'Hares.

When the song was over, Odile began whimpering again, and Grace pushed open the half-door and entered the farmhouse.

'Look, Odile, it's Aintín Grace. She's come to see you,' Tilly exclaimed, clearly delighted to see Grace.

'I did. Dr Ryan was coming out to Mrs Collins, so he gave me a spin.' Grace said as Odile, who normally ran to her, chubby arms outstretched, just cuddled closer to Tilly.

'Is he collecting you on the way back?' Tilly asked.

'He is,' she answered, stroking Odile's cheek with the side of her finger. 'What's wrong, little one, are you not feeling good?'

Odile just shook her head. 'I slept with Tilly and Eloise last night…' she muttered, and Grace shot Tilly a look. It was a worry that Odile would say such things to other people. Up to now she had been too young, but she was becoming so articulate. Tilly and Eloise shared everything, including a bedroom, at the O'Hare's, though for appearances' sake, Eloise kept her things in Marion's old room.

Nobody wanted to tell the innocent little child that she mustn't say such things, but Tilly would have to, because if it got out – the true nature of Tilly and Eloise's relationship – it would draw all manner of problems down on their heads. Such things might be allowed in Dublin or London but not in Knocknashee.

'Cup of tea, Grace?' Eloise offered, ignoring Odile's remark. 'I'm making cheese fondue. Odile loves it, but it won't be ready for a while.' Eloise didn't care who knew she and Tilly were a couple, but it was different for her; she was Swiss and not Catholic and, most importantly, not from this parish.

'Yes, please.' Grace smiled and sat at the kitchen table. 'Is your mam here, Til?'

'She's upstairs. Do you want her?'

Tilly settled Odile on the rocking chair and covered her with a blanket despite the warm day. 'I'll get Dr Ryan to have a look at Odile when he comes back. This isn't like her at all.' Her beautiful face was suffused with worry, but she gave a huge yawn. 'I was out last night because the calves broke out. I was looking for them all over the mountain.'

'Didn't Ronan MacThomais put up the new fencing for you? I thought he was doing that last week?' Grace asked.

'Oh no, he's courting now, and I might as well be invisible. He sent his youngest brother, Tadhg, instead. But that lad's bone idle. If there was work in the bed, he'd sleep on the floor.'

Tall, lithe and muscular from working her own farm, Tilly O'Hare was able to outwork any man and had no patience for weaklings. Grace loved her and felt such gratitude that she was her best friend, but she also knew Tilly had no tolerance for a lot of the male of the species.

'Oh, Tilly, stop, he's just a boy and he tried,' Eloise gently chided. 'She always has a bee in her hat about something,' she said to Grace.

Tilly and Grace caught each other's eye and smiled. Though Eloise had excellent English, sometimes she got phrases a bit wrong and it delighted them.

'What?' Eloise asked, her hands indignantly on her hips.

'It's bonnet, a bee in your *bonnet*.' Grace grinned.

'Bonnet, hat, it's the same thing. Anyway, this poor boy is scared witless of you, Tilly. You need to be more gentle with him.'

Before this could escalate – Tilly and Eloise could be fiery enough if they got into an argument – Grace reached into her cardigan pocket. 'I've had a letter from Richard,' she said, and Tilly paled. 'Alfie's alive, Til, or at least he was a month ago,' Grace said quickly to put her friend out of her misery.

'Oh, thank God...' Tilly exhaled. 'Mam,' she called. 'Mam, come down. Grace is here.'

Eloise hugged Tilly. 'See, I told you. Your brother sounds like the cat with the nine lives, no? It will take more than a bunch of Gestapo knuckleheads to catch him.' She laughed, a deep-throated chuckle.

Mary O'Hare shuffled into the big kitchen, stooped and bent from rheumatism, her fingers swollen and twisted out of shape. The poor woman was in constant pain, but she said she managed it with her own remedies. Mary was a Bean Feasa, a wise woman, and was respected by everyone around here. Even Dr Ryan deferred to her on his patients.

'Tell me, Grace,' she said.

Grace took out the letter and extracted the single thin sheet.

Eloise took the envelope, sighing as she saw the Confoederatio Helvetica stamps with their white cross on a red base.

'It was probably censored, so he wrote in kind of code,' Grace said, handing the letter to Tilly's mother.

Mary shook her head and pushed it back to Grace. 'Read it out loud, love. My eyesight couldn't make out that small writing. And you know I can't read well in English anyway.'

'Or just the parts about Alfie. We don't need to know your private love letters.' Tilly grinned, so relieved her brother was alive.

Eloise sat on the other kitchen chair, and Tilly settled into the rocking chair, pulling Odile onto her lap. Mary O'Hare eased herself painfully into a battered old armchair beside the range that was on winter and summer because they used it for cooking and baking.

Grace began to read. "'Dear Grace, I'm writing to you from Switzerland where I've been happy to meet up with some old friends. I had lunch and recalled the days of *boeuf bourguignon* and *clafoutis* in Paris so long ago. I'm sorry to say that poor B is not doing well at all. In fact, she has an illness that doctors say will be the end of her. Her spirits are good, and she feels she did all she could. I'll tell you all about her when I get home, but I'm afraid that for her, a post-war reunion with her loved ones won't be happening.'"

Odile was nodding off in Tilly's arms – she was definitely sickening for something – and Grace caught Tilly's eye. Grace knew her friend both longed for and dreaded the day Odile's mother came for her. The news that Bernadette would never do that was hard to process. Tilly's eyes were bright with tears as she kissed Odile's head. Mary nodded slowly, and Grace instinctively knew the news was no surprise to her – she had a sense of these things.

She read on. "'I explained all about the situation there and how everyone was fine and happy and well, and she was relieved and very grateful. She asked me to pass on her love and thanks. I gave her the photograph taken on the beach the week before our wedding, and she was very happy to have it."

"'As to the man of that house – I picture you there reading this letter –'" – Grace smiled – "'he is still in the same line of work and doing very well. His enterprise has had remarkable success despite the challenges of operating in wartime, but you all know how determined he is to succeed. He's accompanied now by my friend, who has been persuaded to put his camera down for a while and do some real work!'"

"'I'll be hopeful to meet them in the coming weeks, and I'll write again then, but as they are in B's home country, it might not be as easy to correspond as it is from here. Please don't worry, though, I'll take very good care and do my best to encourage them to take a break. Perhaps a holiday in West Kerry might be just the thing. Though you know how they are addicted to work, but I'll do my best.'"

"'I'm sorry to bring you the news of B. I know it will make you all sad, but the other pair are fine, it seems, which I hope brings you all some relief.'"

"'I can't wait to get back. Love, Richard.'"

The four women sat in silence, absorbing the latest news. Grace had received another letter with this one, just for her, but she'd left that at home.

Unfortunately Richard's letter had not arrived in time for Grace to tell Sarah the good news about Jacob, as her sister-in-law had left Ireland at the end of June.

With Mrs McHale now occupied by her daily routine of chats and reminiscences with Nancy O'Flaherty and her outings with her beau, Dinny McCafferty, Sarah had found herself at a loose end. Every plea to Kirky to let her go to France or anywhere else that wasn't dull and safe had been rejected out of hand. Eventually Sarah had written to some of her British contacts from when she and Richard and Jacob had lived in London. One of them, a Miss Alderton, with whom Sarah had worked previously at the Jewish refugee centre in London, had written back almost immediately.

'As you can imagine, with the situation in Europe, they are working harder than ever,' Sarah had explained to Grace before she left. 'Miss A says they could use my help, if I've got time to spare.' She sighed. 'And let's face it, I've got plenty of that at the moment. In fact, time is all I've got.'

'I'm sorry we haven't been able to track down the canon,' Grace replied. 'Father Iggy has been trying, but he's getting nowhere slowly, he says. Not that we expected it to be any different unfortunately.'

'Well, I'm grateful for the padre trying. But this whole situation is more than frustrating. And not just for me. For Hannah too, I imagine. And poor little Carrie, who waits anxiously every day for news.'

'Have you heard from Hannah recently?'

Sarah nodded. 'She sent me a short letter, just asking how I was and if there was any news. She doesn't want to put much in writing – she's so fearful that her husband will find out before we know what the position is with the canon. I think she's told her husband I'm a distant relative so she can come visit if we hear anything. Which she won't be able to do if I'm not here, of course. But I can't wait around forever, Grace. I need to be doing something.'

She'd paused, as tears welled in her eyes. 'At least at the refugee centre, I can feel like I'm doing something useful, something Jacob would be proud of me for.'

Grace put her arm around Sarah and hugged her. 'He's proud of you no matter what, Sarah. You know that, don't you?'

Sarah nodded again. 'Yes, I do. But working at the centre will help me feel more connected to him.' A look of defiance passed across her face despite her tears.

Grace had managed to persuade Sarah to spend a few days with Miranda Logan, who was staying with friends at a stately pile in Oxfordshire before travelling to London. She had suffered no ill effects from her divorce from the yacht-obsessed Algy and had actually been very charming and funny when she came for the wedding. Despite her earlier concerns that Richard would have regrets, or that Miranda could crook her little finger and try to take him back, nothing could be further from the truth. Miranda said she was really happy for them both, and Grace believed her. She'd quietly asked Grace to encourage Sarah to join her for a break – she'd been shocked at how worn and battered by life her friend was.

'A change is as good as a rest, as they say. It will do you the power of good,' she said. 'And Hannah Monaghan can come here to me if we get any news in her case.'

Sarah had left last week, and when Richard's letter arrived, Grace had telegrammed her to give her the news. She'd had a telegram back, expressing joy and relief from Sarah – and Miranda.

The silence was eventually broken by Mary O'Hare. 'He's a brave man, that husband you have, Grace,' she said.

Grace nodded, her heart swelling with pride. Richard *was* brave. He could have stayed behind the Allied lines as they fought for every yard of France, but he hadn't. He had used his own initiative to cross that occupied country and now was going to re-enter it again, it would seem, to find Alfie and Jacob. She knew from the way he spoke in his private letter that he didn't believe he was going to be able to convince Jacob and Alfie to leave, and he wasn't even sure he should try, but he would for Sarah's and the O'Hares' sake. But Grace also read between the lines that he was doing more than just meeting up with them – somehow he was involved in their work, or he soon would be. He had no way of getting out of occupied France until the Germans were driven out, and that wasn't going to be done in a matter of days. The Germans were resisting fiercely, so it was far from over, and victory, while likely, was by no means guaranteed.

'My poor baby,' Tilly whispered into Odile's hair, the child fast asleep now. The Nazis had shot Odile's father soon after the fall of Paris, and now her mother would die too, having been denied the comfort of holding her child. 'What will we tell her?' she asked her mother.

Mary was resolute and fixed her daughter with a stern gaze. She knew Tilly feared the truth getting out, that not one drop of O'Hare blood ran in the child's veins. 'As far as everyone is concerned, Odile is Alfie and Constance's child. You're her aunt and I'm her grandmother. This news changes nothing. So don't worry, Tilly. We'll have

Father Iggy say a Mass for the repose of the souls of Paul and Bernadette, and we'll raise their child here in love and kindness. When she's old enough, and able for it, you'll tell her the truth about what fine, brave people her parents were.'

Tears streamed down Tilly's cheeks. Eloise got up and hunkered down beside her, placing her hand on Odile's back. 'Your mother is right, Tilly. Odile is ours now – our responsibility – and we will love her and raise her as her parents would want us to.'

'What if they would be horrified to know what...well, what we are?'

Grace was unused to seeing Tilly this unsure or vulnerable, and so she intervened. 'Richard wrote me another letter, Til, with this one, knowing I'd be reading this one out to you all. He told Bernadette all about you and Eloise and Mary and the kind of loving home Odile had, and all she felt was gratitude and relief, so don't worry about that. I got the impression from him that they were kind of bohemian Parisiennes, so how you live wouldn't shock them anyway.'

Tilly absorbed this, and Grace saw the relief there. Then another thought struck her friend and she turned to Eloise. 'But now that I have her for life, it means I'll be staying here. What about you? And our plans to travel and to... I can't ask you to give up your life in Dublin.'

Grace understood now. Tilly was panicking as the landscape of her future had just shifted to be unrecognisable from what she'd imagined. Despite the war, she truly believed Bernadette would one day come back. Not that she wanted rid of Odile, far from it, but she'd always assumed that one day she would have to give her up, and she had a plan to leave, once Mary had died, and live in a more openminded place with Eloise.

Eloise smiled. 'Well, I was going to wait until I had everything settled, but I might as well tell you now.'

'Tell me what?' Tilly asked, clearly stricken. Grace knew her best friend was in constant fear that life in sleepy, conservative Knocknashee would prove too stifling for her cosmopolitan, chic girlfriend.

Though Eloise had never expressed anything but delight at being here.

'Well, you know the way there isn't much work around here?'

Tilly nodded. It was true; farming or fishing was all there was really, unless a family had a shop, and most people lived hand to mouth.

'I was thinking that, after the war, there's going to be a lot of work to be had in England, reconstructing it after all the bombing. So lots of young men and women from here and for miles around will want to go there to seek their fortunes.'

Tilly nodded again. Already word was coming back of how there was more work in England than a man could take on, and the money was good.

'It was Pádraig O Sé of all people who gave me the idea,' Eloise continued. 'He said that most young people couldn't go there because they didn't speak English well, or at all, in some cases, if they didn't go to school because of –' Eloise stopped herself, remembering Grace was there.

'It's all right, Eloise,' Grace said. 'It's true, lots of people didn't send their children to school when Agnes was the principal because they hated my sister so much. So there's a whole generation around here who are undereducated.'

'Well, yes. It's the main barrier for them. They want to go but can't. So I approached Father Iggy about it, and he said' – here Eloise nodded graciously in Grace's direction – 'if Grace was agreeable, I could use the school in the evenings to run night classes in English, and even French and German if people wanted that, to prepare people to go off and make their fortunes.'

Grace was the first to speak. 'I think it's a marvellous idea, and the school is ideal. I've seen so many bright boys and girls do well, but once they leave the classroom, there isn't much for them to do. I try to teach them English, but I have to do most of the day through Irish, and they're not being encouraged at home to learn it for historical reasons. I understand why, but Pádraig O Sé is right. Richard says England is flattened and there's going to be a lot of work over there. If people want to go, then of course having that as an incentive to learn the language is a great idea.'

'Thank you, Grace.' Eloise beamed at her. 'Father Iggy said he was sure you'd support me, and he was right. I've worked for other people for long enough, Tilly. I won't charge much, because people don't have it, but Father Iggy came up with an idea. He said the Church could set up a kind of fund to pay me for the classes, and the people who availed of them would pay back into the fund once they were over there and earning. It would be honour-based, but he thinks most people would be honest and do it. What do you think?'

'He's a genius, that man,' Mary said. 'When you said it first, I thought it was a lovely idea but wondered how could people afford to pay you? Ah, but that's a good plan, right enough. People would pay the money back because their relatives would still be here, and if it got out that Johnny so-and-so was making plenty of money over in England but didn't pay his debts, then the family would be disgraced. *Is rud an-láidir is ea smacht sóisialta.*' She chuckled.

Grace knew she was right about that. The social shame of reneging on a debt like that would be unbearable, so it could work very well.

'Well, Til? What do you think?' Eloise looked to be the uncertain one now.

Tilly's eyes were wide with hope. 'You'd do that? Set up here permanently?'

'I would,' Eloise said quietly.

'For me?' Tilly asked.

'For us, for all three of us.' Eloise placed her hand on Odile's head. 'If you'll have me?'

'I will,' Tilly said softly.

CHAPTER 22

With the school closed for the summer, Grace was listening to a programme of light opera on the wireless. She enjoyed the music – it reminded her of her mother, who had loved Gilbert and Sullivan. The weather was warm, and the children spent all the hours they could on the strand, running in and out of the sea. She didn't need a cardigan at all now, and she saw how her arms and legs were beginning to tan a little in spite of her red hair. She'd never turn golden like Richard, but it was nice not to look as white as a milk bottle.

As she listened, she pulled out her pen and bottle of lilac ink to write her letters. She had written to Richard's parents and they seemed to love hearing from her, although she had no real news to tell them. They replied jointly, Caroline writing one part, Arthur the other. It certainly looked like they were getting on much better these days.

She would also write to Sarah to tell her what she already knew – that Father Iggy had got precisely nowhere with the bishop, who claimed to have no idea where the canon was. Neither she nor the priest believed him, though Father Iggy hadn't said that in so many words. But the trail had gone cold. It was no surprise to Grace that the doors of officialdom would be slammed firmly in the face of the ordinary people when the powers-that-be decided. Charlie had nearly driven himself into an early grave trying to get word of Declan and Siobhán – now Lily Maheady – all those years ago, but despite his efforts, every avenue had come to nothing.

She had just written her address in the top right-hand corner when she heard the front door open. Nobody ever knocked. They just pushed the door in and called. She waited for whoever it was to announce themselves.

She was all alone in the house because Maurice and Patricia had gone to view a house that had come up for sale. The old lady who lived there for years after her husband died had passed on. Her children had emigrated to America and Canada and had no interest in returning, so the house was being sold. Maurice was very interested.

Grace had no objection to her brother and his family staying with her. After all the upheaval of the last few years, she'd been glad of the company. She'd become very close with her long-lost brother and his family, but she also understood they needed a home of their own, and if she was honest, she would love to have the house to herself for when Richard came home.

'I'm in here,' she called from the sitting room as Fr Iggy strolled in. She loved how relaxed her house was now compared to the forbidding days of Agnes when no visitor crossed the threshold. Her friends came and went now and she loved it.

'Hello, Father. This is a surprise. I thought you had the Spillane christening today?'

'Father Lehane, the walking saint that he is, has offered to do it for me, even though he did the ten o'clock as well. So I'm skiving off.' The priest grinned, his eyes huge behind his thick lenses, beads of perspiration on his brow. The weight he'd lost when he was transferred to a parish on the north side of Cork city had all been regained thanks to the baked treats supplied by the ladies of Knocknashee, despite the rationing, and he looked like his old self.

'Eleanor made some elderflower cordial with the children from the flowers on the tree. It's sweetened with Tilly's honey, and it's lovely. Would you have a glass?' she offered.

'I'd love it.'

He followed her into the kitchen to fetch the cordial. Grace pointed outside to the other side of the kitchen yard, where Maurice had built a little table and benches so they could sit beneath the cherry blossom tree planted by their mother, Kathy Fitzgerald. Grace had embroidered some colourful cushions, and it was really a very comfortable little sunny spot out there now.

'Will we sit outside and get a bit of sun on our faces?' she suggested. 'I know it's a small parish, but I feel like I haven't seen you in weeks, apart from on the altar.'

'I know, and between one thing and another, I'm chasing my tail. Father Lynch over in Ballyferriter had to have an operation, and it took longer than they initially thought, so I'm covering Masses there as well, and of course it's wedding season.'

Father Iggy took the glass of cordial and sat on one of the benches under the cherry tree. Grace joined him and sat on the other.

'Any progress with the housekeeping?' she asked.

Father Iggy rolled his eyes to heaven. 'Oh, Grace, don't be talking. It's like a place bears live in, and that's the truth. But we have neither the skill nor the time to be dealing with it. We'll be lucky if we don't get typhoid or cholera or something, but…'

'Gretta O Sé is still hovering?'

'Between you, me and the wall, yes. But she has experience, and a reference, and nobody else has applied, so I…' He exhaled miserably. It was a dilemma.

'I have an idea,' she announced. She had been mulling it over for a while but had been thinking of discussing it with the subject of her idea first.

'I'm all ears.'

'Well…and I haven't breathed a word of this to Mrs McHale yet, but you know she stayed on after the wedding and has made an attachment, as they say?'

'To Dinny McCafferty, I heard.' The priest was normally discreet, but his tone expressed his amazement.

'Well, she was to sail back two weeks ago, but she put it off, and to be honest, I don't think she wants to go back to America at all. She's retired from the bishop's office, and she has no family over there. Every time I met her there, all she talked about was getting home to Ireland.'

Father Iggy's brow furrowed. 'And you think she might stay and become our housekeeper?'

She shrugged. 'I've no idea. But she is of independent means. She owns her own house in Manhattan, so she doesn't need to worry. If she sold it, she would have enough for when she couldn't live with you two any more. And I think she has a notion for Dinny, but his mother wouldn't have a bar of that. Even if she would, you'd be called to administer extreme unction for one or both of them if Mrs McHale had to move in with the widow McCafferty. So maybe this would suit everyone? You won't get years out of the arrangement – she's getting on a bit – but I don't think she's ready to be put out to pasture yet and might like the opportunity.'

Grace watched as he machinated on the idea. 'She could do her line with Dinny but not live with him. And by the time she wanted to retire, surely be to God, Mrs McCafferty would have gone to her reward and they could get married if they liked. Or she could stay living off the proceeds of her house in New York…'

The little priest threw his arms up dramatically and beamed at her. 'Mrs Lewis, you are an out-and-out genius – nothing short of it.' But then he swallowed, looking a little less sure of himself. 'Would she come, do you think, if we offered it to her? She had more of a clerical role in New York, didn't she? It might be a bit beneath her to look after the pair of us eejits.'

She grinned. 'What's that saying, Father Iggy? "A dumb priest never got a parish." I'll ask her if you want me to. She can only say no and you're no worse off than you are now.'

'Thank you, Grace,' he said, taking a sip of his drink and sighing with contentment. 'Now, tell me, any word of Richard?'

'I got a letter – two actually. One I took up to the O'Hares. Alfie is still alive, it would seem, or he was a month ago, and so is Jacob. But Bernadette, Odile's mother, has cancer and hasn't long left. Richard went to see her. He couldn't say much in his letter because everything is read by the authorities, but he sounded sad.'

'I'm sure he just wants to get home to you.' The priest smiled kindly.

Grace breathed out. She was trying to be strong, be brave, be positive, but she was tired of the sensation of worry, of loss, of grief. She just wanted to consolidate her world and have the people she loved around her and safe. But that seemed to be too much to ask.

'Please God, not long now.' It was her stock answer when people asked, but the truth was she had no idea when or even if she would see Richard again. His description of Normandy was so horrific, she could hardly bear to read it: injured bodies turning the ocean red with blood, the sand littered with the corpses of young men, people screaming for a doctor or a priest, the endless thumping, crunching, and sand flying everywhere. His writing was so vivid, it captured the sheer terror of those men perfectly, and for several nights after reading his account, she had woken from a nightmare, imagining Richard bleeding and dying. Sometimes it was Declan's face, sometimes her father's, but it was always the same dream – blood-red water, pink foam, limbs washing in over the remains. She would never tell him about the nightmares. He had needed to share with her what he had seen, and she was glad he could, but the truth was it haunted her.

'There's life in the Germans yet. I called to see Mrs Worth yesterday, and she heard from a friend that those flying bombs are doing desperate wreck in London, almost as bad as the Blitz. Sure, they tell us nothing here in the papers, maybe we're as well off, who knows? But God love them over there in England, as if they haven't endured enough.' The priest shook his head. 'She's trying to cope, put a brave face on it I know, but she's heartbroken, the poor woman.'

Grace nodded. 'She is, but the girls are keeping her busy, and she'll survive. She has no choice.'

'Well, at least the Germans are retreating from Italy, and they've been driven back in France. The Americans are doing well against the Japanese, and if the Russians keep up the pressure on the other side, then please God, this thing will end and people can begin to try to heal.' He sighed. 'Old men quarrel and young men die. It's always the same.'

'All the damage – to people and to countries as well. And for what?' She felt so weary of it all.

'Well, unlike the Great War, this was fought for a good reason, Grace. Hitler's ideas are evil. I don't often mention the quare fella, but if any person on this earth is the devil incarnate, 'tis that lad.'

She smiled. 'You're not much of a one for the devil, true enough. Canon Rafferty was forever threatening us with him, but you don't.'

'I don't think it's necessary. Almost everyone is trying their best with what they have. But he exists, all right, and he's living in Berlin.' She had never seen Father Iggy so dark.

'Speaking of such people' – Grace had long since lost any form of deference for Canon Rafferty – 'still nothing about the canon?'

Father Iggy gazed at his shoes.

'What is it? Do you know something?'

'Nothing official. Nobody in the Church knows where he is. He's not in prison, I don't believe – though he may have been. But an old friend of mine from the seminary, Father Timmy Hackett, he's working in a parish in West Cork, near the town of Castletownbere, a fishing town, very remote. He met the canon when he came to visit me here years ago. I was only a lowly curate then, but Canon Rafferty took notice of Timmy because his uncle is Donal Hackett, famous horse breeder, and he was interested in racing. I met Timmy last week at a funeral of another of our classmates, and he brought it up. He said he saw the canon buying groceries in a little huckster shop down his way a few weeks back. He didn't exchange any words with him, and if it was Canon Rafferty, he wasn't in clerical garb. He was in civilian clothes and looked very down at heel, Father Hackett said. But he thought it might be him.'

'What do you think?' she asked.

Father Iggy rubbed his chin with his hand, a gesture she'd noticed he did when he was thinking. 'I think we should go there and try to find him. I know it might seem like this girl in America is just one person in a world gone insane, but this is one person we can help. And if we can reunite her with her mother, then it's worth it, isn't it?'

'Richard said Jacob told him a line from a Jewish holy book. It says something like "he who saves a single life saves the world entire."'

The priest nodded. 'It's from the Talmud.' He sighed. 'Look, I can't get the child's predicament out of my head, and if the canon is her father – and I've no reason to doubt her mother – then we, the Church, owe her something surely? We'd need to keep it low-key – my superiors would not thank me for meddling. I was more or less told by the bishop when I made enquiries to leave this alone. But Sarah is right – Canon Rafferty might be able to convince this woman's husband to take the child in, and it would go one small step to undo some of the terrible things he did. If he's old and frail now, and surely close to the end of his life, maybe he will want to make amends. If we say that we know he's the girl's father, we might be able to give him the chance to do that.'

Grace thought Father Iggy was giving the canon more credit for having a shred of humanity than he was due but said nothing. 'How would we go there?' she asked. 'I know Sarah would hire a car and drive if she were here, but she has no plans to return from London yet. She's working with the Jewish refugee centre over there. I think she even has Miranda Logan helping her out with fundraising among her society and aristocratic friends – who could have imagined? She still cares about Carrie Dwyer, but the refugee centre is really important at this crucial time in the war. And I think it makes her feel closer to Jacob.'

Father Iggy nodded. 'I'm sure it does, and it's great work she's doing all together.' He took another sip of his drink and looked at her. 'But I thought if you and I went to see him first – assuming we can find him at all – and just ask him to help? Canon Rafferty was very friendly at one stage with this Frank Monaghan. I spoke to the priest in that parish, Father Molloy, last week – did a bit of gentle enquiring – and it seems that Mr Monaghan is a bit stern and unyielding, but he's a good husband and provider. He works hard, and though his wife is much younger than him, he's not a bad man, according to Father Molloy. I didn't go into any details at all, but I was thinking maybe if the canon could be prevailed upon to convince Mr Monaghan to take the girl in, then everyone would be happy.'

Again, Grace bit back a response. Father Iggy wasn't naive, but part of him just refused to believe a man of the cloth could be as evil as Canon Rafferty. She held no such delusions. 'So we should go to Castletownbere and appeal to his better nature?' Her tone must have betrayed her scepticism, because the priest looked hurt.

'He's an ordained priest, Grace, and he has strayed. But didn't God himself welcome the prodigal son who repented? Jesus tells us to forgive, to accept human frailty, not to judge lest we ourselves be judged.'

She could hold her tongue no longer. 'He made a young girl pregnant, Father Iggy. He stole from me and abused my sister in ways I can't even think about and won't ever know the full extent of, but I can guess. He stole Charlie's children from him and sold them for *money*. He sold Hannah into a lonely marriage with man old enough to be her grandfather – for *more money*. He collaborated with the evil regime you just spoke of. If Hitler is the devil, then Rafferty isn't far behind him. It was probably the information he gave that got Declan and John O'Shea and poor Seán O'Connor killed, and God knows how many others. Again, most likely for *money*. So no, Father, I won't be going there with forgiveness in my heart, but I will try to get him to do the right thing for this mother and her child. And if that means blackmailing him, threatening him with the truth or anything else I can think of, I'll do it, because he is not deserving of anyone's compassion.'

Her heart thumped loudly in her chest, and the pulse beat in her temples. She'd never spoken like this to anyone, let alone a priest, but she could no longer hold in the rage.

A long silence hung between them, after these first cross words to ever pass between such good friends.

Eventually Father Iggy sighed. 'I respect your opinion, Grace. And I know why you feel as you do. So will we go to try and find him?'

'But if my methods and motives are very different from yours?'

'Our objective is the same,' the priest said gently. 'You have every right to feel as you do. I'm not condemning you for it, and I'll be honest, I'm angry too. But I'm bound by my faith and the vows I took, and I'll try to abide by them.'

'All right, how will we get there?'

'Mrs Worth said if I ever wanted to borrow her husband's car, I would be more than welcome. I'm not a great driver, but I can manage – if you'll risk it?'

'I'll risk it,' she said with a smile, clinking her cordial glass off his, the argument over.

CHAPTER 23

Chamonix, France

3rd August 1944

The Hotel de la Paix was exactly where Bernadette said it would be, and Richard allowed himself a brief moment of satisfaction that his French was now good enough for him to understand and be understood by others. Nobody would ever think him a local, he knew, but all those hours last year spent in hiding with Jacob with one French romantic novel and a dictionary had paid off. He thought of his hosts at that time, the Ducrots, and offered a silent prayer for them. They were arrested after he and Jacob were found in the woods behind their house, and he prayed that they and their adult son, who was mentally disabled, would have been treated kindly. They had taken an enormous risk in hiding the two Americans. Logic told him they were all dead, but he hoped.

Some children were sitting at a table outside the hotel peeling potatoes. As he approached, their large eyes fixed on him with such depth of fear and mistrust, he felt uncomfortable. The door was open, but there didn't seem to be any adults around. He stood in what would have been the hotel foyer and waited. After about five minutes, in the still, oppressive heat of the day, a tall girl aged about twelve, he thought, with a dark bob and big brown eyes, entered through the front door. Should he give her the coded message? He decided against it.

'Can I help, monsieur?' she asked.

'Yes, I wonder if I could speak to whoever is in charge.' He'd practised the sentence and hoped it was correct.

'Who are you?' she asked directly.

'My name is Harry Anderson.'

'American?' She exuded scepticism from every pore. Like all children in Europe now, she was old beyond her years. Childhood innocence was one of the first casualties of authoritarianism.

He nodded.

'Wait.' She turned away, and then he noticed several more children watching him from behind a doorframe to his left.

He dug into his rucksack, the same one he'd brought with him to France when he landed in Normandy. It was filthy and torn, but it held all he had. In the side pocket were some candy bars, taken from the large stash his father had sent over to Knocknashee before the wedding. He remembered from his last trip that European kids hadn't seen candy for years.

He took the chocolate bars out and offered them to the three children. Slowly they emerged, mistrustful but fascinated.

He put the candy on what was once the reception desk and told the kids to take them. There were two boys, about seven, and a girl of no more than five.

'*Chocolat Américain?*' one of the boys asked. He had a freckled face and both front teeth missing.

Richard nodded with a smile.

'Are you American?' the little girl asked in French, walking to stand right in front of him.

'I am,' he replied.

'Are you here to make the Germans go away?'

The look that crossed her little face broke his heart. Not daring to hope, having seen far too much for a child, America meant safety. An end to all of this.

Richard crouched to be eye level with her, and the two older boys came and crowded behind her. 'Soon that's exactly what's going to happen – you just have to hold on for a little bit longer. But American soldiers and British and Canadians and Australians and French, and Indian and Pakistani and Dutch, and the Russians on the other side, so many countries – all the good countries of the world – are getting together and they are coming. Some of them, they're already here, in the north, and they are driving the Germans back to Germany.'

'But when? It's taking so long...' The little girl sighed.

'I know, sweetheart, but not too much longer now. I promise.'

'Before I'm seven?' she asked.

'How old are you now?'

'Six and two months. My birthday is on the twenty-ninth of May.'

'Oh, definitely ages before that.' He smiled, and as he did, a man appeared. He was missing a leg and used a crutch. He was short and had bristle growing where his hair should be and a livid purple scar on his forearm and hand.

'Monsieur?' His dark eyes were suspicious.

'Ah, *bonjour*. I wanted to see Paulette. The old violin is ready for collection,' Richard said with a nonchalant smile.

The man's face showed no recognition of the code phrase. He simply said, 'Of course, follow me,' and moved slowly back in the direction he had come, behind the concierge desk and down a hallway to an open door. Richard followed the man into the room.

'This is Sister Claire.'

'Thank you, Jacques,' the nun said as the man retreated, closing the door behind him. She turned to Richard. 'Good afternoon to you, Mr...Anderson. How may I help?'

Richard figured she was in her forties, with an open, sensible face and intelligent hazel eyes. He repeated the code phrase.

'And how is Ghislaine?' she replied.

'Not good,' he said, relieved the code had been accepted. 'She's very frail and sick now.'

The nun nodded. 'I'll pray for her.'

'She said I should ask you about making contact with two friends of mine. I have some deliveries for them.'

'And they are?'

He lowered his voice, though the door was closed and the only window looked like it had been painted shut. Outside he could hear the muffled sound of children playing.

'Alfie O'Hare and Jacob Nunez.'

'You can leave whatever it is you need to give to them here, and I will see they get it,' she said, and stood, clearly not wanting to engage in further conversation.

'No, I need to see them. Please…'

'Impossible. Now I must get on. Please see Jacques. He will arrange for whatever it is –'

'I can't do that, ma'am,' he said, but before he could go on, Sister Claire cut across him.

'Do you know what we are doing here, monsieur?' she asked, her French spoken with what sounded like a German accent but he couldn't be sure.

'No. I assume it's some kind of orphanage?'

'Yes, precisely. A refuge for children who have most likely lost everyone and everything they ever loved.'

'And you are doing a wonderful job, but I do need to see –'

'What would you imagine, Mr Anderson, my main priority would be?'

'Keeping them safe.'

'Indeed. So in order to do that, I make decisions. Every day. Thank you for calling.'

'Will you at least please tell them I've got lodgings at 14 Place de la Gare and I would like to see them.' He realised she would say Harry Anderson was looking for them and they might not make the connection. 'Tell Alfie I have a message from Mary and Tilly.'

The woman's face was totally unreadable; she simply gave a slight incline of her head, and Richard knew he was dismissed.

'Au revoir Soeur Clare.'

'Au revoir Monsieur, et bonne chance.'

He walked out of the old building onto the street outside. He checked and there was nobody about – the town seemed deserted in the midday heat – so he took the bag Bernadette had given him from the trunk of the BMW. Wordlessly, Jacques appeared behind him and took it, disappearing back inside the house. *No thanks for risking my life*, he thought with a wry smile. But it was nothing compared to what these people risked every single day. Despite the fact that there was no evidence to suggest it, he guessed those kids were Jews and these adults were shielding them as best they could. That alone was a capital offence for the Nazis.

As he considered his next move, Richard was acutely aware of the German presence in the town. Cars with Nazi insignia, military vehicles, drove up and down occasionally; the scarlet and black flags hung limp from the town hall in the blistering heat, but no servicemen were on the street. There was a panicked air, a sense of anticipation among the locals. News had filtered down that liberation was imminent, but Richard knew that the reality was that the Allies were still a long way off and the fighting was harder than anyone here could imagine. He wouldn't share this information – staying alive and below the radar was all he needed to do.

The small curling notice in the train station offering a room at a house called Chez Moreau had been a long shot. It had been there for a long time, he imagined. So there was a good chance the person was gone, or at least not offering accommodation any more. But short of sleeping in the car again, it was the best option he'd had. Germans were in the town's only functioning hotel, and his paperwork would not withstand any scrutiny. Nor would the flimsy cover story of being Harry Anderson, when his passport said Richard Lewis. If he was picked up, it was all over.

Madame Moreau was indeed there and seemed astonished but delighted at the prospect of a paying guest. She was at pains to point out that without ration cards, she couldn't feed him, and he believed her – the woman was skin and bone. She explained that the Germans had been taking the food from their mouths for so long now, the entire population was waif thin. But she told him she had a clean room for him and that it was a discreet, safe house.

The last part was delivered with a knowing smile, which Richard returned, with no real understanding of what she imagined he was doing. What *was* he doing? The question refused to leave his mind. He'd seen Bernadette for the last time. He'd found out that Alfie and Jacob were alive at least, and he'd delivered help to the resistors. It was time to get back to Grace. He hadn't the faintest idea how he'd do that, but he would.

He'd stay with Madame Moreau tonight, sleep in a bed, and then try to get back across the border into Switzerland. American dollars in his passport had worked surprisingly easily on the way here, and again at a roadblock. He'd just placed fifty-dollar bills inside his papers and handed them over, keeping his eyes forward. He had a loaded pistol in his pocket as well, as a Plan B.

He'd learnt that people involved in nefarious activity didn't like you to make eye contact. It was often just kids manning the patrols now; anyone with any real ability to wield a gun was sent to the front. But even these boys knew the writing on the wall, and it was every man for himself. The Reichsmark wasn't going to be worth the paper it was printed on, and the moment they were liberated, the French would turn on their oppressors with a savagery learnt over four long years of brutal occupation. American dollars might be all that stood between life and death. Nobody wanted to be a hero any more.

If Alfie and Jacob didn't make contact by morning, then they'd have a good reason and he'd have to accept it. He could at least go home with the information he had, and that was enough.

He was starving and wondered how he would get some food. The Hershey's chocolate bars were all he had to eat in his bag, and he'd given them to the kids, and without ration cards, he couldn't go into a shop and buy anything – if there was even anything to buy.

Madame Moreau was on the landing when he came out of his small room to use the facilities.

'Madame!' he exclaimed.

'I'm sorry, Mr Lewis.' He'd had to give her his passport to fill out a form for overnight guests. 'I did not mean to scare you – I was just cleaning...' She waved her hand vaguely in the direction of the landing.

He doubted very much that was what she was doing, but he didn't care. All he could think about was his growling stomach. He'd taken some bread and cheese from Switzerland, but that had been yesterday morning and he'd not eaten since.

'Don't worry, Madame Moreau. I was just wondering – look, I know I don't have a ration card, but is it possible to buy any food? I'm very hungry.'

She looked at his broad, filled-out physique. He felt like a giant in this country at the best of times, and now he was truly Gulliver in the land of the Lilliputians, but it didn't stop him being ravenous. Possibly more than the natives who were used to meagre rations and hunger.

'Monsieur, all extra food is on the black market, and I do not support that, so I am sorry, but no.'

He didn't know if her assertion was based on some moral objection she had to illegal food bartering or if she was just toeing the official line, but either way, she wasn't going to feed him, that much was clear.

'That's fine. I'll survive.' He tried to look cheerful as he walked past her to the bathroom. It was extraordinarily hot, even for a Georgia boy, and he tried not to let his mind wander back to barbeques on the veranda at St Simons, Esme filling the old barrel cooler with ice and bottles of beer while he ate hamburgers and hot dogs, more food than a family here would eat in a month.

He returned to his room and opened the bedroom window, but not a puff of air came through. The heat was deadening and oppressive. Thankfully his landlady had thought to supply a jug of water, warm now too but better than nothing, so he downed a glass, stripped down to his underwear and lay on the bed. He'd give them until tomorrow morning, then he'd drive back, hopefully get back over the border, and then try to figure out his next move. At least from neutral Switzerland, he had some options, and he had money. It wouldn't be even in the ballpark of easy, but especially in the most deprived of times, money still talked.

And if he managed that, then the best reward imaginable was going to be waiting for him. As he dozed off, her face appeared before him, her smile, her beautiful hair, her soft skin, her lips…

CHAPTER 24

He knew there was someone in the room before he was fully awake. His heart quickened, his pulse raced, and his mouth felt dry. The room smelled of cigarette smoke.

He sat up and opened his eyes. Yes, there was someone there, sitting on a chair at the end of his bed.

'Well, well, well, if it isn't the bad penny,' the man said. He had managed once again to change his appearance, but Richard was certain. Alfie O'Hare now had sleek grey hair, cut and combed in a military style, and was clean-shaven. He was dressed in a tan suit with an aqua-blue silk tie and looked every inch the playboy Richard had seen so many of down around Lake Geneva.

'Alfie?'

'Monsieur Gilles Fournier. *Enchanté.*' He smiled.

'OK...' Richard raised an eyebrow and smiled too.

'How've you been?' Alfie asked, speaking once more in his Irish accent.

'Good. Really good. I married Grace.' That news felt like the most important.

'Good for you.' Alfie beamed, 'nice to think some good, normal things are happening alongside this mayhem.'

'Is Jacob OK?'

Alfie nodded. 'Right as rain. A few tight spots since we last met, but like myself, he's the cat with nine lives.' He stretched out luxuriously in the chair, seeming like he hadn't a care in the world.

'And Constance, how is she?' Richard swung his legs off the bed and pulled on his trousers.

Alfie's bonhomie vanished. 'She was picked up five months ago.' His voice was hard. 'Sent to Drancy and from there to the east, not sure where. I've asked, but getting information is close to impossible. She was leading a group over the Alps – done it loads of times – but one of the children got really sick. They had to get a doctor, not one we normally use, and he ran squealing straight to the Gestapo. They were intercepted the following day. Nine people – two families and Constance.'

'Oh, Al – Gilles... I'm so sorry.' Richard thought of the simple gold ring Bernadette had given him for Constance. 'But it won't be long now. Maybe she'll be liberated.'

Alfie gave a quick nod, then swallowed. 'I can hope, but to be honest, the doctor told them Constance was the leader. They don't let us live if they can help it. We're too dangerous.'

Richard took 'us' to mean members of the Resistance.

'Soft-hearted, that was what did for her. I told her over and over. I said if someone gets sick, leave them – we can't lose the group for the sake of one. Or more importantly, a guide like Constance. But she couldn't leave a sick kid, or the mother and father wouldn't, or whatever. I don't know. The kid died anyway – the doctor wasn't able to do anything – and we lost the whole group.'

Though Alfie's words were expressed as anger, it was obvious to Richard that all he felt was grief.

'I remember the first night Jacob and I met her in Paris,' he said. 'She was like a little urchin, all ragged clothes and holes in her boots, cutting her own hair. But even then she exuded something, like she had the bravery of a lion.'

Alfie's jaw was set in a firm line. 'I know. She was something else.

But this stupid mistake – amateur. And she wasn't that. I could wring her neck.'

'And the doctor?' Richard wanted to ask if Alfie could have found out where Constance was being held. It wouldn't have been Alfie's first jailbreak. Collaborator or not, Alfie O'Hare was not a man people refused.

'I slit his throat,' Alfie said, with not a shred of emotion.

Richard should have been shocked, he supposed, but he wasn't. This was not normal; nobody was behaving as if it was. If you collaborated, then you paid the price, simple as that.

'It was what kept us – the Irish, I mean – colonised for so long. Collaborators, paid spies and informers. Collins had a no-tolerance approach in the twenties, and it worked. It drove the English out of Ireland, because nobody would help them. So I adopted the same. People are either with us or against us – no middle ground. That doctor was working against us – I don't care why – so he was executed.'

'I understand,' was all Richard could manage.

'Thanks for the goodies. We were badly in need. I was starting to think Bernadette was in trouble or had been recalled for a cosy chat with Comrade Stalin. I am relieved to know she wasn't –'

'She has cancer,' he said, before Alfie could go any further.

The Irishman winced, ran his hand over his slicked-back grey hair. 'I knew she wasn't well. Bad?'

He nodded, wondering if his distress was personal or professional. It was hard to tell. 'She won't have long. Gruber brought her to every doctor he could find, but they all said the same thing.'

Alfie breathed out as Richard tied his shoelaces. 'Gruber knows his time is up now. He has blood on his hands and Jewish money in his bank account. I've no pity for him. I hope they string him up, but with his resources, he'll probably be fine in Switzerland. Or if not, he might get away to South America. That's their plan. But he adores her. Always did. She can't stand him, but she's such an actress, she makes him believe she loves him too.'

'Well, he certainly left no stone unturned medically, and he seems very devoted.'

'At least she'll be in material comfort. I had hoped she'd see Odile again.' He sounded so sad, Richard felt he should offer some comfort, but Alfie wasn't the kind of man you clapped on the back or put a hand on his shoulder or anything like that.

'I took her a photo of Odile and Grace on the beach. At least she has that.'

'I'm glad. It's something, and in these times, even a tiny thing can make a big difference. Tilly and my mother, are they all right?'

'Going out of their minds worrying about you.' Richard poured another glass of water, embarrassed at the loud growling from his stomach.

Alfie smiled. 'Is Tilly still courting?'

Richard didn't know how much Alfie knew about Tilly and Eloise. He had told Alfie before that they were good friends, and Tilly's brother seemed to take more from it than that, but it was never explicitly stated. 'Ah, well…' He wasn't sure what he should say.

Alfie smiled. 'My sister has not had an eye for lads ever in her life,' he said. 'She's a fine-looking woman, and she could have had the pick of them. But I've always known fellas wouldn't do a thing for her. Mam knows it too.'

'Eloise is a wonderful person, and she and Tilly are very close. Odile absolutely adores her, so they all live up at the farm, the four of them, and they all seem very happy.' His stomach grumbled again.

'Tell her I always knew. If I don't make it, I mean. I hope to tell her myself, but just in case. I always knew, and I'm glad she's got the guts to live life her own way. And tell her as well that I'm grateful for her minding Mam. I should have pulled my weight, and I didn't. So tell her that for me, will you?' He stood up and plunged his hands into his trouser pockets.

'I will,' Richard promised. 'I hope I don't have to, but I will.' His stomach was non-stop growling now.

'Well, come on so.' Alfie made for the door.

'Come on where?'

The Irishman grinned. 'You're after dropping enough hints, man. We better get you a bite to eat before the Jerries think 'tis Yankee tanks coming down the street and not the complaining of your belly.'

He had no time to argue as 'Gilles Fournier' took off down the stairs. Richard followed, dragging his shirt on.

They walked down the street to a streetside bistro and took a seat at an outside table with a gingham tablecloth and a wine bottle dripping old wax as a candle.

Richard knew enough to follow Alfie's lead. The large windows of the bistro were wide open, and inside the building, only a few feet away, were two tables of Germans dining, while the people of the town were half-starved.

One of the officers raised a glass to Alfie, and he returned the man's smile with a wink and a smile of his own.

'Monsieur Fournier, have you made a choice?' A middle-aged man, probably the owner, stood beside them, notebook and pencil in hand.

'Yes, Frederic, we will have the foie gras and two fillet mignon. Oh, and a bottle of the Barolo '31, please.' Alfie smiled, but Richard sensed the cold hatred of the man towards them all, despite his perfectly polite manner.

'Of course.' The man nodded and withdrew.

Before they had time to say another word, the German who had saluted them appeared at their table. He was, according to his uniform, a Wehrmacht officer, his epaulettes showing he held the rank of major. The eagle on the right breast was hand-embroidered with white silk, and his brown leather belt shone.

'Fournier, I must thank you for the present yesterday, most kind. I fear such treats will not feature heavily in my future, so I will savour and enjoy and hope for the best. It is all we can do, is it not?'

Alfie clapped him on the shoulder companionably. 'My pleasure, Major Brunner. Yes, you are right. Hope for the best is all we can do.'

'You mentioned you will be leaving for Switzerland soon. Is that still your plan?' The man had the manner of an avuncular uncle, and Richard had to force himself to remain nonchalant, as if exchanging chit-chat with a high-ranking German officer was a perfectly normal thing to do.

'Initially, yes…' Alfie raised a knowing eyebrow. 'I have to see some friends there. But then I'm not sure.'

He must mean getting out of Europe altogether. How Alfie, one of the most wanted maquisards in the country, was suddenly on friendly terms with the Germans was anyone's guess.

'Well, in case I don't see you again, I wanted to thank you personally for making my time here far less awful than it might have been. I wish you good luck, my friend.' The officer offered his hand for Alfie to shake, which he did, standing up and holding the other man's elbow.

'Oh, my apologies. This is a mutual friend of mine and Herr Gruber's. Harry Anderson from the USA.'

Richard stood, taking the hand offered.

'Harry, this is my friend Major Dietrich Brunner.'

'Delighted to make your acquaintance, Mr Anderson. I trust you are enjoying your time here?' the man asked, as if occupied France with the Allies pushing through German defences daily was a holiday camp. 'It is a very beautiful part of our world, is it not?'

'It really is, and yes, thank you, I am having a very nice time,' Richard managed.

Before the conversation could continue, the waiter appeared holding two plates of foie gras with tiny triangles of toast and a red currant jelly and a bottle of red wine. Richard thought he might lick the pattern off the plate as well as the food, he was so ravenous, but he tried to eat slowly as the German took his leave to rejoin his comrades.

Alfie's face gave nothing away as he chatted about the food, how the foie gras in the eastern part of France, where they were now, was inferior. That it had to come from Périgord in the Dordogne – like what they were eating now. How 1931 was a poor year for Bordeaux, though the port was good, but the Italian Piedmont they were drinking this evening was some of the finest ever.

Richard took his cue from Alfie and made polite conversation in what he hoped was passable French. They talked about the Riviera, what fun had been had there before the war, and Alfie prattled on about this person and that, alleged mutual acquaintances, people with aristocratic names like Gigi and Hortense, Rupert and Boris. Richard played along, laughed at the appropriate times and offered bits of gossip on these fictitious characters as they ate their fillet mignon and buttered carrots in full view of a starving population.

It was deeply uncomfortable, but Richard understood that if he wanted to eat, then this was the only way to do it. Nobody had any food. Like the Ducrots, who had sheltered Jacob and himself, most people around here were farmers. But every single gram of food was requisitioned with no regard for the needs of the people who produced it. Citizens were reduced to eating animal feed, the only food-like stuff that was allowed, only because their overlords wanted the animals well fed in order to maintain yield.

He marvelled at the sheer courage of Alfie O'Hare. The Gestapo would give their eye teeth to get their hands on him, and yet here he was hobnobbing and making jokes right under their noses.

They finished their meal, and Richard felt human again. The groaning, aching pain in his belly was gone, but he thought of the local people here – they had no such respite. A woman with a thin, listless toddler clinging to her leg was sweeping dust out of her house across the road. She gazed at them with ill-disguised contempt – and well she might. If they really had been who they were pretending to be, then they were beneath contempt.

'Madame.' Alfie greeted her with a smile, and as they passed her door, Richard saw him slip a bread roll he must have snatched from the table into her apron pocket.

They strolled back to Richard's digs, chatting amiably, hands in pockets, not a care in the world. Richard found himself wondering in that moment how Alfie, if he survived – and Richard felt he would – could ever adapt to civilian life again.

Back in the house, Madame Moreau was sitting in her little parlour, seemingly just waiting, not reading or anything, perched on her fireside chair. As they returned, she jumped up. 'Someone was looking for you. I said I didn't know where you were. He wanted to wait. He said he was a friend, but I was afraid to say no, and now I don't know…' She was close to tears. 'There is a boy in your bedroom, monsieur. Please do not bring trouble to my house. I am a widow, and I have done nothing wrong…and…'

Alfie answered for him in rapid French with what Richard assumed must be the patois of the region because he could only catch every third word. He placed his hands on her shoulders and spoke quickly and quietly, and whatever he said seemed to calm her down. He took a piece of steak and some carrots wrapped in paper from his pocket and handed the bundle to her. She looked at it as if it was the crown jewels. Richard had not noticed Alfie secreting pieces of his meal into his pockets, but he had done so, while Richard, like the glutton, had eaten all of his. He felt a pang of shame.

Alfie asked her a question – Richard thought it was to describe the boy – and nodded at her response. He'd explained earlier that Jacob stayed out of sight. With his dark complexion, made even more so after a French summer living outside, he was not Aryan-looking in the slightest, and while he could pass as French in a casual interaction, his American accent was still too pronounced, so it was best if he laid low. So it probably wasn't him.

'It's all right, I know who it is,' Alfie murmured, and gestured that Richard should go upstairs ahead of him.

When Richard entered the room, he found Luc, the boy who had helped him escape over the Alps the last time he had been in Switzerland, waiting for him.

'Ah, the *Américain*,' the boy said with a grin.

Richard smiled. Luc had grown in the year since he'd seen him despite the lack of food. He was only around twelve, Richard guessed, and wiry.

'Hello, Luc. What on earth are you doing here?' He was so pleased to see the boy alive and well – helping escapees into Switzerland under the noses of the Germans was a dangerous business.

'He's with us now,' Alfie answered for him, squeezing the boy's shoulder.

'And how is your *maman?*' Richard asked, but instantly regretted it. The shadow that was by now familiar to him crossed the boy's thin face.

'She died a heroine of France,' he said with pride. 'They came, they demanded she tell them where I was, how I was getting people over, but she wouldn't say. I was on a hill above our house. I heard it all.' The voice was not that of a child but of a battle-weary old man. 'But now I am here, and we will end them, forever.'

The slow, deliberate delivery was chilling. Richard had never seen such naked hatred before, and coming from a child so young, it made his blood run cold.

'I'm very sorry to hear that, Luc. She was a brave lady, and I'm sure she's very proud of you.' It was the best he could manage.

The boy nodded. 'She is.'

'Now, Richard,' Alfie said, 'you need to get back to Switzerland to get out of here. Coming into occupied France is one thing – they aren't suspicious of people coming in – but getting out is another matter. It won't be just a case of some dollars in a passport. So I was thinking… You want to get back to Knocknashee and Grace, and we have a bunch of kids that need to be escorted to safety. The Germans know the end is in sight, but if anything, they are doubling their efforts to get people to the east, to camps.'

He lit a cigarette and exhaled, filling the small room with the acrid smell. 'I was thinking Constance was the one to do it, with Luc's help, but she's not here. So how about if you and Luc take the kids? He knows the way, and you've done it before. Would you be willing to do that?'

Richard foolishly had thought he would just drive across the border again, oiling the wheels of his border crossing with cash, but of course Alfie was right. No right-minded person was trying to get *into* German-occupied land, so of course they were going to let him through. But getting out, when the entire world seemed to be trying to flee from this murderous regime, was another matter. The prospect of the gruelling trip up the mountain again, running the gauntlet of the German patrols – he'd had to shoot one or possibly two border guards last time and narrowly escaped himself – filled him with dread. And that was when he only had himself to worry about. Doing it with a bunch of children was terrifying, but he had to try. For Constance, for Bernadette, for Paul. For those kids who deserved a chance to grow up, to fall in love, to have their own children some day. He would do it for them.

'I will,' he replied, and Alfie smiled, turning to Luc.

'See, I told you, kid. You owe me.'

Luc flicked a centime at Alfie, who caught the coin and winked, saying something in rapid French.

'You thought I'd say no?' Richard asked.

Luc just shrugged but gave a small grin.

'Right, we'll do it tonight.' Alfie sucked on the cigarette and exhaled. 'It's Friday, and they usually do shabbat prayers upstairs on a Friday night, so it won't be strange to see activity at the hotel. Obviously the Germans don't know it's shabbat prayers. They think they are all French kids who have been orphaned, and Sister Claire takes pains to ensure they look very Catholic. I'll go there now, check they're ready to go. Richard, try to get some sleep now your belly is full. We'll use your car and squeeze as many kids as we can into it. Meet us at the corner. Park the car in the alleyway beside the boulangerie. We'll be out at nine o'clock. Have the car ready to go. I'll bring blankets to cover them, and whatever food I can get together.'

Alfie was in full organisation mode now, clipped and concise, the bonhomie of earlier gone. 'Have you enough petrol?' he asked, and Richard nodded. There were three cans in the trunk.

'We'll need that space for kids, so fill the tank and leave the rest. I'll try to get it up the mountain some other way – Luc will know where I'll stash it. The same with food and medicine. I'll have whatever we can get sent up.'

'So we drive as far as where I was dropped last time?' Richard asked, trying to sound calm.

'More or less. Luc will be with you. It's best you don't know too much more for now, Richard, so don't ask me anything else,' Alfie said, kindly but firmly.

Richard nodded. The unspoken words hung in the air. *Best he doesn't know so it can't be tortured out of him if he's caught.*

Luc shook Richard's hand. 'See you later, Mr USA,' he said in accented English.

'*A bientôt,*' Richard replied.

Luc went downstairs, and Alfie stood before Richard. 'We won't have time for chats later. Jacob will come. You won't have much time to talk, but at least you can tell his wife he's alive. Give my mother, Tilly and Marion all my love. Tell them I'm sorry for causing them all the worry, and that I'll be home soon, please God.' He reached into his pocket and pulled out a dark beret. 'Put this on your blond tresses, Cary Grant – your head is like a beacon.'

Richard smiled and took the hat. 'This is going to end soon, and the right way, won't it, Alfie?' He heard the uncertainty in his voice and felt like a little boy asking his father for assurances.

Alfie ran his hand over his smooth jaw and shut his eyes. 'I hope so, Richard, because between you and me and the wall, I haven't much more in me.'

Richard knew what he meant. He was the one everyone looked to – even when he was in Spain fighting the fascists during that civil war. Alfie O'Hare was a born leader; his attitude set the tone for everyone else, and everyone took their cues from him. He could never show weakness or vulnerability or the whole thing would come crashing down like a house of cards. But Richard saw the exhaustion in the man's eyes. He'd lost so much, been physically and emotionally tortured, lived in deprivation, constant fear, and now Constance was almost certainly dead. Richard's heart went out to him.

'I know you don't seek accolades or medals, Alfie, but what you've done, the lives you've saved, it will not go unnoticed. People will live, be born, have lives and children because of you, because of your strength. I'm so sorry about Constance. You two were a formidable team, and I know she was the love of your life. But hold on, my friend, please. Mary and Tilly and Marion so desperately want to see you again. Your mother prays every single day for you, and she's sure she'd know if you died, so she's been keeping the faith, as she says.'

Alfie nodded and drew Richard in for a brief strong hug.

'*Go n-éirí an t-ádh leat, mo chara,*' Richard said, and Alfie laughed.

'Miss Fitz isn't only teaching the kids. I see you're getting the *cúpla focal* as well.'

Richard smiled. 'She is. I'm a poor student though.'

'I miss speaking my own language,' Alfie said wistfully. 'I like French and I really like Spanish. English and I have a chequered past – too much water under the bridge between us and our neighbours to ever feel affection for their language. But our Irish language is wonderful.'

'Hopefully soon you'll be on a stool in O'Connor's or Creedon's, having a beer and talking about the harvest, or the weather, or where the mackerel are breaking,' Richard said, smiling.

'I'll look forward to that. Two Knocknashee men. With the help of God, I'll see you there, Richard.' Alfie squeezed his shoulder and was gone.

CHAPTER 25

Knocknashee, County Kerry

August 1944

Grace was at the back of the church after Sunday Mass, lighting a candle each for Mammy and Daddy, Agnes and Declan, when Mrs McHale approached her.

'Grace, I was looking out for you. Have you a minute for a chat?'

'Of course.' Grace smiled. Mrs McHale was dressed in her signature green coat and brown tweed hat, despite the warm weather. Older Irish people didn't allow the weather to dictate what they wore, and Grace noted how easily Mrs McHale blended in in Knocknashee, even after decades in New York. 'Will you come over for a cup of tea?'

'Lovely.' The older woman seemed pleased, and Grace got the impression the conversation she wanted to have would be best in private. The two women walked in companionable silence out of the church, Grace limping a bit today because she hadn't done her exercises last night.

'Any word of Richard?' Mrs McHale asked once they were outside.

'I had a letter ten days ago. He was in Switzerland then. But nothing since.'

'Switzerland? I thought he was going to Normandy where all the fighting is going on?'

'He was there too, but I'm not really sure what he's doing in Switzerland. He wanted to find Sarah's husband – you know, Jacob Nunez?'

'He's a brave lad, our Richard. I pray every day he'll be safe.' Mrs McHale patted Grace's arm as they crossed the street.

Inside Grace's house was quiet. Maurice and Patricia had bought the house they had been looking at. The house was vacant and the price cheap, so they were gradually moving their things in with the owner's permission while the paperwork went through. Grace's place now felt huge and empty, and she found she would miss the hustle and bustle of having the family living there with her.

She filled the kettle and looked in the tin for the rhubarb tart she'd made. The pastry wasn't as sweet as she'd like – they had no sugar, and what honey she had she had used to sweeten the rhubarb, which was so tart it would make you wince – but it was better than nothing.

She cut them each a slice and spooned the top of the milk over them, then made tea.

'Well, Grace, I wanted a bit of advice really, and I thought, who is the most level-headed person in this place? And apart from Nancy, who is a rock of sense, it would be you. I couldn't ask Nancy, of course, because she's been so good to put me up, but I won't outstay my welcome and her daughter is coming with the children to visit in a week's time, so I need to make a plan.'

Grace knew she needed to stay sharp to follow the train of thought. Mrs McHale had a tendency to wander, conversationally speaking. 'Go ahead. I'm happy to help if I can.'

'Well, I was due to go back to New York, as you know, but to tell you the truth, Grace, I've no interest really. I have my little place, of course, but my job is more or less gone. They were only keeping me on out of a sense of charity because I was there since God was a child. But I really think I'd rather stay here. I have friends back in New York, of course, but Grace, when you get to my age, a lot of people die or go to live with their children or go to retirement communities – which sound like God's waiting room, if you ask me…'

Grace stifled a giggle.

'And I know the whole place is talking, so I might as well tell you. I'm kind of friendly with Dinny McCafferty. He asked me up to dance at your wedding, and I haven't had a man ask me to dance since Toby O'Halloran, with breath that smelled of fish, asked me up in St Brendan's Hall in 1911…'

She coloured slightly, and Grace felt a rush of affection for her.

'I was no beauty, not like you, and sure the lads had better girls to catch their eye. Then after the Great War, sure weren't all the boys killed, and even the good-looking girls couldn't get a fella, so there was no hope at all for the likes of me. I got the chance to go to America – I had an uncle, a priest in Yonkers…though he was an awful gambler. He nearly bet the roof off the church before they caught him. Mad for greyhounds, he was, and the funny thing was, 'twas a bite from a dog killed him in the end – he got rabies, the poor old divil…'

Not that it was intentionally funny, but Mrs McHale had a way of delivering a story with so many subplots that it made Grace, and Richard, crack up laughing.

'Well, then I met Des, but sure the poor man's been dead these many years past now, God rest his soul, and I've been on my own longer than I can remember.' Mrs McHale finally paused for breath and looked at Grace expectantly.

'But now you've met Dinny…?'

'Oh yes,' Mrs McHale said. 'And he's nice. Very nice, actually. And quiet. Des was a quiet man too. I prefer men who are quiet, honestly. Sure who could be listening to a fella blathering on night and day? My friend Sheila married a fella that said "hup" at the end of every sentence. No reason, meant nothing, just "What's for the dinner? Hup." Or "I'm going to that funeral. Hup." Sure, that would drive you scatty. It nearly did too – poor Sheila isn't right in the head after all the hupping. She thinks she's a beautiful singer, but she couldn't carry a tune in a bucket. Anyway, no, Dinny suits me well, and he's a lovely dancer, and I love dancing, and he says very nice things to me, and he doesn't drink, and he is well presented. He's clean and tidy and isn't too fat. I couldn't be doing with a big round belly...'

The irony of Mrs McHale being more round than she was tall seemed to be lost on the older woman, and from the description of poor Dinny, she might as well have been describing a beast for sale at the market, but Grace didn't remark on that.

'He seems very nice, certainly,' she said, having never exchanged a single word with the man. She'd seen him at Mass with his mother every Sunday, she looking like she was sucking lemons and he cowed and browbeaten.

'He is. But 'tis the mother is the issue, you see.' Mrs McHale sipped her tea and took a bite of the rhubarb tart, only wincing a little at how sour it was. 'She's like a cut cat, that one, and she'd be impossible if she knew Dinny was courting. He can only barely manage her as it is. That's why we're keeping it low-key, you see.' She sighed. 'I would try to get her to support us, but that woman has more corners than a bag of turf – there's no dealing with her. Poor Dinny's heart is scalded from her, so we can't let the story get out for fear she gets wind of it.'

Grace didn't like to tell her there was no such thing as a secret in Knocknashee.

'So here's my dilemma,' the older woman said, finally getting to the crux of it all. 'I need to get out from under Nancy's feet. She's been so good to me, and we get on like a house on fire, but she has her family to consider and she needs the extra room. I want to stay here and keep things going with Dinny until that auld harridan of a mother of his goes to God. Though what the Almighty will make of her sour puss is anyone's guess. But anyway. So I was thinking of maybe asking if I could rent the old bakery, the Wooden Spoon. I know the woman that had it is gone now, and I know with the rations, there's almost nothing to bake a cake with, but maybe I could try? Maybe it could be a little business I could run? I'd sell my house in New York, and I'd have a few bob, and there's a room above the bakery, I think, so maybe I could fix that up? I know me and stairs don't get on, but it's the best plan I can think of at the moment.'

Grace sipped her tea. She'd been planning to discuss her idea with Mrs McHale this week anyway, so this was perfect timing. Father Iggy had obviously not got around to saying anything. 'I might have a better plan,' she said, and outlined the situation Father Iggy had found himself in and suggested Mrs McHale might like the job of housekeeper for the two priests.

'And the priests wouldn't want someone younger?' Mrs McHale looked incredulous at this stroke of good fortune.

'No, they'd love you to do it. Now, to be truthful, the place is like a bomb hit it, they can't boil an egg, and the clean-up is going to take a while, but once you put manners on the place, it will be lovely. And sure, the priests are pure dotes, so you'll be happy out living there.'

'And you spoke to Father Iggy about this already?' Mrs McHale asked, a beam on her currant-bun face.

'I did. I told him I'd approach you, because it's a bit of a tricky situation with the other applicant.'

Mrs McHale puffed herself out. 'But sure when Bishop McNally from New York wrote and begged Father Iggy to give me the job, he couldn't refuse him now, could he?' she said, her eyes wide and innocent.

Grace had to laugh. The woman was ingenious. 'Of course he couldn't. However much he might want to,' she agreed. Sometimes a little white lie was no harm. 'So will I tell Father Iggy you'll take it? There's a bedroom on the ground floor as well, so you won't have to go upstairs as much, and the pay is all right, I think.'

'I'd do it for free,' Mrs McHale announced. 'And that cobbler's sister is as awkward as a pig in a parlour. I was in there the other day, and she was trying to sweep the floor in the cobbler's shop, and she looked like a bulldog chewing a wasp and making a right hames of it altogether. And Nancy told me she can't cook for toffee, and she's no good at getting by, and wilful waste makes woeful want, as we all know, especially now.' She clapped her hands together gleefully. 'Oh, wait till I tell Dinny! He's going to be like the cat who got the cream, so he will.'

'Well, I'm sure the sooner you can move in, the better. I will warn you, though, it's in a right state,' Grace said with a laugh.

'I'm not one bit shy of hard work, Grace Lewis. And I know Dinny and myself are no spring chickens, but the older the fiddle, the sweeter the tune. I never thought for one second I'd get a chance like this, but now that I have, I'm going to grab it. And 'tis you, Grace, who's making it happen, so I'm very grateful to you.'

'You're very welcome, Mrs McHale, and I'm delighted you're staying. I know Richard will be too.'

'If we can get our boy home to us now, safe and sound, that's all we need.' Mrs McHale reached over and patted Grace's hand. 'Now, tell me, any development on that little girl back in New York? I had a letter from Sarah yesterday. She's writing to Carrie, and telling her she's not giving up, but she sounded very down in the dumps about it all. Sure poor Sarah doesn't know if she's coming or going with Jacob, and she's doing trojan work with all the poor misfortunes that are teeming into London. Ah, she's a great girl altogether. I know Mrs Lewis can be a bit of a cold fish, no doubt about that, and the father would charm the birds from the bushes. They're a quare match and no mistake. But they raised fine children, it has to be said. People you can be proud of.'

Grace didn't like lying to the old woman, but she knew that the expedition she and Father Iggy had planned for tomorrow was best kept quiet. The priest shouldn't be getting involved in it at all; he had been explicitly instructed by the bishop to leave it alone, so he was going out on a limb for her as it was. The fewer people who knew they were going to try to find the canon, the better.

Sarah had written asking for any updates, but Grace had to reply that there weren't. Realistically, the chances of finding him were slim, and even if they did, by some miracle, he most likely wouldn't help them. He was vindictive to the core. Funnily enough, the thought of downfacing him didn't fill her with as much trepidation as once it might have. She had grown up a lot in the years since she first had a run-in with him over Agnes and him spending her money. It was only five or six years, but it felt like a lifetime ago. She was unrecognisable now to the timid girl she was back then.

'No, and I'm not sure we're going to get anywhere, to be honest. Hannah Monaghan called here yesterday out of the blue. Sarah told her I knew about Carrie and she could confide in me. Hannah seemed to think there was no way her husband would accept the child. And that's even if she could prove that Carrie Dwyer *is* her child, and we'd need the canon to do that. So she has resigned herself to knowing she can't approach her until she's eighteen. I know Sarah suggested she write to Carrie, but I'm not sure that's a good idea. Surely the official side of things would have to be in place before she could start corresponding with her?'

Mrs McHale nodded. 'I think so, unfortunately. Over there they're not as trusting as here, but then there's more blackguards too, so they'd be wary of anyone saying they knew a lovely little girl like that. But if anyone can help her, 'tis Sarah – that one has a tongue that would pick a lock, so she has. So we won't give up hope.'

Grace nodded. Sarah had tried her very best while she was here, but her feminist outrage and outspoken condemnation of the patriarchal nature of the Catholic Church hadn't helped. Much as Grace admired her sister-in-law, it would be easier without her.

They chatted on for a while, all about Dinny and his frightful mother, how Mrs McHale was excited to sell her house, and how her neighbour's son, Vito – 'Italian lad who eats too much but has a heart of gold' – was in real estate and engaged to a lovely girl called Adrianna, and they'd most likely buy her place because Adrianna was glued to her own mother like a limpet, and the mother only lived across the street.

Grace told her all about Eloise's plans for the English school, and Mrs McHale was delighted but sad.

'Emigration is grand in theory, Grace, but people belong in their own place, no matter how nice somewhere else is. Don't get me wrong. America was good to me and I loved it, but I always had that longing to come home. I never thought it would happen, I thought I'd die there, but life has a funny way of working out, doesn't it?'

'It does, surely,' Grace agreed, thinking of all the twists and turns of her own life.

'And how's poor Mrs Worth these days? I saw her in O'Donoghue's with the girls and she looked wretched, the poor woman.'

'She's as well as you'd expect. She got a letter from some high-up explaining what happened to Douglas. He was asleep after a double shift, and he was probably so shattered that he didn't hear the air-raid warning. It was a direct hit, so he won't have suffered. That's something, I suppose.'

'God, but doesn't that little runt Hitler have a lot to answer for? May the divil roast him for all eternity is all I can say, the misery he's after causing.'

'I know. Such terrible waste, so many lives ruined.' She sighed. 'But Eleanor is strong, and she has her home and her girls, and she'll make a life for them...'

'Will they stay here, do you think?'

She nodded. 'They will. The girls are locals now, and Eleanor likes the job here, though she's far too qualified for it.'

'But sure she can take over as headmistress when Richard comes back, if you two decide to go off somewhere. Or if you have a baby, please God.'

Grace tried not to voice her worries on that score; she didn't want to hear any platitudes or 'of course you wills' – they didn't help. But she was so worried she would never have a baby. She desperately wanted to be a mother, but she also dreaded denying Richard the chance to be a father. Her face must have betrayed her.

'Ah, Grace, he'll be back. I feel it in my waters that he will. I have a sense of these things. Angelica Totti lived up the street from me. Her boy Syl, he went off to join up at the start, and I knew it the day he walked up the street in his uniform that he was a goner. And sure enough, he was, poor guy. He used to deliver my newspaper when he was a kid on his bike. I can still see him, sailing up the street, throwing the papers into each yard. But I just knew… And his poor mother – the day she got the telegram, I'll never forget it…' She pursed her lips at the sheer sadness of it all.

'It is horrible, all over the world, and mothers in Germany too, but that's not why...'

'What is it so?' Mrs McHale asked kindly.

'Nothing, it's stupid, I'll be fine.' Grace blinked back tears.

'A trouble shared is a trouble halved.'

'I'm just afraid I won't be able to…you know…have a baby, even if Richard does survive.' The tears flowed in earnest then.

To her surprise, Mrs McHale didn't say 'of course you will' or 'try not to worry' or any of that.

'I know how lonely a life without a child of your own can be,' she said. 'Des and I didn't have any, but it wasn't for lack of wanting them. It just wasn't to be. Some women don't mind, they'd prefer it even, but I would have loved to have a baby of my own. So I know why you're worried. What does Dr Warrington say?'

Grace wiped her eyes with the sleeve of her cardigan. 'He said there was no reason I wouldn't conceive, and that as far as he could tell, everything was working normally. But I can't help but worry.'

'Well, the first step to having a family is having that handsome husband of yours back here, so let's focus on that first. But Grace, if it doesn't work out, and you and Richard can't have your own, remember there are lots of children in the world now who will need a home, so maybe that's a way to be a mother if not through the normal way.' She smiled. 'There's more than one way to skin a cat, you know.'

Grace felt better thinking about that. She'd been raised by her own parents until she was ten, but then Hugh and Lizzie Warrington had stepped in as sort of surrogate parents – even now they were like a mother and father to her. Tilly was Odile's mother in all but blood; Charlie was Kate and Paudie's father, just as much as he was Seámus's and Lily's; and Lily herself was Joey and Sylvia Maheady's daughter every bit as much as their youngest daughter, Ivy, who was not adopted. Yes, there was more than one way to be a parent, and if things didn't go the way she hoped, Mrs McHale was right – there were options.

She smiled. 'That's the most helpful thing I've heard in a long time,

Mrs McHale. Thank you. So maybe that's our future, please God, if we have one.'

'You have, of course. It's going to be fine.' Mrs McHale was sure.

CHAPTER 26

Father Iggy pulled into the side of the road outside Tilly's farm where Grace had spent the night last night. She'd eventually confided about the trip to try to find the canon to Tilly, who had suggested they leave from her place as opposed to from Grace's house, as that would have the whole town's tongues wagging. Especially since Agnes being seen driving off in the canon's car in years gone by was a conversation topic nobody ever tired of.

Douglas Worth's black Ford had been parked up for ages until Eleanor decided she'd better learn to drive, and she'd lent the car to Father Iggy for the day, no questions asked.

Grace got into the passenger seat, and they chugged off down the hill and around the back of the graveyard rather than drive though Knocknashee, and soon they were out on the main road to Dingle.

The journey was going to take several hours because they would need to cross over two mountain ranges on what were little more than sheep tracks. The Beara Peninsula was as remote and even wilder than their own, Grace had heard, but she'd never been there.

'Hannah Monaghan came to see me yesterday,' Grace told him as they began the long journey. 'Sarah wrote to her and told her I knew everything and that she could confide in me. She didn't stay long, but she wanted to know if there was any update on her daughter. Since she found out about her being in an orphanage, she's been going out of her mind with worry.'

'The poor woman. Has she spoken to her husband yet?'

'No, she doesn't want to unless there's a chance she can get the girl back. But I asked her how likely it was that he'd accept the child even if we could get the canon to agree to confirm her as Carrie's mother. She started crying then, saying she didn't think he would. He is very proud, cares very much about his standing and presents himself as above reproach, a pillar of the community and the Church, "holier than thou", if you know what I mean.'

'That might be our secret weapon, though,' Father Iggy said, deep in thought. 'I was praying about this, and if he's such a paragon of virtue, he won't want anyone knowing he has a less than snow-white past when it comes to his wife. He basically paid the canon for her – paid more when she had a son. That's not exactly paragon-of-virtue behaviour now, is it?'

'Are you suggesting blackmail, Father Iggy?' She laughed.

'Well, that's a terrible word, Grace. I'm just suggesting we pull any lever we have to reunite this child with her mother. Both of them are distraught at this stage and would be much better off together.'

'Does the end justify the means sometimes, do you think?'

The priest sighed. 'I don't know. But look at the world now, the carnage that's going on to defeat Hitler. Millions dead, and nobody is asking if this is morally the right thing to do. It just has to be done, and that's all about it. Maybe this is something like that?'

'I think so,' she agreed.

Grace had been taken by surprise when Hannah Monaghan had shown up at her house yesterday. Grace was curious about the woman at first, but she had warmed to her. It was hard not to. Hannah's face when she recalled what had happened to her, her agony at the loss of her baby daughter and the way she gripped Grace's hand and begged her to help would not leave Grace's mind. She felt the woman's anguish, and it had connected to something within herself. Something that had come out in her conversation with Mrs McHale – the fear and loss she felt for a child of her own who was not yet born or who might never be born. She had some inkling of what Hannah was going through, though she had yet to become a mother herself. After talking to Hannah, she was more certain than ever she had to do something to help.

The pair travelled on to Killarney, and Father Iggy dragged it out of Grace how she'd managed to convince the bishop to send him back to Knocknashee after a long stint in Cork. She recalled the summons to the bishop's palace – it felt like a lifetime ago – and how the bishop had asked her to remain silent on the subject of the canon and his involvement with the Germans, and how she, more or less, put the reinstatement of Father Iggy down as the terms of her silence.

The little priest had hooted with laughter at this. 'You're some operator, Miss Fitz. You look sweet, like butter wouldn't melt in your mouth, but I'll tell you what, I'm glad I'm your friend and not your adversary. Blackmailing bishops, sidestepping the cobbler's sister to install the wonderous Mrs McHale, outmanoeuvring your man Francis Sheehan – and remember when we got rid of Kit Gallagher and gave the job to Dymphna? Not to mention the whole business with Charlie and Lily. You're like the guardian angel of the parish, Grace, and most of the time nobody knows 'tis you behind the scenes pulling all the strings.'

Grace laughed at this. She never saw herself in those terms, but she supposed he was right to an extent. Things just sort of happened to her more than her seeking out complications in life, but she did seem to have become the kind of person who got things done. She hoped her parents would be proud and not see her as a meddling young woman sticking her beak into other people's business.

As if he could read her mind, Father Iggy went on. 'Truly, Grace, you're remarkable. All you've endured, and yet you constantly seek to improve things for other people. You're what Mary calls an old soul, you know that?'

She nodded. Mary O'Hare often said that to her – that she'd been here before. Mary was of the opinion that we came to this earth many times, in different capacities, and those who were wise, who sought to help rather than harm, who tried to understand rather than contradict, were the older souls, nearing the end of the life cycles. It wasn't exactly a Catholic belief, so it made Grace a little uncomfortable sometimes when Mary went on with what the canon would have called 'old pagan claptrap', but Father Iggy was fascinated by her and her views on existential matters and never dismissed her at all.

'I don't think I am anything special, Father. I just seem to find myself in situations and I try to do the right thing. I don't always do it. I could be less sharp with Pádraig O Sé sometimes, and Charlie asked me to speak to Dymphna to see if I could find out why she's in such grumpy form, but I chickened out because on the day I called, she was fuming over something Kate had done. I didn't really want to do it anyway, it's best to stay out of other people's marriages I think. So I made an excuse and left.'

Father Iggy was busy navigating around a flock of sheep, who were all over the small road with no sign of anyone shepherding them. 'Ah, sure the one thing this job teaches you is nobody knows what goes on behind closed doors. But my own mother, I remember, when she was about that age, going through the change, as they call it, she was fierce irritable altogether. Eat you without salt, she would, and she'd been the sweetest woman for three counties up to then. Nobody said a word, but I remember seeing the perspiration running off her, or seeing her crying over nothing, and I went to my father about it. I was worried, you know. I thought she might be very sick or something. But sure he hadn't a notion and was, according to himself, only getting dog's abuse from her for doing nothing.'

'I don't know much about it either. You'd think for a thing that happens to half the population, there'd be some talk, but no. Lizzie told me she had a very hard time around then too. Some women do, I think. She's fine now, but Lizzie said she was hot all the time and very emotional. Hugh found a woman in Dublin through a nurse he knew – she was a Native American woman, would you believe – and she made her a potion of some kind using an herb that grows in America called black cohosh. Lizzie said it really helped. Mary O'Hare asked Sarah to find her some seeds or roots of it whenever she went back to the States. Esme brought them with her when she came over for the wedding, and now Mary is growing it in the woods behind the farm. I was considering mentioning it to Dymphna, but she's in no mood for conversations and unasked-for advice these days.'

'That's the worst kind, right enough.' Father Iggy made a face, and she laughed.

'I told Charlie about it, though, and he suggested it one evening to her and she didn't bite his head off. I hear she went up to Mary, and according to Charlie, things are much better since. She told him how it felt, feeling tired and hot and moody all the time, and he had spoken to Mary himself first, and she explained the change to him, so he's not taking everything so personally since. They're back talking, and so things have taken a turn for the better there.'

'Ah, sure it can't have been easy for Dymphna over the past while, between that and especially with Lily coming back,' Father Iggy mused. 'She's a lovely girl, but you could see how it would have been hard for Charlie's family. They were used to being the centre of his world, and then this exotic young woman turns up and everyone is upset. Charlie is trying to please everyone and feels like he's getting it all wrong, and he's just trying his best too.'

He'd hit the nail on the head about a major source of stress in the McKenna household, and Grace marvelled at how insightful he was. For a man who had no personal experience of relationships or having children, he could see things very clearly. No wonder people went to him for advice on all kinds of things.

'Well, it's just life, isn't it? If it's not one thing, it's another,' she said. 'But at least they're figuring it out a bit better now. Charlie and Dymphna go for a walk now every evening, hand in hand. So that's a good sign. And Kate looks less murderous than she did. She's at that age, neither fish, flesh nor good red herring as my mother used to say.'

The priest rolled down the window to let some air into the stuffy car. 'You'd wonder at Mother Nature all the same, wouldn't you?'

'How do you mean?'

'Well, I'm not one to criticise the creator, God knows, but it seems like a bit of a timing fault to have women who are dealing with the change having to manage children who are becoming adults and all the high jinks that involves, and then trying to care for old sick parents, all at the same time, often with a husband who is going half deaf and only wants to read the paper or go for a pint. 'Tisn't fair on the women, I often think.'

She chuckled. 'Be careful, Father, or Tilly and Sarah will have you joining the suffragettes.'

He gave her a sidelong glance. 'The feminist priest – can you just imagine? But I do think it's unfair. Men can sometimes get away with murder – going from being minded by their mothers to being minded by their wives. Do you know I heard a man at a funeral the other day tell the lady of the house to ask his wife if he took sugar in his tea? He didn't know because he never made his own tea.'

'Well, Father, you're not exactly a domestic goddess yourself, are you?' she nudged him playfully.

He groaned. 'True for you, Grace. I'm a pure solid disaster, and that's the truth. I have nightmares that Mrs McHale will marry Dinny when Mrs McCafferty dies and we'll be left stranded again. I'm praying the mother holds on for another few years.' He gave her a mischievous wink.

She waggled her finger in mock admonishment. 'Don't let Mrs McHale hear you saying that – she's praying for the opposite.'

'Sure we're probably cancelling each other out in that case,' Father Iggy replied with a laugh.

Eventually they drove into the fishing town of Castletownbere on the end of the Beara Peninsula.

'Now what?' Grace asked.

'Well, my friend said the shop where he thinks he might have seen the canon was at the end of the main street. A little huckster shop, not the main grocer's. So maybe we go in there and ask? I'll do it if you like – the collar tends to get people talking.'

'Should you? I mean, they'd be far more likely to tell you the truth, but if it gets back to the bishop that you're asking questions, you'll be in trouble.'

'I will, I suppose. But sure I'll jump off that bridge when I come to it,' he said as he drove through the town.

She surveyed the brightly coloured fishing boats tied up at the quayside; there were more out in the bay plying their trade. The small grocer's shop was the last commercial premises at the end of the town, no more really than the downstairs room of a terraced house. It was not painted and blended into the grey streetscape, with nothing outside to indicate it even was a shop.

'I think we should both go in, share the blame,' she said, getting out of the car once Father Iggy parked it.

The door was open, and they walked straight in. The aroma inside was earthy and warm but not unpleasant. To their right were shelves, and on them were baskets of freshly dug potatoes and bunches of carrots, a basket of turnips and some pots of jam.

On the other side ran a counter, and behind it stood a pleasant-faced man in his forties wearing a brown overall.

'Good afternoon, Father, how can I help you?'

'Well, I'm hoping you can,' Father Iggy began. 'I'm looking for an old friend of mine. He was seen in this shop not so long ago. He'd be in his sixties, tall, balding, grey hair, with protruding eyebrows, and he has a slight lisp when he speaks?'

The man thought for a moment. 'There's a man comes in, lives up at the old O'Sullivan place, I think. He hasn't been around here before, and he doesn't say much, to be honest, so I don't have his name, but he might be who you're after?'

'Could well be.' The priest smiled. 'And where is this place?'

'Carry on out the road there' – the shopkeeper pointed left – 'and when you come to a fork, take the hill to the right. Keep going up until you come to a big farmhouse – there's a rusty plough out in front. Turn right there and keep going up. There's a cottage up there, and I think that's where he's staying.'

'Thank you very much, and God bless you,' Father Iggy said as they left. The ease with which they'd got the information surprised Grace, but then people were very deferential to the clergy, so she supposed that was just how priests were treated.

They followed the instructions, and sure enough within ten minutes they were outside a small whitewashed cottage. It looked uninhabited; ragged grey net curtains hung in the windows, and weeds grew through the gravel outside.

They approached the front door. Father Iggy knocked, but no sound came from within. He knocked again and then went to the window to peer inside. The glass was filthy, so it wasn't easy to see in, but Grace thought she saw some movement.

She nodded to Father Iggy, who went back to the door and continued rapping on it with his knuckles.

Eventually, after a full ten minutes of this, the door opened and there he was.

Canon Rafferty.

CHAPTER 27

CHAMONIX, FRANCE

Richard did exactly as Alfie had told him and parked the car, facing out, in the alleyway beside the bakery. He'd reversed about ten feet into the alleyway, but it was narrow, and he'd tried to leave enough space for the children to squeeze by his door and get in the back and the trunk. The town was in darkness; nobody was about. The café where he and Alfie had eaten earlier was now closed, and every house had shutters up.

The Hotel de la Paix was at the other end of this block, with each block being no more than five or six buildings long. All they had to do was get the children out of the hotel, along the street and into his car. High around the little town, the snow from the Alps glistened, even in the dark night, as the moon shone down. It was clear and warm and an excellent night for the Resistance – on nights like these, bright, clear and lit by the moon, flights could land.

Richard's palms were sweating on the steering wheel, and his heart was thumping. If a German appeared, he'd decided to say he was planning a long drive to Lyon and wanted to get going overnight because it was too hot to drive by day. It was not the greatest excuse, but it was the best he could come up with.

It was 8:57 by his watch, three minutes to the rendezvous. The lights were off in his car, and it was black, so he hoped that even if a German patrol did pass, he would go unnoticed.

The seconds ticked painfully by. Still no sign of life. Then he heard footsteps – was it boots? He slid down as best he could into the step-well so if someone passed by, all they would see would be the car, not him. Although with his height and bulk, it was difficult.

He was wearing the beret and a navy-blue pullover Grace had knitted him. The pullover was too warm, but it was the only dark thing he had brought.

The footsteps sounded more like high heels now, sort of clip-clopping along, and he wondered who on earth would risk being interrogated by wandering about at this hour, but he stayed down. The footsteps faded as the person went down the street, and he exhaled.

Moments later he started again as a shuffling sound came from deeper down the alleyway behind the car. Then the back door of the car was wrenched open and he realised they must have brought the children around the back of the buildings rather than up the street.

Several small pairs of terrified eyes gazed at him as Luc ushered the children into the trunk and then the back seat, all the time without one of them making a sound. Richard got out and helped them, squeezing them in as best he could. Luc went around the passenger side and put a small girl of no more than four into the stepwell and then got in himself.

Just as Richard was about to get into the driver's seat, he saw him. Jacob. At the back of the lane, walking towards him. Richard was so relieved to see his best friend, he almost cried. He figured Jacob must have offered to accompany the children instead of Alfie so he could see Richard.

As Jacob reached him, he smiled and drew Richard into an emotional embrace.

'Thank God you're alive, Jacob,' Richard breathed, much relieved to see that Jacob looked tired and thin but otherwise unharmed. He was a little shocked but also reassured to feel the hard outline of a gun beneath his brother-in-law's jacket.

'Good to see you too, Richard,' Jacob whispered into his ear. 'Thanks for doing this. Give this to Sarah, will you?' He slipped an envelope into Richard's trouser pocket, and murmured, 'Tell her a hundred hearts could not hold the love.'

Richard nodded, aware that his eyes were welling with tears. 'Jacob...'

But Jacob was moving silently towards the back of the alleyway, gesturing at Richard to get going.

'We need to go, *Américain*,' Luc hissed as Richard got back into the car.

He nodded and started the engine. As he did, he was dazzled by a sudden searchlight no more than five or six feet ahead of him. Someone was standing in the entrance to the alleyway. It was so blinding, he couldn't see how many people there were.

'Halt!' The shouted order rang through the still night. '*Raus aus dem Auto!*'

Whatever was going to happen next, there was no way Richard was going to stop or get out of the car.

'Drive, just drive!' Luc screamed. 'Now!'

He didn't stop to think. He put his foot on the accelerator, released the clutch and floored it. The thump of a body hitting first the hood and then the windshield made some of the children whimper, but Luc shouted, 'Don't stop, don't stop!'

He turned the wheel and sped down the street, bellows and gunshots ringing out behind him. There was no way he could go back; he had to get out of there. Within minutes they were out in the countryside, Luc giving him directions and urging him to go faster, faster. If the Germans were in pursuit, they needed to outpace them. Luckily the BMW was a sports model with a powerful engine.

Richard didn't dare look behind – he let Luc do that. He just concentrated on getting as far from Chamonix as was possible. Higher and higher they climbed, up corkscrew hills that tore at the engine of the BMW, but he didn't care.

'We've lost them, nobody is following for now,' Luc said with a sigh of relief as he turned to face forward.

They'd be abandoning the car soon anyway. Hopefully it could be taken by Alfie's people and reused, but either way, he would ignore the engine's protests at being raced up huge inclines. The vertiginous drops either side of the road were terrifying, but again, Richard couldn't allow them to register; it would slow him down. He just needed to focus on driving this car up these mountains with the little kids inside it safely and quickly. No other thought could be allowed into his brain right now.

Once there was no more road, the scree was impossible to grip with the tyres. They skidded terrifyingly several times, failing to gain purchase on the loose road surface at that angle. Luc told him to stop. Richard drove the car into an old wooden barn, and they helped the children out.

In a pile in the corner were some canvas sacks, and Luc handed one each to the children, who, Richard now realised, numbered twelve. Three emerged from the trunk, while the back seat held eight, four sitting on the laps of another four. The little one in the stepwell in front of Luc was the last one.

They were tiny, some not much more than toddlers, and others were seven or eight, he guessed. One boy, a little guy with round glasses, smiled at him. 'Nice driving,' he said.

'Thanks,' Richard replied.

The air was cold and clear up here in the mountains. The inky sky was full of stars, and the huge pearlescent moon hung low. He was glad now of Grace's sweater.

Luc gathered all the children around him and crouched down to be at eye level with them. He spoke slowly, so Richard was able to understand what he said.

'Now we walk up over that mountain there. All right?' He pointed to a snowy peak, impossibly high. 'It will be difficult, and we will all be tired, but we must try our hardest. If you absolutely cannot walk, then Richard and I will carry you, but just for a little while. On the other side of that mountain is the country of...?' He smiled, as if this was a quiz in school.

'Switzerland,' a shy-looking tall girl said.

'Yes, Switzerland, and that is not controlled by the Germans. So once we get there, we are safe.' Luc gave them an encouraging grin.

Richard marvelled at him. He was only a kid himself, not much older than these, but he was a man now, and his childhood was far behind him.

'Are our parents there?' a little girl of around five with blond plaits asked.

Luc cast Richard a glance; suddenly Luc was just a kid and could not answer that question.

'We don't know, little one,' Richard said, 'but we know who is *not* there, and that is the Nazis. So should we go?'

With looks ranging from excitement to terror, the children nodded. They slung their canvas bags with cannisters of water and some bits of bread and some fruit in them over their little shoulders and began to climb.

Five hours later, as dawn was breaking and the children were almost falling down with exhaustion, Luc led them to a small chalet in a little bower. All around were stands of evergreen trees that hid the house from view.

The group approached in single file, too shattered to even speak. Inside was an old woman, who had a pot of something that smelled of herbs on the hearth. She handed out small cups of the broth to the children first, who were now frozen as well as totally drained. They finished their warm broth and were told to lie down, some on the settle and some on rugs on the floor around the fire. Within moments they were all fast asleep.

Richard accepted a cup of the steaming broth. He thought how he would love a hunk of bread to dip in it, but he, like everyone else, would have to be grateful for the heat and the nourishment the broth alone provided.

He went outside and leant on the windowsill to drink it. The small chalet room was overcrowded with all the children, and he felt the need for some space for himself. He would need to rest as well. His legs and back ached; he'd carried a little girl called Berta for the last five or six miles. She had started out as barely the weight of a feather, but by the time they reached the chalet, she felt as heavy as a ton of bricks.

The woman of the house came out and, to his surprise, spoke to him in English. Her accent was American. 'Long way from home, eh?' she said. She was younger than he'd originally thought, possibly sixty, with long grey hair, a weather-beaten face and intense green eyes.

'You too, by the sounds of it?'

She nodded. 'From the Smoky Mountains, fifty miles from Knoxville, Tennessee. I came over as a nurse in the last war and met a Frenchman. The rest is history. You?'

'Savannah, Georgia,' he replied, feeling inordinately happy to meet a fellow American. 'Is your husband still here?'

'Nah, the Spanish flu took Pierre, but by then I had traded the Smokies for the Alps and there was no going back for me. I've lived up here ever since.'

'I can see why. It's so beautiful.' He sighed with pleasure as the warm soup filled his stomach.

'It will be again when we get the Boche out.'

She took out a packet of cigarettes and offered him one, which he refused with thanks. She lit up by striking a match off the rough plaster around the door – it reminded him of the cowboys in the western movies. She was like Calamity Jane.

'What's your name?' she asked.

'Richard Lewis. You?'

She smiled. 'Clarissa Davison. Nice to meet you.'

'Have you spoken to anyone, from, well...anyone involved with this? In the last few hours, I mean?' Richard knew they trusted this woman, of course, but it was still best to be circumspect.

Clarissa puffed on her cigarette. 'Luc said it was pretty hairy, you guys getting away. You must have done some skilful driving to shake them off your tail. Well done.'

'I was too scared to look behind me, so I just drove as fast as I could. No skill, just terror,' he admitted with a self-deprecating laugh. Then he remembered the sickening thump on the windscreen. 'But I reckon I got at least one of the Jerries with the car.'

She nodded. 'You did. Good job.'

There was something bitter in her tone that unsettled Richard.

Then she said, 'I've got a radio up here. It helps me stay informed about who, or what, might be coming my way. You understand?'

He nodded. The skin on his arms began to prickle, his instincts screaming at him that something was very wrong.

Clarissa's face was unreadable as she continued. 'Look, Richard, I got some coded messages earlier, before you and Luc arrived. They told me to tell you we lost the escort guy who was accompanying the kids. He shot a second German after you ran over the other one, but not before the Kraut gave returning fire. It was a bad hit.'

No. Richard felt his stomach lurch as the realisation hit him. Jacob was the only other adult there. But he couldn't be dead. How could that be right? He had survived so much for so long. He should have been dead ten times over by now. But this night, of all nights? He refused to believe it. How could this be?

'The thing is' – the look Clarissa threw him made him shiver – 'nobody could get to the guy, so…the German commander, Brunner, hung his body up outside the town hall as a warning to anyone considering resisting.'

He gasped as her words hit him like a punch to the gut. The avuncular German officer he and Alfie had met in the café earlier had done this despicable thing?

She put a hand on his arm. 'I'm sorry. He was your friend?'

All he could do was nod.

She gave him a sad smile. 'He was a brave man, Richard, that's for sure.' Her voice was bitter again, this time laced with hatred and anger, which he now fully shared. 'The population is behind us now, and it's all over for them. Brunner will pay for his actions. You can bet on that.'

He nodded again. He had no doubt that if Brunner's good friend

Gilles Fournier found him any time soon, it would not go well for the German. And he was glad at the thought.

Luc joined them, his young face despondent and weary. *'Je suis vraiment désolé, mon ami.'* The boy put his hand on Richard's arm, his words of condolence heartfelt. This kid knew better than anyone what this was like.

Tears stung the back of Richard's eyes at the unfairness of it all. But then in the grand scheme of this terrible war, Jacob was just one more dead body. Luc's mother, Constance, Paul, the Ducrots, so many others. Why not Jacob? Resisting the regime was not a game; it was deadly dangerous, and Jacob knew it. Since Richard first met him years ago in Savannah, all Jacob Nunez wanted to do was get over here and do his bit against the Nazis. He'd been so frustrated at having to just comment from the sidelines. He wanted to come to fight for his people, and he knew the risks.

Richard fought back the tears. This was no time for emotions. He had a job to do. He knew that so many times it would have been easier for Alfie or Bernadette or even for Jacob to give up and weep; they'd all lost so much, endured so much pain, physical and emotional. But they didn't succumb to it. They stayed strong and focused and single-minded. That was what was needed now. He would steel himself. He would get these children to safety, and he would put grieving for the best friend he'd ever had on hold, until he could allow himself to feel it. It was in this moment, he longed for Grace. She was his safe haven, the person he could be truly honest with. *Soon.* He'd get home to her no matter what it took. But for now, to honour his friend who had sacrificed everything in this horrible, horrible war, he would do what he had promised Jacob he would do.

'Come inside, get some rest,' Clarissa said quietly, leading them both into the chalet. 'There's a cot upstairs you two can sleep on. I'll stay awake and keep watch.'

CHAPTER 28

CASTLETOWNBERE, COUNTY CORK

The canon just stood there and didn't say a word for a long moment. Then he shuffled back into the house, leaving the door open. He seemed to move a bit slower now, but he did not otherwise appear to have aged any more in the two years since Grace had seen him, and she realised he was one of those people who looked the same age for years.

She and Father Iggy followed him into the house. The room they entered was sparse, just a table with one chair, as well as a dresser with a small collection of paltry utensils and a few provisions on it. There was an old pot-bellied stove in the fireplace. Off this room was another room. The door was ajar, and Grace could see it was a bedroom containing a single iron bed with a thin mattress, a single blanket and a flat pillow. Altogether it was a miserable dwelling, without a single thing to soften it. No rug or cushion or picture even – what was there was purely functional.

'Hello, Michael,' Father Iggy said, to Grace's surprise. She had never heard anyone address the canon by his first name.

'What do you want, Iggy?' the man replied with a weary sigh.

'Grace and I –'

The canon rudely cut in over him. 'Ah, Miss Fitzgerald, you really are getting your pound of flesh, aren't you? Will there ever be a time when I won't have you harassing me?' His tone was sneering, his s's sibilant, as she remembered.

She decided to ignore the barb and just get to the point. 'We're here on business, Canon,' she said. 'There's a child in an orphanage in New York, whose name is Carrie Dwyer. Her adoptive parents were killed, and we want to reunite her with her birth mother, who is, we believe, Hannah Monaghan.' She was relieved at how steady her voice sounded. She certainly didn't feel it – even being in his presence was deeply unsettling.

'Do that then,' the canon said, sitting on the only chair and leaving them standing. Grace noticed he hadn't reacted at all to the mention of Hannah's name, although he also hadn't denied knowing who she was.

'We can't without your help, Michael.' Father Iggy's voice was soft, reasonable.

'Why should I help her?' The canon jerked his head at Grace. 'God knows, that cripple has done nothing but cause me pain. I'll be damned if I help her now.'

Grace tried to hide her shock at a priest using such language to describe her, but she remained stoic. He wanted a reaction. He wasn't getting it.

'You know as well as I do, none of this is Grace's fault, Michael.' Father Iggy was firm but still kind. 'But you have a chance now, as a man of God, to do the right thing. This little girl in New York has nobody, but if she can be returned to her mother, then at least that's one small gesture of goodwill, something for the balance sheet.'

The laugh, a hissing, horrible thing, seemed to bubble up from inside the older man. 'You believe that still, Iggy? That there's going to be a day of reckoning for us all? That we'll stand before the man in the sky and he'll judge us and then it's paradise or eternal damnation?'

Grace shuddered at the sarcasm and disdain that dripped from the canon's words.

'I do. And like us all, your day will come, and it would be nice to have some good thing you did –'

'To offset the rest, is it? And I suppose you're without sin, are you, Iggy?' The same mocking tone.

'Not at all, nothing like it. I'm the same as everyone, just trying to balance up the score. And this is your chance to do that. Something drew you to the priesthood, Michael. You didn't have to commit your life to God, but you did. You took some wrong turns, but you are only human, and if you can do this one good thing, I think it will make you feel better. But more importantly, it will help this child.'

A small smile played on the canon's thin lips, and Grace tried not to look at his face, with the long, grey eyebrows that seemed to hang over his small, mean eyes, the weak chin, the sloped shoulders.

'No,' he said sullenly. 'Now get out.'

She caught Father Iggy's eye. Appealing to Canon Rafferty's better nature had failed – as she knew it would. He simply didn't have one. They would have to use the other tactic.

'I know who the child's father is.' She eyed him steadily as she spoke. 'You will write a letter to the orphanage in New York confirming Hannah Monaghan is Carrie's mother, and another letter to Frank Monaghan, explaining the situation and impressing on him the need to welcome this child into his home. Failing to do so will result in your paternity being revealed to the bishop, as well as Frank Monaghan's role in essentially purchasing a bride through you. I know he paid you one hundred pounds on the day of the wedding and a further hundred when she gave birth to a son. All of this will come out, Canon, and whatever shred of a reputation you have left will be destroyed.'

The silence hung heavily in the room as the three of them waited. Grace could feel her heart beat rapidly in her chest, but she clenched her fists by her sides to stop her hands trembling. Any show of weakness was something he would notice and capitalise on.

'I heard you married again. To a filthy-rich American, no less,' the canon said at last, his face twisted into an unpleasant sneer. 'Not bad going for a cripple, I have to say.'

'My life is none of your business,' she answered quietly.

His grey eyes flashed with anger. 'But it would seem, Miss Fitzgerald, that mine is repeatedly made yours. Isn't that a curious thing? Maybe if you minded your own business, and didn't stick your nose where it doesn't belong, we'd all be happier. What is this girl to you, anyway?'

'That's not the point, Michael.' Father Iggy tried again. 'You've broken every vow we made. Your soul is in mortal danger. What Grace does or doesn't do is nothing to do with it. I'm begging you, Michael, as one priest to another, do the right thing. There is always a place for redemption, you know that. This is your chance.'

The canon steepled his fingers, tapping them on his thin mouth, deep in thought. Long seconds passed. 'I want five hundred pounds. In cash. And a new life in America. If you will give me that, I'll go to that place in New York in person and have them release the child into the care of her mother. And I'll ensure Frank Monaghan complies. He'll need two hundred pounds to agree.'

Father Iggy looked like he'd been punched in the stomach and Grace felt a pang of pity for her friend. He had truly believed that it would be possible to appeal to the canon's better nature, that his vows as a man of God would mean something to him. But she wasn't at all surprised. Rafferty was rotten, mean and greedy to the core.

'Fine,' she said. It was an extortionate sum, but she knew Sarah's quest to help Carrie Dwyer was one small light of hope in a sea of despair for her sister-in-law. Sarah wanted this child to be provided with a home, so she would put up the money the canon was demanding. Grace was sure of that.

The canon sniffed loudly, and she couldn't help thinking that he was somewhat surprised by her agreeing to his outrageous demands. 'Come back with the money, book me passage, and set me up with a house. I want to live in South Carolina – the climate there will suit me. I'll go via New York and –'

Grace thought quickly. 'Book your own passage, and I'll see you are reimbursed. But the money won't be handed over until the paperwork is signed and sealed.' Sarah had told her that the ideal scenario would be for Carrie's birth mother and her husband to present themselves at the orphanage in New York with the canon, who could confirm Hannah's maternity, and the couple would then take Carrie home. If that huge sum was to be handed over to this horrible man, then she would go for the ideal scenario, and he would have to play it her way.

'It will be in a bank account for you in America, and you'll be given the details when we are sure Carrie is safe and released into the legal care of her mother. And father.'

The canon was about to object, but she held up her hand for silence – years of teaching had given her the skill to silence a room with a gesture. 'Frank and Hannah Monaghan will have to go as well. He will have to adopt Carrie legally, so there can be no grey area. Once all that is done, you can go wherever you wish. We won't be finding you a home – you'll take your money and leave, and you will never hear from me again. That's one option. The other is I go to the bishop and tell him everything.

'We both know whatever minimal protection of the Church you now enjoy' – she glanced around the hovel pointedly – 'would be removed if I were to reveal that you impregnated a young woman and then abandoned both her and her child to an institution before selling your own infant daughter to a couple in America, plus selling the girl whose life you had destroyed into a marriage with a man decades older than her. And all to satisfy nothing more than your own despicable desires and for your own financial gain. Also, my husband is a journalist, and I am sure he could find a way to sell such a sensational story as this to a number of publications with fewer scruples than the ones he usually writes for. You'd be all over the newspapers, Canon. And for all you say you don't care, the release of this information would make you even more of a pariah than you already are – we both know that's the truth. You would not be welcome anywhere, and you would have no resources.

'So the choice is yours. Do what I ask or suffer the consequences.' She paused for breath and noticed both the canon and Father Iggy were staring at her in astonishment. She inhaled deeply and continued.

'Additionally, you will write a letter now, in front of me, telling the truth of Carrie Dwyer's parentage, and sign and date it. Father Iggy can be a witness. Those are my terms – take them or leave them.'

'And if Monaghan refuses?' the canon asked. Grace had to fight back a surge of satisfaction – she was winning.

She composed herself and replied, 'It's up to you to make sure he doesn't. Also, please impress upon him the need to be kind to this child. We will be watching, and if he treats her badly, then his role in the whole sordid business could be revealed.'

'And you're just going to stand there, are you?' The canon now rounded on Father Iggy. 'While this...this...*harridan*...blackmails me?'

Father Iggy looked sad. 'You have no one to blame but yourself, Michael. You're the architect of your own misfortune. Take some responsibility for once, will you?'

'Do we have a deal or not?' Grace asked, smiling inwardly at her use of the Americanism.

'This is not –' the canon tried again.

'Yes or no?'

'All right, fine. Yes. I'll speak to Monaghan, and once he agrees, I'll book us passage. I have your word the money, including the cost of the fare, will be there once it's all done?'

She nodded. 'The money will be in Lewis Holdings in Savannah, Georgia. My father-in-law owns that and once we are clear the money can be transferred to an account of your choosing. Just as soon as we give the authorisation.'

'And what if you renege on it?' the canon asked.

'I won't. *I* am a person of my word.'

'Trust her, Michael, she will keep her end of the bargain,' Father Iggy urged.

'Fine. Get out, the pair of you. I'll notify you when I've spoken to Monaghan.'

Grace dug in her bag for a piece of paper and a pen.

'Write.' she instructed. The canon did as she bid him, his spindly writing telling the story of Carrie's parentage. He signed it wordlessly and handed it to her.

Her job done, Grace turned and left, without a backward glance.

CHAPTER 29

KNOCKNASHEE, COUNTY KERRY

15TH SEPTEMBER 1944

'So we can see here, the Russians are coming into Riga, and then to Bulgaria. The Canadians are after capturing Dieppe – that's very important as a port. And of course Paris has been liberated, and so has Brussels...'

Grace was in the middle of explaining the progress of the war, using the huge world map Father Iggy had insisted on buying for the school years ago and a pointer stick her sister Agnes had only used for slapping children, when Eleanor knocked on her door. The children were settling back to school nicely after the summer holiday, and the news of the war was getting better day by day.

'All right, everyone, I'd like you all to draw a map of Europe in your copybook, and insert the cities of Dublin, London, Paris, Amsterdam, Rome, Barcelona and Berlin while I'm gone. You can copy it from the big map.'

The Allies were almost through France, apart from a few pockets in the east, and they were making great progress up from the south as well. It finally felt like it might all be over.

'There's a lady here to see you,' Eleanor said. 'I told her it would be best to come back after school, but she said it would only take a minute.'

Grace looked out the window and saw Hannah Monaghan in the schoolyard. 'That's fine, Eleanor. They can work away while I'm talking to her, thanks.'

'Leave your door open. I'll keep an ear out,' Eleanor said, retreating to the younger classroom, where she was doing an art project on autumn leaves. Grace and Eleanor now alternated which class they each taught. It made a nice change for the children and for themselves too.

It was good to see Eleanor back at work. The summer had dragged on for her, as she was lost in a sea of grief, but she seemed a bit better now the new term had started. Grace knew from experience, teaching was a good way to take your mind off things. You had no business bringing personal stuff to the classroom, and sometimes that was a bit of a relief. Olivia, Joanne and Libby had taken great solace from their friends, and while they too were mourning their father, they were children, and their ability to bounce back was remarkable.

Charlie met her as she left the school building and handed her a bundle of envelopes. One, she was delighted to note, was from Richard, the postmark dated only four days ago. She heaved a sigh of relief.

'Dymphna asked if you'd come for your tea this evening,' Charlie said. 'She's worked out a recipe for a cake that needs no sugar, and she wants us all to try it.' He laughed. 'Oh, and Lily's back in her second year of university, can you believe that? She sent a picture – it arrived this morning – of her all ready to go for the new term. Dymphna has it stuck up on the wall.' The pride in his voice was clear, and the relief that his wife and family were at last coming to accept Lily was welcome.

'I'd love to. Eloise has her first English class here this evening. She is booked out, would you believe, and Tilly is dropping her down, so can I bring her and Odile too?'

'More the merrier,' Charlie called as he cycled off on his rounds.

Tilly had confided in her that Dymphna had gone to Mary O'Hare and got some kind of a tincture that was helping her greatly with the hot flushes, and so things seemed much better for everyone in that house. Grace was glad she'd not interfered directly herself. She and Dymphna had had a big chat one day last week about how hard it was for everyone and how Dymphna had simply been overwhelmed by it all. Managing a toddler, having a pair of school-goers who had all their own problems, caring for her very cranky mother and then trying to navigate her husband's long-lost American daughter, all while dealing with the change. No wonder the poor woman had been under pressure. Grace had offered to mind the children one night so she and Charlie could go to the pictures, and they'd taken her up on it. While they were out, she'd enlisted Kate and Paudie to help her do a big clear-out of the cupboards and the larder, and Dymphna had almost cried when she came home, she was so grateful.

Grace had also remembered something Eleanor said – just because a woman was going through the change, it didn't mean there was no reason for her to be furious; it was just that normally women put up with everyone expecting them to do everything, and one day, something just snaps. That was exactly what had happened with Dymphna, but now that it was being addressed, and Charlie and the children were seeing things a bit more from Dymphna's point of view, life for everyone was much better.

Grace crossed the yard to where Hannah Monaghan stood waiting for her. It was still warm, as the cooler autumnal air had yet to make itself known, and the trees in the village were a riot of reds, golds and orange.

'Hannah,' she said with a smile, 'how are you?'

'Oh, Mrs Lewis, I had to come and tell you. I can't believe it.' The other woman's hazel eyes were bright with excitement, and she looked like a completely different woman to the downtrodden creature Grace had met some months ago.

'Frank was out all day yesterday – I don't know where – but he came back and said that he and I are going to America to adopt Carrie, to take her home with us. We leave on the twenty-ninth of this month.

'He said he was shocked and very upset that I have had a child out of wedlock. Although I can't believe that could be much of a surprise to him given all the hints about fallen women he's been dropping over the years, and even he couldn't have seriously thought I'd have married a man old enough to be my grandfather if I didn't have some shameful reason to be grateful for a marriage. Anyway, Frank says he's willing to overlook everything in the interests of charity and mercy.

'Canon Rafferty' – her face clouded at the mention of his name – 'is coming with us because he's going to make sure it's all done legally. To be honest, the thought of even seeing the canon makes me feel sick, but I don't care. If I can get my baby back, it's going to be worth it.' She blushed. 'Well, I know she's a child now, but still…I never ever thought…even for a moment.

'We told the boys too. Frank's sister is going to take care of them while we're away. The only thing is, Mrs Lewis, Frank says we can't say that I'm Carrie's mother.'

Grace could see the disappointment etched on the woman's face as she spoke.

'We're going to say she's an orphaned child of an old friend. Frank was in America for a year or two when he was young, so the story will work.' Tears welled in her eyes. 'I wanted so badly to be able to tell Carrie that I'm her mother, but Frank says I have to see it from his point of view and how would it make him look if other people knew about…' She sighed. 'But beggars can't be choosers – that's right, isn't it, Mrs Lewis? I mean, Frank just came up to me and said it straight out – I didn't even have to plead or anything. And he said he'll try to be fair to her even if she is a bast –' She stopped herself repeating that awful word. 'Well, he's going to try…' Tears spilled down her cheeks now. 'It's just, Mrs Lewis, I…I never thought Frank cared about me, but by doing this…'

Grace kept her face calm, suppressing her internal outrage. How could she ever reveal to this poor woman that her husband was a mercenary, heartless man who was only doing this because he was afraid of the truth getting out? And, of course, for money. Best let her believe he was doing something kind for her – after all these years, it was the least she could have.

'I'm delighted for you, Hannah,' she said, smiling brightly at the woman. 'This is wonderful news. Have you written to Sarah?'

Hannah nodded. 'I sent her a telegram this morning on my way here. None of this would be happening if it wasn't for her – and for you. I can't ever repay either of you, you know.'

'Not at all, Hannah, we did nothing. Sarah will be over the moon that it all worked out for you, I know.'

Hannah thanked her profusely again, then rushed away to get her bus home. Grace returned to her pupils, as she could hear the decibel level in her classroom rising even out in the schoolyard.

Of course, Sarah was already fully aware of the Monaghans' planned trip to the States. Grace had written to her, outlining the meeting with the canon and the deal they'd struck. She added that she hoped she hadn't overstepped with agreeing to that amount of money, as it was an enormous sum. Sarah had replied immediately, assuring Grace she'd done precisely the right thing and confirming that the money would be there to be withdrawn once the papers were signed.

The rest of the day flew by, and before Grace knew it, the bell rang for the end of the schoolday. As she was tidying up, Fiachra O'Flynn arrived with a telegram for her.

'Ah, Fiachra, how are you?' she asked kindly.

'I'm all right, Miss Fitz,' he said though he looked forlorn. 'Did you hear how Lily's getting on grand in college in America? She's in her second year now.'

'I did. Charlie told me this morning.'

'Imagine Lily as a doctor. It's hard to believe, isn't it?'

'Not really, Fiachra. To be honest, Lily's a very bright girl and she's very…ambitious. I think she'll make a great doctor. Do you not agree?'

The lad looked at her, and she could see the conflict in his face. Finally he gave in and nodded miserably. 'Aye, that she will, Miss Fitz,' he said. 'And more power to her, I suppose.' He paused a moment and then gave a deep sigh. 'I suppose we won't see her any more in Knocknashee now.'

Grace smiled. 'Oh, I think we will, Fiachra. Lily will be back to see Charlie and Dymphna and the family.'

She hated to confirm his worst fears but there was no pont in encouraging something that had no future.

'Yes, I suppose she will.' He didn't say out loud 'but not me', but Grace could feel it linger unspoken between them. 'What will I do?' He looked so desolate, it was almost comical.

'I'll tell you what you should do,' she replied. 'You should wash and iron your best shirt and trousers and take yourself off to the dance in Dingle next Saturday night. Sure aren't the young bucks from here only mad to be going in there? Find yourself a nice girl, ask her up to dance and buy her a cup of tea and a bun. If I was you, that's what I'd do.'

'But nobody will be like Lily…' he protested.

'That's true, nobody will, but there are plenty of fish in the sea, Fiachra…'

'There's only one salmon,' he responded with a doleful shake of his head.

'Indeed, and that's not true at all, Fiachra O'Flynn. There are plenty of lovely girls who'd love to be asked up by a fine, handsome lad like yourself from a good family and with a steady job.'

'So I should just forget about her? That's what Charlie says too, and my mam, and my sister…'

'Did you ever hear the saying, Fiachra, "what's for you will not pass you by"?'

He nodded. 'My mam says it often. But I was so sure Lily was the one for me, but she has other plans and I'm not part of them…'

'Then you have to forget her, Fiachra,' she said solemnly. 'There's nothing else for it.' She smiled at him gently. 'But you know, just because Lily is special – which she is – doesn't mean she's the best that's out there for you.'

He sighed. 'Thanks for trying to cheer me up, Miss Fitz.'

Grace caught his arm as he turned to go. 'Fiachra?'

'Miss Fitz?'

'My telegram?'

'Oh yeah. Sorry, Miss Fitz.' The lad blushed and handed Grace the buff-coloured envelope.

'We're ready to go now, Grace.' Eleanor Worth appeared at the door of the classroom, her eldest daughter behind her. 'Can we help you with anything? Oh, hello, Fiachra.'

'Hello, Mrs Worth. I hope you're keeping well yourself.'

'I am indeed, thank you.' Eleanor turned to Grace. 'If you're ready, we can lock up.'

'I'd better be off so, Miss Fitz,' Fiachra said. Grace stifled a smile. The young postman looked like he was afraid they'd lock him in if he stayed a minute longer. To her amusement, he bolted for the classroom door and headed out into the yard in search of his bike.

To Grace's surprise, Olivia Worth made to follow him out.

'Where are you going, young lady?' Eleanor asked.

Olivia blushed and blurted out, 'I…I just need to ask Fiachra about…his sister. She's in my class.'

Grace was forced to stifle a giggle as Eleanor murmured, 'As if I didn't know already,' under her breath. 'Go on then,' Eleanor said to her eldest daughter. 'But don't delay the lad. He has work to do.'

'I won't, Mammy.' Olivia beamed, and Grace and Eleanor watched as she struck up a conversation with the young man in the schoolyard.

'She's fourteen, and far too young to be thinking of such things. I will need to keep a stern eye on it all,' Eleanor said. But there was an affectionate twinkle in her eye.

'Of course you will, but Fiachra is a nice lad, Eleanor – I've known him all his life. Now you go ahead. I've just a few things to finish off here, and I'll lock up myself after that.'

As soon as Eleanor left, Grace opened the telegram Fiachra had delivered to her.

Arranged as discussed. Passage booked on SS Carleton *departing Queenstown Sept 29. Expect to be reimbursed.*

No signature, but it could only be from the canon.

Grace locked up the school and made her way home. Then she made herself a well-earned cup of tea and sat down in her kitchen to read Richard's letter.

Dearest darling Grace,

I'm writing this from Montreux in Switzerland. France is all but liberated, but the dying weeks of the occupation were among the deadliest, the Nazis anxious to cover their tracks, I guess.

I have some very sad news. Jacob is dead.

I met Alfie in Chamonix, a little town near the Alps. He asked that I send his love to his mother and sisters and a promise that he'll come home as soon as he can. He recruited me to help him transfer some Jewish children over the mountains into Switzerland, which I agreed to do. Jacob came the night I collected them. We met briefly, and he gave me a letter for Sarah. Seconds later, he was dead, shot by a German who had caught us trying to escape. I'll fill you in in greater detail when I come home, but poor Jacob gave his life to help save those twelve little boys and girls, Grace. He died a hero.

When I found out, I was up in the Alps, hiding out in a cabin, and I didn't allow myself to feel it. There was too much at stake for me to fall to pieces. But now I feel overwhelmed with all of the emotions. The grief and loss for myself—he was my best friend, and I loved him so much—but even more so for Sarah and his family. And just the sheer waste of it all.

He was so brave, Grace. He could have stayed in the US. He could have stayed in London. He could have come back with me from Switzerland last year. But Jacob always took the hard option because he wanted to help. He didn't die in vain—he saved twelve little kids and so many more we'll never know about—but I am haunted by that night. I could have saved him. I could have gone back. He was wounded but didn't die right away. He suffered, Grace, and that knowledge keeps me awake at night. I think maybe I could have shot the German myself, or done something. God, I don't know. I was just focused on getting those little kids out of there, and Luc, who was with me, was yelling at me to drive faster, and so I did, and it wasn't until hours and hours later that I found out Jacob was killed.

Even writing it now, it's hard to believe. I miss him, Grace. So much. It's like something is stuck in my chest.

Allen Dulles is posting this in the diplomatic pouch for me, so I can be a bit more candid than I normally would be. He's been very helpful actually.

I'll come back now via London and see Sarah, to tell her in person. Though how I'll do that, I just don't know. I hope to get out tonight, so by the time you read this, I might well be in London already. It's costing a small fortune, but I don't care. I just want to get back to you. A small private company is offering flights to the highest bidder. Even as Europe is in total chaos, someone is always looking to make a buck.

I might bring Sarah back to Knocknashee with me, if she'll come. She'll need us in the coming weeks.

There is an organization here in Switzerland that is taking care of child refugees; we handed the kids over to them. They'll try to reunite as many as they can with their families, though looking at the carnage and the number of displaced people, that won't be easy. Poor little things thought their parents might be here, but of course they are not. God alone knows where they might be.

Bernadette died too. I spoke to her husband yesterday. I went to the house, because as far as he's concerned, I'm just Harry, an old friend from Paris, and he was distraught. He brought me in, gave me a drink, and told me that she died in his arms a week ago. He cried as he told me, sobbing. And honestly, Grace, it was bizarre. This is a man of vast wealth, all gotten through the exploitation of innocent people, but part of me felt sorry for him. He loved his Ghislaine with all his heart. He has no idea who she really was. He asked me if I knew who the child in the photo he found under her pillow is. You can't imagine how strange it was, a Nazi sympathiser, in floods of tears, holding a picture of you and Odile and asking me if I know who you both are.

Of course I denied knowing either of you, but he wondered if Ghislaine had a child before he knew her. He said that if he found out that she did, he would want to find her and ensure she was all right out of love for Ghislaine. He knows nothing beyond the photo, so we are safe, but it was an eerie moment.

I feel so tired, Grace. Everyone says the war is nearly over, but there's a lot more to do yet, for Europeans anyway, and the USA fights on in the

Pacific. All I want to do now is come home, fall into bed with you, and block out the entire world.

Kirky will be having a canary by now—I've been out of contact for so long. I sent a telegram to say I was alive but Jacob didn't make it, but I'll have to write to him soon. And to my parents. But for now, they are all getting a telegram and you are the only one I'm writing a letter to.

I'll be home very soon, my darling. I can't wait to see you.

All my love, now and forever,

Richard xoxoxox

CHAPTER 30

London, England

September 1944

Richard sat in the Associated Press office lounge where he'd arranged to meet Sarah. She was living with Miss Alderton and Miss Alderton's very elderly mother, so she said it was best to meet someplace else. He would have preferred somewhere more private, but London was teeming with people and privacy was in short supply. He settled in a corner booth and hoped they wouldn't be disturbed.

'Well, struth, if it isn't my guardian angel!'

Richard looked up from the copy of the *Capital* he'd managed to grab from the stand inside the door to see Warren King, the Australian journalist whose brother Ed had got Richard across France, waving at him.

Richard stood, happy to see him. 'Hi, Warren.' He smiled.

'G'day, mate, great to see ya. I didn't hear, and I was getting worried.' Warren shook Richard's hand enthusiastically.

'Here I am, like a bad penny. And thanks to Ed for the ride. How is he?'

'Right as rain, last I heard.' Warren grinned. 'But forget about him. Did you hear what happened?'

'No, I'm not back all that long...' He knew the AP offices were a hive of gossip, so he was glad of the distraction.

'I only got a flamin' award.' He lowered his voice. 'Or should I say, *you* did.'

'What?' Richard had no idea what he was on about.

'You know I'm a sports writer, yeah?'

He nodded as Warren took a seat opposite him.

'Footy, cricket, the gee-gees, rugby – you name it, I can write about it and you'd feel like you were right there, on the side of the action. But this war stuff was too flamin' hard, mate, couldn't do it. So when you gave me the piece you wrote, it saved my bacon, let me tell ya.'

Richard smiled. 'Glad to help.'

'Well, I filed it, and mate, you're not gonna believe this, but my editor reckons it's the best bit of writing he's seen in his whole career. He said that *to me*. Now he probably smelled a rat 'cause my next piece was back to my usual rubbish standard, but he printed it – the piece you wrote – and it only got nominated for a journalism prize and it won!'

Richard couldn't help but laugh.

Warren dug in his pocket and pulled out a wad of notes. 'The prize is some old plaque or something, whatever about that. But I also got a two-hundred-quid bonus, so here you go.' He threw a wad of notes on the table.

'No, that's your money, Warren. I don't want it.'

'Well, I can't do that, mate. I was keeping it for when I saw you. I don't need the dosh. I'm happy to be left here, with my editor waiting – in vain, it has to be said – for my next flash of genius.'

As they discussed it, Sarah arrived, looking even more dishevelled than usual after being caught in a downpour. Her dark wavy hair that she clearly cut herself hung in damp tendrils around her square jaw. And today she was wearing a dress that might once have been blue but now looked like a shapeless grey bag. On her feet were men's boots, and thick grey socks bunched around her ankles. Their mother would have a stroke if she saw her only daughter, Richard thought.

'Warren, this is my sister, Sarah. Sarah Nunez, Warren King, a fellow journalist.'

'We met before. How are you, Warren?' Sarah asked, sitting beside Richard. She noticed the money on the table. 'What's the cash about?'

'Long story,' Richard said, not wishing to go into it.

'I owe this to your brother, but he doesn't want to take it,' Warren said with a sigh.

'Well, if neither of you want it, there are around seventy kids who just arrived from France this morning with what they stand up in, and the charity looking after them could sure use it?'

The two men looked at each other. Richard shrugged.

'Fair enough, it's yours,' Warren said.

Sarah took the money and shoved it into her leather satchel, which Richard recognised as Jacob's.

'OK, mate, I'll leave you to it.' Warren clearly sensed he wasn't needed there. For all his guff, he was more clued in than he ever let on. He didn't pretend to know anything, and as a result found out so much more than anyone else, even if his political corresponding left something to be desired.

'See you, Warren, take care. And pass on my regards to Ed,' Richard said as he walked off.

'Will do, mate.' Warren gave a cheery wave and was gone.

Sarah turned to look at Richard then, her back to the room. No greeting, no exclamation that he was alive – she only had one question on her mind.

Before Richard could summon the words, she saved him. 'He's dead, isn't he?' Her dark eyes filled with pain.

'He is,' Richard said quietly.

'Tell me everything.' He could see she was concentrating on breathing, but she needed to know. Slowly, and in as much detail as he could recall, he told her the whole story.

'So it wasn't for nothing,' she said when he'd finished.

'Absolutely not. He, Alfie, Constance and Luc have gotten so many people to safety over those mountains – we'll never know for sure how many lives they saved. And if Jacob had not brought the kids to me that night, it would have been Alfie and he'd be dead now. Jacob didn't do anything wrong. It was just bad luck. The Germans are so jumpy these days. It's more dangerous than ever over there.'

'How did you and Alfie just sit in a café, eating, with them beside you?' she asked.

'It's Alfie. He's amazing, like a chameleon. He can be whatever he needs to be in any situation.'

'I wish you could have had more time with Jacob.' She had yet to cry. Maybe she had no more tears.

'Me too. But he did have time to give me this, for you.' He reached into his jacket pocket and took out the envelope Jacob had slipped him that fateful night.

'Have you read it?' she asked.

'Of course not. It's for you.'

She took the envelope and sat looking at it.

'Do you want to get out of here?' he asked. 'Maybe go to the park? The sun's out again.'

She nodded, holding the envelope, gazing down at it. 'His last post,' she whispered.

'And it was to you,' he said, putting his arm protectively around her shoulder.

They walked into Hyde Park, and Richard found an empty bench. 'Should I go?' he asked, but she shook her head, patting the seat beside her.

He sat there as she read the letter. Then she passed it to him. 'You don't have to –'

'Read it,' she said, her eyes bright.

Mea levavot ihiyu meat midai kdei lehakhil et kol ha'ahava sheli elaikh.
Sarah,

I learned the phrase above from a fifteen-year-old girl I was leading over the mountains, so I think it means 'a hundred hearts could not hold all the love I have for you.' But then again, she could have been messing with me. If it means 'you're a useless sack of chicken heads,' forgive me. I meant to say the heart thing.

I don't have many regrets, but one is leaving you. The other is not telling you every single day how precious you are to me—always have been and always will be.

I know you're worried and probably mad as hell at me for not coming back with Richard, but I have to stay. I have to help, and I am helping—I am doing something. It's not that I care more about them than I do about you. They just need me more right now. I'm sorry if I got frustrated before about not being able to do anything. That wasn't your fault, but I took it out on you sometimes, so I'm sorry.

Alfie is a true hero. If I don't make it, take care of him when this is over, if you can. He's not going to find adjusting to normal life easy. He says he's going to go home. Hopefully we'll all be together in Knocknashee—that's my dream. You and me, Richard and Grace, Alfie and all that cast of characters that make up that crazy Irish village.

If it's at all possible, I will come back to you, my Sarah, but if it's not, then please, get on with your life. Live and love again. All I ever want is for you to be happy. When things get rough here, I think of you in London, drinking coffee in our bed, wearing my shirt. Or in Savannah, when I saved you from a life of wealth and ease to give you a life of poverty, cold, and danger.

You gave up so much for me, but know this, Sarah Lewis Nunez, there is nothing—NOTHING—I wouldn't give up for you. I consider myself so blessed to have known love like this. Many people live their whole lives and never feel it.

If I die tomorrow, then I know I have loved, and loved more deeply than many men do in a lifetime. You are so special and so beautiful and funny and so very kind, and the world is a better place for having Sarah Lewis from Savannah in it.

Be happy, my darling wife.
Always,
Your husband, Jacob

Richard gulped. 'Oh God,' he breathed.

'What?' Sarah asked.

He turned to her, tears streaming down his face, and reached for her, pulling her into an embrace.

'"Tell her a hundred hearts couldn't hold the love,"' he whispered as he held her close. 'They were Jacob's last words to me.'

There, on a bench in Hyde Park, with battle-battered London trying to limp along all around them, they cried together for Jacob Nunez.

CHAPTER 31

Mid-Atlantic Ocean

30th September 1944

Two days into the voyage to New York from Cork, Hannah Monaghan lay in her bunk aboard the SS *Carleton*, kept awake by the sounds of her husband's noisy snoring. She could hardly believe this was happening, even now. The gentle rumbling of the huge ship's engines was soothing, and if it wasn't for the sporadic loud snoring coming from Frank, she would be sleeping peacefully herself.

It had been the same last night. She had opted to spend most of the time since boarding in their cabin. The ship was full of injured American soldiers being repatriated, and she had no interest whatsoever in being anywhere near the canon, so to pass the long hours at sea, she stayed in their tiny second-class accommodation, reading, writing letters to her long-lost daughter and to her sons, explaining things for when they would be older. Two down – they had three more days of the voyage to go.

THE LAST POST

On the previous evening, the ship's captain had made them all stand on deck in the freezing cold for an evacuation drill. Frank had been furious, especially since the canon, who was travelling in a first-class cabin, didn't have to participate. Apparently those passengers were given their safety briefing in the comfort of the salon. Frank had complained, but the purser just laughed, saying that if the ship was hit, the Jerries didn't care who was in what class, so everyone was going down together.

Hannah must have dozed off, because she was awoken at about three o'clock in the morning by the evacuation alarm going off. She tried to get Frank to get up, but he refused, saying it was just another drill and he wasn't playing their stupid games, so she went to the deck alone.

Frank was right, it seemed, but Hannah endured it, shivering in a row with the other women and children as they were allocated to a lifeboat. They were instructed to memorise their boat; hers was number fifteen on the port side, two-thirds of the way down. They were given instructions on how, in the event of an attack, they were to dress warmly, take nothing with them and get into their allocated boats in a quick and orderly way.

Someone asked where the men were to board their boats, and the purser just gave him a funny look. 'Ladies and gentlemen, as you are no doubt aware, we are above capacity, given the needs of war. Women, children and servicemen are to be given priority – in that order.'

'So are you telling us there are not enough lifeboats for everyone?' the man asked again.

Hannah was glad Frank had refused to come to the drill, because if he had been here with her, he would be the one complaining and she would have been mortified.

'We will do our best to keep everyone safe, sir. You've been allocated a lifeboat. Now you may return to your cabins, but rest assured there will be other drills. It is incumbent upon you to ensure you are at your muster station assigned to you on boarding within four minutes of the alarm sounding. There is considerable U-boat activity in these waters all of the time, so I suggest you sleep in your warm clothing. Good night.'

Hannah made a mental note to tell Frank that in the morning. He insisted on dressing for bed each night in his crisply ironed pyjamas, buttoned up to the neck. The thought that German U-boats were under the ship kept her awake in terror, but Frank didn't seem to care. He and the canon were enjoying the hospitality of the first-class lounge, eating and drinking and putting it all on an account that Frank said the canon was going to pick up.

Only this morning he had revealed that the canon intended to stay on in America, that they and Carrie would be coming home without the priest. That came as a wonderful relief. Hannah didn't want Carrie to have to spend any time with the man who was her father. It was not going to be easy, pretending to the child that she wasn't her real mother, but she would do it. And maybe, please God, in years to come, when Frank died, she could tell her daughter the truth. It was sinful to think this way, she knew, wishing her husband dead, and she would never say it aloud, but in truth she lived for the day. She knew her sons would be welcoming to Carrie; they were sweet boys, and she loved them so much. But like her, they were wary and fearful of their father. He was the disciplinarian, and it broke her heart when he beat them. He said it was necessary to keep them in line but she didn't agree. Some day, hopefully in the not-too-distant future, they would all be free of him.

Frank grunted and broke wind, the noxious smell filling the airless cabin. She covered her nose with the blanket. He'd drunk too much again tonight – she could always tell – coming back glittery-eyed and demanding she perform her 'wifely duties', as he called it.

She did as he told her, like she always did, and when he finished, he rolled off her and went to his own bunk. Even at his age, and even when full of drink, he was still able to perform. She knew it made him proud. She hoped she wouldn't get pregnant again. She had enough children. But that was not her decision to make, as Frank had pointed out on the one occasion she dared raise the topic.

Carrie. It was a lovely name. She'd called her little girl Bridget when she was born, after Hannah's own mother, but obviously her adopted parents named her Carrie. She tried to picture her face but failed. She longed to see her with a physical ache. She had to keep reminding herself that the girl was thirteen years old now, not an infant as she was the last time Hannah had seen her.

The screech of the alarm cut through her thoughts.

She'd done as instructed and gone to bed dressed, so she got up and put on her boots and warm coat, then fastened her life belt over it.

'Frank...' She shook him. 'Frank, come on. We need to go – the alarm.'

'I'm not going, woman, I told you.' He turned over and pulled the blanket over his bony shoulder.

She persisted. 'Please, Frank, come on. They said we have to –'

'Get off me!' he roared, and she jumped.

She knew him well enough after all these years to dare not try again. Instead she left the cabin alone and trundled up the gangway with the other passengers, making her way to lifeboat fifteen. It was probably just another drill.

Something was different, though. The crew were not joking with each other and relaxing. They were all in a focused hive of activity.

A crew member was standing with a clipboard beside boat fifteen. 'Name?' he asked.

'Er, Hannah Monaghan. Is this drill real?'

The crewman nodded solemnly. 'Yes, ma'am, hit by a U-boat fifteen minutes ago. We have to evacuate. Please get into the boat.'

Panic surged through her, jangling her nerves. 'Oh, I have to go back down – my husband didn't come up with me!' She grabbed the crewman's arm, but he just shook it off. He was already checking some other people off his list. 'Please, sir, my husband...'

'Just get in the lifeboat, ma'am, now,' he snapped, and she recoiled. She couldn't just get in a lifeboat and leave Frank. She tried to walk back against the swarms of people heading towards the lifeboat stations but was stopped by a burly crew member with a flaming-red beard.

'Please, sir, I must go back down...'

He stood before her, blocking her way. 'No. Can't allow it. Go immediately to your assigned boat, ma'am.'

'But I –' she protested, fighting back tears.

'Now!' he shouted, and she found herself in a moving swell of people, being carried back to the lifeboats. She saw number fifteen was almost full. Her brain whirred. What was she doing? She couldn't get left behind. Her boys, Carrie... She had to get on the lifeboat. Suddenly that was all that mattered. Frank would be all right. He always was. And surely someone would check the cabins?

Hannah clambered over the side, landing painfully on her hip, and dragged herself to a seat on one of the cross planks.

As she squeezed in at the end of the seat, a woman with three small children crushed beside her. Hannah helped her move them along the seat. One dropped a teddy bear and squealed. Hannah picked it up and handed it back.

In front of and behind her, she could hear frantic voices as people scrambled into lifeboats. It was pitch-dark and biting cold. She held on to the ropes as lifeboat fifteen, full of passengers, was lowered onto the dark, choppy sea. Mothers clung to their crying children, older women sat still, coats pulled tightly around them, young girls cried. The voices from high up on the deck became faint as the boat hit the water, and a young crewman rowed them out into the inky night, away from the ship. The water, the spray, the wind were all bitterly cold, and Hannah felt her teeth chatter as the cold seeped in through her coat.

Looking back at the ship, the *SS Carleton* looked fine to her, but the ensign on their lifeboat, who was called Malov, told them the ship had a huge hole in her bow, far below the waterline, and was taking on water.

She tried to focus on breathing. What about Frank? The canon? All the paperwork that they needed to claim Carrie? All she had was what she stood in, nothing else. Frank had all their money and papers. She tried to calm herself. Surely Frank would be on one of the other boats; he had to be. She shivered uncontrollably, her teeth clenched as the icy waves and freezing wind numbed all physical sensation. Would she die here? Was this how her life ended? Who would care for her boys? Thoughts went round and round as her body seemed to acclimatise to the frozen conditions.

'How long till she sinks?' an American woman asked.

'No idea. Not long, I'd imagine. I was on the *SS Valiant* when she was hit, and she went down in less than fifteen minutes, but she had incendiaries aboard. We're not carrying anything like that, so longer maybe...'

'This is your second sinking?' the woman asked incredulously.

'Yes, ma'am,' the ensign replied as he rowed determinedly.

Would that happen now? Was Frank still on there? What about the canon? She just knew he'd survive – people like him always did.

Each lifeboat had a light, and soon they were far enough from the ship to just see a twinkle of lights on the ocean. Ensign Malov stopped rowing.

'We're far enough away not to be dragged into the downpull if she sinks,' he said, resting the oars on his lap and taking a drink of water from his canteen. Despite the cold, he was sweating. 'The captain sent up a distress signal, and there will be other ships travelling in convoy, so we'll be rescued, don't worry.'

The lifeboat was buffeted by the choppy seas. Hannah, sitting on the edge of the boat, was soaked by water splashing over the side.

She offered up a prayer. *Please, Lord, let me see my children. Let me get Carrie and see my boys again. Please, God.*

'So now we just wait?' a woman behind her asked.

'As I told this lady, a distress call has been sent. The crew are probably still on board trying to make contact with a rescue ship nearby,' the ensign replied, but Hannah could sense his feigned calm. He was trained not to panic, but he was worried.

'So the U-boat might still be here, under us?' one of the younger women asked, her voice rising in alarm. Hannah guessed the girl could be no more than seventeen.

'They're after big ships, not civilians. Please just try to remain calm.'

In her pocket Hannah had the rosary beads her mother had given her when she went to the horrible place to have Carrie. She started saying the prayers she'd known by heart since childhood.

For hours they sat there, frozen to the bone, the *Carleton* slowly sinking before their eyes. Hannah could no longer feel the waves as they splashed against her. The woman with the three children asked if one of her girls could lean against her, and of course she obliged. The child had slipped down and was now lying in her sodden lap, amazingly asleep. Hannah kept one arm around her to stop the child slipping to the floor, which was now covered with six inches of seawater that had come in over the side. Nobody had spoken for ages.

It was impossible to tell how much time had passed. Hours definitely, but she didn't know how many. She prayed for God to save them, to save her for her children. She prayed for Frank. She even said a prayer for the canon. She could no longer feel the beads of the rosary, but she mumbled her prayers over and over, the sound giving her some comfort. Around her, some other women were doing the same. Others were glassy-eyed, staring straight ahead. More were still weeping.

Then she saw them. She might have been the first one in their boat to see them, but there were lights on the horizon. The ship came closer, painfully slowly, and then they all saw it – the American flag to the fore. It took what felt like forever to reach them, but eventually the huge merchant ship loomed beside them. The ensign rowed them to the starboard side, where the other lifeboats all congregated and were lashed together by the crew for safety. One by one the passengers in each overcrowded lifeboat were rescued, each person told to place a sling under their arms to be pulled aboard the *MV Austin*, painstakingly and carefully. The ship they were aboard had gone beneath the waves hours ago.

Hannah had to be helped into the harness as her fingers refused to work, but as the webbing belt bit under her arms, she could feel it digging in. She shut her eyes, trying to block out the panic as she was hoisted higher and higher, the rain whipping viciously against her face, her hair in her mouth, her feet dangling into nothingness. Strong hands pulled her over the railings, and she was carried by two men to an area inside where a station for women to undress behind a screen had been set up. Her fingers ached and tingled painfully, but she was just about able to remove her sodden clothing and put on the clean, dry clothes supplied: a man's shirt, trousers and socks. She was given a length of twine to use as a belt, as the trousers were much too big, and she rolled up the legs. She was then ushered to an area where blankets and hot drinks were being given out as the crew tried to find room for everyone.

Other women searched frantically for their spouses or other family members, but Hannah just sat on the makeshift bunk she was given. She ate the food handed to her and eventually slept on and off.

The next three days passed in a blur. Hannah felt somehow removed from her body. She knew she should go and look for Frank, or even the canon, but she couldn't. It was as if she were paralysed. Physically and emotionally. She sat and ate and drank what she was given, speaking to nobody, hours passing by. All she thought about were her boys and Carrie. She needed to get to them. Every time the problems of how she would survive appeared in her mind – how she would be reunited with Frank, what would they do with no passports or money – she felt overwhelming exhaustion and her brain refused to focus. Frank would not be good in this situation; he liked to be in control and didn't do well with taking instructions. She could not deal with him now, making demands, issuing orders to the crew who were doing their best. He would come looking for her, she knew, and he'd find her soon enough. She had moved to a corner and settled there, only leaving to go to the toilet.

Eventually, three days later, the ship pulled into the passenger port of Ellis Island.

Because they had no possessions or paperwork, each survivor was taken to a room to be interviewed. She gave her name to the kind woman when it was her turn and asked about Frank. She'd not seen him on the ship, but he might have been in another part. The woman scanned a sheet of printed names, checked it twice and broke the news gently that Francis John Monaghan was not listed among the survivors.

Hannah heard the blood rush in her ears and felt a myriad of emotions: guilt – she should have looked harder for him; panic – what would she do now; loneliness – she was totally alone all the way over in America, with no money or papers or anything; and yes, she hated to name it, but relief. If Frank was gone, she had control of her own life. For the first time ever, she was a free woman. She tried to quell the feelings; it was too much.

She forced herself to speak. 'We were travelling with another man, a friend…' Her voice choked on the word 'friend', but the woman looked at her with compassion. 'Michael Rafferty.'

The woman checked her list. 'I'm afraid I don't see –'

'He was in first class.'

The woman checked the list again. 'I'm so sorry. He's listed as lost as well. Many of the men didn't make it. The ship was over capacity, you see. My deepest condolences, Mrs Monaghan. Is there someone we can call?'

'I don't really know anyone…' She tried to take this all in. The canon was dead. Frank was dead. How could this be? Her boys would grow up without their father. She was a widow now.

As the woman filled in a form, she allowed herself to begin to process what had happened. It was like poking at a sore tooth with your tongue, testing to see how much it hurt. But she found it didn't hurt. The canon was gone, lying at the bottom of the cold, dark Atlantic. Gone. He couldn't hurt anyone else now. Frank was more complicated. He was not a terrible man. He had provided for her, for their children. He'd been willing to take Carrie in – for which she would always be grateful. A tear slipped down her cheek. In the end he'd done a kind thing for her, for no gain, nothing in it for him, just out of love. Though he never said the words, somehow, in his own way, Frank Monaghan must have loved her.

'Please don't worry.' The woman's words cut through her thoughts. 'If you go out that door and turn to your left, you'll see a large hall with red doors. The Sisters of Charity have set up in there, and they will help you with clothing and food and a place to stay until you figure everything out. They'll help you make contact with family back home too.' The official stood and helped Hannah rise from the chair. She was more shaken than she'd realised.

'Thank you,' she managed.

'Of course, and again, my deepest condolences.'

'Thank you,' she repeated, feeling like it was she who was underwater, not the canon and Frank. They were gone. Both of them. Gone forever. The words drummed like a tattoo on the doors of her brain.

The nuns were kind and practical, and once they found out the purpose of her visit, they made contact with the Graham School, and even arranged transport for her to go there. In the meantime she was given, along with other survivors, a bed and some dry clothes at the convent.

Two days after she was told her husband and the canon were dead, Hannah found herself in a hand-me-down primrose-yellow dress and coat, by far the nicest garments she'd ever worn, a pair of shoes just a little too tight and a cream cloche hat, loaded in a taxi and driving to a place called Hastings-on-Hudson in New York.

In her mind she had conjured up a cold, harsh Dickensian-type institution, but as the taxi approached, she realised with relief she could not have been more wrong. The Graham School was a beautiful red-brick building on the crest of a hill, overlooking the Hudson River. It was surrounded by playing fields and farms, and as they got closer, she could see a playground for children. It was idyllic.

She was a nervous wreck. What if without the canon's testimony they refused to believe she was Carrie's mother?

The taxi driver chatted all the way, telling her how the Graham School had been founded by the wife of one of America's founding fathers, Alexander Hamilton. His wife, Eliza, outlived him by many years and had set up the first orphanage in the city.

Normally Hannah would have been fascinated by his stories, but she was trying to focus and present herself as a balanced, stable person for these authorities so they would allow her to take Carrie. On arriving at the school, the driver assured her he'd been paid and left her there, telling her to have them call when she needed to be collected. She'd been given a loan by the sisters to tide her over, which she would ensure was paid back, every penny, once she got back to Ireland. She knew Frank had left everything to her and the boys. He had no other relatives and had explained to her a few years ago that while she was his beneficiary, she was to ensure one of the boys took over the business and that the others were to be financially supported by his estate. He never mentioned what she was supposed to do when he died.

She knew for a fact her husband had quite a bit of money. Not that he ever consulted her or informed her about anything, but she'd seen his bank book and had been astonished. The shop and house – a huge, hard-to-clean mausoleum that she hated – were now hers too.

They were expecting her at this Graham School, but they were also expecting Frank and the canon. How would it go now that it was just Hannah on her own? She wished she had Mrs Lewis or Mrs Nunez with her; they were the reason she was even here. She marvelled at women like them, so well able for the world. She wondered how one got to be that way.

Steeling herself, Hannah walked up to what looked like an administration building of some kind.

The woman on the desk seemed happy to see her and led her down to an office where a middle-aged woman with horn-rimmed spectacles and red hair in a bun looked up with a smile. 'Ah, Mrs Monaghan, we've been expecting you. My name is Ophelia Palmer. I am the head of legal affairs.' She stood and approached Hannah, hand outstretched. As Miss Palmer glanced behind her, looking for Frank, Hannah took the opportunity to blurt out the whole story.

'Oh my goodness, I heard about the *Carleton* but had no idea you were aboard.' The woman seemed nonplussed. 'And your husband and Canon Rafferty? I'm so very, very sorry. This is a terrible tragedy. Please, let me get you a drink?'

'I'm fine, honestly, thank you.' She just needed to know if there was now going to be a problem.

'Well, I'm assuming you still want to go ahead? Or has the change in circumstances…?'

'I want to go ahead,' Hannah said with conviction. 'It was what my husband and I wanted.'

'Very well. And can I just say how brave you are, doing this, especially now, after all that's happened. I'm not sure I could be as strong as you in the same situation.' The woman was the epitome of efficiency and seemed relieved she was not expected to offer more emotional support. 'Now I'm assuming all of your paperwork went down with the ship?'

Hannah felt her mouth go dry. She had no choice but to nod. Was this the end?

'No matter,' Miss Palmer said. 'We have a letter here, sent by Canon Rafferty a few weeks ago, outlining the case and confirming that you, Mrs Hannah Monaghan, are the natural mother of Carol Dwyer. And that in light of the demise of her adoptive parents, you wish to resume custody of your daughter. Is that correct?'

'Yes, very much so.' The relief, the fear, the dread, began to dissipate. It was going to be all right.

'And assuming you are the beneficiary of your late husband's estate, you are still in a financial position to care for her?'

'That's correct, yes,' she heard herself say.

'Very good. It will take a few days – a petition must be made to the court – but I do not envisage any issues. Now, would you like to meet your daughter, Mrs Monaghan?' Ophelia Palmer smiled.

Hannah swallowed. 'Very much.'

'I believe Carrie's in the stables – she's mad about horses. She's been reading up about Ireland from our library, and she has told me that Ireland is very green. So maybe she'll get to befriend some horses there.'

Prior to Frank's death, Hannah would have dreaded to hear this. Frank would no doubt comment that 'a child out of an orphanage would want to lower her expectations and not think she's going to be cavorting round the country on horseback as if she were gentry.'

She breathed in. 'If Carrie wants a horse of her own, I'll buy her one.'

'Well, I'm sure that would be a dream come true for her. She grew up in Brooklyn – not much room for paddocks there – but she loves country life. Perhaps it's her Irish roots.'

The woman went to the door and gestured that Hannah should go ahead of her. 'Let's go reunite you with your daughter, Mrs Monaghan. She's so excited to meet you.'

EPILOGUE

Knocknashee, County Kerry

June 1950

Grace watched her handsome husband as he fixed his tie in the oval mirror over the fireplace. It was unusual to see him in formal clothes, and he took her breath away. She was used to him being in the raggedy navy jumper she knit for him years ago and a pair of canvas trousers patched so often they were more patch than trousers.

His first book, a collection of essays about ordinary people in wartime London, had been accepted by a very prestigious publisher and had been such a literary and commercial success, he'd been offered a three-book deal. So Richard divided his time between writing his first novel and taking care of their two beautiful but lively children while she worked in the school. She was five weeks late with her period, so she was sure she was expecting again, and she was over the moon. Hugh Warrington had been right – there was nothing whatsoever wrong with her, and once Richard came home, she conceived easily. The pregnancies and births were easy enough, and she would go through it a hundred times for her precious little ones.

Their first-born was a boy, named after Jacob, and their daughter, Eliza, was named after Lizzie Warrington, who was flourishing in her role as grandma. She and Hugh were both retired now so had plenty of time for visits, and the children loved to see them.

Five-year-old Jacob ran in, screaming as three-year-old Eliza chased him with sticky fingers.

'Enough, both of you,' Grace said. The unusual volume in her voice caused them to stop in their tracks.

'She's going to stick me, Mammy. She's got jam on her!' Jacob hid behind Grace, and she feared for her royal-blue silk dress.

'Nobody is sticking anyone,' Richard said, turning from the mirror. He took Eliza's sticky hands and led her to the kitchen sink while Grace did the same with Jacob, together they washed both children's hands.

Richard sat the children on the draining board and spoke. They gave him their complete attention.

'Right, you guys, listen up.' He said it in a funny voice that made them giggle. 'What day is today?'

'The special day,' they chorused in English. Richard spoke exclusively in English to them, though his Irish was improving slowly, and everyone else spoke in Irish, so they were bilingual. Though when Jacob realised that their friend Odile, who was a very sophisticated ten-year-old, could speak French and German as well as Irish and English, he had decided he wanted to do that too. If Odile told Jacob to jump off a cliff, he'd do it, such was the level of his devotion.

'Exactly. So we are all going to be on our best behaviour. Deal?' Richard looked mock-stern.

'Deal,' they both squealed.

'And you can come to the first bit, in the church, but then Nana Lizzie is taking you two home and Mammy and Daddy are staying for a little while, all right?'

'Is Odile coming back to our house with Nana Lizzie?' Jacob asked eagerly.

'No, Odile is staying with Auntie Tilly and Tante Eloise today,' Grace replied. 'But she's coming down here tomorrow, and she said she's going to let you ride Aonbharr on the beach. *If* you're good.'

'Is everyone staying except us?' Jacob sounded very hard done by.

'No, Kate and Paudie are taking Seámus home so Charlie and Dymphna can stay too.'

'And we can definitely see everyone again tomorrow?' Jacob needed the details copper-fastened.

'Everyone. The party tomorrow will be much better fun because it's during the day, and we won't be all dressed up and worried about getting sticky fingers on us,' Richard said, ruffling his son's sandy-blond curls. 'Today is the boring bit in the church,' he whispered, and Grace thumped his arm.

'The church is not the boring bit. Don't listen to Daddy.' She made admonishing eyes at Richard, who just laughed.

Hugh came downstairs in his suit, Lizzie behind him in a lovely floral dress. They were both the picture of health.

'Nana Lizzie, I hurted my finger.' Eliza held up her baby finger and showed Lizzie a microscopic cut from two weeks ago.

'Oh, best take a look at that. We might need an ambulance,' Hugh said, putting on his glasses and examining the tiny finger.

'Will she be all right?' Lizzie asked, mock-concerned, and Eliza beamed, lapping up the attention.

'Oh, I don't know. It's a bad cut,' Hugh said in a serious voice. 'But my diagnosis is, if she gets an ice cream later, that will do the trick, I think.' He winked as Eliza and Jacob giggled.

'Daidó, carry me?' Eliza said, using her best baby voice. They called Hugh Daidó, the Irish word for grandpa, but Lizzie was Nana Lizzie. Richard's mother had nearly physically recoiled at being called Mamó, the Irish word for granny, so they settled on Grandma Caroline, and Arthur was just Pops.

Richard, Grace and the children had been in Savannah for the summer last year, and the children were spoiled rotten by their grandparents. It was as if Caroline was trying to make up for all the time she missed with Richard. He'd spent the whole holiday marvelling that 'she never did that with us' as Caroline played games and did colouring and even licked ice creams at the beach. Arthur took them up in his plane, and they all went island-hopping on his yacht. Grace wondered if they would ever have any idea how lucky they were.

'She's well able to walk, Hugh,' Grace objected, but Hugh shushed her.

'Sure she's light as a feather, and I love it,' he whispered.

Grace and Richard hung back as they watched the Warringtons take their children down the path.

'You look stunning, by the way, Mrs Lewis,' Richard murmured in her ear.

She laughed. 'As do you – now that you're wearing trousers that are not falling asunder.'

'Get out of here – you love the bohemian look,' he teased. 'I see how you look at me when my hair is standing on end and I'm deep in creativity. All that lusting after me...' He squeezed her waist playfully as she pushed him out the door.

'How you can get lust out of frustration, I'll never know...' she joked as she took his arm.

Charlie and Dymphna were already halfway up the hill, with little Seámus running to catch up with Kate and Paudie, all in their finery. Eleanor had parked her black Ford, and the three girls were getting out – poised young ladies now, not the poor skinny little creatures they'd been when they arrived eight long years ago.

Olivia, now twenty and working as a nurse in the hospital in Dingle, was engaged to Fiachra O'Flynn, who had finally got over Dr Lily Maheady, who, it seems, was 'dating an attorney' – a concept nobody in Knocknashee understood until Richard explained that dating meant being involved romantically and an attorney was a solicitor. Fiachra now hung on every word Olivia said.

Eleanor had remarried to a man named Bill McEvoy. The couple had met at a teacher training day in Killarney two years ago. Bill wasn't driving today because his arm was in a sling. He was a physical education teacher in the school where Maurice was now principal and had taken a bad knock when demonstrating a tackle in hurling.

The student followed his instruction a little too seriously and ended up fracturing Bill's arm. He'd laughingly told them the story and said he was more embarrassed than in pain, though the boy's parents were most apologetic.

Everyone turned at the sound of the horses' hooves on the cobbles. Tilly was at the reins, and the jaunting car was decked out with ribbons and flowers. Beside her, on the front seat, was Odile, waving to everyone like she was the Queen of Sheba, with Eloise beside her. Tilly, Grace thought, looked magnificent, like Queen Meadhbh or Granuaile. She was wearing a green tweed trouser suit, with a white blouse.

In the back, on the seats behind the driver, was Mary O'Hare, who had to be wrangled into a beige dress and coat and, according to Tilly, surgically separated from her wellington boots. The old woman beamed with pride as she sat beside her son, Alfie, in full morning dress and looking like a film star.

Alfie O'Hare had come back to Knocknashee in 1946, tired, broken and a bit lost. His mother's love, his sister's support and the friendship of Grace, Richard, Eloise and Sarah, when she visited, had restored him to life. He spent a lot of time with Sarah. They were both a bit bewildered as to how to go on after the war – him without Constance, her without Jacob. Life seemed so empty for them.

Alfie needed a purpose, and Sarah was still working very hard in London with the refugees. The end of the war had only been the beginning for so many people. Millions displaced, homes gone, families annihilated, orphans made – there was so much work to be done.

Sarah had suggested that once he was ready, he should go over, join her in London. She'd put him to work, and to everyone's surprise, two years ago he did just that.

Grace and Richard waved as the O'Hares passed, and eventually everyone gathered in the church.

Grace and Richard took a child each and sat them on their laps, with Hugh and Lizzie either side in case of an escapee. Caroline Lewis turned in the pew and smiled at her grandchildren. She was still a little awed by small children, but they seemed to find her fascinating.

The Lewis parents were staying with Grace and Richard and the children for the wedding, and so far it was going really well. Last night Grace had walked into the sitting room to find Eliza's fingers adorned in priceless sapphires and emeralds as she wore Grandma Caroline's rings. Eliza had explained that Odile had a diamond ring – Richard had delivered the rings left to her by her mother, Bernadette Dreyfus, as he'd been asked to do – and she wore it sometimes, supervised by Tilly. Eliza longed to have one like it, and to everyone's surprise, Grandma Caroline had obliged.

Maurice and Patricia were expecting another baby any day now – a surprise after so long, as their youngest, Molly, was almost twelve now. They were not here this morning but would pop to the party tomorrow if Patricia was up to it. Molly and fourteen-year-old Cáit refused to miss out on the wedding so were coming with Grace and Richard to the reception.

Nathan and Rebecca and their daughters sat in the front pew on one side of Caroline Lewis. Esme Carter, on her second visit to Ireland, sat on the other.

With the congregation gathered, the church organ started up with the wedding march, and everyone turned around.

Grace stifled a laugh. Sarah had never lost it. She was wearing a dazzlingly white, exquisitely cut full suit, complete with wing-tip dress shirt, bow tie, waistcoat, tails and pleated trousers. She beamed with delight at the reaction of the gathered congregation as she linked Arthur's arm. A bride in trousers might be unusual in America, but it was unheard of in Knocknashee. But Sarah Lewis always did things her own way – it was one of the many reasons Alfie O'Hare loved her, and one of the many reasons he had proposed on Christmas Day in front of everyone who had gathered at the O'Hare farm for the Christmas celebrations.

Grace sat in the pew and remembered that Christmas, how she had welled up as Alfie stood, tapped his glass and asked for a bit of silence. The children were all playing in the parlour, so it was just the adults gathered round.

'Thanks to everyone who made this the best Christmas I've ever had,' he'd said, his voice gravelly and deep. Alfie was handsome in a battle-scarred way, but there was something very compelling about him. 'I shouldn't be here, really, and many of my friends and people I loved didn't make it. But I never thought that after all that happened, I would find love, of all things.' He laughed at the very notion.

'But I did find it. In the shape of the kindest, most compassionate, most decent, quirkiest, most opinionated woman I've ever met.' He looked at Sarah, who grinned.

'The fact that she's incredibly beautiful helps, of course.' His tone turned serious. 'But when I came home, as you know, I was not in a good way. To be honest, I wondered why I'd been spared. I didn't see the point. But all of you, your friendship and love and patience… I'm sorry, I wasn't always easy, I know…'

'Understatement of the century,' Tilly quipped, and everyone chuckled. It was true; Alfie had been very difficult to deal with at times – often he was so angry he had to go off climbing the mountains on his own and would disappear for days. When that happened, he was so morose, he'd drag a nation down with him. But over time he got better.

'I know. I am really sorry, but it was you all helped bring me back. One person, though, who understood what I'd lost, because she lost it too, was my saviour. I think we might have saved each other a little bit, but that turned into love, and we both know, in the end, that is all that matters.'

He knelt beside Sarah at the table and produced a ring. 'Will you marry me, Sarah Lewis Nunez?'

Sarah had allowed him to slip the ring on her finger. Then she looked down at him and said simply, 'Yes.'

The wedding ceremony, performed by Father Iggy, was beautiful. Mrs McHale had done the flowers, and even Peggy Donnelly and Nancy O'Flaherty, who were recognised as the altar flower experts in the village, had to admit they had never seen anything like it.

Dinny's mother's extensive garden had been raided – only possible because the old woman had, thankfully for all concerned, gone to her reward the previous winter.

Father Iggy lived in terror of Mrs McHale saying she was leaving to get married too. But Mrs McHale and Dinny were happy enough as they were – 'courting with a view to marriage'.

'Some day. But not today. Not tomorrow either, if the truth be known,' Mrs McHale had confided to Grace with a chuckle. 'No harm to keep a bit of mystery, though.'

Father Iggy gave a beautiful sermon about service to others, love, resilience and compassion – qualities both the bride and groom had in spades, individually and as a couple – and how they had all the tools necessary for a long and happy marriage.

As the organ played and the bride and groom walked hand in hand down the aisle of Knocknashee church, Richard took Grace's hand. 'Should we go for a walk while all the milling around is going on?' he suggested. 'Let Hugh and Lizzie mind the kids?'

'Let's,' she replied.

The reception was in a hotel in Dingle, and Bobby the Bus had been pressed into commission to transport everyone back and forth, under the watchful gaze of Sergeant Keane, who extracted a promise from Bobby that no drink would be consumed until tomorrow for the after-party sponsored by the Lewis family, when he could drink Lough Erne dry if he wanted.

Lizzie and Hugh were happy to oblige, and Richard and Grace slipped out the side gate of the churchyard and walked down to the pier and along to the beach. The place was deserted since everyone was at the wedding.

They walked hand in hand. Her limp was so much better now. Lizzie did the exercises with her whenever she visited, and Richard insisted on employing a young physiotherapist to come twice a week. The bathroom had been upgraded and now housed a large soaking bath and a tiled floor. She had been sad to replace the one Declan made her, but the old cow trough had sprung several leaks.

Richard helped her over the rocks until they got to the flat rock. She'd had so many picnics on that rock with Tilly. She'd raged at Agnes there and thrown her frustrations in a bottle out to sea at that exact spot, and that bottle had found its way to St Simons Island in

Georgia, USA, to be found by a lovely dog called Doodle, long dead now.

'Imagine if you'd never written that letter,' Richard said as he sat beside her, his arm around her, her head on his shoulder. 'I can't imagine my life...'

'You'd probably be a millionaire banker married to Miranda.' She laughed.

'Well, the bank would have gone under years ago, and I don't think I'd have had the stamina for Miranda.' He chuckled.

Miranda Logan had visited earlier in the year with her latest fling – a Russian ballet dancer with smouldering black eyes and powerful muscled legs like Grace had never seen. Their bedroom antics had kept the whole house awake.

'You definitely wouldn't.' She nudged him playfully. 'You were snoring by ten o'clock last night.'

'Making things up is exhausting work, I'll have you know.' He kissed the top of her head.

'I don't doubt it.' She gazed out to sea. 'The Canon will be dead nearly six years this year, can you believe it? There was a time I thought he'd haunt me forever.'

'I really hope there's a God, because I love the idea that he'd have to explain himself,' Richard mused.

'All's well that ends well, I suppose. Hannah is so happy, and Carrie and herself are so close. It's like they were never apart. She just finished her Leaving Certificate and hopes to get a job in the civil service. There's a new department of fisheries being set up here, so she applied for that. I wrote her a reference, so I'm hopeful she gets it. She could have done a secretarial course or something, but she doesn't want to leave home. She's so involved with her young brothers too – it's lovely to see.'

'It is,' he agreed.

'Oh, by the way, I think we might have a new little Lewis joining us in the New Year,' she said nonchalantly.

'What? Really?' Richard beamed. 'That's amazing. I did wonder. You seem even more...curvaceous...' He winked.

'Really?' She raised an eyebrow.

'Oh, Grace.' He kissed her then. On and on they kissed, only stopping when they realised three seals were watching them with their sad brown eyes.

'I love you,' he said, his voice thick with emotion. 'I thank God every day for you, that you wrote that letter, that I had you to come back to, that I survived the war when so many didn't.'

'And I love you too, Richard. I love us, our family, our two little rascals and this new one...' She took his hand and placed it on her tummy. He bent and kissed her stomach.

'Hello in there, this is your daddy. I can't wait to meet you. Try not to make your mama too sick, OK? She's got a lot on her plate with your crazy brother and sister. So you be a good little boy or girl and grow healthy and strong, and we'll see you very soon.'

They sat in contented silence for a few moments, his arm around her shoulder as she leant into him, the seals swimming around them, gannets and gulls circling as the azure Atlantic that had both given and taken so much glinted in the sunlight.

As the soft breeze lifted her copper curls from her face, Grace felt the love not just of her husband but of all those who'd gone before. Her parents, Agnes, Declan, Jacob, and Bernadette and Constance, whom she'd never met but felt she knew. After all they'd gone through, this was exactly where they all wanted Grace and Richard to be – happy, together and in love.

'So have you decided on a title for the new book?' she asked.

'I think so.'

'Well, go on then. Don't keep me in suspense.' She nestled closer to him.

He turned, placed a finger under her chin and tilted her face for a kiss. 'I think it has to be called *Lilac Ink*.'

The end.

AFTERWORD

Dear Readers,

Thank you for staying with me and Richard and Grace all this time. I had no idea that it would go on this long or take so many twists and turns, but it would've been lonely without you, so thank you for keeping me company. It's sad to say goodbye isn't it? It is for me too. But the time has come.

Seven books is a long series, and so once I finished this book I needed to take some time out to allow the creative well to refill.

I was worried what, if anything, could follow this story. But one day, my husband and I went for a ramble around a neglected, but once beautiful old house near where we live. Truth to tell, it was where my husband grew up, but his family sold it years ago, and the last owner had passed away, so we were just being nosy.

It is a listed building and is surrounded by architectural gems and archeology going back thousands of years. As we tramped through overgrown orchards, and scaled ivy- clad walls, an idea occurred to me. What would this house say to us if it could speak?

So my new book was born.

AFTERWORD

Here's a sneak peek!

Prologue

I've seen dark times. Darker than you can ever imagine now.

I've also seen good times, so good that it was impossible at that time to imagine another tear would ever be shed for all eternity under this roof.

But the wheel is always turning, nothing stays the same. That is both comforting and terrifying, I know.

I can adapt. I know that about myself. I can be whatever is necessary in any given time. A sanctuary, a home, a fortress, a keeper of secrets, a prison, a place to be free. I've been so many things to so many people down through the years. Before I stood as you see me now, I looked different, I suited the world I was built for.

And while in each generation the outside world looks different, different clothes, different politics, different ways of entertaining, different languages even, the things that unite my people are constant.

Have I seen love stories? Indeed. Plenty of them, some destined to succeed, others doomed to fail.

Betrayals? Oh yes.

And I've kept silent company on those the dark nights of the soul with my people as they paced the floors, not knowing what the future held. Fearful, watchful, anticipating.

I've played host to great gatherings of soaring intellect, where ideas took flight.

I've housed the smallest of minds, those who saw no way but their own.

I've braced myself for attack so often I've lost count. I've been battered and bruised, I've wondered many times if this was the end, but it never is. Because no matter what, I go on. And those who live beneath my roof are my people. I will always wrap my walls around them, they choose me, or perhaps I choose them, I'm never quite sure.

What I do know for certain is that no matter what comes, I can survive so long as the people I protect, protect me in return. I don't need to be spectacular, though I have been, in my time. Oh, I wish you could have seen me then. I was something to behold, and no mistake. I was truly magnificent once. But these days, I am old, so very, very old, and I've been alone for a while now, so I don't mind if the ivy creeps and the squirrels scamper and the birds nest in my eaves. The little birds and animals are company, and I care for them. I provide shelter. I might rise again, be spectacular once more, who knows?

Every generation thinks they have the monopoly on suffering, on wonder, on terror, on passion, or on excitement. But from my perspective, that of centuries of silent observation, nothing could be further from the truth. People fail to understand that regardless of which numbers are etched on the calendar, men and women are just the same. The things that drive people in this twenty-first century - love, passion, revenge, greed, kindness, empathy, jealousy, duty - are precisely the same things that drove people when first I came to be. And reactions are predictable, if you watch long enough. Because however shocking a situation seems, let me assure you of this, it has all happened before.

AFTERWORD

I'm glad you came to join me. I like company. And I never know when this will all end. Maybe it never will, or maybe my time is up. Nobody knows. But it's nice not to feel alone. Especially now.

Dark clouds are gathering again. I can always sense it.

But I am ready. As always. To face the next chapter.

* * *

I (really!!) hope this piques your interest. If you would like to preorder the ebook, you can click HERE

Of course, as always, pop over to www.jeangrainger.com to join my readers' club and I'll send you a free novel to download as a welcome gift.

And finally, if you could leave a review of The Last Post wherever you get books, I'd be delighted.

GLOSSARY - FOCLOIR

Garsún – young boy
Cailleach – a witch
Poitín – an illegal alcoholic spirit made with potatoes
Tabhair dom do lámh – give me your hand (an Irish tune)
Domhain – World
Ceann Trá – the village of Ventry on the Dingle Peninsula
Óinseach – a simpleton
Sidhe – fairies
Tuatha De Danann – a mythical ancient tribe of Ireland who had magical qualities.
Fir Bolg – a tribe who were the enemies of the Tuatha De Danann
go dtuga Dia suaimhneas dó – May god grant him peace
Ar dheis Dé go raibh a anam dílis – may his gentle soul rest at God's right hand
Ní bheidh a leithéad arís ann. – We won't see the likes of him again
Bean feasa – a wise woman, an old woman with magical skills
A stór – my love
Mo chroí – my heart (endearment)
Is fearr beagán den ghaol, ná mórán den charthanas – Kinship is more important than charity.
Rud an- laidir is ea smacht sóisialta – Social pressure is a powerful thing
Go neirí an t-ádh leat – good luck – literally may the luck rise up for you.
Cúpla focail – a few words – it means a little bit of Irish – to have the 'cúpla focail'
Mo chara – my friend
To make a hames of something – to make a mess of it due to ineptitude
Je suis vraiment desolée mon ami – I've truly sorry my friend. (French)
Queen Medhbh – a figure from Irish mythology. And Irish warrior queen feared and loved.
Grainnuaile – An Irish Pirate woman from the fifteenth century. Feared on the high seas. Met Queen Elizabeth the first to negotiate.
Jaunting car – an elaborate carriage pulled by a horse.

ACKNOWLEDGMENTS

I never set out to write a seven-book series. But Grace and Richard wound their stories around our hearts and refused to let go. There were so many times I wondered if it would ever end, because just when I thought it was finished, it wasn't. I don't have as much control over this as you might think. 😀

I loved writing it, and I'm sad it's over.

Thank you for sticking with us all this time.

Over the course of writing this, I had my own share of loss and grief and in some ways telling their stories was cathartic. My wonderful parents both died within the last three years, and the hole they've left is unfathomable. There may not have been any blood or sweat in the creation of this series, but there were plenty of tears.

When I started writing in 2010, I wrote a book that garnered not the slightest modicum of interest in book land. I was at the point of giving up, when one lone editor, called Helen Falconer, took me on. The book, *The Tour*, was a complete dog's dinner but undaunted, and with humour and mesmerising skill she fixed it. I watched and learned in awe as she deconstructed the story and put it all back together, properly this time.

What began as an author-editor relationship went on to become one of the most significant and precious friendships of my life. As well as being an incredible author and poet herself, Helen and I worked on every book of mine together. Often arguing fiercely, other times collapsing into uncontrollable laughter, always loving each other.

Her husband and mine became friends then, and we frequently

had food and wine fuelled debates, laughs and conversations that went into the small hours. Helen was brave, clever, opinionated, funny, kind and special. She was also a one-off. I never met anyone like her and I doubt I ever will again.

She left for the stars, quite suddenly, on the first of February 2025, and took our hearts with her. On the day before she died, she assured me I could do this writing malarky without her, but that she would always be looking over my shoulder, rolling her eyes and laughing.

My wonderful team, Carol, Diarmuid and Barbara knew exactly what she meant to me, personally and professionally, and so they held me up in those dark days. Grace and Richard's world became a kind of sanctuary, away from the reality of all I'd lost.

I want to say a special word of thanks to my other wonderful editor, Abby, who went so far beyond her brief of copy-editor to help me. Despite having her own loss to cope with, she and her husband and their adorable shelties, welcomed me to their Arizona home and took care of my battered heart. I will never forget their kindness.

None of this magical author life would ever have happened if it hadn't been for Helen Falconer. I'd still be teaching English and History in a secondary school, never knowing that this other life was possible. So in more ways than I can count, I owe everything to her.

I miss her all the time, I want to share the victories and I need her inimitably sanguine courage on the darker days. But I don't think our people ever leave us, so with Helen and my parents at my back I close the door on this chapter and wait to see what's next.

Thank you for reading my stories,
Ar dheis Dé go raibh a h-anamacha dílis,
May their souls rest at God's right hand.
Jean Grainger December 2025

ABOUT THE AUTHOR

Jean Grainger is a USA Today bestselling Irish author. She writes historical and contemporary Irish fiction and her work has very flatteringly been compared to the late great Maeve Binchy.

She lives in a stone cottage in Cork with her lovely husband Diarmuid and the youngest two of her four children. The older two come home for a break when adulting gets too exhausting. There are a variety of animals there too, all led by two cute but clueless microdogs called Scrappy and Scoobi.

ALSO BY JEAN GRAINGER

The Tour Series

The Tour

Safe at the Edge of the World

The Story of Grenville King

The Homecoming of Bubbles O'Leary

Finding Billie Romano

Kayla's Trick

The Carmel Sheehan Story

Letters of Freedom

The Future's Not Ours To See

What Will Be

The Robinswood Story

What Once Was True

Return To Robinswood

Trials and Tribulations

The Star and the Shamrock Series

The Star and the Shamrock

The Emerald Horizon

The Hard Way Home

The World Starts Anew

The Queenstown Series

Last Port of Call

The West's Awake

The Harp and the Rose

Roaring Liberty

Standalone Books

So Much Owed

Shadow of a Century

Under Heaven's Shining Stars

Catriona's War

Sisters of the Southern Cross

The Kilteegan Bridge Series

The Trouble with Secrets

What Divides Us

More Harm Than Good

When Irish Eyes Are Lying

A Silent Understanding

The Mags Munroe Story

The Existential Worries of Mags Munroe

Growing Wild in the Shade

Each to their Own

Closer Than You Think

Chance your Arm

The Aisling Series

For All The World

A Beautiful Ferocity

Rivers of Wrath

The Gem of Ireland's Crown

The Knocknashee Series

Lilac Ink

Yesterday's Paper

History's Pages

Sincerely, Grace

Folded Corners

Allied Flames

The Last Post

The Dunmara Story

If Walls Could Talk

Made in the USA
Las Vegas, NV
04 February 2026